In Search of Life

Dedication

My purpose in writing this book is to interest others in reading the Bible. I hope that this narrative will make the reader think carefully, ask questions and turn to the Bible for answers.

Above all, it has been my earnest hope and prayer for some very special people that has motivated me to write this story. I hope they will take the opportunity to read this fictional account and think deeply upon the issues it presents.

It is to these friends that I truly dedicate this book. May God bless them.

In Search of Life

ANNA TIKVAH

FIRST PRINTING

Stallard & Potter
2 Jervois Street,
Torrensville,
South Australia, 5031
September 2003

Published by CSSS

85 Suffolk Road,
Hawthorndene,
South Australia, 5051
Email: csssadelaide@
webshield.net.au
Website: www.csss.org.au

SECOND PRINTING
August 2006

THIRD PRINTING
February 2015

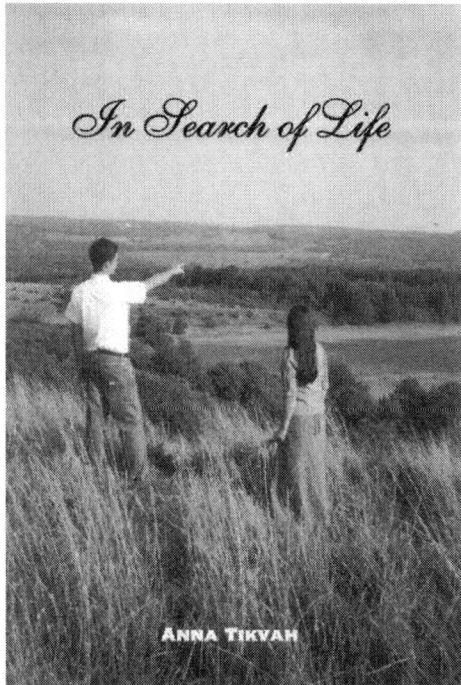

In Search of Life

ANNA TIKVAH

Original Cover

REVISED AND FOURTH PRINTING:
Kindle Direct, Amazon
November 2023
ISBN: 9798866393565

New Cover by Chris & AI, Cilla Tuckson and Jessica Fish

In Search of Life is the first in a series of four books:

Who Are You Looking For?

An Invitation to Forever

Eleven Weeks

Chapters

CHAPTER 1

The Funeral

Rain drizzled down the brightly coloured umbrellas and splashed to the ground. The fog was so thick that the people standing around in a circle were shrouded in a misty haze. In the middle lay a coffin with one simple bouquet of roses perfectly centred on the dark wood. A short, stocky, elderly man was proclaiming the last words of comfort, but oddly enough, no one was crying. Only one woman in a dark dress stood with tears in her eyes. She was thin, almost frail-looking with light brown hair pulled loosely back and pretty blue eyes that seemed full of pain. Draped around her shoulders was the arm of a young girl in her teens. Thin like her mother, Verity Lovell wore a black coat, but she was taller with long, brown hair and coffee-coloured eyes.

Today here in the rain, her big brown eyes held a mix of emotion. She herself was not crying and she wondered why her mother was. Yes, the man in the coffin was her father, Dan Lovell, but everyone at the funeral knew that he had been an abusive alcoholic for the last ten years. Verity was quite aware that many in the crowd thought her mother was foolish to have stayed by his side right to the end. When her father had finally died after a lengthy illness, there had been a sense of relief for all of them. Deep inside, she felt guilty for feeling so happy at a funeral, but she had to admit that was how she felt! Now there would be no more drunken rages to endure, no more waking up at night to hear her father yelling at her mother. Maybe now the meagre wage that her mother managed to earn each week would provide food for all of them. It had been so infuriating to watch her father down bottle after bottle to his own derangement, when they had all been so desperately hungry! So, why on earth did her mother look so sad?

What now, was Reverend Tobias saying? That her father, Dan Lovell was looking down from heaven on them? That God was a forgiving God and could see past such a sickness to the true heart of a man? That her father was going to dwell in peace with Jesus, forever?

Perplexed, Verity looked quizzically at her mother, but Kara Lovell only put her finger to her lips.

Why would God invite such a man to heaven? She couldn't even imagine her father being thankful for such a good place. He had always mocked 'good people', sneered at churches and tossed aside the Bible as a book of myths! The thought of her father up in heaven surrounded by angels seemed like such an ironic fate that she almost laughed.

Glancing up at her older brother Thomas beside her, she wondered if he found this funny as well. Thomas however, was staring at the ground. His hair, no longer slicked carefully back, had become a wet mass of curls. She was happy to have his arm around her shoulder and see his best friend Ken on his other side. Thomas was so fortunate to have always had Ken. They had played together since they were tiny tots on the front lawn. Through all the difficult years with Dad, Thomas had taken refuge in this friendship. In many ways Thomas was more a part of Ken's family than his own.

When Reverend Tobias finally concluded with a prayer, everyone was greatly relieved to escape from the rain and head back to the church.

As soon as they were all in the car, Verity blurted out the question that was confusing her. "Mom," she exclaimed in perplexity, "why did Reverend Tobias say that Dad was in heaven? Dad wouldn't have even wanted to go there!"

Kara turned around to look at her daughter. There was a slight look of exasperation on her face. Ever since Verity had learned to speak, she had questioned everything. When she was little, the questions weren't difficult for Kara to answer; they just required lots

3

of patience. However, in the last few years, the questions had become steadily more difficult and many times Kara felt unable to help. With a measure of compassion, she reached over to gently pat Verity's arm. "God *is* a merciful God," she said softly. "Perhaps He saw that underneath all the bad behaviour, your father had a good heart. If it wasn't for alcohol…"

Thomas broke in with a laugh. "When you're alive they scare you with burning in hell—and when you're dead, they say everyone goes to heaven!"

Kara glared reproachfully at Thomas as Ken's father started the car, but Thomas continued anyway. "It's all just a big hoax; everyone says something different. I don't think I believe in God at all!"

Verity ignored her brother's developing atheism. "Where in the Bible does it explain about who goes to heaven?" she begged.

Her mother sighed. "The Bible? I don't know, Honey—I've never read it. Reverend Tobias has though. He must know."

Musing this over in her own mind as they headed back to the church, Verity decided that she had to find the answer to this question. As horrible as he had been, she wasn't sure that she wanted her dad to be burning in hell… but it just didn't make any sense for him to be in heaven!

Ken's dad led the procession of cars back to the church where a luncheon was to be served. Thomas attempted to change the conversation and began speaking to Ken's father about the camping trip they had invited him to join. "Will we really travel for two weeks, Mr. Norton?"

"Yes, Thomas, two weeks up in Jasper National Park. We'll take you to see the Rocky Mountains, Lake Louise, glaciers and anything else you like!"

The excitement showed on Thomas' face! Verity knew that her brother would have been excited just to stay at Ken's house for

4

two weeks. But to travel?! As a family they had never been able to travel anywhere. This was going to be the adventure of a lifetime!

Smiling, Verity was glad Thomas had this to look forward to. Her brother was very special to her. They'd had their share of fights and arguments, but Thomas had always been there for her when she needed him. In her younger years she had run to him many times for protection. Whether it had been the bully at school or fear of her father's rages, she knew Thomas would help her out. Now that they were in their teens, he had become one of her best friends. While they disagreed on many issues, she felt completely comfortable discussing anything with him.

Breaking from her own thoughts, Verity realized her mother was speaking of heaven. "It must be wonderful," Kara reflected dreamily, "to be up in heaven with the angels. To be up where the grass is always green and flowers bloom all around. Beautiful music will float through the skies, and it will always be light!" Kara laughed a little. "And imagine looking down on your own funeral and hearing what everyone is saying about you!"

"How do you know that's what will happen?" Verity asked. Her mother rarely spoke of such things. They hadn't been able to attend church regularly and religion had been taboo when her dad was around. Until today Verity had not given much thought to life after death.

"Well Dear, that's just what Reverend Tobias always says. He's been a minister for many years, so he should know."

"Does it say that in the Bible?"

"I'm sure it must, in *many* places. Why don't you ask him yourself?" Kara encouraged.

They pulled into the church parking lot and Verity got out quickly. She'd resolved to do just that—she would ask the minister! As she made her way up the steps, she noticed that people weren't fussing over her in the same way. The funeral was over, Dan Lovell was finally buried, the food was good, and most people were happily eating, laughing, and talking with their neighbours. Verity saw Reverend Tobias and his wife in a corner, enjoying a bacon quiche. "Perfect," she thought, "I'll go right over."

However, before she could make it across the room, a tall grey-haired woman, her face strikingly similar to Verity's, enveloped her in a warm embrace. "Verity, my darling, I'm so glad to see you!"

Taking a step back, the dark-haired girl was quite pleased to see that this woman was her Aunt Judy Kolmer.

"You must have grown a foot since I last saw you!" exclaimed her aunt admiringly. "You look all grown up, in fact. How old are you now?"

"I'm almost sixteen, Aunt Judy," she beamed. "It's so wonderful to see you again!"

Aunt Judy apologized for not being at the funeral service. "I so wanted to be there for my brother's funeral! I will always miss the Dan I used to know!" Her face clouded over for a moment and she dabbed at her eyes with a tissue. Then she went on to explain, "My plane was delayed for hours and I had so much trouble hailing a taxi! At least I'm here now! Anyway, I have a wonderful idea for all of you!" she said enthusiastically, her dark eyes lighting up with a sparkle. "I must speak to your mother about it first, though!"

With a pat on her arm, Aunt Judy hurried off to Verity's mother who was coming toward them with open arms.

Verity smiled to herself. She had always liked her Aunt Judy. Her aunt knew the truth about the alcohol problems and the struggles they had endured. What ever would they have done without Aunt Judy's frequent phone calls and generous gifts of money? Someday Verity hoped she could visit her aunt in the far away province of Ontario, where she owned a remarkably successful grocery store. If only her dad had been more like Aunt Judy, maybe they would have lived in a big country home like hers and helped the poor out instead of being the beggars!

Curious about what the wonderful plan could be, Verity watched her mother and Aunt Judy discussing something quite animatedly together. Then she remembered her important questions for Reverend Tobias. Seeing he was still in the corner, she hurried over.

"How are you doing, poor girl?" he asked compassionately as she sat down beside them.

"Have you had a bite to eat?" his wife inquired kindly.

"Not yet," she smiled. "Reverend Tobias, I need to ask you a question. How do you know that my dad is in heaven?"

The minister paused, surprised. "Well, you see, my dear," he began, "everyone has an immortal soul. When we die, the soul lives on and the angels carry it to heaven to be with God forever."

"Where does it explain about that in the Bible?" Verity asked.

Reverend Tobias cleared his throat and reached for his napkin. He wiped his face, set down his food and walked over to his coat. From the inside pocket he pulled out a very small Bible. "Now Verity," he said authoritatively, as he returned, "there are lots of places where the Bible speaks of heaven as being our future dwelling place. Here's one in John chapter fourteen, verse two: *'In my Father's house are many rooms; if it were not so, I would have told you. I am going there to prepare a place for you.'*"

Reverend Tobias also showed Verity Second Kings chapter two, verses one to eleven, where Elisha saw Elijah taken up to heaven in a whirlwind. "In Hebrews chapter ten, verse thirty-four," he added, "it states that *'ye have in heaven a better and an enduring substance.'*"

It was all said so fast that Verity didn't have a chance to look at the verses carefully. "You wouldn't happen to have a pen and paper, would you?" she asked, wishing she'd thought to get that first.

Mrs. Tobias kindly produced both items from her purse and Verity asked the minister to state the verses once more, so that she could write them down.

"Does everyone go to heaven?" Verity inquired politely, after jotting down the references.

"Well, no," Reverend Tobias replied, his face reddening slightly, "if a person is exceedingly wicked, they go to hell and burn forever."

"Where does it explain in the Bible about who goes where?" Verity probed further. She hoped there would be a verse somewhere that would clearly state the qualifications for making it to heaven. "I can see that good people might go there," she continued, "but my dad, you know he wasn't a good man. He never came to church, and he made fun of people who believed in God. Why would he go to heaven?"

Reverend Tobias glanced uneasily at his wife, but she only shook her head. "Verity, you must understand, Dear, that, of course I'm not God," he explained. "I can't say for sure what God would choose for your father but it's my understanding that our Creator is very merciful. Hell is a horrible, horrible punishment. Only the worst sinners go there! Your father was a very sick man; it wasn't really his fault that he became an alcoholic and lost control when he was drunk. So, I believe God will see all that and give him a place above."

"I see," Verity said slowly, realising that there was a lot she didn't understand about God, about death, even about life. She was an exceptionally deep thinker for a young girl, but religion wasn't a topic she had ever pondered so seriously before. Now it all seemed incredibly important, and she felt an overwhelming desire to find the answers. She was just about to ask Reverend Tobias to show her some passages about God's mercy, when his wife spoke up.

"I think your mother wants to speak to you, Verity, Dear," announced Mrs. Tobias. Verity looked up and saw her mother standing alone waving at her, trying to get her attention.

"Thank-you, Reverend Tobias," Verity nodded, returning the pen and tucking the piece of paper into her pocket before she hurried across the room.

Kara's face was alight with joy. "Verity, I have wonderful news for all of us!" she exclaimed. "Aunt Judy has invited us to come and live with her in Ontario! It's been quite lonely for her since Uncle Ned passed away and you know she has that huge house out in the country. She's even offered me a job at the grocery store and occasional work for you and Thomas!"

Verity drew in a deep breath trying to take this all in. Saskatchewan had always been her home. This would mean leaving behind all the people she had grown up with, and beginning grade eleven at a strange school! On the other hand, she knew her mom was struggling to keep a steady job. Working for Aunt Judy would mean fair and reliable employment and they would get to live in a big house in the country! Home had only ever been one crowded rental unit after another, always in the centre of town surrounded by pavement and cement walls. Aunt Judy's offer sure sounded inviting!

But then, there was Thomas…

"Mom, I like the idea," Verity spoke hesitantly, "but Thomas won't, I know it!"

They both looked over at Thomas. There in the foyer he bantered about with Ken, obviously comparing which of them was taller. "They're like brothers," whispered Mom. "He's really had the best of friends." She gazed a moment more and then turned sharply away. "It is going to break his heart. You're right, Verity. But I feel I *must* take this opportunity! We've always been so desperately poor; life has been so hard! I can't go on like this forever…!"

At this moment Kara Lovell, who had maintained her composure all morning, broke down sobbing into her daughter's arms.

"It's okay, Mom," Verity said reassuringly, holding her close. "It's true. You've put up with so much and worked so hard. This is a wonderful opportunity for you, for all of us!"

Aunt Judy seeing and hearing the sudden change in emotions, hurried over, as did several others. "Kara, are you okay? What's happened?" she asked with deep concern. Hearing only sobs, Aunt Judy turned to Verity. "What's wrong with your mother?"

"Nothing," smiled Verity, "except that she wants to take you up on your offer to live in Ontario."

"Then it's all settled!" clapped her aunt joyfully.

"What's this?" broke in a deep, concerned voice. "Who's going to Ontario?"

Gazing back over her shoulder, Verity saw that Thomas and Ken had walked over to join them. She knew that this news would be devastating for him. It didn't seem to her that this was the right time or place to tell Thomas about the offer.

Aunt Judy however, thought differently. "You're going to Ontario, Thomas! All of you are going to come and live with me. Your mom can work in the grocery store…"

She didn't get any further because a wild-eyed Thomas burst out, "You've got to be joking! We aren't leaving here! This is our home! I'm not leaving my friends!"

Kara raised her tear-stained face and pleaded, "It's a wonderful offer, Thomas! Please, for my sake, accept it!"

Thomas gazed around in shocked dismay, astonished that such a life-shattering decision had been made so quickly without any input from him! Then, unable to endure the idea, he turned in despair and took off from the room, with Ken following close behind.

CHAPTER 2

Good-bye

Now that her father was dead, Verity hoped that all would be peaceful and calm at home. Unfortunately, this was not to be. The decision to move to Ontario was causing great friction between Thomas and his mother. In the evenings it was now her brother's angry voice that Verity heard when Kara arrived home from work. Thomas' roots ran deep in Saskatchewan. At school the good-looking, athletic youth was popular with most of his peers and many young ladies. His friends were all that mattered to him, all that he'd ever had in life. The last thing he wanted was to be dragged a thousand kilometres across Canada to begin life anew.

Verity had a few girlfriends that she would miss but she'd never enjoyed the popularity Thomas had. All through public school, while her classmates had wanted to run and play games, Verity had preferred to pick up a book and read. She'd always been the girl who asked too many questions; the girl who thought through everything far too seriously. Although she had her place in the group and was by no means considered a social outcast, she didn't feel very close to anyone in Saskatchewan. In a sense, with all the difficulties they had faced at home, while Thomas had found a form of escape in his social life, Verity had kept her nose in a book. Whenever she was overwhelmed by fear or pain, she would find a quiet place to hide away and take refuge in the latest novel she was reading. Then she could flee far off to worlds where every manifestation of evil was eventually vanquished, and the hero always triumphant. Books were easy to transport and readily available. She was confident that there would be many more in Ontario.

Day after day, Thomas tried his best to find another family to live with in Saskatchewan. He was determined not to leave, but so far no one had agreed to take him in. Ken's family was the most likely option, but his parents felt it was best for Thomas to have the opportunity to broaden his horizons. "It's not that we don't care about you or want you here, Thomas," Ken's dad had explained, "it's just that in the bigger picture, we think this move will open more doors for you down the road."

Finally, Kara sat down with her son one night. Compassionately, she pleaded that since this was his last year of high school, he would have to endure only ten months in Ontario and then he would be able to come back, get a job and live independently. "Thomas, please," she begged, "don't ask me to give up this wonderful opportunity when it only affects *one* year of your life! This may be the only chance I get."

Grudgingly, Thomas agreed but a storm cloud of anger and bitterness had entered his heart. He was further incensed when he realized that on top of leaving his hometown, he was also going to miss out on the trip he'd been so excited about! Aunt Judy had gone ahead and paid for their tickets to come out! To re-arrange for Thomas to join them three weeks later would cost money they didn't have, and could potentially upset Aunt Judy. Kara felt too beholden to risk that.

Thomas could hardly endure the disappointment. Not only was he upset with his mother and his aunt, this further aggravated the grudge he held against the man who had disappointed him all of his life. If it wasn't for the alcohol abuse, his father could have continued managing the huge farm operation he had once been responsible for. Without the alcohol, Thomas and Verity could have come home to a peaceful, loving home, instead of fear and uncertainty. They had never felt safe inviting friends over. Toys and possessions had constantly been pawned off for yet another drop of the dementing fluid. In all Thomas' proudest moments at school, his father's face was the one that was always missing. Then there had been that awful day where his dad had embarrassed him in front of all his friends. Now here, after his father's death, there was still another blow: they couldn't even stay in Saskatchewan, where at least he had adopted himself into his friends' families!

As the departure day loomed closer, Thomas tried again to convince his mom at least to let him go on the trip. "I'd be fine flying on my own, Mom," he argued. "I know Aunt Judy won't mind. Sure, I would be three weeks behind all of you but at least I'd be there a day before school starts!"

"Thomas," Kara replied wearily yet again, wondering if she was making the right decision, "Aunt Judy has booked and paid for these tickets. I don't want to mess things up by changing dates!"

The weeks that followed were very busy trying to work out travel details, saying good-bye to friends and giving away furniture to anyone who wanted it. Kara laughed that at least they didn't have to spend much time packing; there were only a few items worth taking along.

Cleaning out the closet one day, Thomas dragged out a large box of photo albums. Gingerly, he opened the one lying on top. He hadn't looked at them for years. For a moment he gazed, puzzled at the little boy's face that smiled happily from the black and white picture. Then in repulsion, he slammed the album shut. "Let's throw out this one! It's him!"

Kara stopped him before he could do any damage. "Thomas," she spoke, her voice trembling, "I'll sort through these."

Perplexed, Thomas argued, "Why would you even keep an album of Dad? Why on earth would you want to remember him?"

Wondering the same thing herself, Verity looked up to see a look of pain cross her mother's face. "He wasn't always... the way you remember," Kara choked. Her eyes scanned the room, looking for a new job for Thomas—something that would take him out of the house! At last, she looked over at the old kitchen chairs.

"Please, Thomas," she begged, "could you take those wooden chairs to Mrs. McMillan? I promised them to her."

Shaking his head in utter disbelief, Thomas obeyed.

Saying good-bye at the airport a week later, was an experience Verity felt sure she would never forget. So many people had come to see them off! After lots of hugs and tears, she felt relieved to be finally sitting on the plane. Thomas had put on a strong front in the airport but now he sat despondently a few rows ahead.

"Thomas looks like his life is just about to end," she commented to her mother, who was beside her.

"I know," Kara replied sadly. "If my head hadn't been in such a muddle the last few weeks, maybe I would have found a way to let him go on that trip. It's just been one more bitter pill to swallow."

Verity sighed. Even deep within herself, there were so many conflicting emotions. Her mind drifted back to the party they had been at the night before. Ken and a few of Thomas' closest friends had organized a going-away party for him, generously inviting Verity and her friends as well. It had been such a wonderful evening! Thomas had been so alive, so jovial, so animated. She wondered what his friends at school would think if they saw how dejected he looked now. It was strange that a person could be the life of the party in one situation and so sullen and withdrawn in the next. Yet, in the last few weeks he had bounced back and forth between those two extremes day after day.

The plane taxied down the runway and took off, climbing steeply up into the air. Verity leaned over to look out the window, fascinated by her first flight, watching houses and cars recede quickly until they were only tiny dots far below. When clouds blocked the view from the little window, Verity pulled out the large good-bye card she'd been given. She still felt surprised as she read over all the names and autographs that had been signed. A couple of her friends had taken up one whole side of the card expressing their grief. There were many notes stating how much this or that person was going to miss her. Some had written that they wished they could be more like her! Or that their mother wished they could be! While she had never felt lonely at school, she certainly hadn't realized any of them had cared so much. But then, maybe this was just how people wrote when good-byes had to be said. Even Ken had signed the card, "I'll never forget you! Keep asking questions! Love Ken."

She wished she could read Thomas' card as well, but so far he hadn't let her. Not only had he been given a big card, but he had also received presents and individual cards from over half the students in his class!

For the next few hours, she talked to her mom off and on and continued to enjoy the scenery when there was a break in the clouds. In her heart she was glad to be off on their new adventure. She was sorry to leave behind the people she had grown up with, but she was quite happy to escape the old life and memories. The new opportunities were becoming more exciting every moment. Before long she was looking out the window at the huge expanse of Toronto below her!

CHAPTER 3

A New Home

Aunt Judy met them at the airport and they all piled into her shiny, new Jeep. "Nice Jeep!" Thomas said, looking slightly impressed.

After driving for two hours, the last winding road to Aunt Judy's place thrilled Verity. Beauty lay on every side. Each hill felt like a roller coaster, dipping way down into forest-lined valleys and then coming up again so high that one could see far off into the distance. On both sides of the road lay farmers' fields and lovely country homes. Tall maples covered the hills with thick pines nestled close by.

"Aunt Judy, does *your* place look this beautiful?" Verity asked, fascinated.

Laughing, Aunt Judy bragged, "My place has the best view of all!"

They finally reached the highest hill they had seen in the distance and there on the right was Aunt Judy's grey stone house.

"Wow!" Verity said, impressed, as she gazed at the view in the backyard. "I can see for miles around and it's all trees and fields and rolling hills!"

"Go on, take a run out to that ridge over there," Aunt Judy said pointing. "Then you'll really feel on top of the world."

Verity pulled on Thomas' arm. "Come on. Stop wishing you were somewhere else! Let's go!"

There was just the tiniest hint of excitement on her brother's face as they went racing together across the mowed grass and up a winding pathway that led out to the hill. After a minute or two, they came to a place where the footpath ended, and the ridge dropped off steeply on all three sides at least fifty metres down.

"Hey, in the winter we could toboggan here!" Thomas exclaimed.

It was a long way down and a few large, mature trees grew at the bottom. Verity questioned the safety of such a venture, but she nodded in agreement.

"And there's even a lake over there!" Thomas said, pointing to a shimmering-blue body of water.

Shading her eyes, Verity could see it, although it was half hidden amongst trees. Part way down the hill, Verity found a delightful little nook. It was sheltered from the wind and curved perfectly to provide a backrest, yet still wide open to the view.

"The perfect reading spot!" she thought. "This is where I'll come to read all my books!"

In the last couple of weeks, she had been thinking a lot about what happened after death. She felt that if she had a Bible of her own, she wouldn't have to wait for other people to give her answers. She could find them out for herself. If Christianity was based upon the Bible, then surely somewhere within the pages of that book lay the answers to her questions. Somewhere there had to be a verse that explained just how good a person needed to be to go up to heaven. And what was heaven like? What would you actually do there every day? Did anyone ever get bored? The more she thought about it, the more questions she had.

There was only a week left before her birthday and she hoped that someone – perhaps Aunt Judy – would ask her if there was anything she wanted.

The sun was low in the sky and turning the world a lovely golden colour as she and Thomas walked down the hill to explore their new surroundings. They found several apple trees, loaded with small wild apples. A dirt road ran by the property at the bottom and a winding trail led into the forest. After making their way back up the hill again, they stood one last time on the top. A gentle breeze picked up Verity's long, dark brown hair and twisted it around her. Gazing out at the tall maple trees, the distant blue hills, the shimmering lake in the valley, she had a sensation that this was home. "I feel like this is where I belong," she said softly to Thomas. "This has to be the most beautiful place in the world!"

Thomas shook his head. "It's not what kind of view you have or how nice your house is that makes you belong—it's the people! It's where your friends are—and my friends are back in Saskatchewan!"

Verity wished she hadn't spoken. For a few moments Thomas had looked happy to be here until she had reminded him of what he'd left. As they walked back to the house in silence, Verity was delighted with everything she saw, but she wisely kept her feelings to herself.

When they came inside, Aunt Judy wanted to show them all through her home. It was huge! As they toured room after room, Verity began to think it would be easy to get lost in this place.

Sitting down to a lovely meal of Caesar salad, roast chicken, baked potatoes and two kinds of cooked vegetables, Verity glanced over at Thomas who was digging in with delight. On the plane he had refused to eat anything but now he had obviously decided to end his protest!

"Verity," Aunt Judy was saying, "since your birthday is next week, is there anything in particular you would like?"

Pausing to finish a mouthful of roast chicken, Verity was delighted. Here was her opportunity!

"Well, Aunt Judy, it's very kind of you to ask! What I would like more than anything else right now—is a Bible!"

Aunt Judy and Kara looked rather surprised and Thomas snickered loudly. "Have you gone nuts?!" he asked.

Sunday morning, Aunt Judy suggested they all take a drive into town for a tour of Grandville. It was Aunt Judy's day off and she wanted to show them the high school they would attend. Thomas and Verity were looking forward to seeing the grocery store that she owned as well. In fact, Verity was bursting with curiosity. She wanted to see the whole town, the stores, the people that she might go to school with, and what churches she could attend.

The first stop was Kolmer's IGA, Aunt Judy's grocery store, which was open on Sunday. Aunt Judy showed them every section of her store proudly, giving the history of what it had been like when she and Uncle Ned had bought it many years ago and what they had done to upgrade it. Privately, Verity was a little bored until they reached the bakery. "Now, my dears," Aunt Judy directed, "I want you to try these cheese bagels. We've just begun making them and they are the best! Especially when they're still hot and fresh from the oven."

The bagels were delicious!

Since Aunt Judy had a few management matters to attend to, Verity asked if she could take a walk around town. She asked Thomas if he wanted to come but he had found a bench in the sunshine and was content to sit and eat.

Grandville was quite a small town. It was easy to find the main centre. Walking quickly, she made her way to Broadway and passed by a couple of churches within the first block. There was an old, very large, Roman Catholic Church with a tall steeple and pretty stained-glass windows. A little further down stood a beautiful stone church with a clock tower that now had an "Art Gallery" sign in front. She wondered why it wasn't a church any longer.

At the main intersection, Verity could see that this was the old downtown section. Almost all the storefronts looked as though they had been there for at least a century. A few of the shop windows held her attention as she gazed at the various objects displayed in them. It was rather busy in this area of Grandville and many people passed by her on the sidewalks. Some glanced curiously in her direction, while others brushed past her as though she were just another lamppost. A few shared smiles and nods with her.

Continuing her walk further east she saw a modern 'Gilgal Bible Chapel'. She could hear the voices of people singing to a lively beat and the sign in front said, 'All Welcome'. "Maybe I'll go there someday," she thought. "It kind of looks like our church back home."

Gazing up the road further, she thought perhaps she had come to the end of Grandville's downtown district, so she decided to go back to the IGA a different way. As she went around the block, she came across a plain white church with a large sign advertising a public talk that evening. She glanced over at the sign. It said, *'God's Promises to Man. Do You Know Them? Will You Take Part in Them?'*

"God's promises," she echoed in her mind. "I have no idea what those are." After a few moments of reflection, she wondered if the sign was referring to the promise of going to heaven.

As she began walking past the building, she could hear a rousing hymn being sung inside. She paused to listen carefully. Some of the phrases reaching her ears puzzled her. They didn't fit into the picture she had of life after death. *"Hail! Jesus comes again, Hallelujah, amen. He comes o'er earth to reign…"* and then, *"True Heir to David's throne, he'll claim it as his own; his power shall then be known…"*

"Hmm, that's strange," she thought. "Why would Jesus come back to reign on earth when all the good people have gone to heaven to be with him?"

She was mulling this over, when a shiny, red Jeep pulled up beside her. "Would you like to come see the school now, Dear?" Aunt Judy asked.

"For sure!" Verity said, getting in, as a tingle of excitement ran up her spine.

"Thomas and your mother walked over from the store," her aunt answered, in response to Verity's look of surprise that they weren't also in the Jeep. "This is the school your father and mother and I all went to. We spent many happy years here and I'm sure you will too."

Verity looked up amused. "My father was actually happy?"

A look of astonishment passed over Aunt Judy's face, followed slowly by a nod of understanding. "My dear, your father wasn't always the way you remember him. I suppose all your memories are of a sick, old drunk; and yet, I'm sure when you were four or five, he was a very different man. Don't you remember any happy times with him?"

"No, I don't!" Verity stated flatly. "I only remember him being angry or totally drunk. In fact, I try my best not to even think about him."

Aunt Judy's eyes looked rather misty when Verity turned to see why she wasn't responding. "I have some pictures of better days," Aunt Judy said at last.

"I don't want to see anything about him." Verity shuddered.

"And yet," Aunt Judy went on slowly, "you're a lot like him..."

"No way!" interjected Verity with alarm in her dark eyes. "Please, Aunt Judy, don't ever say that!!"

"Verity!" her aunt pleaded. "He was my brother! I still love him! I used to play with him when we were kids. We grew up together. I enjoyed being with Dan!"

Thankfully, they had arrived at the high school and Verity was happy to jump out and discuss something else. They walked all the way around the brown brick building. Aunt Judy pointed out entrances and peeked in windows to show them where different classes would be held. The school was in good condition but much smaller than the one they had been used to back in Saskatchewan.

Aunt Judy wanted to show them the football field and ball diamonds, but Verity was feeling a little tired from all the walking that morning. Sometimes her lower back hurt when she exercised a lot. She decided to have a rest on the grass beside the school as the others walked off to the grounds. It was a beautiful summer day. A slight breeze brought relief from the hot sun shining down. Sitting back contented, she watched people coming and going in the neighbourhood nearby. A group of teenage girls walked past, laughing and chatting to one another. Verity wondered if any of them might become her friends. An older lady was out in her backyard watering her flowers while her husband mowed the lawn. Quite a few children were playing on the playground equipment at the primary school across the way. Up ahead, a dark green car pulled into a driveway and two men in suits and a white-haired lady got out. One looked to be about Thomas' age. It really was fun to observe all the people in the town, who were strangers now, but not for long. Who would she get to know? Who would she hang around with? Would it be easy to fit in? If only school began tomorrow!

When the sports field tour had been completed, Verity could see from the look on Thomas' face that the morning's excursion had only served to increase his homesickness. She jumped up, reaching out to take his arm. "You'll soon have lots of new friends..." she started to say but he yanked his arm away.

"Just ten months and then I'm out of here! I can't wait!" he snarled, his blue eyes flashing. "I don't want any new friends!"

Verity felt hurt. Why did Thomas have to be so horrible about this? Was he going to continue to be so angry in school? Or was this just the way he was acting with his family?

CHAPTER 4

A New Book

Augding. There weren't any friends to invite over,
A ugust fourteenth came quickly and Verity celebrated her
sixteenth birthday. There weren't any friends to invite over,
but she was used to that. With her dad having been so sick
and unpredictable she could only vaguely remember the last time
she'd had friends at her party.

"Oh, Mom," she exclaimed, holding up the new clothes she'd
just unwrapped. "These are so beautiful and they're even brand
new!"

"Yes, they're new. You do like the colours and everything?"

"They're perfect!"

Kara had always done her best to find good clothing at second
hand stores, but until now new clothes were an unaffordable luxury.

There were a two hair scrunchies from Thomas and they were
even the right colour to go with her new outfits. It was a step up
from his usual gift of a chocolate bar and gum. "Oh thank-you,
Thomas!" she exclaimed, "This is just what I needed—and they
even match!"

"I hope you aren't fussy about translations, Verity," Aunt Judy
said apologetically, handing her a rectangular gift wrapped in the
most beautiful paper Verity had ever seen. "I always thought a Bible
was a Bible. I had no idea there were so many different versions.
Finally, I asked the saleslady what the difference was. She told me
that the original Bible was written in some other languages, I can't
remember which, and today there are several English translations to
choose from. One that she showed me was authorized by a King
hundreds of years ago, and therefore used rather old English. There
was another Bible that was a paraphrase, which she said wasn't

really very accurate—just someone putting the Bible into his own words. There were several others too—but she personally recommended the New International Version. Apparently, it uses modern language but is still quite accurate."

"I wouldn't know the difference," Verity shrugged, as she took the soft cover book out of its wrappings and fingered the gilt edges. "I'm just so happy to have a Bible of my own. Now I can find all the answers to my questions! Thanks, Aunt Judy!"

Early the next morning, Aunt Judy and Kara left for work again, promising that tomorrow both Thomas and Verity could come in and work for some pocket money. As soon as they were alone, Thomas spoke up disdainfully, "Why on earth would you ask for a Bible as a birthday present? If you want a book for your present, at least pick something that's not ancient and outdated!"

Verity looked up from finishing her breakfast. "There are some questions that are bothering me," she replied, "and I think I'll find the answers in the Bible."

"It's just a book of myths and fables. You'll never understand it," Thomas scoffed, as he smoothed back his dark curls and headed towards the front door.

His words sounded exactly like something her father would have said and Verity couldn't restrain herself. "You're just like Dad," she sighed, "always putting down religion."

"I am not like Dad!" Thomas whirled around angrily. "I may not be religious, but I don't go around beating people up!"

Verity watched him head off dejectedly to the forest. She sighed again deeply. At home she could hardly remember seeing Thomas alone and now out here in the country, he really had no choice. How she hoped he would find at least one good friend at school.

Ah yes, school! Taking her bowl over to the dishwasher, she finished loading the rest of the dishes and turned it on. There were only two weeks left before school began. She wanted to get lots of reading done before things got busy. With Mom and Aunt Judy gone most of the day and even a couple of evenings each week, she was very happy to have something to do. The list of chores they left her each morning only took about an hour and then she had to occupy herself until it was time to prepare supper.

"I sure hope I can find answers in here," she thought, feeling a little intimidated, as she picked up her new book. It really was so huge and there were so many different books inside to make up the whole. "Kings, Chronicles, Psalms, Isaiah…" she murmured, flipping through. "Now where should I start?" She remembered hearing a few things about the New Testament and began turning to Matthew. "But then," she mused to herself, "with any other book I would start at the very beginning, so maybe that's what I should do."

Feeling good about that decision, she grabbed a notebook and pen and headed out to the hill. It was the perfect place for concentration and peace, a place where Thomas wouldn't disturb her. She ran up the pathway. Curiosity and excitement were welling up within. What would she discover now that she had the opportunity to look at the Bible for herself?

After tramping down the long grass, Verity settled comfortably into the nook on the hill. She gazed at the words on the cover, 'The Holy Bible'. She had read many books before, but none of them had professed they were 'holy'. Was this book really written by God? Did God even exist? If He did, did He hope that everyone would read the message that He had written?

Pondering these matters, she admired the beauty all around her. She could see across the valley for miles, the rolling hills fading off near the horizon in pale blue curves. Green leafy trees below waved gently in the light summer breeze. Up above in the huge expanse of sapphire-blue sky, sharp-eyed hawks flew in wide circles, their tiny eyes looking hundreds of feet below for their next meal. Verity felt fairly confident that there was a God, but she couldn't have proved His existence to anyone else.

The very first verse in Genesis began with the statement, *"In the beginning God created the heavens and the earth."*

"This is interesting!" she mused, after reading the whole chapter. "The Bible begins by claiming that God created the whole world in just six days. This must be the very first thing God wants us to know." As she glanced over the chapter again, thinking about what she had learned in school, she felt uneasy. How did evolution fit into this whole picture? Did God start evolution? But no, God said He created the world in six days—not millions of years. Did the Bible begin with a lie? Or was evolution a lie? Or was there some other way to see both together? She picked up her notepad. Already she had questions to jot down.

In chapter two she read the details of how God had created man out of the dust and *"breathed into his nostrils the breath of life, and the man became a living being."*

Verity carried on reading for a while, wrapped up in the story of Adam and Eve. After they had sinned because a talking serpent had lied to Eve, she wondered why God barred them from eating from the tree of life and living forever. This seemed confusing. In what sense was God worried about Adam and Eve living forever? Was it possible that they could have lived forever *on the earth?* Or did this refer to the afterlife? Perhaps Adam and Eve didn't have immortal souls yet? More questions!

In chapter four, Verity was amazed that Cain became the first murderer. He even lied to God. "Wow," she thought, "God just created the world and already He needs a jail!" As a punishment, God sent Cain far away.

Reading through chapter five, she was astonished how long people were living. "Is this for real?" she wondered. "How could people live over nine hundred years?" Over and over in the chapter it was also recorded that people lived and then they died. Why wasn't anything written about where they went next?

When she came to Enoch in the same chapter, she read, *"Enoch walked with God; then he was no more, because God took him away."*

"It doesn't say where God took him to," she puzzled, "but it must be heaven." Was Enoch the only good man? Had no one else been taken away? She felt a little unsure about her dad's chances for heaven, if Enoch was the only person so far that had been good enough.

Verity was quite surprised to discover in Genesis chapter six, that people were so wicked God had to wipe them all out with a flood and start over again with Noah and his family. "Okay," she thought, "now these people must be really bad sinners if God wants to destroy them all! So why doesn't God say they are all going to hell?"

Reading about the rainbow after the flood was surprising. "Wow!" she thought, "I didn't know a rainbow is the symbol of God's promise to never flood the earth again! Until now I've only thought about the pot of gold at the end—never about a promise from God!" Then she remembered her walk around town and the sign about God's promises. Was the rainbow one of promises?

The story of Abram began in chapter twelve and was quite captivating. "God must have really liked this man to have made him so many promises!" she remarked to herself. More promises! "But why did God say He would give Abram all the land he could *see* forever, for himself and his descendants? Did this mean Abram would never die or just that he would keep all the land as long as he lived? Why did God use the word 'forever'?"

Verity was puzzled again when she came to chapter twenty. Abram (now Abraham) was living in Abimelech's land. "Why isn't Abraham living in the land God gave him?" she wondered. "Didn't he like it?" She was even more confused in chapter twenty-three. "This doesn't make sense. Why would Abraham have to *buy* land for his wife's grave? Why wouldn't he use the land he was given?"

She sighed deeply as she looked at the long list of questions she had jotted down. "It would be really nice," she said aloud to no one in particular, "to have someone I could talk to about all of this!" Almost two hours had passed and instead of finding the answers she was looking for, her reading had simply engendered many more questions! And the Bible was such a huge book!

Her thoughts were suddenly interrupted by a rustling sound of approaching footsteps. She turned quickly to see who was coming. It was Thomas. He was just as surprised to see her as she was to see him. Tears filled his deep blue eyes and he held a letter in his hand. "Oh, so this is where you've disappeared to!" he muttered, as he turned around to go back to the house.

"Thomas, what's wrong?" Verity cried, jumping up and running after him. At first, Thomas wouldn't respond.

Verity grabbed his arm. "Thomas, what's the matter? Did you get some bad news?"

Instead of speaking, Thomas opened the envelope and pulled out a photo. Verity looked at it. Ken stood by a crystal-clear lake with jagged mountains in the background. Verity guessed the photo had been taken at Lake Louise. Instead of a smile, Ken looked downcast. Written across the bottom of the photo in gel marker were the words, "Everything is fantastic... except you're not here!"

"Oh, Thomas," she said sadly, "I'm so sorry you had to miss out on that wonderful trip!"

Pulling his arm away, he exclaimed angrily, "Nothing's fair!" He picked up a rock and threw it far into the valley. "I'm supposed to be all happy and thankful that Aunt Judy brought us here—and I'm not! In fact, I hate it! I wish we were back in Saskatchewan! So, what if we lived in a run-down shack. At least we had friends! At least I was happy!"

Verity knew better than to try to reason with him.

Thomas understood she didn't feel the same. "Go back to your reading," he shrugged. "I didn't mean to bother you!"

He could have said the words sincerely, but Verity heard the contempt in his voice. As she watched him trudge off, she wondered what it would take for him to see things differently; or whether he ever would. For quite a while she just sat on the hill staring out to the horizon. School started next week, and Thomas certainly didn't seem to be settling in! She struggled to think of what could be done for him. Unfortunately, she didn't get any bright ideas.

CHAPTER 5

A Bad Start

In the last week before school, Verity made the most of her quiet, peaceful days. Out in the country, as they were, there weren't many opportunities for social outings except when Aunt Judy brought them in to work in the store once a week. The closest neighbours commuted an hour every day to a big city for work. Across the road, a large potato farm sprawled on the gently rolling slopes. The couple that lived there had two children but they weren't even old enough to attend school yet.

Day after sunny day, Verity spent most of her time tucked away in the hill reading her new Bible. Here and there the stories touched her heart so much that tears came to her eyes. The life of Joseph, beginning in Genesis chapter thirty-seven, read like a highly dramatic play. She could see it all clearly before her eyes; the jealousy of his brothers, the love he shared with his father and his deep devotion to God. It shocked her to read of Joseph's envious brothers selling him as a slave to a group of Ishmaelites travelling to Egypt. When she read of Potiphar's wife trying unsuccessfully to seduce the handsome, young Joseph, she shook her head in amazement. The story had every element of a Hollywood movie and yet it was wholesome and discreetly written with strong moral lessons. Finally, when Joseph, now second only to Pharaoh, revealed himself to his brothers, the love and forgiveness he expressed melted her heart. The story was so good, she read it twice.

On Friday morning Verity awoke early. Today she and Thomas were to go into town and meet with the guidance counsellor at the high school to finalize their course selections. Then Aunt Judy had promised to find a few jobs at the store to keep them busy for the afternoon. It was rather exciting to have a whole day in town. Would they meet anyone interesting today? If only Thomas could find a friend like Ken, Verity was sure he would stop being so

31

miserable. It would be great to have him happy again! How she longed for a peaceful home. In her mind, all that was needed now was for Thomas to find one good friend!

Rolling over in bed, she checked to see what time it was. It was only six a.m.! There were still four hours to go before they were going to leave, but she was too excited to go back to sleep. Reaching over for her Bible, she pulled herself up in bed. Since they were going to be out for the whole day, it'd be good to get some reading done now.

Having finished Genesis, she opened up her Bible to the next book, Exodus. It was easy to get caught up in the story of Moses and the horrible Pharaoh who wanted all the Israelite baby boys to be drowned in the river! How ironic that Pharaoh's own daughter found little baby Moses floating in a basket and decided to adopt him!

In Exodus chapter six, she came across a verse where God told Moses He was going to bring Israel into the land He had promised to Abraham, Isaac and Jacob. Here was that promise being repeated again! Why was this land so important?

Moses had the difficult job of trying to convince Pharaoh to let the nation of Israel leave Egypt. Pharaoh had been using the Israelites as his slave labour force. If he were to let them all go, only Egyptians would be left to do all the hard work and they weren't likely to want to work for nothing!

"I wonder if the Israelites built any of the pyramids?" she mused.

God sent plague after plague, but Pharaoh stubbornly refused to let the Israelites go. Why didn't he see that he couldn't fight against God? It wasn't until all the firstborn children and animals had died, including Pharaoh's own son that he decided to let Israel go. But then, the next day he changed his mind and gathered his whole army together to chase after the Israelites. When the Israelites cried because they were trapped between a huge sea and the approaching Egyptians, God parted the water for them and they walked through the sea on a dry path!

"Wow!" she thought, "they were so lucky to see such a miracle! Now they will know for sure that God is real and able to do anything!" After the Israelites had crossed between two walls of water, on dry ground, the Egyptians chased after them. God brought the sea back together and the Egyptians were drowned. It was such a demonstration of God's power! In their thankfulness, the Israelites sang and the women danced to praise God for their freedom. But only a couple of days later in the story, the Israelites began complaining that they had nothing to eat.

In surprise Verity thought, "With all the power their God has shown them, I'm sure if they just asked Him nicely, He could make food on the spot!" She shook her head. "Why didn't these people trust God? They were shown a miracle almost every day and yet they seemed unable to believe that God could provide in the next situation."

The last half of Exodus dealt primarily with many of the laws and regulations God had for the nation of Israel. It impressed her how fair and well-thought-out God's rules were. For example, in Exodus chapter twenty-two, if a thief stole another man's ox, then he had to pay two oxen back as punishment for his crime. If he couldn't pay back for his crime, then he was to be sold as a servant for up to six years. "Much better for him to work and pay back his crime, than to sit in a jail and do nothing," she thought.

Poor people were allowed to help themselves to what was left over from other people's crops. "I guess that was God's way of providing a welfare program," she reckoned, remembering many trips to the foodbank.

Hearing a door bang in the hallway, Verity glanced over again at the clock. It was almost seven-thirty and time for breakfast. In a flash she was out of bed, truly looking forward to the day.

The meeting with the guidance counsellor took almost an hour. Everything in the school seemed exciting and intimidating at the same time. The long, plain hallways were so quiet and empty that it was hard to believe they would be full of students next week.

As Thomas and Verity headed back to the IGA they passed a large group of teens in their bathing suits, heading to the local pool. "I wish we were going for a swim," she said, looking longingly after the group and noting that a few of them were looking back at her.

"I don't," Thomas muttered.

"But it would be such a great way to meet people!"

"I don't want to meet anyone!"

"You don't?"

"No! I'm only here for ten months and then I'm going back home. What's the use of getting to know people I'll never see again?"

Glancing up with alarm, Verity wondered if Thomas really intended to be anti-social.

They spent the afternoon at the store. Verity was given the job of watering the fall chrysanthemums in the outdoor garden centre. Thomas had to collect carts and bring them back in. There were plenty of moms with small children milling about the store and several elderly couples, but not many teens.

Having watered, deadheaded, and reorganized all the plants, Verity started to help stock shelves and stack cardboard boxes. Thomas was sorting through the fresh produce, pulling out old stock and replacing it with new. Suddenly, to Verity's great delight, in walked the same group of teens they had passed earlier! From where she was positioned by the cereal aisle, she could see that a couple of the girls noticed Thomas right away. His back was to them as they whispered and glanced at each other. Then smoothing back their hair and joining arms they approached him.

"Excuse me," the blonde one giggled. "Do you work here?"

"I don't think we've seen you before," said the other tall, athletic girl. "Are you new to the area?"

Without even so much as a smile, Thomas pointed at another employee working in the meat department. "If you want to know anything—that's the guy to ask."

It was plain to see that the two girls were disappointed. Thomas had even turned his back on them. Surely, he must have known that the girls were more interested in talking, than in finding groceries! In a huff they walked off to join their group of friends.

Verity could hardly believe what she'd just seen. Thomas had been absolutely rude! She could hear the girls relaying how unfriendly he was. What a shame! They didn't appreciate all that Thomas had been through and what was behind the miserable look on his face. She wished she could run up and explain that Thomas wasn't really that mean—that he was just lonely and angry and homesick. But she knew such action would make her brother furious.

Was Thomas really going to shut himself off from other people for a year? How could he ever exist in such a state when he was used to being popular? Why didn't he want to make new friends and start a new life like she did?

CHAPTER 6

In Need of Help

On the last Saturday before school began, it rained all day. Unable to go out to the hill, Verity went up to her room instead. Aunt Judy had decorated this room in a wonderful fashion. Everything matched in a lovely rose print. There was a big solid bed with lots of cushions, ruffles, and a little reading light in just the right spot. A huge window filled half of the wall opposite the bed. In front of the window a soft burgundy sofa stretched across, welcoming anyone to sit and enjoy the view. There was a lovely wooden desk in one corner and a matching dresser in the other. It was luxurious!

Bunching up the pillows on her bed, she reached for her Bible lying on the bedside table. She had finished the first four books, filled many pages of her notebook and was about to start the book of Deuteronomy.

Not far into Deuteronomy, she came across chapter six, verse four, *"Hear O Israel: The LORD our God, the LORD is one."* "That seems odd," she thought. "Why does God feel it's necessary to state that He is *one* God? Wouldn't that be obvious?" She added another question to her notepad.

The experiences of the children of Israel in the wilderness had been an eye opener. At times the narrative changed from a story to very factual information about their worship practices and instructions for building a tabernacle. As she was primarily searching for answers about life after death, she skimmed through the factual details fairly quickly. The stories however, were fascinating to her eager mind. What kept repeating itself over and over again was how quickly people went astray from God's commands. There only ever seemed to be a handful of people out of thousands, who were faithful to God. All the others were continually disobeying, complaining, being faithless and wanting to worship idols.

"Why would anyone want to worship an idol?" she wondered aloud. "And yet there must have been some compelling reason. God forbids making idols in the Ten Commandments."

She was also surprised to see a different side of God than the one Reverend Tobias usually spoke of. Several times in the wilderness, thousands of Israelites were wiped out for complaining or disobeying God's laws. It appeared to Verity that God got angry a lot and when He was angry many people were destroyed rather quickly. "I thought it was wrong to get angry," she said to herself. "I wonder if there are times when it's okay to be angry?" This led her to think again about life after death. If God was so upset with all these people that He killed them, would He then turn around and offer them a place in heaven? The chances of her father being up in heaven with God were becoming more remote. "And yet," she puzzled aloud, "God doesn't threaten any of the Israelites with going to hell, or offer any of them the reward of heaven."

So far, the Old Testament hadn't yielded much detail about heaven or hell. For that reason, she decided to begin reading the New Testament everyday as well. It seemed to her that Reverend Tobias had usually quoted from the New Testament, not the Old—so perhaps Jesus would have more to say about life after death.

As there wasn't much else to do that rainy Saturday, she just carried on reading the gospel of Matthew. Again and again, she saw the phrase, 'the kingdom of heaven,' which she jotted down on her pad of paper. But in Matthew chapter five she came across verse five that stated, *'Blessed are the meek, for they will inherit the earth.'* That reminded her of the promise God had made to Abraham, Isaac and Jacob about inheriting the land forever. Then in Matthew chapter eight, verse eleven she read about Abraham, Isaac and Jacob sitting down in the 'kingdom of heaven' at a big feast. When would that take place?

An hour later, she came across Matthew chapter nineteen, where in verses twenty-three to twenty-four, Jesus said it would be hard for even a rich man to get into the kingdom of heaven. If it was hard for a rich man to go to heaven, what about her dad?

That evening, after she had cooked dinner, eaten it with the others and retired to bed, Verity came across a passage that made her sit straight up and shudder. *"...But suppose that servant is wicked and says to himself, 'My master is staying away a long time,' and he then begins to beat his fellow servants and to eat and drink with the drunkards. The master of that servant will come on a day when he does not expect him and at an hour he is not aware of. He will cut him to pieces and assign him a place with the hypocrites, where there shall be weeping and gnashing of teeth."*

Did verses forty-eight to fifty-one of Matthew twenty-four, really mean what they said? Because if they did, then it didn't sound like God offered much hope for someone who had lived like her father had.

Every now and then Verity tried to express one of her many questions to the other members of her household around the supper table. She was getting used to the fact that no one else had even considered the question, never mind the answer. However, the more she read, the more she had an overwhelming desire to discuss what she was finding with someone else. On the Sunday evening before school began, she tried again.

"Why do you suppose anyone would want to worship an idol?" she asked, as the lasagne was being served.

"Why do you suppose anyone would want to worship God?" mocked Thomas.

"Thomas!" rebuked Kara sharply, "don't ever talk like that around here!"

Turning to Verity, Kara said wearily, "I have no idea about idols but I do feel you are spending too much time reading that Bible!"

Verity was dismayed. "Mom, how could anyone spend too much time reading the Bible?"

Kara shook her head. "Verity, it's putting a lot of funny thoughts in your head. We don't have Reverend Tobias here to sort you out."

"Funny ideas? Mom, you're a Christian! Isn't Christianity based on the Bible?"

"Well, yes, of course," stammered her mother. "But you need a pastor or someone with a full understanding to help you get it all straight! Last night, Verity, you asked why God said He was only one God, when Reverend Tobias used to say, 'God is three in one'! You are too young to understand the Bible by yourself!"

That evening as Verity got ready for bed, the pain in her back shot down her leg. "I must have twisted wrong," she thought dismissively, as the pain subsided.

Pondering what her mother had said had dinner, she wondered if her mom and Thomas were right. After all, she had gone searching for answers and instead she was just finding more and more questions! She looked at her Bible lying on the bedside table, a blue ribbon marking her place only such a little way into the whole book. Instead of her usual excitement about curling up in bed to continue her quest, she felt a great wave of despair wash over. "Maybe I won't bother reading tonight," she decided with a sigh. "I'll do something else instead."

As she gazed around the room for ideas of just what she might do, her eyes fell on a new picture hanging on the wall. "Aunt Judy must have hung it in here!" she guessed. She shuffled across the room in her slippers and then stopped short, realizing who it was that smiled out at her. The man in the picture was her dad and he was holding a little girl in his arms at a cottage.

"That's me!" she gasped, recognizing her brown hair and eyes. Suddenly, she remembered this very moment. Her father had taken her down to the lake, while her mom had been busy making dinner. She had been afraid to put her face in the water but with Dad's patient—yes, patient—little games he had finally convinced her to try it. Both faces were smiling triumphantly because they had just overcome a tremendous hurdle. Why had she forgotten that moment? She actually had one good memory! Were there more tucked away?

A corner of her heart brightened and then a totally unconnected thought came into her mind; she didn't know why. It suddenly occurred to her to pray! She had never prayed on her own before. "If that difficult book is really God's Word," she said aloud, "then why not pray to God for His help in understanding it?"

Throwing off the despair, she reflected on how God had brought about all kinds of unexpected events when people had decided to pray to Him for help. In fact, wasn't that the whole lesson she had been learning from Israel in the wilderness? They had constantly provoked God to anger because whenever they needed help, they complained. If they had truly appreciated His might and power and love, they would have seen their needs and humbly asked God for help. She was able to read about *their* circumstances and observe that surely a God that could open a sea and let them walk on dry land was capable of providing water in a desert; so now, what about her own life?!

With a great sense of relief she prayed, "Dear God, I am so very thankful to be alive. I am so glad You have written a book so that I can know about You. Please, please help me understand what I'm reading. And if there's anyone around here who could help explain the Bible to me, please let me find them. Amen."

With a quiet assurance in her heart, believing that all was now in God's hands, she laid her head upon her pillow and fell asleep.

CHAPTER 7

A Special Invitation

Tuesday was the first day of school. Both Thomas and Verity arrived in the morning very confident that they knew which entrance to go through but not at all sure what they would find inside. After stopping at the office and getting helpful directions, they eventually found their way to class.

The first teacher Verity met was Mr. Symons. A tall, middle-aged man, with kind blue eyes and a friendly smile, greeted all the grade eleven math students as they filed into the room. What Verity noticed first was his tie. It was dark black silk with planets floating around, and written at the bottom were the words, *'In the beginning God created...'*

It didn't take long before the first 'wise guy' put up his hand to ask, "Mr. Symons, aren't you aware that Evolution is a proven theory?"

Mr. Symons grinned. "Shane Black, aren't you aware that Evolution is not a proven theory at all?" [1]

Everyone in the class hoped that this argument would continue, but the rest of the seventy-minute period focused mainly on math. Verity liked Mr. Symons' pleasant manner and she could follow his logic amazingly well. She wished though, that they could have discussed his tie a little longer.

Towards the end of the day, Verity noticed that one girl with shoulder-length, light brown hair seemed to be in all her classes. The teachers referred to her as 'Purity'.

---

[1] (1) DISMANTLED EVOLUTION | Official Trailer [HD] | Documentary - YouTube

"Is that really her name?" Verity wondered, "or a nickname?" Once, Purity turned to glance quickly at Verity and in that brief instant their eyes had met. It is hard to judge a person's character in only one glance, but there was a sweet and lovely light that shone from Purity's grey-green eyes. While lots of other girls were using every free moment to gossip loudly about boys and parties, Purity sat quietly, diligently beginning the assigned homework. Verity was quite curious about this girl. Even Purity's modest skirt and top were quite distinct from the scant clothing many others wore. Did she always dress this way?

In each class that they had been in together, Purity had kept to herself, not having much to do with anyone around her. "Either she's new like me," thought Verity, "or she isn't very interested in having friends."

Most of the students were quite friendly and Verity was enjoying meeting so many new people. At the end of the day, she left feeling there were many people she would like to know better.

Thomas had passed her a few times in the hall and Verity could tell that his day was not going well. She sighed. Her brother looked so miserable that it would be hard for anyone to think he would be worth getting to know.

At supper that night, Thomas expressed all his disappointments of the day. "It's a dumb school! There wasn't one friendly person! I didn't see anyone I'd want for a friend anyway! I hate this place! I can't wait until I'm eighteen and out of here!"

"Did you try to be friendly to anyone, Thomas?" asked his mother cautiously.

"Try to be friendly!?" erupted Thomas. "I'm the stranger— they should be making an effort to be friendly to me!"

Verity thought it might be best not to mention her good day right then. Later, when Thomas had retired to his room, she felt free to tell her mom all the things that had happened. "And Mom," she finished, "I really like my math teacher, Mr. Symons! He was wearing this tie that said, *'In the beginning God created...!'*"

The first couple of weeks of school seemed to fly by. Every day Verity became more confident of friendships and her place in the school. She was intrigued by Purity, but the quiet girl was hardly ever around when there was an opportunity to talk, so it was rather difficult to get to know her. Mr. Symons always got a smile from her though and Verity wondered if he had been her teacher last year, or if Purity knew him some other way.

Across from her in math class, sat Emily who was always friendly and constantly needing Verity's help to figure out her homework. She had short, black hair and seemed to get along with everyone. It didn't take much effort to be Emily's friend.

Verity's favourite teacher was still Mr. Symons. Not only did he explain math lessons well, but he also often made little comments or asked leading questions to encourage his students to think about life and see the 'bigger picture'.

In contrast to her math teacher, Mr. Connor was the science teacher. Right away, Verity could see he had no time for God. The second week of school he delved into the 'Big Bang Theory', teaching how life evolved from the first simple cell, as though there were no other alternatives to consider.

"Another question to sort through!" Verity commented to herself. "Am I going to take the Bible for what it says, or is some of it just myth?"

Yet, in science class she made another friend, a petite girl named Kate with red, curly hair. Whenever Mr. Connor talked for too long, Kate was sure to liven things up by sending funny little notes.

So, Verity was feeling quite welcome at the school and happy to be there—but unfortunately her brother was not. Whenever she passed him in the halls, he barely acknowledged her presence, and he was always alone. She had even overheard a few of the grade twelve students discussing how grumpy he was. Some had suggested that Thomas thought he was better than everyone else, while others thought he was just a grouch. Then she heard them repeating the story of how snobby he had been in the grocery store to Sandy and Roxanne!

If only they understood! If only she knew them well enough to explain!

Stepping off the school bus one lovely September afternoon, Verity noticed that Thomas wasn't running to get the mail as usual. Ken had written once a week at first but since school began, not a single letter had arrived from him.

She watched her brother trudge despondently up the driveway as she walked over to the mailbox. "Thomas must've had a really bad day!" she thought, feeling a little sorry for him. "He's even given up thinking there might be a letter." She shook her head sadly. "I don't know how it can get any worse though—really, he talks to no one, and no one talks to him!"

When she opened the mailbox, all worry about Thomas faded as she grasped the pale green flyer that lay on top of all the newspapers. The word 'Bible' caught her eye. It was an advertisement for a series of six seminars designed to teach people how to read the Bible for themselves! She carefully read the information inside the front page: *"If you find reading the Bible difficult or frustrating at times, then these seminars are for you. They are aimed at equipping you with the skills and determination to understand Scriptural doctrines for yourself and benefit from a new appreciation of the Bible. Whether you are familiar with the Bible or are new to reading it, you will walk away with loads of information and new energy to begin reading more effectively..."*

"Wow! It's like they designed this course for me!" she exclaimed aloud. "This is going to help me understand the Bible for myself!!" She scanned the flyer further. "What you will learn…" she read; then in delight she exclaimed, "they are going to deal with what happens at death! Oh! And there's a class on 'The Bible interprets itself'! Maybe I will get some of my questions answered!" At the bottom was the assurance, "It's totally free and there are no obligations—ever!"

"That's good," she thought, "Mom will like *free!*"

Flipping to the back of the page she couldn't believe her eyes! There were photos of both presenters, and one was Mr. Symons! He and a Mr. Henderson were to be the presenters for the upcoming six nights.

Verity fairly flew into the house to show her mother the good news. However, her mother didn't seem to appreciate what a wonderful opportunity this was. With pursed lips she read through the flyer silently as Verity stood by anxiously imploring, "Mom, it's exactly what I need! You said I needed someone to help me understand the Bible! I prayed to God for help—and here it is!"

"Verity, it's not put on by our church. I don't know if you'll be taught things that are right or not."

"But Mom," she pleaded, "Mr. Symons is doing it! He's my favourite teacher at school!"

"I don't know why you have to be so consumed by this Verity! You scare me!"

"Mom, I just want to find out exactly what happens to people when they die. At least," she murmured, remembering, "that's all I wondered at first and now I guess I've found a hundred more questions!"

Kara Lovell opened the flyer and examined the schedule again, then sighed. "It's too bad the subject of 'Life and Death in the

Bible' isn't on the first night of the series!" She paused. "Well, I'll talk it over with your aunt and tell you my decision later."

Verity felt like she was holding her breath all evening. Why did her mom have to get so upset about her being interested in religion? There were lots of worse activities a young teen could become involved in. Why be upset about studying the Bible?

Later, after supper, Verity overheard Aunt Judy and her mom discussing the whole matter. Ascending to her ears, loud and clear, was Aunt Judy's response. "Kara, it's only natural. She's gone through her father's death and that's raised a lot of questions in her young mind. I have known Craig and Beth Symons for years and I am sure you have nothing to fear. I don't really know exactly what they believe but their church has been in town for as long as I can remember."

As she waited in suspense for her mother's decision, Verity remembered to pray for God's help in deciding this. Prayer had become an important part of every day. It was such a relief to hand over such difficult matters to an all-powerful Being!

When her mother came up at last to her room, she spoke reluctantly. "Verity, I have decided I will allow you to go, if you give me an honest run-down every night after the class. However, I can't drive you there. Aunt Judy works straight through on Tuesday evenings. So, you can only go—if you can find a ride."

Verity gave her mother a big hug and said, "Thanks so much, Mom! I'm sure God will help me find a ride!"

CHAPTER 8

A Discussion and A New Friend

P assing Thomas in the hall the next day at school, Verity was amazed to see him walking side-by-side with another guy and *laughing!* She turned to take a closer look at the fellow with Thomas. He was a stocky, coarse-looking fellow, who might have been handsome if he were better groomed. Wearing a hard-rock t-shirt and baggy pants that threatened to fall down at any moment, he appeared to have a 'don't care' attitude. He was sharing a joke quite loudly with Thomas and the vulgar language pierced Verity's ears. "Oh no," she thought, "this may be worse than Thomas having no friends at all!"

Entering math class, Verity noticed Mr. Symons had on a new tie. This one was light grey with a rainbow and Noah's ark. Already kids were asking questions about the tie, probably because to most, a good discussion was much better than a math lesson.

"So, Mr. Symons," Shane Black taunted, "do you really believe that myth about the flood? Isn't it kind of impossible that there could be enough water to cover the *whole* earth?"

"Well, Shane, before God created the world, the planet was covered with water,[1] so we know there is enough. The Bible tells us that the flood waters came up from the fountains of the deep, beneath the dry land,[2] and from forty days of rain from the sky. And it is very possible that the full uplift of the mountains occurred *after* the flood, in order to drain the land dry.[3] Mt. Everest might not have been so tall when God first created the world. You'll find some really

---

[1] Genesis 1:1-10; Psalm 104:5-9
[2] Genesis 7:11; 8:2
[3] Mountains After the Flood: The Backstory (isgenesishistory.com)

interesting, speculative theories about how this happened if you do some research.

"Like what?" Shane answered. "Give me one example."

Everyone was listening curiously.

"Well, one theory that I find intriguing involves a water canopy.[4] If you read Genesis chapter one carefully, you'll see that right in the beginning God tells us that the atmosphere in which we breathe, was in between water, both below and above. Some scientists have understood this to mean that before the flood there was a thick band of water surrounding the entire world." He drew a little diagram on the chalkboard to illustrate his point. "Not only would this band of water, or canopy, have provided enough water to rain for forty days, but while it remained above the atmosphere it would have acted like the glass on a greenhouse. The thick band of water, probably in a vapour form, or ice, would have kept in the heat on the earth—accounting for why we find mammoths and other warm-climate animals in the Siberian ice caps today, totally preserved in a frozen state. We know those animals can't exist in such a cold location but obviously they once did. At one time the whole earth must have been much more moderate in temperature. This water canopy theory, and it is *just a speculative theory*, would also explain how people lived so long before the flood."

"How long did they live?" another student asked.

Mr. Symons was happy to answer. "Before the great deluge, people lived for over nine hundred years. After the flood, the life-span drops dramatically. If this layer of water above the atmosphere did exist, it would filter out the ultra-violet rays that contribute to the ageing process. Without the ultra-violet rays coming through and

---

John C. Whitcomb and Henry M. Morris, The Genesis Flood. 1961.
9781596383951.pdf (storage.googleapis.com)
Andrew A. Snelling. The Genesis Flood Revisited. 2009
The Genesis Flood Revisited (masterbooks.com)

with the benefits of a wonderfully moderated climate, people and animals would have been able to live much longer."

Pausing, Mr. Symons added, "There are objections to this theory, with some researchers suggesting that the earth would get too hot if all this water fell in forty days. So, it is speculation. However, from the Bible record and evidence all over the Earth, including seashells on top of Mt. Everest, I believe the Global Flood is an established historical fact."

"Scientists today promote Evolution, not speculative theories," Shane protested.

"Ah, but remember, Shane," Mr. Symons smiled, "Evolution itself is only a *theory* of history – not science. Evolution is just another possible, speculative theory based on the evidence we find. And there are numerous good scientists today who still promote Creation and the existence of Intelligent Design. They just aren't given many platforms to publish their findings, like those who promote Evolution. But if you search, you will find well-reasoned theories by scientists with full credentials, that are far more believable than Evolution."[5]

Shane Black considered himself to be a great debater and loved nothing better than a good argument, so he tried again. "Mr. Symons, if there really are scientists who believe this stuff about creation, then how come our science textbooks don't even mention it as an alternative?"

"That's a decision on the part of the Canadian educational system, Shane. It's not because there is a lack of good materials to use."

---

[5] Ask John Mackay | Creation Questions & Answers - NOAH'S FLOOD: Where did the water come from, and where did it go?

Creation.com - How did the waters of Noah's Flood drain

Another student put up his hand. "I'm a Christian but I also believe in Evolution. My Minister says that Genesis is just a compilation of good stories. It's not meant to be taken literally."

At this point Mr. Symons stopped and smiled. "I could really go on about this all day. It's a subject I find fascinating. There's so much that could be said about Genesis. Let me just say this, it comes down to our attitude on how we approach the Bible. Do we say, 'My beliefs are right, so the Bible has to fit around them?' Or do we say, 'The Bible is God's inspired Word. It's right—so I'll let it teach me?'"

He paused with chalk in hand. "Now, I am supposed to be your math teacher," he laughed. "So, let's get on with today's math lesson."

Verity was enthralled. Mr. Symons had just suggested a good answer to her question about why people lived so long! He had even answered some questions that she had not thought of yet. His attitude to the Bible struck a resonant chord in her heart. She had to get to those seminars! "I wonder," she thought suddenly, "if Mr. Symons might know someone who could give me a ride?"

After class, Verity waited until everyone had filed out and then she went up shyly. "Mr. Symons," she began, "I saw your picture on the flyer that came yesterday; the one about reading the Bible."

Her teacher nodded with interest.

"I'd really like to come but my mom can't drive me. She says I can go, but she doesn't have a car that night."

Mr. Symons smiled. "Verity, if you would like to come to the Seminars, we will do everything we can to help you get there! Where do you live?"

"Near the little town of Pineridge."

"Really?" he laughed. "I'm just a few kilometres from there myself. I'd be happy to pick you up!"

It had all come together so easily. Would prayer always work so well?

When Verity relayed this news to her mother, Kara was much less enthusiastic. Secretly she had been hoping the lack of a ride would end the whole problem. Aunt Judy suggested she should call the Symons and make sure everything was truly okay by them.

Mr. Symons helped to calm Kara Lovell's fears. As she hung up the phone, she turned to Verity. "All right, Honey, it's settled. Mr. and Mrs. Symons are quite happy to give you a ride Tuesday to the Bible seminars. I just hope all this works out for good!"

"What?!" Thomas scorned, overhearing the discussion as he passed by. "You're going to a Bible seminar now? Are you planning to be a Minister some day—or something crazy like that?"

Verity decided not to bother answering him. She knew he wasn't looking for an answer anyway. Lately he was getting his digs in every chance he got. Why he wanted to give her such a hard time she did not know. They had been so close only months ago. Somewhere back in Saskatchewan was the brother she loved. Who was this person they had brought with them?

That night in her room, after she had thanked God for answering her prayer, she turned back to her Bible. September was almost over and Verity was finishing the book of Judges. Both Joshua and Judges had been very difficult for her to understand. She really questioned why there was so much killing in Joshua. "I thought murder was wrong. Why is God commanding His people to kill even women and children? In fact, God is even upset with the Israelites when they don't kill everyone!"

Also, Judges was filled with some rather gruesome stories, more killing, lying, cheating and people worshipping idols. Over and over, she read a recurring phrase, *"the children of Israel did evil."*

"Why did God want to record all these stories?" she wondered. "Wouldn't it have been better to leave out such horrid things?"

Tonight, as she opened her Bible to read the last three chapters of Judges, she couldn't believe how awful the story was. It was savage! She hoped the book of Ruth wouldn't be so violent.

Thomas was quite boastful as they waited for the school bus the next morning. "Yep, I've finally found a friend who thinks like I do. Hank says, 'God's just a crutch for the weak!' Besides, who wants to believe in God when there's so much fun to be had!"

Verity looked at him strangely. "Fun? You haven't been interested in having fun since we got here!?"

Thomas rolled his eyes disdainfully. "I mean *real* fun! Not anything you know about!"

Eyeing him suspiciously, Verity asked, "How do you define this 'fun' you're talking about?"

"You wouldn't understand, my poor, boringly-good, little sister!"

Nothing Verity said would coax any further details out of Thomas, but she felt very wary about his new friend, Hank Hamann.

A few days later, at lunch, Verity was ambling down the hall on her way to the library with a huge stack of books to look through. Purity was coming down the hall in the other direction. It was rather surprising to see her still in school during lunch hour. As usual, she was wearing a modest, yet attractive outfit, and walking alone. Verity glanced over at her, trying hard to make eye contact. She was just about to invite Purity to do homework in the library when someone walked straight into her. Or maybe she walked straight into him. Whatever way it was, her books and papers went flying all over the hall.

"I'm very sorry," she heard someone say. Glancing up into a concerned but amused face, Verity quickly realised she had been looking at Purity instead of watching where she was going.

"No, I'm sorry. It was my fault," she apologized, feeling rather embarrassed.

The tall, young fellow just smiled as he bent over and started gathering up her books. Verity hastily picked up her important papers as other students filed through, trying their best to avoid stepping on things. At last, all the books were rescued, and the young man good-naturedly stacked what he had gathered on top of her pile.

"Thank-you so much," Verity smiled.

"No problem," he said nodding. Then with a twinkle in his amber-brown eyes, he added, "Next time I'll watch where I'm going!"

Verity smiled at the gentle rebuke and carried on to the library to do her homework.

On her way back to class, Verity passed Thomas and Hank lazing around. "So is the party at your place?" she heard Thomas ask, before he noticed her.

What Hank answered, Verity did not hear. But the word 'party' was enough to send off an alarm in her head. Was this kind of 'fun' Thomas had mentioned a few days ago? Maybe it was just a friendly get-together or a dance. Why did she feel so worried that Thomas was getting himself into trouble? Surely Thomas had seen enough of his father's problems with alcohol to avoid that kind of a party. Hadn't he?

CHAPTER 9

How Readest Thou?

The first seminar night was October the second, and Verity was in a wonderful state of excitement. Downstairs, her mom and Thomas were having a heated discussion about why he had been so sick Saturday morning. Verity was just happy she hadn't caught it. To have to miss the first night of the seminars because of the flu would have been terrible!

The flyer had said to come in comfortable, casual clothes but Verity was having a hard time deciding just what to wear. This seemed so much more important than going to school so in the end she decided to dress up.

When the Symons arrived, Verity was already waiting outside with her Bible in hand. Kara came out briefly to greet them and thank them for picking up her daughter.

As Mr. Symons drove down the driveway, Mrs. Symons turned and introduced herself and her two girls, who were riding in the backseat with Verity. She was a tall, attractive woman with coffee-brown eyes and long chestnut hair tied back in a braid. Her pleasant smile and friendly manner quickly put Verity at ease. Verity learned that the oldest girl beside her with thick, wavy blond hair and brown eyes was Lindsay and she was ten. The younger girl, Jessica, had short blond hair and big blue eyes. She seemed rather tall for a seven-year-old. On her lap, clutched very tightly, was a large bag of 'things to do'.

Mrs. Symons explained that altogether they had four children and the older son, Taylor, was old enough to baby-sit his four-year-old brother.

After Verity had made sure she understood who everyone was in the Symons' family, Mr. Symons queried, "I've heard that you just moved here this summer, Verity, is that right?"

"Yes," she replied. "We used to live in Saskatchewan. When my dad died, my aunt invited us here to live with her."

"Oh, I'm sorry to hear you lost your father!" Mrs. Symons said sympathetically.

"Well," Verity hesitated, "he was an alcoholic. My mother's life is much better now that he is gone."

Mr. and Mrs. Symons glanced at one another silently.

"What do you know about the Bible, Verity?" Mr. Symons asked pleasantly.

"Very little, sir. I started reading it after my father died. You see, at the funeral our minister said my father had gone to heaven and that didn't make sense to me. My dad wasn't a good man! So, I started off trying to find out what the Bible says about life after death."

Verity happened to glance over at the two girls and saw that they were listening to her story with astonishment. "I am just so excited about the seminars," she added, "because now that I've been reading the Bible, I have hundreds of questions!"

"Well, here we are," Mr. Symons announced with a laugh, as they pulled up to the library. "Time to start answering some of those questions!"

A lot of people showed up for the evening and the room began to feel rather packed. Verity was impressed that so many people wanted to know more about the Bible. There were people of all ages. Several had brought their Bibles and others borrowed them from a stack at the back of the room. Some were smartly dressed, while others looked like they had just been out jogging. All in all, she guessed there were about fifty people present. There were even a few young children that had come along with their parents. Verity noticed that Lindsay and Jessica were sitting next to Mrs. Symons at the back, with their colouring books and markers arranged nicely in front of them. The 'things to do' bag lay limp on the table.

Everyone was given a white binder with the course contents inside. As Verity waited for the class to begin, she looked through the notes inside her binder. There was a handy little time chart in one of the side pockets and lots of other information.

Mr. Symons explained that since they were discussing God's message to mankind, they should ask for His guidance. He then began the evening with a prayer to God.

The presenters kept up a quick pace and for Verity, it was fascinating. Mr. Henderson, a tall slender man with slightly balding, grey hair, gave an overview of the Bible. He demonstrated that the Bible itself claimed total inspiration from God. Turning to Second Timothy chapter three, verses fourteen to seventeen, he showed how the Scriptures themselves stated they were sufficient to provide hope, bring salvation, and give direction for daily living.

Then he directed everyone's attention to a poem in their binders called 'How Readest Thou?' which described the different attitudes people might have when reading the Bible. He read the poem through and discussed the best approach.

As Mr. Symons went through his section on 'The Bible Interprets Itself,' his words brought such encouragement to Verity. "A basic principle of reading the Bible more effectively," he stated, "lies in this simple fact: the answers to your questions about what the Bible teaches are found in the Bible."

"Now," he went on to say, "to understand the Bible, there are three things you should always do. Look first to the Bible for answers to your questions. Read the whole Bible, to find answers to your questions. And write your questions down, as it may be a while before you find the answers."

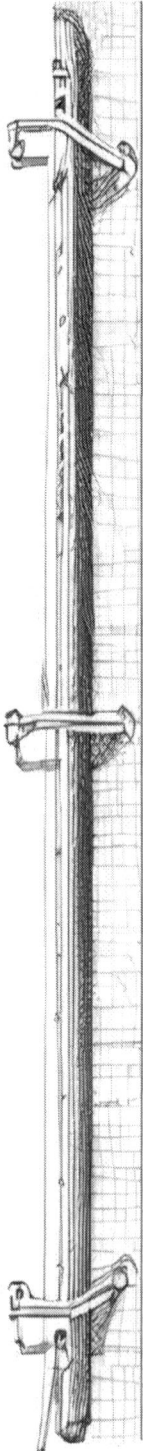

HOW READEST THOU? (Anonymous)

It is one thing to read the Bible through,
Another thing to learn and read and do.
Some read it with desire to learn, and read
But to their subject pay but little heed;
Some read it as their duty every week,
But no instruction from the Bible seek;
While others read it with but little care,
With no regard to how they read or where;
Some read it as a History, to know
How people lived two thousand years ago,
Some read it to bring themselves into repute,
By showing others how they can dispute;
While others read because their neighbors do,
To see how long it takes to read it through.
Some read it for the wonders that are there,
How David killed a lion and a bear;
While others read it with uncommon care,
Hoping to find some contradictions there.
Some read as though it did not speak to them
But to the people at Jerusalem.
One reads it as a book of mysteries,
And won't believe the very thing he sees;
One reads with father's specs upon his head,
And sees the thing just as his father said;
Some read to prove a pre adopted creed,
Hence understanding but little as they read,
For every passage in the book they bend
To make it suit that all important end.
Some people read, as I have often thought,
To teach the Book, instead of being taught;
And some there are who read it out of spite,
I fear there are but few who read it right.
One thing I find, and you may find it too,
The more you read, the more you find it true;
But this to find, an open eye is needful,
With often prayer, and humble heart all heedful;
The man who reads with pride or inattention,
Will only find full causes of dissension,
The man who reads with modest penetration,
Will find the joy of comfort and salvation.

"Wow!" thought Verity, "that's just what I'm doing. I guess I need to carry on and not give up."

"A good way to help you understand what you are reading in the Scriptures," Mr. Symons continued, "is to use cross-references. Not every Bible has these, but there are many Bibles available today with these references down the centre column or the side of each page. A cross-reference links to other relevant verses in the Bible to give more information on the phrase to which they are attached."

To demonstrate how the Bible answers itself and how cross-references help, Mr. Symons gave an example. "When someone reads Matthew chapter twenty-seven, verse forty-six, they may ask: 'Why did Jesus say on the cross, *'My God, my God, why hast thou forsaken me?'*'"

To help him answer the question he had posed, Mr. Symons turned on his power-point projector. An enlarged page of a Bible showing Matthew chapter twenty-seven, came onto the screen. Pointing to a centre column down the middle of the page, he explained that these were the cross-references. He then pointed back to verse forty-six, where a tiny "z" was by the phrase, *'why hast thou forsaken me?'* In the centre column of cross-references, a corresponding "z" was next to a reference, Psalm twenty-two, verse one.

Looking up Psalm twenty-two, Mr. Symons read verse one. *"My God, my God, why hast thou forsaken me? Why art thou so far from helping me, and from the words of my roaring?"* The beginning sentence was the same as the words Jesus had spoken!

"Seeing that this psalm records the same words that Jesus spoke, what might this indicate to us?" he asked.

An older man put up his hand, "Perhaps Jesus was quoting the psalm?" he said tentatively.

"Good thinking," Mr. Symons encouraged. "Let's look further on in this psalm and see if there is any reason for Jesus to do that. Would anyone like to read verses six to seven?"

Verity read them. *"'But I am a worm and not a man, scorned by men and despised by the people. All who see me mock me; they hurl insults, shaking their heads; 'He trusts in the LORD; let the LORD rescue him. Let him deliver him, since he delights in him.'"*

With a twinkle in his eyes, Mr. Symons asked, "Does anyone hear an echo back to Christ's crucifixion?"

There was a shuffling of pages as everyone turned quickly back to Matthew chapter twenty-seven to scan the page for an 'echo.' Before long a young woman in a tracksuit put up her hand. "Verse forty-three," she said excitedly. "It says, *'He trusts in God. Let God rescue him now if he wants him, for he said; I am the Son of God.'* That's exactly what people were saying as they looked at Jesus on the cross!"

Nodding, Mr. Symons smiled. "Correct! And what does it say just above that in verse thirty-nine?"

The young woman answered, "It says, *'Those who passed by hurled insults at him, shaking their heads.'*"

Mr. Symons continued on through the psalm, looking at verses thirteen to eighteen and comparing them with Matthew chapter twenty-seven. The psalm accurately foretold how the assembly of the wicked would pierce Jesus' hands and feet, how he would hang naked in view of everyone, even that his garments would be parted among them and they would cast lots for his vesture!

"Jesus was quoting those words of the psalm," he explained, "so that anyone familiar with the Scriptures would hear an echo back to Psalm twenty-two and read through all of it. If they did, they would see how exactly this psalm described Jesus' crucifixion. When they came to verse twenty-four in the psalm, they would realise that God said He had not forsaken Christ but had heard his cry for help. The psalm proves that everything which went on that dark day was entirely in God's hands! Those who hated Jesus thought his crucifixion was proof that he couldn't have been the Messiah, or God wouldn't have let him die. Instead, if they'd read Psalm twenty-two, they would have seen that Jesus' crucifixion proved that he *was* the Messiah—all this had been prophesied long ago! Jesus' death was an essential part of God's plan of salvation!"

Verity was enjoying the presentations so much that the hour and a half flew by. Before she knew it, Mr. Henderson was closing with his section on 'Why the Bible is Difficult to Read'.

"God's Word is difficult to read for a reason," he was saying. "God's Word is only understood by those who are willing to pray for guidance, and put in time and energy to seek for the truth. How many people enjoy the challenge of a crossword puzzle? Yet how few are willing to take on the challenge of answering the questions presented in God's Word? Doing a crossword puzzle might help you to learn a few facts you didn't know before; it might even improve your spelling. However, have a look at the ways reading the Bible can benefit you!"

Mr. Henderson clicked a button and Second Timothy three, verses fifteen to seventeen, came up on the screen. *"...you have known the Holy Scriptures, which are able to make you wise for salvation through faith in Christ Jesus. All Scripture is God-breathed and is useful for teaching, rebuking, correcting and training in righteousness, so that the man of God may be thoroughly equipped for every good work."*

"Notice that the Bible can make us wise unto salvation!" he pointed out. "There are many products advertised today that promise to add years to our lives. People will pay exorbitant prices to try these things out. Only the Bible though, can promise to give us *salvation*—to save us eternally! Isn't that worth devoting some time and energy to find?"

Mr. Henderson carried on, "Yes, the Bible can be difficult. Yet in His Word, God has promised to give understanding to those who seek it diligently."

He closed, referring to Matthew chapter seven, verses seven to eight, and reading James chapter one, verses five to six. *"If any of you lacks wisdom, he should ask God, who gives generously to all without finding fault, and it will be given to him. But when he asks, he must believe and not doubt, because he who doubts is like a wave of the sea, blown and tossed by the wind.'"*

Verity was very thankful as she crawled into bed that night. She had a new confidence that someday, with God's help, she would find the answers to all her questions.

CHAPTER 10

Letting Your Light Shine

That week in school, Verity felt very positive about her new life in Ontario. She was glad to be in Grandville High and so thankful to have met Mr. Symons. Walking happily off to class one morning, she noticed a tall, familiar young man coming toward her. He hastily jumped to one side, making an exaggerated attempt to avoid her.

Slightly embarrassed, Verity laughed. "Thanks for watching where you're going!" she called out.

He nodded with a grin, and she passed on to class.

The sun was shining warm and bright outside during class, promising at least one more summery day before the cold set in. When the lunch bell rang and Purity left to go to her locker alone, Verity suddenly had an idea. "Hey Purity," she called out, walking quickly toward her. "Do you mind if I have lunch with you today?"

Purity looked surprised but she smiled. "That would be great," she said. "I was going to walk to the park. It's so nice out."

The two girls pushed open the big, black doors and stepped out into the warm October sunshine. Many other students were outside as well, trying to catch the last bit of summer while they had the chance. As they walked along the sidewalk to the park, they admired all the trees decked out in their brilliant fall colours. The bright reds and oranges were a striking contrast against the blue sky. It was truly an artist's delight! The park was close to the school and full of large mature oak and maple trees.

"It's like God gives us one last jolt of colour before the whole world turns white!" Verity remarked.

Purity glanced at her with a pleased expression and then bent to pick up one of the orange leaves blowing around on the grass. "This is my favourite colour," she said. "I love the contrast with the bright orange on the tips and the green veins showing through."

"They are beautiful," Verity agreed, "but I like the red ones best."

Finding a bench, they sat down in the sunshine. Purity was quiet for a moment with her head down before she began to eat. Verity wondered if she was feeling okay but before she could ask, Purity opened her eyes and began unpacking the lunch bag she carried.

"I hope you don't mind me joining you?" Verity asked hesitantly, as they snacked on their sandwiches. "I've been wanting to get to know you better but you're never around when there's time to talk."

"Oh, really?" Purity pondered, "I don't mind being by myself."

"But don't you ever feel lonely?"

"Yes, sometimes, but… well, I don't really fit in...here."

"Why," Verity asked kindly.

"I'm religious," she said awkwardly. "I don't have much in common with anyone at school." With a wistful smile she added, "Most people think I'm weird." She shrugged. "So, I'd rather be on my own."

Verity considered this for a minute or two. She respected Purity for daring to be different, but she wondered if this was the right outcome. "Do you think Jesus should have just kept to himself as well?" she asked at last.

Purity frowned. "Well, no, he came here to preach…" then she stopped and questioned, "What are you getting at?"

Verity put her hand on Purity's arm. "Please don't be upset with me. I like you. I can tell you are a nice person, and everyone knows you have good morals. But it seems to me that you could have such a good influence on other people if you were friendlier. Didn't Jesus say we are to let our light shine and not hide it?"

Puzzled, Purity gazed at Verity. She wasn't used to having school chums fault her on a religious basis. "What religion are you?"

"I'm not any religion," Verity replied. "I'm just reading the Bible and trying to find out what it means." After a slight pause she added, "This week I went to a seminar on the Bible. Mr. Symons was one of the speakers and there was another man, Mr. Henderson…"

Purity was looking at her wide-eyed. "That's my dad!" she exclaimed. "Mr. Henderson is my dad. You went to the Bible seminars?"

For a moment they looked at each other in wonder and then they both started to laugh. "You're going to those seminars!" Purity repeated, as though she could hardly believe it. "I'm sure you will love them! I went last year and even though I've been brought up reading the Bible, they were still very interesting for me!"

Now that their lunches were finished, it was time to start heading back for school. They continued discussing the seminars and examining the pretty leaves along the way.

Approaching the school, Verity could see a few students standing outside the main entrance. There was a tall fellow with tawny-brown hair who looked familiar, and Verity strained her eyes to see if he was the same young man she had bumped into before. Sure enough, as they came closer, she could see that he was.

Seeing that the two girls were headed his way, the young man courteously opened the door for them. "Good afternoon, ladies," he said with mock politeness.

"Thank you," they smiled, both feeling a little self-conscious.

"Who is he?" Verity asked when they were safely out of hearing. There was something about this boy's friendly manner that was intriguing. He was vaguely like Ken. She wondered if he might be a good friend for Thomas and... maybe even herself.

"He's Peter Bryant," Purity answered. "He's in grade 12. That's all I know about him."

"Grade 12," Verity thought to herself. "How can I help Thomas and Peter be friends?

CHAPTER 11

Confusing Promises

Summer felt truly over as Verity sat curled up reading the Bible on her sofa. It had been a frosty Friday and most of the brightly coloured leaves had blown off in the high winds last night. Now all the big maples and oaks looked bare and dead—their painted leaves littered the entire lawn.

Since it was Friday, the house was very quiet because Mom and Aunt Judy always worked until late. Verity had finished her homework quickly before making grilled cheese for herself and Thomas and now she had a couple hours left to carry on with her search.

She heard a door bang downstairs and her mind momentarily drifted to thoughts about her brother. Thomas had seemed in a good humour today. He seemed to get along well with Hank, even though this was a very different friendship than the one he had enjoyed with Ken. Tonight, after dinner, he had mumbled something about schoolwork and retired to his room. She was pleased he was doing his homework. Maybe he was settling in.

After finally getting through Joshua and Judges, Verity had found Ruth and First Samuel delightful stories again. There were still struggles between good and evil but to her relief there wasn't so much killing and destruction. She was enthralled with the story of David, a humble shepherd boy who had been chosen by God to be king. The last few nights, she had been so interested that she'd decided to keep reading in Samuel rather than go on to the New Testament.

Second Samuel chapter seven had another promise from God. This time the promise was made to David, who had become the king of Israel. Once again God had used that word 'forever' in relation to David's throne. She read the verse over a fourth time to herself. *"The*

LORD declares to you that the LORD himself will establish a house for you: When your days are over and you rest with your fathers, I will raise up your offspring to succeed you, who will come from your own body, and I will establish his kingdom. He is the one who will build a house for my Name, and I will establish the throne of his kingdom forever... Your house and your kingdom will endure forever before me, your throne will be established forever."

Where was David's throne today? There wasn't a king in the modern nation of Israel—so what could 'forever' mean? Trying to put into practice what she had learned from the seminar, she examined the cross-references in her centre margin, and one led her to Luke chapter one, verses thirty-one to thirty-three. In speaking to his mother, Mary, the angel said that Jesus would sit on David's throne forever.

"But Jesus didn't reign like a king in Matthew's gospel. If Jesus is up with God in heaven, when and why will he ever sit on a man's throne on earth? Why does it speak in these terms?"

It suddenly occurred to her to call Mr. Symons. He had said he would be happy to answer her questions at any time.

Mrs. Symons answered the call. Verity was very disappointed when she learned Mr. Symons was at a youth group that evening. "But Verity, I'll try to answer your questions if you like," Mrs. Symons offered.

Verity explained about the promise and her confusion.

"Oh, you've just come across one of the most important promises in the whole Bible!" Mrs. Symons said enthusiastically.

"I have?"

"Yes! What is God promising David?"

"That he would have a son; that his son would build God a house, and that his kingdom would last forever."

"Very good!" said Mrs. Symons, "Did David *have* a son?"

"Yes, lots of them."

"Right. And God chose Solomon to be the next king, didn't He? Did Solomon's kingdom last forever?"

"Well, no one is called a king in Israel today." Verity answered.

"That's correct. And the kingdom in Israel only lasted approximately three to four hundred years after Solomon. Then the Babylonians took the Israelites captive, and they never again had a king on a throne. So, Solomon was David's son and he did build God a temple, but his kingdom certainly didn't last forever."

"Okay," agreed Verity, "so what is God promising?"

Mrs. Symons carried on explaining. "Now you remembered to use your cross- references," she praised, "and you found Luke chapter one, verse thirty-three. What do verses thirty-one and thirty-three say?"

Verity turned back to the reference. "They say, *'You will be with child and give birth to a son, and you are to give him the name Jesus. He will be great and will be called the Son of the Most High. The Lord God will give him the throne of his father David, and he will reign over the house of Jacob forever; his kingdom will never end.'"*

Mrs. Symons asked, "So, who is really the promised son that will reign on David's throne?"

"I guess it must be Jesus," Verity deduced.

"Did Jesus reign as a king while he was on the earth?"

"No, not at all," Verity answered.

"And where was David's throne?"

"Jerusalem."

"So, if Jesus didn't reign in Jerusalem as a king when he was on earth the first time, then this must need to happen in the future," Mrs. Symons stated. "Now Verity, in my King James Version of Second Samuel chapter seven, verse sixteen," she continued, "it says that David's throne will be established forever before him. David will get to see this happen!" She paused a moment and then asked, "You started reading the Bible in Genesis, didn't you?"

"Yes," Verity responded, feeling this was all very interesting, but she just didn't understand how God was going to work it all out.

"Oh good," said Mrs. Symons, "now, if you've already been through Genesis, you probably remember the promises God made to a man called Abraham."

"I do. And God said 'forever' to him as well," Verity replied. "I was also confused about that promise, because Abraham ended up having to buy land to bury his wife, when God had already told him he could have all the land he could see!"

"Ah, yes," Mrs. Symons answered, "if you turn to Acts chapter seven, verses two to five, Stephen talks about that very promise. Maybe his words will shed some light on this."

Verity found the place and read the passage slowly to herself. "It says that God didn't give Abraham any of the land He promised... okay, so that's why Abraham had to buy land!" She paused, trying to put it all together. "But why wouldn't God keep His promise?"

"Let's look at one more passage and then you might be able to answer that yourself," Mrs. Symons said encouragingly. "Turn to Hebrews chapter eleven, verses eight to sixteen."

It took Verity a while to find Hebrews, but at last she did, and she read it over slowly again. With a sigh, she said meekly, "Now I'm more confused than ever, Mrs. Symons. Abraham didn't get his promise, but he expected to get it in the future! And he's looking for a heavenly country. Does that mean God will make him the same sort land up in heaven?"

"Well, Verity," answered Mrs. Symons gently, "let's go over what we've learned from these verses. It's always more exciting if you can see the answer for yourself. Abraham was promised land," she stated slowly. "He never received any of it and he didn't expect to—because he knew he would get it in the future. Are you okay with that?" she asked.

When Verity gave her assent, Mrs. Symons continued, "Now, David was promised a son, who we discovered was Jesus. He was also promised that he would see his son's kingdom established forever. So, how do you think Abraham will get to have his promised land *forever* and David be able to see his son Jesus ruling from Jerusalem *forever?*"

"Well, the only way I can see it happening is if they are both alive again on the earth," Verity concluded hesitantly. "But then Jesus will have to come back down from heaven..."

"That's it, Verity! And as you read through the New Testament you will find many other passages that refer to Jesus returning to earth to reign as King.[1] The resurrection of the dead and the granting of eternal life is also linked to Jesus' return.[2] Now, just to show you something really exciting, let's look up Galatians chapter three, verses twenty-six to twenty-nine."

Verity read the verses out loud. *"'You are all sons of God through faith in Christ Jesus, for all of you who were baptized into Christ have clothed yourselves with Christ. There is neither Jew nor Greek, slave nor free, male nor female, for you are all one in Christ Jesus. If you belong to Christ, then you are Abraham's seed, and heirs according to the promise.'"*

---

[1] John 19:12-19; 1 Corinthians 15:22–26; Revelation 17:14; 19:16
[2] 1 Thessalonians 4:13-18; John 5:21-29; Daniel 12:1-3

"Wow," said Verity tentatively, "is this saying that if we get baptized then we will inherit Abraham's promises also?" She hesitated, still trying to fit everything in. "But why would God bring everyone back to earth when they are already enjoying heaven?"

Mrs. Symons paused for a moment, then she said, "Verity, I could answer that question for you right now, but I think you will enjoy finding the answer yourself. On the last night of the seminars, we usually give out a study-sheet on this very topic. I think, since you have thought so much about this, that it would be really good for you to do it now." With a pause, she added, "Your determination is wonderful to see! Jesus encourages us to seek—and that if we do seek we will find.[3] I'm sure Mr. Symons will be happy to explain the study-sheet to you after school on Monday."

"Oh, I hope so, Mrs. Symons! I would be so glad to understand all of this." Her head was in a bit of a whirl after all this new information. It was quite interesting, but something didn't sit right with Verity. Heaven had always seemed like such a wonderful place to go to, so why would anyone want to come back to the earth?

Towards the end of the phone call, Verity became aware of a horn honking nearby and a door banging downstairs. As she hung up the phone and looked out the window, she was sure she saw Thomas getting into a car on the road. It drove off, screeching the tires and swaying from side to side. Her hands flew to her face. Where, oh where was Thomas going?

---

[3] Matthew 7:7

CHAPTER 12

The Lack of Hope

S aturday mornings were usually very quiet for Verity. She was always the first one up. On this particular morning she woke up to a sleet storm wailing away outside, hitting the front windows with gale force. Summer was well and truly over.

As she sat at the table eating a muffin, she noticed an unfamiliar photograph album in front of her. Guessing that perhaps Aunt Judy had left it there for her, she opened the old, worn cover and gazed curiously inside. The front page held a black and white photo of two little children playing happily outside an old farmhouse. She knew the pictures were too old to be Thomas and herself, so who were they? Finally recognising her deceased grandparents, she realised the children must be Aunt Judy and her dad. As she turned the pages, the children became more and more mature in their looks. Both of them seemed happy and carefree. The questions repeated themselves in her mind yet again. What was it that went wrong with Dad? Why did he change?

So intent was she on examining the faces, that she didn't hear Aunt Judy come in until she spoke. "Doesn't Thomas look like your dad?"

"Yes," she agreed flatly, "he does." Then with a shake of her head she asked, "Aunt Judy, I don't understand. Why did Dad change? What went wrong?"

Aunt Judy tilted her head to one side. "Verity, your dad was a nice, happy little boy, who asked a lot of questions like you! There was only one problem: he never really knew what he wanted. He had no long-term goals. Now, myself, I've always known that I wanted to make a lot of money and live in California. When I'm fifty that's where I plan to be. Everyone needs something in life to look forward to; something to work towards!"

Aunt Judy helped herself to a muffin and carried on, "Now back to your dad, he and your mother were happily married and everything was fine—I think he even used to go to church with your mom. They moved out to Saskatchewan because your dad thought he wanted to get into agriculture. He was soon the second man in charge of a huge, successful farm operation. Your dad always liked to drink socially but one day he showed up late for work very drunk. He made some costly, bad decisions for the company and that was that. They fired him the next day! He took it hard and became really depressed. That made him drink even more and before we all knew it, he had a severe addiction; he was an alcoholic. For a while there was enough money to carry on as he wanted, but he was unable to find another job and soon he went bankrupt. I guess that's what you remember most—a sick, addicted man desperate for another drink and no money to buy one."

"Yes," said Verity, looking far away, "and on top of that, Dad became violent and we all lived in fear. We never knew when the next rampage would be, or what would set him off. I had completely forgotten that he was ever patient until I saw that picture you hung in my room."

Aunt Judy put her arm around Verity. "I know you went through a lot, Darling! I always told your mom she should leave him and move out here with us. But your mom wouldn't leave because she said she still loved the man he used to be. Remember that! It isn't good for you to go on hating your father. You will be better off to forgive him and dwell on the good memories."

Verity nodded as tears filled her eyes. "I didn't know I had any good memories until I saw that picture. We never had pictures hanging at home because my dad couldn't stand them." She paused, thinking hard. "Aunt Judy, are you trying to help Thomas, as well?"

Aunt Judy hesitated. "I have tried," she said, looking away with a sigh, "but Thomas takes everything down as soon as I put it up. I found the cutest little picture of your dad reading Thomas a story in bed when he was only two. It didn't stay on the wall for even a day. I don't know where Thomas puts the pictures, but I hope he doesn't throw them out."

Suddenly remembering something, Aunt Judy looked up with a smile. "Just one second, Verity," she said, heading off to her room. "I found a little treasure for you the other day!"

Verity wondered what she would bring back. Another picture? Another memory?

However, Aunt Judy came back with a small book in her hands, smiling triumphantly. "Look at this!" she exclaimed delightedly. "This is our old family Bible! I found it Thursday when I was sorting through the mess in the attic. Since you're so interested in reading the Bible, I think you should have it."

Verity took the old book and examined it with pleasure. It was a King James Version, rather worn but still in good shape.

"Thanks Aunt Judy, this will be great to look through!" she replied. As she quickly thumbed through the pages, Verity could see that someone had marked certain passages and left little notes.

At this point, Kara stumbled into the kitchen, yawning. "Goodness, it's ten o'clock and I've had a huge sleep in!" Looking around, she anxiously asked, "Where's Thomas?"

"He's still in bed, I think," Verity shrugged. She had heard him come home late in the night. "He might have hung out with Hank last night."

Frowning, Kara went down to the basement room to check on her son. When she came up, concern lay in every line. "He's been sick again, Judy, and he won't wake up!" The concern suddenly gave way to tears and Kara collapsed into a chair. "I can't go through this again, Judy!" she sobbed. "He's going down the same path his father did and he's only *seventeen!* What am I going to do?!"

"It's just a growing thing, Kara. He'll learn!"

"But Thomas was never like this back home!" she sobbed. "He's so angry now. Maybe he can't forgive his father…or *me*… for pulling him away from his friends…"

"Or maybe it's a lack of hope," Verity offered quietly.

Aunt Judy stood behind, rubbing Kara's shoulders. "We won't let this keep happening," she said firmly. "From now on that boy can no longer be left alone."

"But I need to work and…"

Aunt Judy interrupted, "Now Kara, listen to me. I know you didn't want Thomas to work a lot of hours so that he could concentrate on his last year of schooling. But I don't think he's been spending too much time on homework, as it is. Let's put him on the work schedule for every Friday evening and weekends. That way we can make sure he misses any future parties."

CHAPTER 13

A Bible at School

"Verity! It's time to get up, Dear," Kara called from the stairs. It didn't take Verity long to recall that today was the day Mr. Symons had promised to help her after school. Last night at the seminar he had apologized for being busy Monday and Tuesday. He agreed with his wife that Verity would find the study-sheet really helpful, so he'd asked her to meet him today after school.

For a few minutes longer she lay in bed, contemplating what she had learned last night. In the 'Overview of the Bible' section, Mr. Henderson had dealt with each book from Genesis to Psalms. He had briefly explained the main theme from each, when it was written, and by whom. Now she felt that Joshua and Judges made a little more sense. The book of Joshua dealt with the Israelites taking possession of the 'promised' land. Mr. Henderson read a quote from Genesis chapter fifteen, verses thirteen to twenty-one. He then explained that when God had promised the land of Canaan to Abraham and his descendants, He also told him that his descendants had to wait four hundred years before they could take over the land. They had to wait until the people that lived in Canaan became wicked enough to deserve God's total destruction. When those four hundred years had elapsed, the Canaanite people had indeed become so perverse that God said the *'land would vomit them out'* if He didn't intervene.[1] He warned the Israelites that if they didn't follow His command to kill all the Canaanites, their children would learn perversity. And if the Israelites were to act in the same morally corrupt way, they too would be cast out of the land...which they were many years later.[2]

---

[1] Leviticus 18:15-30; Deuteronomy 9:5
[2] Leviticus 20:22; Ezekiel 36:17-20; Ezekiel 22:7-15

Unfortunately, the Israelites didn't obey God's commands completely. Instead, they kept many of the Canaanites to be their slaves. They didn't even finish taking all of the land that God had promised them but left many of the nations untouched.

The book of Judges was all about the disastrous consequences of not obeying God's orders. Just as God had warned them, the Canaanites taught Israel all their wicked practices, which led them into idol worship and perverse behaviour. There was a continuous cycle in the book of Judges. The Israelites would forget God and sin against Him—so God would send punishments, most often in the form of Israel being attacked by the other people around them. Because of this, the Israelites would see the worthlessness of their idols and cry to God for help. Then God would raise up a 'judge', someone to be their leader and deliver them from their enemies. But, when things became peaceful and prosperous, then Israel would turn away from God and disobey His commands again. The same cycle occurred repeatedly. Mr. Henderson explained that in Judges, every person did what was right in their own eyes.[3] Instead of allowing God's Word to guide them, they determined for themselves what was right or wrong. This led to the strange accounts of people thinking they were doing right, but in reality, acting in ways that were abhorrent to God.

The lesson Mr. Henderson brought out at the end of his section was that God, as the Creator of us all, knows what is best and He has the authority to make the rules. If God directly gives the command to kill others because He deems them worthy of destruction, then we would be disobeying Him if we refused. If God says we are not to kill, then we would be sinning if we chose to kill. In the New Testament, God has told us through Jesus, not to draw a sword against others,[4] to love our enemies and do good to those who hate us.[5]

---

[3] Judges 17:6
[4] Matt. 26:52
[5] Matt. 5:38–48

On her mother's second call, Verity came back to reality. She threw off her warm blankets, sprang out of bed—and nearly fell to the ground. A funny tingle was in her leg and for a moment it had refused to support her weight. "Silly leg," she thought, as the tingle dissipated and she felt normal again.

Gathering her books for school, she saw her Bible sitting on the dining room table and decided to grab it for the afterschool session. Thomas saw her pop it into her backpack. "Are you really going to take that thing to school?" he questioned disdainfully.

Verity grinned at him. "Yes, I think I'll take you and Hank aside and let you in on what you're missing!"

Looking at Thomas, Verity didn't see at first the response she had anticipated. For just a second a deep emptiness lay in his eyes, but it was quickly overtaken by defiance. "You're the one missing out, not me!" he said with an air of superiority, striding off for the bus.

In that brief instant, Verity had seen that Thomas' defences were not so sure and absolute as he made out. "Maybe," she thought to herself, "just maybe, he is still reachable."

During science class that morning, as Mr. Connor droned on about the Geological Record and millions of years, Verity's mind drifted back to a point Mr. Henderson had made at the seminar the night before. He had referred to a verse that said that Jesus' 'soul was not left in hell,' but was resurrected. This had bothered her last night and was uppermost in her mind now. Why would Jesus' soul be put in hell for the three days he was dead, when he was the most righteous person that had ever lived?

When lunch hour came, Verity excused herself from eating with Purity, Emily and Kate and hurried down to the library to see if she could find the passage again. Maybe she had misunderstood. She was glad she had brought her Bible with her so she could figure this verse out. Flipping quickly through the pages, she remembered the passage was near the beginning of Acts. Soon she found it in the second chapter, verse thirty-one.

"Hmm, that's interesting," she pondered to herself, "here in my NIV Bible it says that *'he was not abandoned to the grave.'* I was sure Mr. Henderson read the word 'hell' from his version." Scanning the verse quickly again, she was surprised not to see the word 'soul' either. As she was sticking a little piece of paper in the spot to remind her to ask Mr. Symons about it later that day, she had a feeling someone was standing very close behind her. Quickly turning around, she looked up and saw the tall young man she had once bumped into, gazing over her shoulder.

"Is that a Bible you have there?" he asked.

"Yes," she nodded, a little shy.

Peter pulled a chair out and sat down beside her. "I don't think we've been introduced properly. I'm Peter Bryant and I've been trying hard not to collide with you again."

Verity laughed. "I'm Verity Lovell."

"So, are you religious?" he questioned, motioning towards her Bible.

"I'm very *interested* in religion," she smiled. "I've been reading the Bible a lot lately."

"Really?" Peter seemed to want her to carry on.

"I started out with one question and now that I've been reading the Bible, I have at least a hundred more!"

Peter chuckled. "So, what was your first question?"

She drew in a deep breath. "Well, I just wanted to know what happens after death. Where do we go? Who goes where?"

Peter shrugged. "That's easy. Good people go to heaven, bad people go to hell."

"And where would I find that in the Bible?"

"Gee, it's everywhere," Peter began. "Let's see if I can show you a passage." He picked up her Bible, thinking deeply. "Okay, I'm sure I remember this one." Searching through the gospels, Peter finally came to Luke chapter twenty-three, verses forty-two to forty-three. "This is when Jesus was dying on the cross," he explained. "One of the thieves that was crucified with him repented, and asked Jesus to remember him when he came into his kingdom; so, Jesus said, *'today you will be with me in paradise.'"*

Verity marvelled. "Now I'm really mixed up! Was Jesus in heaven or hell when he died?"

Seeing that Peter looked confused, she tried to explain, "Well, last night at the Bible seminar that I've been going to, Mr. Henderson said that during those three days and nights that Jesus was dead, his soul was actually *in hell*. But when I looked up Acts two – the same passage – in my Bible just now, it didn't say anything about a soul or hell."

Peter still looked puzzled. "What Bible seminars are these?"

"Didn't you get a green flyer about a month ago, called 'Learn to Read the Bible Effectively'?" she asked. "Actually, Mr. Symons, my math teacher, is the one of the speakers! I've learned so much in just two nights."

Peter shook his head. "I don't remember seeing a flyer like that but then I hardly ever look at the mail. Religion *is* a very important part of my life though."

"Oh," she replied, thrilled that Peter shared her interest. "So, do you ever have questions about the Bible?"

"You mean me personally?"

She nodded.

"Not really, I guess. Our Pastor does such a great job explaining everything that I don't usually have any questions," he shrugged.

Feeling quite comfortable now, Verity decided to present her own case before Peter. "Well then, let me tell you what first started me thinking about all this. My dad died a few months ago..."

Peter looked startled. "Oh, I'm sorry to hear that..."

"Well, he was an alcoholic and he made life very tough for our family. He had no time for God or religion. At the funeral, the minister said my dad was probably in heaven looking down on all of us. It almost made me laugh because it would've been rather ironic. So, I started reading the Bible to see if I could find out who actually gets to go where."

"That is a tough one," Peter replied, shaking his head. "None of us can really say for sure, who goes where, I guess... but I do know we all have an immortal soul that goes to one place or the other."

Verity was just about to ask if Peter knew where the Bible said that, when she saw Hank and Thomas come in... and they were walking towards her!

"Hey, Thomas, your sister has a Bible and she's reading it with Beanpole!" Hank laughed loudly.

Peter turned sharply, just in time to see Hank reaching for Verity's Bible.

"There's only one place for trash like this!" Hank stated harshly.

Before Hank could grab the Bible, Peter firmly laid his hand down on top of it.

Verity felt indignation welling up within her but keeping it in check, she asked, "How do you know it's trash? Have you ever read it?"

Quite aware that he was causing a scene, Hank strolled off with Thomas, ignoring her question and broadcasting to everyone in the library, "So Beanpole is sticking up for the Minister-in-training! Wait till I tell all the guys!"

Verity felt her cheeks flushing hotly. Only her brother had teased her about training to be a 'minister'! How could Thomas sink so low as to spout off to Hank about her? Where had his loyalty gone? A sharp sword of betrayal pierced her heart. Thomas didn't even turn to look at her. He just sauntered off with Hank down the hall.

Verity didn't know what to say or where to look, but Peter spoke gently with wonder, "Is Thomas your brother?"

She nodded miserably, wishing either her face would cool down or Peter would leave.

"I never would have guessed it," he went on in surprise. "He's so different from you…"

It was suddenly all too much, and Verity's eyes misted over. "You just don't understand him—no one here has given him a chance. Back home he had such good friends! He didn't want to leave… he's angry about so many things." With that she burst into tears and sprang from her chair, relieved to hear the school bell ring. Lunch was over.

Feeling rather humiliated, Verity dashed off to class without looking behind. An hour ago, Peter had been a friendly stranger— and now she had spilled her life's story to him, ending up in tears! It wasn't the introduction she'd hoped to make for Thomas or herself.

By the time the day was over, Verity had calmed down and only felt rather foolish about the whole episode. It really was almost laughable. She hoped Peter would think so too, but she knew that she was going to feel embarrassed the next time she met him.

With her Bible in hand, she made her way to the Math office for her appointment with Mr. Symons. He was still helping one of his students but that only took a few more minutes and then he ushered her in.

"Verity," he began, "we usually leave this exercise to the last night, because by then we've discussed all the different study tools. This study-sheet is where we put what you've learned into practice. So, what I'm trying to say is, I hope you don't find this too overwhelming all at once."

"I hope not too," she smiled.

"Okay," Mr. Symons went on, stacking some big heavy reference books on his desk. "Do you understand that the Old Testament was first written in the Hebrew language and the New Testament was first written in Greek?"

She nodded, although this was new to her.

"So, when a translator sits down to make an English Bible from the original Hebrew or Greek, he has to make many decisions as he goes along. He has to decide how best to translate each original word into an appropriate English word."

Mr. Symons paused as he tried to think of a way to simplify what he was saying. "Let's say," he began, "that you saw the French word 'garçon' and you wanted to write an English equivalent. Well, you could choose from 'boy,' 'lad,' 'guy,' 'fellow,' 'male'… get the point?"

Verity nodded. "You are saying that there's more than one English word that I could use for 'garçon.'"

"Exactly," he smiled. "And whatever language a translator is using, he has to make those kinds of decisions for most words. Take another example," he carried on, "just so you see why this is so important—last night we talked about Jesus' soul being in hell for three days when he was dead…"

Verity raised her hand.

"Yes?" he laughed.

"I'm so glad that you brought up that verse, Mr. Symons. I looked it up today in my Bible and it didn't say anything about hell or soul."

Mr. Symons glanced at her Bible. "Is that an NIV you have there?"

"Yes."

He nodded. "In the Greek language there is a word 'hades.' In our English Bibles, the translators have at various times translated this word as 'grave, pit or hell.'"

"They all mean the same thing?!"

"Yes. Every time a translator comes to the word 'hades' he has to think, 'now, should I put in hell, grave or pit?' So here in Acts chapter two, your NIV has accurately put 'grave.' If it used only the words 'grave' or 'pit' for all the places 'hades' occurs, then it would greatly help to remove the misconception that there is a fiery place of torment."

Verity was stunned. "Are you saying there's no hell?"

Mr. Symons smiled. "Did you know that people used to say they would 'hell their potatoes'? They only meant that they would bury them in the dirt. Along the way, sometime during the last few centuries, 'hell' has come to mean much more than it did in the Bible. When a person reads the word 'hell' in the Bible, they see a very different visual picture than when they read 'grave' or 'pit'— yet it's all the same Greek or Hebrew word."

"So, if I was reading a Greek Bible," Verity said slowly, "then I would see just 'hades' in all the passages, instead of 'grave' in some and 'pit' in others and..."

Mr. Symons was nodding. "Exactly!" He smiled at her with a little shake of his head. "I must say, Verity, you're very perceptive!"

Reaching for a heavy book on top of the pile, he continued kindly. "There's a lot more I could say about 'hell' but let's save that for later. Right now, let's see if we can figure out 'soul.'" As he opened up the big book, he said, "I don't want to scare you with these reference books.[6] Yes, they're big, but if you can make your way around a dictionary, you'll have no trouble figuring out how to use these. I'm sure after finishing this study-sheet, you'll be a pro!"

"This book here is called 'Strong's Exhaustive Concordance,'" he explained, showing her various pages. "It lists every single word in the King James Bible alphabetically. You would use this book if you wanted to find out what a word from the Bible meant in its original language."

Pushing it in front of her, he nodded. "Now see if you can find the word 'soul.'"

Verity found it easily. It really was just like a dictionary. Every phrase in the Bible that had the word 'soul' in it appeared chronologically underneath the word 'soul,' all the way from Genesis to Revelation.

Mr. Symons showed her the little numbers beside the phrases and then he turned to the back of the book to what was called a 'Hebrew Dictionary.' There was also a 'Greek Dictionary' for the New Testament words. It was easy to then use the number given for 'soul'—5315 and find the definition. Under the number 5315 was the Hebrew word 'nephesh.'

"Wow!" Verity exclaimed, reading the definition, *"a breathing creature, appetite, beast, body, breath, dead, desire...* it

---

[6] Strong's Concordance, Lexicon and many other study aids can now be easily referenced on your phone or computer. Try the free App MySword - Free Android Bible or e-Sword HD: Bible Study to Go for Apple

goes on and on!" She paused, rather puzzled, searching over the list a few times. "But nowhere does it say 'immortal soul.'"

Mr. Symons nodded. "When you look up 'soul' in the Greek Dictionary at the back, the definition will give the impression that the soul is immortal, because that is what Mr. Strong believed. Just keep in mind that while these definitions list the ways in which each word is used, they also include Strong's personal opinion on the meaning. Be careful to examine the passages that are listed. That is the best way to determine how the Bible actually uses or defines a word."

With a smile, he reached for the second book. "Now I don't want to confuse you," he began, "but I want you to be able to use this book as well." He showed her the cover of the second book. "This is 'Englishman's Hebrew-Chaldee Concordance of the Old Testament.' Don't be scared by the long name. It's simply a book that lists all the places where a particular Hebrew word occurs regardless of how its been translated into English."

Seeing her puzzled brow, he tried to explain very carefully. "This book will give all the places where 'nephesh' is used in the entire Old Testament, regardless of whether the translators have used 'soul,' 'life,' or 'creature' in English. Do you follow me?"

Verity sighed. "Maybe when you show me, I'll understand."

Mr. Symons chuckled. "It is a lot to take in all at once!" Opening it up, he explained, "Now, I'll use the same number we found for 'soul' in Strong's Concordance to find 'nephesh' in here."

He turned to the exact number and showed Verity the difference between the two books. Strong's listed phrases with the English word 'soul' in them. In Englishman's, under the Hebrew word 'nephesh' there were many more phrases, some with 'soul,' some with 'life,' some with 'body,' and several other related words.

"So, in Englishman's," he stated, "we have a much more complete picture of how the Hebrew word 'nephesh' is used in the entire Old Testament."

Verity skimmed the pages quickly. She could hardly wait to begin.

"Now the third book," he said, motioning to it, "is just like Englishman's, except it's for the New Testament Greek words. After you've done this investigation into what a 'soul' really is, we can meet again if you'd like."

"That would be fantastic!" Verity exclaimed. "This is a much quicker way to answer my question than reading through the whole Bible!"

"Yes, in some ways," Mr. Symons replied. "But this is like using a magnifying glass to see the details on a snowflake. A detailed study like this will give you some very important information but reading the whole Bible gives you the big picture. That will always be the most valuable thing to do! Oh, and one more thing," he said, picking up some photocopied sheets from his desk. "Since we don't have enough of these reference books to let everyone in the seminars borrow them, we've photocopied the relevant pages. You might as well take these photocopies home with you. Then you can highlight verses you find helpful and refer to them easily if you need to."

Verity felt quite excited as they headed out to drive home. This was like detective work! She was about to do some deep investigation. Perhaps she would finally find the answer to her very first question!

WHAT IS A 'SOUL'?

what-is-a-soul-worksheet.pdf (wordpress.com)

1. What do you think of when you hear the English word 'soul'?

_____

2. Who or what do you think has a soul? _____

3. Is there a difference between having a soul and being a soul?

_____

The first place that the English word 'soul' appears in the KJV Bible is Genesis 2:7: *"And the LORD <Y@hovah> God <'elohiym> formed <yatsar> man <'adam> of the dust <`aphar> of <min> the ground, <'adamah> and breathed <naphach> into his nostrils <'aph> the breath <n@shamah> of life; <chay> and man <'adam> became a living <chay> soul. <nephesh>"*

(Free Bible App- **MySword- Free Android Bible** OR **e-Sword HD: Bible Study to Go**)

4. What is the Hebrew word for 'soul'? _____

Hebrew # _____

What is the Strong's definition for this word?

_____

5. What is the Greek word for 'soul'? _____

Greek # _____

What is the Strong's definition for this word?

_____

6. Consider the first time the word 'soul' is used for a man in Genesis 2:7. Based on this verse (above), what is the composition of a soul?

_____ + _____ = _____

TAKE THE INVESTIGATION DEEPER

If you are interested in a more extensive investigation, use your Bible App to look at the Hebrew and Greek #'s for 'soul.' A sample list follows. See what characteristics apply to a "soul":

1. Who or what is a soul?

_____

2. What physical activities is a 'soul' capable of?

_____

_____

3. List any passages that suggest a soul lives forever:

_____

_____

4. List any passages that suggest a soul doesn't live forever:

_____

_____

6. Find a Church Catechism or Statement of Belief online and record what they say about the "soul:

_____

_____

7. Do a search on the phrase 'immortal soul' and list the passages you find:

_____

8. Based on your research, write your own definition of "soul":
A soul is _____

_____

The definitions below are taken from Strong's Concordance and Lexicon along with a sample of some of the relevant verses extracted from Englishman's Hebrew and Greek Concordance.

[H5315] (nephesh/neh'-fesh) from 5314; properly, a breathing creature, i.e. animal of (abstractly) vitality; used very widely in a literal, accommodated or figurative sense (bodily or mental):--any, appetite, beast, body, breath, creature, X dead(-ly), desire, X (dis-)contented, X fish, ghost, + greedy, he, heart(-y), (hath, X jeopardy of) life (X in jeopardy), lust, man, me, mind, mortally, one, own, person, pleasure, (her-, him-, my-, thy-)self, them (your)-selves, + slay, soul, + tablet, they, thing, (X she) will, X would have it.

Ge 1:20. the moving creature *that hath* (marg. *soul*) life,
   2:7. man became a living *soul*.
    19. every living *creature*,
   9:5 your blood of *your lives*
    —will I require *the life of* man.
   9:10 every *living creature* that is with you,
   12:5 *the souls* that they had gotten
    13 *my soul* shall live because of thee.

Nu 6:6 shall come at no dead *body* (lit. dead *soul*).
   19:11 He that toucheth the dead *body* of any man
   31:19 whosoever hath killed *any person*,

1Sa 2:35 in mine heart and *in my mind*
   18:1 *that the soul of* Jonathan was knit *with the soul of* David, and Jonathan loved him *as his own soul*.
   22:23 he that seeketh *my life* seeketh *thy life*

Es 7:3 let *my life* be given me at my petition,
   7 Haman stood up to make request for *his life*
Job 2:6 but save *his life*.
   6:7 The things that *my soul* refused to touch

Ps 11:5 him that loveth violence *his soul* hateth.
   16:10 thou wilt not leave *my soul* in hell;
   19:7 converting *the soul*:
   22:29 and none can keep alive *his own soul.*

Eze 13:19 to slay *the souls* that should not die,
      and to save *the souls* alive that should
      not live,
   18:4 all *souls* are mine; *as the soul of* the
      father, *so also the soul of* the son is mine:
      the soul that sinneth, it shall die.
   20 *The soul* that sinneth, it shall die.

[G5590] (psuche/psoo-khay') from 5594; breath, i.e. (by
implication) spirit, abstractly or concretely (the animal
sentient principle only; thus distinguished on the one hand
from 4151, which is the rational and immortal soul; and on
the other from 2222, which is mere vitality, even of plants:
these terms thus exactly correspond respectively to the
Hebrew 5315):--heart (+ -ily), life, mind, soul, + us, + you.

Mt 2:20 which sought the young child's *life.*
   6:25 Take no thought for your *life,* what ye
      —Is not the *life* more than meat,
   10:28 not able to kill the *soul:*
      —to destroy both *soul* and body in hell.
   39 He that findeth his *life* shall lose it:
   12:18 in whom my *soul* is well pleased:
   20:28 to give his *life* a ransom for many.

Lu 9:56 is not come to destroy men's *lives,* but to
   12:19 And I will say to my *soul, Soul,* thou hast
      much goods
   20 this night thy *soul* shall be required
   22 Take no thought for your *life,* what
   23 The *life* is more than meat,

Col 3:23 And whatsoever ye do, do it *heartily,*
Heb 12:3 lest ye be wearied and faint in your *minds.*
Jas 5:20 shall save a *soul* from death,
1Pe 3:20 few, that is, eight *souls* were saved
2Pe 2:8 vexed his righteous *soul* from day to day
   14 beguiling unstable *souls:*

CHAPTER 14

Finding the Answer

It wasn't until early Saturday morning that Verity found time to do the study-sheet. All was peaceful and quiet. Thomas had grudgingly gone to work last night, so he and everyone else were still asleep.

Verity stretched out by the coffee table and began the study-sheet entitled 'What is a Soul?' She had her NIV and the old King James Bible in front of her, as well as the photocopied reference pages from Mr. Symons. She filled in the Greek and Hebrew numbers at the top of the sheet and the meanings for the word 'soul.'

The next question asked if the phrase 'immortal soul' ever occurred in the Bible. Determined to find this, she quickly skimmed through the concordance looking at every verse with the word 'soul' in it. At last, she had to write 'no.' There wasn't even one instance in either the Old or New Testaments where the phrase 'immortal soul' could be found.

Next she looked carefully at all the occurrences of the two words frequently translated as the English word 'soul'—'nephesh' in the Hebrew and 'psuche' in the Greek. There were questions about the various characteristics of the soul, which took her at least an hour to answer, but by the end she was greatly amazed.

"Wow!" she exclaimed to herself. "I would never have thought it, but a soul can eat, it can sin, die, worship idols, be given up for others, it can even be hit! Over and over again, 'nephesh' is also translated as 'person,' or 'life,' or even 'creature'! And whatever a soul is—animals have it too!"

There were a few passages she had written down during her search, which seemed to indicate that a soul left the body at death— namely Genesis thirty-five, verse eighteen and First Kings seventeen, verses twenty-one to twenty-two. However, after seeing all the different English words that the translators had used freely for 'nephesh,' she tried substituting the word 'life' in place of 'soul.' When she did that, those two passages fit in perfectly with the others.

She marvelled that the passage Mr. Henderson had showed them, where he had said Jesus' soul wasn't left in hell, contained the Greek word 'psuche.' In her NIV, 'psuche' had been translated 'body,' but now she knew that the translators could have, just as accurately, used the word soul as in the King James.

In the last few months, she had read through much of the Old Testament, without realising that souls could eat, sin, touch and die. Her NIV translation, in its efforts to make God's word easier to understand, had not used the word 'soul' in passages that didn't fit the 'immortal soul' theory. Verity began turning up various passages in her NIV to see how the Hebrew word "nephesh" had been translated.

Leviticus chapter seven, verse twenty-seven read, *"If anyone eats blood, that person must be cut off from his people."*

"Interesting," she thought. "So, I read that passage in my NIV without realising the words 'anyone' and 'person' were really the word 'soul'! Therefore, I didn't know that a soul could eat."

Next, she looked at Joshua chapter ten, verses thirty-two, thirty-five, thirty- seven and thirty-nine. She decided to turn up this passage in both her King James Bible and the NIV. To her surprise, in the old King James all the verses were already highlighted with a big question mark to one side! She read the highlighted verses *"... they smote it with the edge of the sword and utterly destroyed all the souls that were therein."* When she looked in her NIV, it simply stated that, *"everyone was destroyed."*

"Wow! Souls can be destroyed!" she said to herself, shaking her head in amazement.

She compared the King James Version of Ezekiel chapter eighteen, verse four – *"The soul that sinneth, it shall die"*, to her NIV version – *"The soul who sins, is the one who will die."*

"That's a telling verse," she thought. "If I was that far along in my reading, I would have discovered here that a soul can sin and also die!"

Verity carried on for quite a while, finding that although her NIV Bible sometimes accurately put in other related words instead of 'soul,' in the process it covered up many of the most revealing verses about 'nephesh.' She wondered why the translators didn't just consistently translate 'nephesh' as 'person,' 'life' or 'creature' all the way through the whole Bible? Whenever she saw the word 'soul,' a very different visual image came into her mind, than when she saw the words 'body' or 'life.' It was the same confusion as 'hell' versus the 'grave.' She wondered, "Where did this idea of 'an immortal soul' come from?"

"If I didn't use these reference books and discover how God used the word 'nephesh,'" she considered, "then I might never have realised that since a soul can die it can't possibly be immortal."

She leaned back rather amazed. This was quite a dawning revelation to her searching mind. She sat there for a while pondering what other beliefs she had that could no longer be true without the existence of an 'immortal soul.'

"If we don't have something inside us that lives on," she thought, "then I guess when we are dead, that's it. We must be just plain dead, and in the ground." She remembered again the passage about Jesus and the comments Mr. Symons had made about 'hell.' "Maybe, when the King James says that Jesus' soul was in hell for three days," she considered, "that is the same as stating that his body lay in the grave for three days. He didn't go off to heaven and he didn't go down to a fiery torment—he just lay dead in the grave."

Her thoughts would have carried on much further but Thomas, now awake, was coming up the stairs. "So, what new questions have you thought up for us, Reverend Verity?!" he said sarcastically, gazing at the Bibles and reference books spread out all over the living room floor.

Slowly, still in a state of shock, she turned to look at him. "Actually, I've finally discovered my answer!"

Thomas reacted to the strange expression on her face. "And what is the answer?" he asked, continuing his mocking tone.

"There is no immortal soul, Thomas! When we die, that's it. Nothing floats off to some other place."

Astonished, Thomas asked, "So Dad isn't in heaven?"

"No," she said softly, "I guess he's just dead... in the ground."

For a moment Thomas looked serious, very serious, but he was not going to let his guard down for long. "I never believed in people going off to heaven or hell anyway!" he scoffed, marching out to the kitchen.

Verity nodded slowly, looking off out the window. "Then I guess you were right."

"What?" he said, looking back in surprise, "Did you say I was right?"

She laughed. "You may be right about that, but you aren't right about God. He *does* exist!"

"So, when we die, that's it?" Thomas asked cautiously.

Verity shook her head slowly. "Death can't be the end. Abraham must be alive again to get the land God promised him. David must be alive again to see Jesus sit on his throne. So, I guess the dead stay dead, until the resurrection. Reverend Tobias used to talk about the resurrection, Thomas. Remember?"

Thomas was busy pouring himself some cereal, but Verity continued anyway. "The resurrection never made much sense to me before. Why would we want our bodies back when we've been living happily in heaven without them? But," she continued, thinking out loud, "if when we die we *stay* dead in the ground, then the resurrection is the *beginning* of life after death! And without the resurrection we have no hope of ever being alive again. So, it's not about living forever in heaven— it's about living forever on the earth!"

All the pieces were coming together. Jumping up, Verity clapped her hands. "That's why Abraham was promised land on earth, *forever!* And that's why Jesus will reign on David's throne, *forever!* It's for the future, *after* the resurrection! People will live forever on the earth then! Yes, I've got it! It all makes perfect sense!"

Thomas looked at her as though she was a raving lunatic. "Wait till I tell Hank about this!" he said, rolling his eyes.

Verity froze. Why did Thomas always have to knock her down, every chance he got? Could he not stand to see her happy? "Thomas, I can't believe you'd make fun of me to that horrible Hank Hamann!"

"Hank's not horrible! He's the only person who has been nice to me since I came here. We have a lot in common."

"Thomas, if Ken was here, he wouldn't want to hang out with Hank, and you know it!"

"If Ken was here, then I wouldn't need…" Thomas stopped short, realising he was setting himself up, but Verity had seen the pain in his eyes.

"Thomas," she said gently, "if you weren't so miserable all the time, the nice kids would be friendly to you."

"What nice kids?" he shot back. "Or do you mean Peter Bryant?" he asked sarcastically. "He's hardly spoken a word to me… At least," he mumbled, "he hasn't until the last few days."

Verity face coloured at the mention of Peter's name, but what was it Thomas had said? "He's spoken to you in the last couple of days?"

"Oh yeah, he's trying really hard to be my friend now…" Thomas pounded the table with his fist. "Anyway, I don't know why I'm talking to you so much. You're my wacko sister! I like Hank, okay? I have a lot of fun with him—it's the only time I feel good anymore! At least he's not stuck up like *your* friend Purity!"

"She's not stuck up!"

"Oh yes, she is! I never saw anyone who fits her name better than that girl. Everyone I talk to says she's the biggest snob they've ever met. She never stays for lunch; she doesn't go to dances or anything besides classes; most people have never even heard her speak!"

"Then how do they know she's a snob?" Verity questioned indignantly.

"What?"

"Well, if they haven't talked to her and if you haven't talked to her, then how do you know she's a snob? Maybe she's just shy!"

Thomas shook his head, determinedly. "I'm not going to talk to a goody-goody like her! I'm not in her league!"

"That's too bad," Verity remarked. "Then I guess you'll never discover that there may be other people just as lonely as you!"

Thomas had had enough. Donning his winter coat quickly, he took off outside to get the snow off the Jeep. It was almost time for him to drive in with Aunt Judy to work.

Verity stood by the window watching him head out and wishing she knew how to help him.

At last, remembering the elation she had felt before Thomas spoiled her joy, she turned back to the coffee table and picked up the photocopied pages. It would be good to highlight the most telling verses so she could find them quickly if she needed to.

Thinking of Peter, she wondered if he would talk to her again. It was encouraging to hear that he was trying to be a friend to Thomas. Perhaps she would keep the pages in her backpack just in case. "Maybe, just maybe," she said hopefully, "I'll get a chance to show these to him sometime."

CHAPTER 15

It's a Gift

W hen the Symons arrived to pick Verity up for the seminar, Jessica got out of the car so that Verity could sit in the middle. Verity loved the colourful pictures they had made for her, which had 'I love you!' written on them. Jessica had brought her a big red apple, which she gratefully accepted. "It looks delicious!" she exclaimed. "I'll eat it for my lunch tomorrow," she promised. She then launched in to share her discoveries about the 'soul' to the Symons.

"Verity, I'm impressed by how well you've seen all the implications from that study," Mr. Symons said. "You're right about the resurrection being so important. The apostle Paul felt there was no advantage for him if the dead don't rise.[1] Everyone may just as well eat and drink for tomorrow they could die and life will be over. If you read through all of First Corinthians fifteen, you will find that the resurrection is the most important hope that God has given us. That wouldn't be the case if we had immortal souls that went to heaven when we died. If you have an immortal soul, resurrection might be a bonus, but it is no longer a necessity."

Turning around in her seat, Mrs. Symons added, "In that same chapter Paul states clearly that without the resurrection, those that have fallen asleep in Christ have *perished*."

"Yes, and Jesus often spoke of the dead as being asleep,"[2] Mr. Symons said in agreement. "He didn't see death as a finality, just something that he will wake us from when he returns."

Verity nodded thoughtfully. "So, now I'm wondering *who* will be resurrected to live forever when Jesus reigns from

---

[1] 1 Corinthians 15:32

[2] John 11:11–13, 24–25 and 1 Thessalonians 4:13–17

Jerusalem? Is this something that will happen to everyone? Or will some people stay dead?"

"Those are great questions, Verity!" Mr. Symons replied. "If you wouldn't mind reading from Romans chapter six, verses twenty to twenty-three, we could determine what God has promised on this subject."

Verity turned it up in her Bible and read, *"'When you were slaves to sin, you were free from the control of righteousness. What benefit did you reap at that time from the things you are now ashamed of? Those things result in death! But now that you have been set free from sin and have become slaves to God, the benefit you reap leads to holiness, and the result is eternal life. For the wages of sin is death, but the gift of God is eternal life in Christ Jesus our Lord.'"*

"What do *you* think?" Mr. Symons asked, "Will everyone get to live forever?"

Somewhat unsure, Verity responded, "It sounds like you have to serve God to get eternal life."

Both the Symons nodded. "That's what I read as well," replied Mr. Symons, "Eternal life isn't referred to here as a human 'right' that we all deserve. Eternal life is a *gift* that God gives to those who willingly become servants to Him. In other words, if we don't choose to follow God's commands, mortality is what we are left with. Without God, we are born, we live and we die. There is nothing more."

"Really?" Verity asked incredulously.

"Ephesians chapter two is quite helpful here," Mrs. Symons put in. "Verity, what does your version say in verses one to three?"

Looking it up as quickly as she could, Verity read the passage. *"'As for you, you were dead in your transgressions and sins, in which you used to live when you followed the ways of this world and of the ruler of the kingdom of the air, the spirit who is now at work in those who are disobedient. All of us also lived among them at one time, gratifying the cravings of our sinful nature and following its desires and thoughts. Like the rest, we were by nature objects of wrath.'"*

"Is there any hope offered here to people who are just living a life of pleasure for themselves?" Mr. Symons asked.

"Well, it refers to them as being 'dead in their transgressions and sins,'" repeated Verity uncertainly.

"That's right," Mr. Symons replied. "If you don't mind, read verses twelve to thirteen as well."

Verity was happy to carry on. *"'Remember that at that time you were separate from Christ, excluded from citizenship in Israel and foreigners to the covenants of promise, without hope and without God in the world. But now in Christ Jesus you who once were far away have been brought near through the blood of Christ.'"*

"Wow!" she responded. "That's pretty strong language!"

Mrs. Symons nodded seriously. "And notice that the promises are mentioned again. Without Christ we are *'foreigners to the covenants of promise.'"*

They had reached the library so Verity thanked the Symons for the ride and followed them into the room. Jessica took her hand as they walked toward the table.

"Do you enjoy the seminars as much as I do?" Verity asked her, realising that the two girls had been a little left out during the conversation in the car.

"Oh yes!" Jessica replied enthusiastically. "We get to colour with all the other kids."

"They all sit and colour with you?" Verity asked in surprise.

"Well, they start off sitting with their parents," the little girl explained factually, "but when they get bored they come back and do stuff with us."

"So, that's why you carry that big bag?"

"Yes, I have my favourite books and lots of markers—even some dolls."

Before the seminar began, Verity thought carefully over the discussion in the car and re-examined the Ephesians passage. It seemed that being "in Christ" was what made the difference between having a hope or being excluded from the promises. That reminded her of the passage Mrs. Symons had shown her a few weeks ago that linked Abraham's promises to a hope she could share in. At last, she found it again due to the bright yellow she had highlighted it with. Galatians chapter three, verses twenty-seven to twenty-nine tied it all together very nicely. *"For as many of you as have been baptized into Christ have put on Christ. There is neither Jew nor Greek, there is neither bond nor free, there is neither male nor female: for ye are all one in Christ Jesus. And if ye be Christ's, then are ye Abraham's seed, and heirs according to the promise."*

As always, more and more pieces of the puzzle fell into place as she listened to the presentations. The overview of the books of the Bible dealt tonight with First and Second Kings all the way to the book of Nahum. Mr. Henderson explained that King Solomon's early rule over Israel was a foretaste of the kingdom to come under Christ. All the nations were at peace and brought gifts to him. Solomon's wisdom was so great that his fame spread far and wide. People came from many other countries to hear him speak and ask questions. Solomon also built a magnificent temple for God in Jerusalem. All these things pointed forward to what Christ will do in even greater ways when he returns to rule the earth. The future temple that Christ will one day build, detailed in Ezekiel chapters forty to forty-eight, will be much more glorious than the magnificent temple that Solomon built. However, while Solomon began his reign in such a promising way, he failed to follow the commands of the law in Deuteronomy chapter seventeen and the result was, as the law had predicted—his heart was turned away from God. He married many wives who were idol worshippers, he gathered great riches to himself and horses from Egypt. Sadly, therefore, he gave into idol worship and became so proud that he would no longer listen to God's rebuke. Perhaps the words that he penned later in Ecclesiastes four, verse thirteen, were a reflection on his wayward life, *"better is a poor and wise child than an old and foolish king, who will no more be admonished."*

During the instruction on using Bible study tools, Verity felt rather smug. She was way ahead on this one! Mr. Symons explained to the rest of the class how to use the concordance and other reference books.

After this, Mr. Henderson handed out a practice sheet for using the study tools. He gave everyone fifteen minutes to see if they could find all the answers. The verse to be examined was, *"Blessed are the meek, for they shall inherit the earth."* Verity was surprised to see that in the Greek dictionary of Strong's Concordance, 'meek' could also mean 'humble'.

Looking at their cross-references they discovered that Jesus wasn't the first one to speak these words. Psalm thirty-seven, verse eleven also said, *"the meek shall inherit the earth."* Four other places in the same psalm spoke about the righteous inheriting the land and dwelling in it forever.

"That's just like what was promised to Abraham," she said to herself. Looking up the word 'inherit,' Verity scanned all the passages where it appeared in the Bible. She noted that God had frequently promised that people would inherit the earth, but never heaven.

When Mr. Henderson took up the study-sheet, he pointed out that in Psalm thirty-seven, not only did it promise that the meek would inherit the earth; conversely, it also said the wicked would perish and be cut off.

Remembering back to the chapters she had read in Matthew, Verity felt she had to ask what the 'kingdom of heaven' referred to. It didn't seem to fit.

Mr. Henderson was quite happy to respond. "Well, in Scripture there are two kingdoms set in contrast one to the other. One is the kingdom of men, which is what we are in right now. Men, and occasionally women, are in the positions of government. They rule over the nations, they make the laws and other people submit to them. When Jesus returns to rule the earth, it will no longer be the 'kingdom of men,' it will be the 'Kingdom of God,' or as Matthew states –'the kingdom of heaven.' It will be a divine Kingdom on earth."

Another lady put up her hand and asked about Jesus' promise to the thief on the cross. "Why then did Jesus say in Luke chapter twenty-three, verse forty-three, *'Verily I say unto thee, today shalt thou be with me in paradise'?* If paradise is on earth, what did Jesus mean?"

"Good question, Kelly," Mr. Symons replied. "Now we've already seen that Jesus was in 'hell' or the grave for three days following his death.[3] So, we know he didn't mean that he and the thief were going to heaven that very day. Remember also what Jesus said to Mary when he was resurrected, *'Touch me not, for I am not yet ascended to my Father.'*[4] Therefore, Jesus must not have gone to heaven until *after* his resurrection—forty days after, in fact!"

Seeing another hand up, Mr. Henderson let the man ask his question. "If all that time went by as you say, then what did Jesus mean when he said 'Today'?"

Nodding, Mr. Henderson answered, "The difficulty is rather easily dispelled by changing the punctuation of the verse. The

---

[3] Acts 2:22-27
[4] John 20:17

original Scriptures, you see, had no punctuation; this was added at the translators' discretion. The verse can legitimately be punctuated and read this way, *'Verily, I say unto thee today, thou shalt be with me in paradise.'"*

Looking around and seeing a few sceptical faces, he asked, "Does anyone want to take a guess as to the meaning of 'paradise'?"

Kelly put up her hand. "I always thought it was another way to describe heaven."

Mr. Henderson passed her the concordance. "Now that we've learned how to use this book, let's check it out in here."

After searching through slowly, Kelly looked up in surprise. "The definition is *'a park, or an Eden, a place of future happiness.'"*

"That's right," Mr. Henderson said, "and we know from other passages in the Bible that the earth will be restored to a paradise condition[5] when Jesus returns. So, it's at that time that the thief will be resurrected and, as he requested, be with Jesus when he comes into his Kingdom."

When the class finished Verity looked back to where the girls sat. Sure enough, a little girl about two years old sat with Lindsay, still looking at a book. Jessica was helping a small boy get some refreshments. In fact, his plate was *loaded* with snacks! They really were the cutest girls!

On the way home in the car, Mrs. Symons said gently, "Verity, I hear your brother Thomas isn't doing very well in school. Why do you think he is having so much trouble?"

Verity sighed. "I don't know. Back home in Saskatchewan, Thomas had so many friends and he was a good student. You'd never know it from looking at him here, but Thomas really gets close to people and his friends meant everything to him. So, he didn't want

---

[5] Isaiah 35, 51:3, 60:13–19, 65:17–22, etc.

to move to Ontario with us and he's angry over that and lots of other things! There's still all the hurt he feels about what happened with Dad. He just can't let it go!"

"Verity," spoke Mr. Symons hesitantly. "I'm quite worried about Thomas. Hank Hamann and his buddies aren't going to help your brother out of this. They'll only lead him into more trouble— deep trouble!"

Verity could tell Mr. Symons would liked to have said more, but with his two young daughters sitting in the backseat, he was trying to be discreet. "I'm worried too," she expressed, "especially since overhearing a conversation or two."

Jessica was looking up at her with big wide eyes, but Lindsay was falling asleep and didn't seem to be listening to what was being discussed.

"I've noticed in the last few days that a few of the better students are trying to include Thomas, so I've actually drawn up a new seating plan to move him beside them."

"Oh, that's a great idea!"

As they pulled up to Verity's home, Mrs. Symons turned and laid her hand on Verity's arm. "We'll pray for him too, Dear. When things are beyond our control, the best thing we can do is pray!"

"I will too!" whispered Jessica, squeezing her hand.

Verity smiled and thanked them all as she hopped out.

"That's something I'll add to my prayers as well," she determined, climbing the stairs to bed.

THE MEEK SHALL INHERIT THE EARTH

"Blessed are the meek; for they shall inherit the earth." Matthew 5:5

1. Using Strong's Concordance look up the word for 'meek.'
Greek # _____ Word _____
Strong's Definition: _____

2. Using the center margin of your Bible, see if there are any relevant cross-references: _____
_____
_____

3. Look up the word 'inherit.' Using the list of passages where the English word 'inherit' occurs, check out other passages of the Bible that speak of a promised future reward:

_____
_____
_____
_____
_____
_____

> [G4239] (praus/prah-ooce') apparently a primary word; mild, i.e. (by implication) humble:--meek. See also 4235. see G4235

This is a selection of verses from *Strong's Concordance* where the word ***inherit*** occurs.

Ge 15:7 to give thee this land to inherit it.
  28:4 that thou mayest inherit the land
Ex 32:13 seed, and they shall inherit it for ever.
Le 20:24 Ye shall inherit their land, and I will
Jos 1:6 shalt thou divide for an inheritance the
1Sa 2:8 to make them inherit the throne of glory
Ps 25:13 and his seed shall inherit the earth.
  37:9 the LORD, they shall inherit the earth.
  11 But the meek shall inherit the earth;

1Co 6:9 shall not inherit the kingdom of God?
  10 shall inherit the kingdom of God.
  15:50 and blood cannot inherit the kingdom
    doth corruption inherit incorruption.
Ga 5:21 shall not inherit the kingdom of God.
Heb 6:12 faith and patience inherit the promises.
1Pe 3:9 called, that ye should inherit a blessing.
Rev 21:7 that overcometh shall inherit all things

CHAPTER 16

Compassion

A s Verity ambled down the hall for science class that morning she saw Peter coming the other way. Since their discussion in the library when she'd left in tears, they hadn't seen each other. Waving cheerfully as he turned into his classroom, Peter called out, "Good morning, Verity."

Happily, Verity returned the greeting. The smile stayed on her face as she entered her class.

Mr. Connor discussed a special project that morning. They were to work in pairs and develop an oral presentation with supporting posters and a five-page essay. They could choose any topic dealing with either the beginning of life, or how animals had evolved from one kind to another.

On the way to their next class, Purity asked, "So what topic are you planning to choose, Verity?"

"I think I'll do mine on the evidence for Special Creation – that's the beginning of life as I see it!"

"What a great idea!" Purity marvelled. "Could I work with you?"

"Sure!" Verity exclaimed, grateful to have Purity on her side. "We could each do a different aspect supporting Creation. I'm sure Mr. Symons would be willing to help us out."

Verity was very pleased that Purity had asked to work with her. The blond girl was a rather shy, timid person and Verity realised that it was difficult for her to reach out to other people, but since their walk to the park there was a new comradery.

After math class, the two girls approached Mr. Symons with their ideas. He was most enthusiastic about helping them. "I'd love to help!" he said. "There are still a lot of scientists today who are also Creationists! They've written excellent material to refute the theory of evolution and to support Special Creation— scientifically! However, neither the media nor the educational system informs the general public of their research, as belief in Creation is considered 'out of date.'"

As he wiped the chalkboards to prepare for his next class, he continued, "Did you know that before Darwin almost all scientists believed in Creation? Isaac Newton, for example, is well known today for his scientific discoveries; but he claimed he studied science for what he could learn about God. In fact, Isaac Newton wrote more articles on the subject of religion than he ever did about science!" Pausing to organise his notes, he added, "I have a couple of books that will be most helpful to you girls. I will try to remember to bring them tomorrow."

Sure enough Mr. Symons brought the books the next day. Every spare moment that week they worked together reading and planning their presentations. There was a lot of information to search through and determine what would fit in best with the requirements of their assignment.

"I don't know how we're going to be able to do a good job on this, just working at lunch," Verity said the next Monday, flipping through 'In the Minds of Men.' "This book has so much good information. Why don't you come back to my house after school and stay overnight?"

Purity looked hesitant. "I'm not sure I'd be allowed... but maybe you could come to my house. I can ask tonight."

It didn't matter to Verity whose house they went to. "Okay," she said, "I'm free any night, except Tuesday of course!"

After getting her mother's approval, Verity followed Purity to her bus Thursday afternoon with a great deal of curiosity. She knew

Mr. Henderson from the seminars but she didn't feel as close to him as she did to Mr. Symons. What would the Henderson family be like?

The Hendersons lived out of town in the opposite direction from Aunt Judy's home. Here all the land lay flat with much of it cleared for farming. A few forests still stood in places but for the most part, level open fields stretched far into the horizon. At last, the bus pulled up to a modern, red brick bungalow.

Verity walked down the driveway with Purity and her three younger siblings. The youngest two were very excited to have a visitor coming to their home. When Verity asked them their names, she realised that Purity wasn't the only Henderson with an unusual name.

"My name's Jed," said the oldest boy, "that's short for Jedidiah. It's from the Bible."

"And my name's Jerry," said the next red-haired boy. "That's short for Jeremiah. It's from the Bible too!"

"And what's your name?" Verity asked the youngest child, squatting down to her level.

"I'm Melita!" she said quite proudly. Little Melita didn't seem to be afflicted with any degree of shyness.

"Where does Verity come from?" Jed asked inquisitively. "I've never heard that name before."

Verity had to laugh. Here she was thinking how unusual their names were and they were thinking the same about hers! "I'm named after my grandmother," she explained. "Verity is French for 'truth.' When I was little, my mom used to tell me that I couldn't tell lies because my name meant 'truth!'"

"So, you never told lies?" Jerry wanted to know.

"Well, I can't say I never did, or I'd be lying," she laughed again, "but I sure try hard not to!"

When they all trooped into the house, a wonderful aroma of baking bread and fresh cookies greeted them. The best part was that Mrs. Henderson, a tall, blonde woman, generously invited them to help themselves. Verity tried to get to know everyone, finding it quite interesting to see Purity in the position of 'big sister.' The younger children asked Verity one question after another, much to Purity's embarrassment.

It was already four-thirty before the two girls were able to escape upstairs to Purity's room. The desk in the corner was too small for both to work at, so they sprawled out on the bed to read and take notes.

Verity was thoroughly enjoying the books Mr. Symons had loaned them. She had never supposed there was so much sound evidence that God was the Creator. In fact, the more she read, the more she began to see that evolution was based upon premises that couldn't be tested, that had never been observed, and that required much more faith to believe in than did the concept of a Creator God. "It really is unfair that this side of the argument isn't presented in science class!" she remarked to Purity. "I wish I could take an hour for my oral presentation instead of just ten minutes."

Purity looked up with surprise.

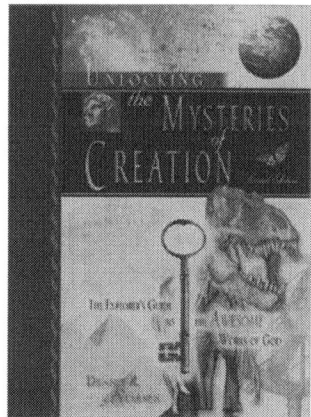

A few moments later, Verity spoke again. "If only I could find some way of fitting in all this information on Noah's Flood. 'Unlocking the Mysteries of Creation'[1] says this is the key that so

[1] Dennis R. Petersen. Publisher: Master Books; Reprint edition (Sept. 2002) ISBN: 0890513716
See also Evolution's Achilles' Heels (creation.com)

many geologists are missing. They want to presume that everything has always continued as we see it today—they don't believe that a global catastrophe like the Flood ever occurred. I just read here that to create a fossil there must be lots of mud and instant burial, not millions of years of something being slowly covered with sand. That makes so much sense, Purity! Of course, if a dinosaur lay dead on the ground for thousands of years, it would simply rot and disintegrate into nothing, not be preserved as a fossil! The fossil record indicates a massive burial— instantly—that covered millions of animals. And then there had to be tremendous pressure—like the flood waters would provide—to compact that mud into sedimentary rock![2] Oh, I wish I could think of how to fit the Flood into my presentation!"

The last words were said in real agony, for in reading these books Verity had come to see that the Flood had affected geology all over the earth. She wanted to speak about the Grand Canyon, the order in which fossils had been buried, how Carbon-14 dating systems were thrown off, how fossil fuels had been created... it just went on and on.

Then to top it all off, the book quoted a passage, Second Peter chapter three, verses three to six: *"First of all, you must understand that in the last days scoffers will come, scoffing and following their own evil desires. They will say, 'Where is this 'coming' he promised? Ever since our fathers died, everything goes on as it has been since the beginning of creation.' But they deliberately forget that long ago by God's word the heavens existed and the earth was formed out of water and by water. By these waters also the world of that time was deluged and destroyed."*

Reading that verse sent a shiver down her spine. God predicted two thousand years ago that people would assume everything had been the same since life began, and that people would 'deliberately forget' that God made the world and that there

---

[2] Where Do Fossils Fit Into the Bible? (isgenesishistory.com)

had been a Global flood! The book she was reading stated that most geologists don't take into account the tremendous upheavals the earth would have gone through, firstly in the creation process and secondly in the world being submerged with water at least twenty feet above the highest mountains![3]

It didn't seem very long before Mrs. Henderson called everyone for supper— and what a delicious meal she had prepared! Mr. Henderson was home and quite pleased to see their visitor. Until now, Verity had only seen a very serious side of him. Relaxed at home with his family, he was much more jovial, and courteously inquired about Verity's life-story, making her feel quite welcome and important.

"I'm really happy you two girls have chosen to do this presentation on Creation," he said approvingly.

Mrs. Henderson nodded. "I hear it was your idea, Verity! You must have a lot of courage."

Verity shook her head. "I don't know if its courage, Mrs. Henderson. I've just been amazed how strong the evidence is for Special Creation! People in our Science class might never get a chance to hear this other side unless we tell them."

Purity looked a little surprised. "Aren't you a little nervous about doing it though?"

Verity shrugged. "Yes, a little. But the weight of evidence is on the side of creation, not evolution. We don't need to be nervous."

After the supper dishes were cleared up, the Hendersons sat down to read from the Bible. Mr. Henderson explained that this was something they did every night. They would read three or four chapters of the Bible following a reading guide, which allowed them to finish the Old Testament and read through the New Testament twice within a year.

---

[3] Genesis 7:20

"Is that just for this year?" Verity asked.

"Oh no," Purity smiled. "We do the same thing every year."

"Wow! I guess you really get to know the Bible then!" Verity said, impressed.

All of the readings were interesting, especially when they could ask any question they wanted and Mr. Henderson gave clear, carefully reasoned answers.

However, the reading that really stood out in Verity's mind afterwards was Daniel chapter two. It was the account of King Nebuchadnezzar in Babylon and a dream he'd had that troubled him. In his dream he saw a huge statue of a man with a gold head, silver arms and belly, bronze thighs and iron legs. The statue's feet were a mixture of iron and clay. Suddenly, a large stone was cut from the mountain and smashed the image to pieces. Then the stone grew so big it filled the whole earth.

Nebuchadnezzar didn't know that his dream had come from God but he was so bothered by it that he was desperate to find out what it meant.

After the king had almost killed his wise men because they were unable to tell him both what happened in the dream and *also* what it meant—finally Daniel assured the king that he would ask God for the meaning. God did give Daniel the interpretation. It was a dream of the future! The gold head represented the kingdom of Babylon, which would be overthrown by the silver arms—the kingdom of the Medes and Persians. Then the silver arms would be overthrown by the bronze thighs—the kingdom of Greece, which would itself be overthrown by the iron legs—the kingdom of Rome. Finally, when Rome fell, the legs of iron weren't overthrown by another worldwide empire but rather parts of the iron lived on, mixed with worthless clay until a stone came down and smashed the whole image.

The stone, Mr. Henderson explained, was Jesus at his return to the earth. He would subdue all the nations of the world and rule in dominion over the whole earth, fulfilling verse forty-four of the chapter, *"And in the days of these kings shall the God of heaven set up a kingdom, which shall never be destroyed: and the kingdom shall not be left to other people, but it shall break in pieces and consume all these kingdoms, and it shall stand for ever."*

Verity was delighted. "So, it's another one of God's promises, this time made to King Nebuchadnezzar and Daniel!"

"Yes," agreed Mr. Henderson, "another promise about a kingdom on earth, *forever;* just like we discussed this week at the seminars."

"I really enjoyed the section on the 'Purpose of God Revealed,'" Verity nodded, remembering.

"It does change your perspective on things," agreed Mr. Henderson, "when you come to realise that God created the world for a reason. His purpose is that *'the whole world will be filled with His glory.'*"[4]

"What does that mean?" Verity asked. "How will the whole earth be filled with God's glory?"

Mrs. Henderson answered, "When all the people on the earth are demonstrating God's characteristics, then God's glory will fill the whole earth."

Everyone nodded and Mr. Henderson said, "That's the day we are all looking forward to."

This brought to Verity's active mind a new question she had been wondering about. "If everyone is made immortal in this kingdom, why would Jesus need to rule over them?"

---

[4] Numbers 14:21

For a moment Mr. Henderson had to figure out just what Verity meant. Then he understood. "Jesus isn't going to rule over the immortal people, Verity. In fact, those he gives the gift of eternal life will rule *with* him in this Kingdom."

Seeing Verity's look of surprise, he showed her Revelation chapter five, verse nine to ten. *"And they sung a new song, saying, Thou art worthy to take the book, and to open the seals thereof: for thou wast slain, and hast redeemed us to God by thy blood out of every kindred, and tongue, and people, and nation; And hast made us unto our God kings and priests: and we shall reign on the earth."*

"Well, who's being ruled over then?" she asked, perplexed.

"If Jesus returned tomorrow, Verity," he began, "would there only be Jesus and the people he resurrects on earth?"

"No, I guess there would also be all the people who are living on the earth at that time."

"Right," he nodded. "Jesus isn't going to just obliterate all those people; he's going to ask those who survive Armageddon to serve him as King.[5] As we read in Daniel chapter two, this will require a 'rod of iron' in some cases. There are other prophecies that indicate many countries won't like being told to submit to Jesus, and they will come out to fight him."[6]

This was all new to Verity—people fighting against Jesus at his return, and a Jesus who used a 'rod of iron' on them!

Seeing her wide-eyed look, Mr. Henderson continued, "Let me explain things in the order I believe they will happen. The first thing Jesus will do when he returns is to raise the dead and gather his followers.[7] After judging them, he will give immortality to the

---

[5] Zechariah 14
[6] Psalm 2; Zechariah 12:1–10; Revelation 19:9–20, etc.
[7] 1 Thessalonians 4:16–18

faithful. Around this time, there will be devastating earthquakes, and a terrible war in Israel.[8]

Even when Jesus has delivered Israel from this battle and set himself up as King, Psalm two tells us that many will not appreciate who Jesus Christ is, and will gather to try and overthrow his government. Of course, they won't succeed and after they have been defeated, *then* Jesus will reign in peace over all the earth. Those who survive these great wars will be the subjects of this worldwide Kingdom. They will be the people that will be ruled over by Christ and his immortal saints. These survivors will have to be taught God's ways. Isaiah speaks of the *'veil that is spread over all the nations'*[9] being destroyed. Then the whole earth will finally know of God in truth. All nations will go up to Jerusalem to learn more."[10]

"But why would people fight against Jesus?" Verity asked in alarm.

"Many religions are looking for an Antichrist to come before Jesus does," Mr. Henderson began. "Without reading the Bible carefully, especially the Epistles of John, they don't appreciate that Antichrist has been here since the very first century. Several things they expect this future Antichrist to do are exactly the things that Jesus himself will do. So, these people will see Jesus as this impostor and come to destroy him."[11]

"That's scary!" Verity responded.

"Yes, it is," he agreed. "It will be a sad consequence for those who aren't careful to hold fast to the Word of God and instead choose to follow the 'clever' delusions of men."

---

[8] Zechariah 14:1–5; Ezekiel 38 and 39

[9] Isaiah 25:7

[10] Isaiah 2:2–5; Isaiah 29:10–24; 30:18–21

[11] For more about Antichrist, see Book 2 in the Anna Tikvah series "Who Are You Looking For?"

As they ended the Bible readings with more enlightening discussions, Verity thought how much she would learn if she had the wonderful opportunity to discuss God's Word like this every night!

It was nearly ten o'clock when the girls finally decided to put aside their presentation and get some sleep. They had accomplished a lot, and both felt confident that they would be ready next week. Verity had reluctantly given up on including evidence for the Flood. She would liked to have discussed it if her topic had been Geology— but unfortunately it wasn't.

Purity insisted that Verity should sleep in her bed while she crawled into a sleeping bag on the floor.

A big, full moon lit up the night sky and streamed its way in through the window. Verity nestled down in the soft, cozy blankets and thought over how great the evening had been. She realised now that Purity was a warm, sweet person. It had just taken a little while to get to know her better.

"I'm so glad you moved here," Purity remarked softly.

"You are?"

"Yes! I used to hate going to school."

"You hated school? But you do so well!" Verity exclaimed.

"I didn't hate learning... I just didn't like being so alone. I was always so different from everyone else. Now that you're here, I know I can count on at least one friendly face."

Verity leaned over the side of the bed so she could see Purity. "I thought you liked being alone?" she smiled.

"Well," Purity sighed, "I would rather be alone than with a group of people telling dirty jokes or planning how they can get drunk on the weekend... but it's wonderful to have a friend!"

"I am your friend, Purity," Verity said, smiling, "and it is nice to know that when I'm with you, we can talk about things that really matter. I really appreciate your friendship as well! But," she continued, shuffling around so her head could rest on her arm, "don't forget that many of those people who tell dirty jokes and plan to get drunk every weekend don't have anything better in life. They haven't grown up like you, reading the Bible every day with your family. Like... my brother for instance..."

"Yes. He's rather scary," agreed Purity.

That wasn't the train of thought Verity had intended, so she was a little taken aback. "Scary?"

Rather embarrassed, Purity tried to explain herself. "Well, the friends he hangs out with are not very nice. Hank Hamann is always getting into trouble with the police and... well, your brother has such a mean look on his face, I'm scared to talk to him."

Verity was quiet for a few moments letting this revelation sink in. This was Purity's impression of Thomas! Purity had never seen any other side of him. For all Purity knew, Thomas had always been that way. "I guess that's the way other people at school view him too," she said regretfully, thinking of Peter's reaction.

"That's not your view?" Purity asked, interested.

Verity plumped up her pillow under her arms. "Thomas has only been like that since we came here."

"Really?" Purity gasped.

"Yes, and I love Thomas. It hurts me to see him so angry. Back in Saskatchewan we had a very rough childhood, but Thomas was always my friend. I tagged along after him and his friends whenever I could. He had great friends back home. I'm sure even you would like them—Ken especially! When my dad got drunk and was mean to me, Thomas always did his best to make me feel better, especially if my mom was at work. I did the same for him."

"Your dad got drunk and hurt you?!"

Verity realised her friend didn't know much about her life in Saskatchewan. "Yes, he was an alcoholic. He had such a drinking problem, he couldn't hold down a job. While he was drunk, he would get really angry. When Thomas was younger, he would stick up for Dad because he really cared about him. But then, on Thomas' thirteenth birthday, Dad came home in a drunken rage. He embarrassed Thomas terribly in front of his friends. After that my brother started hating him. Then my dad died and we moved here, so Thomas had to leave all his friends. I think that was more than he could bear. I don't know why he's hanging around with Hank but I know he'd be happier if he made better friends."

Purity had been listening intently and when Verity was finished it was a while before she knew what to say. At last, she said softly, "I'm sorry. I guess I judged Thomas harshly without really knowing the situation. I didn't know either of you went through such a rough time."

With a sigh, Verity answered thoughtfully, "I know it's still Thomas' fault that so many people misunderstand him. It's his choice to go around looking so miserable and choosing bad friends. But it just seems things are going worse and worse for him. I wish so much I could help him find his way out of this!"

"You are helping by example, Verity."

She sighed again deeply, "He only seems to get angrier the more I try to do what's right."

"Maybe you're pricking his conscience," Purity suggested.

"Maybe," Verity reflected.

They were quiet for a while and Verity was starting to think that Purity was asleep when she heard her whisper. "Verity?"

"Yes?"

"I've thought a lot about what you've said tonight. I'm going to try and be friendly to your brother. But it will be hard!"

"Why?"

She sighed. "I'm afraid that if I say 'Hi,' he might growl an insult back at me... or ignore me completely."

Verity laughed quietly. She was actually quite curious to see what would happen if Purity said hello to Thomas! "He might growl," she agreed with a smile, "but at least he won't be able to call you a snob, anymore."

"He calls me a snob?" Purity repeated in astonishment.

Nodding, Verity could see that Purity was really thinking this through. After another period of silence, Purity spoke softly again, "I guess in some ways I have been rather snobby." She sighed. Then a glow of kindness came over her face and she whispered to Verity, "Why don't we say a prayer for your brother?"

Very thankful for Purity's concern, Verity bowed her head as Purity, in a simple manner, asked for God to "please help Thomas."

CHAPTER 17

The Creation Presentation

The next day at lunch when the two girls arrived at the library with their Creation books in hand, Verity was elated to see that Peter and Thomas were deep in conversation at another table! She felt like tiptoeing so in they wouldn't be disturbed.

But just as she and Purity were about to start work on a poster, Hank Hamann arrived. Unfortunately, he noticed both girls right away. His eyes narrowed as he coarsely called out, "Hey, Reverend Verity, are you as pure as Purity?"

When Verity didn't answer he tried again, "Is anyone here as pure as Purity?" Seeing Thomas stand up, Hank laughed loudly, "Hey, what about you Thomas, are you that pure?"

Purity's face was a bright pink.

Verity wondered if her friend wished she had been given a nice, normal name, like… Sara or Jane.

"Not me!" said Thomas harshly. "I'm not that pure!"

They both laughed rudely and walked out of the library, leaving behind two rather embarrassed girls. If Purity had feared talking to Thomas before, it would be twice as hard now!

With a sigh, Peter rose from his seat and walked over to their table. "Well, that wasn't nice," he said regretfully. "And Thomas and I were actually having a decent conversation before Hank came in."

"Thank you for trying," Verity smiled gratefully.

"Of course," Peter shrugged. "I like your brother."

Seeing the books Mr. Symons had lent them lying on the table, the tall young man picked up the bigger one eagerly. "'In the

Minds of Men!'[1] he exclaimed. "Say, this is a really good book! I read it last year! Did you borrow it from Mr. Symons?"

When the girls nodded, Peter asked, "Anyway, what are you working on?" Happy to forget what had just occurred, the girls explained their plans.

Peter looked impressed but he said with a wry grin, "I suppose you're prepared to get a D on this project? Mr. Connor doesn't take too kindly to anyone opposing evolution!"

The girls glanced at one another; they hadn't quite planned on a D! "Well," Verity said at last, "other people in the class need to know that there is more evidence for creation than they'll ever find for evolution. This may be their only opportunity to hear some of that evidence."

"Good for you both!" Peter nodded. "Well, I've got to go play a basketball game. See you around!"

On Sunday evening, the day before the presentation, Verity asked at supper if she could practise in front of the family. Mom and Aunt Judy readily agreed.

Thomas shrugged. "I guess I might as well hear what lame excuses you have."

Verity set up her posters, drew a deep breath and began. "I would like to present the evidence for Special Creation. By Special Creation I mean that God created the world and life on it. What we see today didn't just evolve. Mathematically, several calculations show that life on earth cannot be more than seven to ten thousand years old. Take, for example, the population of the earth. Today," she said, pointing to her chart, "families average 3.6 children and

---

[1] In the Minds of Men: Darwin and the New World Order by Ian T. Taylor, TFE Pub; 4th edition (October 1999) ASIN: 0969178891
In The Minds Of Men Darwin And The New World Order Evolution Darwinism nwo illuminati freemasons : Free Download, Borrow, and Streaming : Internet Archive

the annual population grows 2 %. The population we have today could easily have developed from a single family in just four thousand years, if the growth rate were reduced to only .5 % per year, that is, an average of only 2.5 children per family. This would be a fourth of the present rate of growth and easily allows for loss of life due to famines, disease, and major wars. So, we can see this fits well within the framework of a global flood four to five thousand years ago."

Mom and Aunt Judy were nodding politely.

"However," she continued, "if we take the evolutionary model, we will have to say that the first people evolved at least a million years ago. At this same small growth rate of .5 % a year, we would have today, this number of people living right now." She pointed to the enormous number at the bottom of her poster, "ten with two thousand, and one hundred zeros, after it!"

Noting that Thomas was working hard at not being interested, Verity then switched to a picture of the sun. She explained that the sun continuously pours out vast quantities of energy of which planet Earth receives only a small part. If the sun were to be slightly hotter or cooler than it is today, life could not exist on earth. "Many scientists believe," she continued, "that the sun is shrinking by approximately .1 % per century. That may not seem like much to worry about now but if we use that calculation and work backwards, we can see that in only twenty million years, the surface of the sun would have been touching the earth! Obviously, life couldn't have been evolving on earth for millions of years because it would have been far too hot!"

Her presentation ended with two final examples. When the first rocket landed on the moon, there was almost a complete lack of atmospheric dust. This surprised many scientists who had calculated several centimetres or metres of dust based on their premise that the solar system had existed so long.[2]

With a bird's eye view of Niagara Falls, Verity explained how the rate of erosion along the gorge equated to somewhere between four and seven thousand years of activity. Verity then held up the two books that Mr. Symons had loaned her, 'Unlocking the Mysteries of Creation' by Dennis R. Peterson and 'In the Minds of Men' by Ian Taylor—and recommended them both to her audience. "These will be a great help for those of you who wish to know more."

Mom and Aunt Judy clapped their hands. "Wonderful job, you're a natural presenter!" Aunt Judy praised.

Thomas simply shrugged and headed off to his room.

The presentation the next day went well. Verity did feel a little nervous standing in front of her classmates. She avoided glancing in Shane Black's direction so she wouldn't have to see his sceptical, taunting look. Thankfully, her new friends Emily and Kate seemed quite interested, so she focused in on them. Unfortunately, at the end when she wanted to advertise the books, she could only hold up one. She had searched the whole house that morning, but the bigger book seemed to have disappeared.

Purity had a little trouble getting started as she wasn't very confident about public speaking. With somewhat faltering speech, she presented evidence to show that one species of animal cannot reproduce with another species. Therefore, animals couldn't have evolved from one kind into another kind. Looking first at a mule, the product of a horse and donkey, two closely related animals within the same species, she pointed out that mules are always infertile. Then she held up a picture of an animal that was a cross between a lion and a tiger. Once again, it was healthy and interesting

---

[2] See also Age of the earth (creation.com) 101 evidences for a young age of the earth and the universe

to look at, but it couldn't produce offspring. "These animals," she said, "are very close genetically yet their crossbreeds can't reproduce and continue this line. If a donkey and a horse can't produce fertile offspring, what hope is there for a fish to evolve into a land-dwelling creature and be able to have offspring? If one species really does evolve into another, then why don't we see transitional species today? According to evolution, this process should still be going on and everything should be evolving into something better. Instead, all of nature shows us that animals, plants and people all reproduce only within their own species. Maple trees produce new maple trees. Monarch butterflies produce monarch butterflies. Apes produce baby apes."

Holding up a large poster with the many breeds of dogs represented on it, Purity explained how that selective breeding is able to alter the canines' appearance, height, personality and colouring, but a dog will always remain a dog. "Selective breeding can greatly modify the offspring based on the genetic material *already available* within the dog family, but it will never produce something genetically *new* to the species, like horns or wings."[3]

Holding up a picture of a finch, Purity carried on. "Finches for instance can hatch with broad beaks or slim beaks. Depending upon the hardness of the seeds that year, the beak may determine which birds survive best. So yes, within the genetics of a finch lie certain variations for beak development, but a finch will always be a finch; there are no genetics available for it to turn into even another species of bird."

Although Purity spoke nervously, in the end the examples still came out loud and clear in favour of Special Creation.

Mr. Connor grudgingly gave them a C plus. "For the effort", he said. "The substance is rather weak."

---

[3] Three Myths About Species Changing Over Time - Media Center (creation.com)

CHAPTER 18

Peter Is Shocked

With the approach of mid-term exams in early November, Verity was kept very busy fitting in homework, Bible reading, and the Tuesday night seminars. November twelfth was the last 'Learn to Read the Bible Effectively' seminar. However, Mr. Henderson had suggested those who were interested could continue with Mr. Symons and himself, reading through Genesis and applying the study skills they had learned.

The 'soul' study-sheet had provoked a great deal of lively discussion which most people found quite interesting.

Nevertheless, a few seemed unwilling to accept that the Bible did not support a belief they held very dear. One older man, Henry, who had been rather quiet for the previous five evenings, now asked Mr. Symons to explain several New Testament passages. With every passage, Mr. Symons kindly directed Henry back to the context of the verse and reminded him that the word 'soul' really referred to a living being, their mind, their life, their existence.

"What about Matthew chapter ten, verse twenty-eight?" questioned Henry further, "It reads, *'Do not be afraid of those who kill the body but cannot kill the soul.'* See! The soul and body are two distinct things—one can be killed, and one can't."

"You're saying then," replied Mr. Symons, "that the soul can't be killed?"

"That's right!"

"Well, if a soul is truly immortal and can't die—then what does the rest of the verse mean?"

Henry read tentatively, *"'Rather be afraid of the One who can destroy both soul and body in hell.'"*

"Who can 'destroy both soul and body,' Henry?"

"God of course. He can destroy anything."

"Does God destroy *'immortal* souls'?"

"He could," Henry responded hypothetically, although he had never considered this before.

Mr. Symons asked everyone to look carefully at the passage and the verses around it to understand what point Jesus was trying to get across.

It took a few moments before anyone answered but Sally thought she could see the point. "Is it that people can kill other people, but only God can choose to give us life again, or leave us dead?"

"That's it, Sally," Mr. Symons smiled encouragingly. "People can kill other people—and many followers of Christ were killed for their beliefs. But those followers had the hope of resurrection and life forever. Only God has the power to destroy both our bodies and our lives. If God leaves us dead in the grave—which is what hell is—then we have no hope. Without God resurrecting us, our bodies stay dead and so does any hope of living again!"

Another hand went up. This time it was Sarah. "You keep saying that hell is the grave. How would you ever possibly explain Mark chapter nine, verses forty-three to forty-eight that way? I'll read it out for you," she offered. *"'...And if thy hand offend thee, cut it off: it is better for thee to enter into life maimed, than having two hands to go into hell, into the fire that never shall be quenched... Where their worm dieth not, and the fire is not quenched...'"*

Sarah looked up and Mr. Symons nodded apologetically. "We have been talking about hell as the grave without fully explaining the subject," he began. "Who would like to look up the word for 'hell' here?"

As it had been her question, Sarah offered to do this research. Within a few minutes she read out the information from the back of Strong's Concordance. "It's the word 'Gehenna' and it means the *valley of the son of Hinnom; a valley of Jerusalem, used as a name for the place (or state) of everlasting punishment —hell.'*"

Mr. Symons nodded, "In the New Testament," he explained, "there are a few different Greek words translated as 'hell.' The most common one is 'hades' which is also used as the grave or pit, but 'gehenna' is a different Greek word." Passing Sarah a Bible Dictionary, he suggested, "Now, since this is an actual place in Jerusalem, let's find out what it was used for. Look up the word 'Gehenna', please, Sarah."

There was quite a lengthy article written about 'Gehenna' in Hasting's Dictionary of the Bible. The basic idea was that Gehenna was a place to throw garbage. Even dead carcases of criminals or animals were dumped there. A fire was kept continuously burning so that everything would be consumed.

Mr. Symons pointed out that if this passage in Mark nine really referred to the popular belief of a fiery underground place of torment, one would have to believe also that worms were also immortal; as in the passage Sarah had read it said, *"their worm dieth not."*

"Instead," he went on to say, "the fire not being quenched and the undying worm speak of total destruction. Those two things continue on until there is nothing left to be consumed. In this Mark nine passage, Jesus is warning people in a parable form that if they keep being lead astray by a particular temptation in their lives, it is better to cut off that temptation than to be thrown into Gehenna as a criminal and perish forever. With the exception of the 'lake of fire' in Revelation[1] and the parable of Lazarus,[2] all the passages in the New Testament that discuss 'hell' as a fiery place use this same word

---

[1] Revelation 20:14-15
[2] Luke 16:23

'Gehenna.' But the usual Greek word translated as hell is 'hades' and it is synonymous with the grave."[3]

Verity was still thinking about the seminar discussion the next day as she gathered her textbooks that she needed to complete her homework. Purity was waiting as they had planned to go to the library during lunch hour. When they saw Thomas and Hank come around the corner, they both looked at each other in dismay.

"Well, if it isn't Reverend Verity and Miss Perfectly Pure!" Hank laughed loudly.

Thomas looked slightly annoyed. "Hey, Verity," he said, "I need some money."

"For what?" she asked suspiciously.

"I just need it! You don't need to know why."

"I'm not giving you any money unless you tell me why," she replied firmly.

Purity pulled ten dollars from her pencil case. "Here, you can have this," she offered timidly.

Thomas was taken off guard. "Are you sure?"

She nodded, turning rather pink.

Hank laughed crudely. "If only Miss Perfectly Pure knew what that ten dollars was going to buy!"

Thomas turned around sharply and the two of them lumbered off outside.

---

[3] 1 Corinthians 15:55; Acts 2:27-31
See also The New Testament 'hell' | Original Gospel
(1) Hell and Mr. Fudge (2012) | Full Movie | Mackenzie Astin | Keri Lynn
Pratt | Wes Robertson - YouTube

"I can't believe he didn't even say thank-you!" Verity said with disgust. "Purity that was awfully nice of you to give him money, but I don't think you should do it again."

"I was only trying to be friendly," she pleaded.

"That part was good," Verity agreed, "but I'm worried that money will be buying drinks... Oh, well!"

Realising she had homework in every subject, Verity decided to bring her whole backpack to the library. They met there with Emily and Kate and settled down to study.

As they all worked on various assignments, Emily, who was searching magazines for articles on 'environmental issues', suddenly giggled. "Look at this cartoon!" She passed it around so they all could see. A sad looking fellow wearing big, thick glasses was standing open-mouthed at St. Peter's pearly gates. St. Peter was explaining that to get into heaven, the distressed student had to answer a math question about two trains travelling at different speeds.

Purity shook her head in disdain. "People don't go to heaven!"

Emily and Kate looked up in astonishment. "What? Of course they do!"

Verity smiled. "I used to think people went to heaven too, but since I've looked at it more carefully, I've learned that isn't what the Bible teaches."

"Really?"

Verity pulled out her soul study-sheet. Briefly, she tried to explain about the Hebrew and Greek words. "Look here at all the things the Bible says about 'souls,' they can eat, die, sin, be killed..."

She was interrupted as a tall young man pulled his chair over to their table. "Hi," Peter nodded, as he sat down beside her. "I overheard your conversation. What's this about souls?"

Verity passed him the sheet. "Let me show you where I got this information from, Peter." She pulled out the photocopied pages Mr. Symons had given her. "These are taken from a concordance of the Old Testament. It lists all the places where a Hebrew word occurs, regardless of how it has been translated into English." Looking quickly around, Verity saw that everyone, except Purity, looked confused. She tried to explain it the way Mr. Symons had explained it to her.

Peter took the pages in his hands and looked them over carefully. "So, you're saying that 'nephesh' is the Hebrew word for soul, and it's been translated different ways in the English?"

"Yes!" she nodded enthusiastically. "You can look at them all if you want but let me just point out a few."

Emily and Kate jumped up to look at the list as well. "Look at this," Verity said, excitement surging through her again as she pointed to the passages she had highlighted. "In Numbers chapter six, verse six, *'a person is to come at 'no dead body.'* That word for 'body' is the same word used for 'soul.' The passage could legitimately read, 'a person is to come at no dead soul!' So, a soul can be a corpse! Psalm twenty-two, verse twenty-nine says, *'none can keep alive his own soul.'* Joshua chapter eleven, verse eleven says, *'they smote all the souls that were therein, utterly destroying them.'* Ezekiel chapter eighteen, verse four says, *'the soul that sinneth it shall die...'* " She would have liked to carry on but a quick glance at Peter's white, tense face made her stop.

He was looking at her very seriously. "Verity, do you mind if I borrow these pages tonight?"

"No, that would be fine," she said.

Without another word, Peter picked up the papers and strode out of the library. He didn't even nod good-bye.

"Whew," exclaimed Kate, "he's upset!"

Emily looked like she was in shock too. "Verity, this is major stuff here! Are you sure it's right?"

"It's only what the Bible says," Verity shrugged, her spirits dampened. It had been so exciting for her to discover what really happened after death that she expected everyone else to be just as excited.

But the difference was this; for many months now, Verity had been wondering about life after death and seeking to know what the truth was. Until today, none of the others had even given the subject more than a moment's consideration. And without first considering the question, the answer isn't always appreciated.

CHAPTER 19

A Visit to the Symons' Home

T he next afternoon when Verity came home, her mom announced that Mrs. Symons had called to invite them all for dinner on Saturday. "She mentioned that there are additional seminars planned on Genesis. Did you know about that Verity?"

Verity's hand flew to her face. "Oh Mom! Mr. Symons did mention that Tuesday night at the last session and I forgot to tell you. We're going to read the Bible together and discuss it. Do you mind if I go?"

"Well, I've been reading through the notes you bring home every week and so far I haven't come across anything to worry about." She looked at her daughter seriously. "I guess I'll decide after we have dinner with the Symons."

When Saturday evening finally arrived, Thomas was most reluctant to go along, but since he was no longer allowed to stay home alone, he had no choice.

It was only a short ride down the roller coaster road to the Symons.' Verity always loved driving on that road but as they pulled up to the Symons' modest, green coloured house, she felt a little anxious. So much depended on how well this evening went. During her ride to the seminars with the Symons that week, Verity had discussed her mother's concerns with them so they were well aware that Kara had objections. Now Verity wondered what questions would be asked and what answers would be given. She was more convinced than ever that she wanted to find her answers in the Bible. The study-sheets had been so helpful in giving her direction on how to find these answers for herself. It would be so interesting to read through Genesis with everyone else. Yet, her mom still seemed suspicious and fearful of what this was all about.

Walking up the pathway, Verity glanced over at Thomas. He was wearing his sour expression. She knew how resentful he was that he had to come. How she hoped that the Symons would see through his sullenness and be able to help him.

Aunt Judy was the least apprehensive about this visit. She had known the Symons for years. Because of grocery store business she knew almost everyone in town by their first names, plus all the neighbourhood gossip. Aunt Judy therefore needed no introduction as the Symons came out the door and greeted her on their front step. "Hello, Craig and Beth," she responded, shaking their hands. "It's so kind of you to invite us over!"

Kara was also warmly greeted by Beth Symons, who inquired how well they were all settling in and asked if they would like some tea.

Lindsay and Jessica were eagerly awaiting their favourite friend Verity. They politely greeted the visitors. They gazed at Thomas perhaps a little longer than they should have. With all they had heard about him they were very curious to see what he was actually like. As soon as Verity had removed her coat, they eagerly grabbed her hands to show her a surprise they had in their room. Verity laughed, as she hadn't yet taken off her shoes and she needed her hands to do so.

Mrs. Symons was trying to introduce all the guests to her children and now that everyone had taken off their coats and hung them up, Verity could see the two boys standing a little further down the hallway. "This is Taylor, our oldest," Mrs. Symons said, hugging him close. Taylor looked to be about thirteen by Verity's estimation, with dark hair and eyes like his mother. With a smile Taylor patted his brother's head, saying, "And this is Allan, the youngest. Tell everyone how old you are, Allan."

With a cheerful little face, Allan proudly held up four fingers and said, "I'm four years old! Almost five!"

As Verity followed the girls upstairs, she saw cute little Allan with his long- lashed brown eyes take Thomas' hand and cheerfully ask, "Can you play with me?!" Unable to resist the trusting little chap, Thomas allowed himself to be led into the living room where a big box of Duplo stood waiting.

Before Verity could enter the girl's bedroom, she was told to shut her eyes and not open them until they said it was okay. Wondering whatever this could be about, she obeyed the instructions and was led into the room. When the girls gave the word, Verity opened her eyes and saw that Lindsay was holding a crudely wrapped present out to her. "Open it. It's for you!" Jessica said, bouncing up and down, her pretty blue eyes sparkling with excitement.

"It's from both of us," Lindsay informed her excitedly.

There was lots of tape on the wrapping paper and it took Verity a while to get through it. Finally, she pulled out a little wooden plaque with woolly sheep and the words, "The Lord is my Shepherd".

"Did you girls make this for me?" she asked admiringly. "Yes!" laughed Jessica, "we made it this morning."

"Mom said we could," Lindsay nodded seriously. "I wrote the words and Jessica glued on the sheep."

Verity made a big fuss over how beautiful the present was and how much she appreciated it. Then the girls invited her to go downstairs and colour pictures with them.

That sounded great to Verity as she could then keep an ear open to the adults' conversation as well. Walking into the living room, she noticed that Thomas was well into building. Big towers, colourful houses and everything else that Allan asked for were being constructed. She marvelled at how easily the little boy had drawn out the real Thomas. Taylor had joined in too and it seemed they were all having fun with the four-year old's toys!

The adults stayed in the kitchen as Beth served tea and calmly went about fixing dinner. Their voices carried well to Verity's ears. She could hear Mr. Symons asking Aunt Judy how the grocery store was doing.

So far things were going great and everyone seemed to be getting along fine. Verity sighed happily.

When the announcement came that dinner was ready, Lindsay was very eager to show everyone where they were to sit. She had been put in charge of setting the table and was quite delighted to organise all the adults. The seating arrangements made Verity smile. She was in between Jessica and Lindsay, while Taylor and Allan flanked Thomas.

Mr. Symons bowed his head and thanked God for the food. The earnestness in his voice struck Verity. He prayed that God would soon send His Son to the earth to set up His Kingdom. He prayed as though he couldn't wait for the day! She had noticed that about his prayers before, at the seminars. They weren't just words he repeated out of habit; his prayers were said with so much feeling!

The meal was delicious. There was savoury roast chicken and gravy with mashed potatoes and corn. Then Mrs. Symons passed around sautéed purple cabbage and Parmesan green beans. Everyone was happily enjoying the meal, when Aunt Judy spoke up.

"I hope you don't mind Craig, if we ask you a few questions?" she inquired confidently.

"Not at all," he replied cheerfully.

"Well, since Verity would like to attend the next six seminars, Kara and I just want to be sure what she is getting into."

"Of course," Craig agreed.

"What exactly is the name of your religion?" Aunt Judy inquired politely.

"We are called Christadelphians," he replied. "'Christa' is Greek for 'Christ' and 'adelphos' is Greek for 'brethren.'"

"Oh, so it means, 'Christ's brethren'?"

Craig Symons nodded. "Or brethren in Christ. Jesus said, *'My mother and my brethren are these which hear the word of God and do it.'*[1] So the name Christadelphian, simply follows from this passage."

"Is it just for the men?" Kara inquired, a little confused.

"No," Craig smiled. "I'm using the term 'Brethren' like I would 'mankind'. We are brothers *and sisters* in Christ."

"Have Christadelphians been around for very long?" Kara questioned, still a little anxious.

Verity was quite interested to know this as well. She had never discussed this with the Symons.

"What is important, Kara," replied Craig gently, "is not the name 'Christadelphian' but the beliefs. People with different religious names down through the centuries have believed the same Gospel message that we do. Whenever a group of individuals chose to use only the Bible as their authority, they often came to the same Biblical beliefs as Christadelphians have today. There are copies of their writings and books - for example, The Polish Brethren.[2] You would also likely know the Apostles' Creed, written not long after Christ's ascension.[3] That is a Creed we totally agree with."

Passing around the roast chicken, Mr. Symons carried on, "It's helpful if you know a little of the religious history during the last two thousand years. For instance, in the dark ages—the sixteenth century—reading the Bible was forbidden by the Church."

---

[1] Luke 8:19–21
[2] Polish Brethren - Wikipedia
[3] Apostles' Creed - Wikipedia

He nodded at the look of shock on all their faces. "That's right," he said, "in fact, those who were found reading the Bible were burned at the stake by the Church. Priests gave their Church services in Latin so that the common people were left in ignorance about what was being said. Finally, at great risk to their lives, a few men managed to translate the Bible into English and distribute copies underground. This led to the Protestant Reformation, when people came to discover that what they read in the Bible condemned the actions of the clergy. There are writings from people at this time period that we would accept as being true Bible beliefs.[4] What's important to God is not the name people choose to call themselves, but whether they understand and preach God's Word as He has written it. We gave ourselves the name 'Christadelphian' in the mid-1800s when we had to register our group with the government."

"Oh, so you've been around for well over a hundred years then!" Kara said, somewhat relieved.

"Okay," nodded Aunt Judy, satisfied with the answers so far. "Now, what exactly is your motivation for putting on these seminars? It must take up so much of your time and be fairly expensive."

Verity again was eager to hear his response. These were all questions she had not thought to ask.

"Motivation?" Craig laughed a little, as he poured himself a glass of water. "Judy, I have so much motivation to do the seminars! We all do. I guess one of the primary reasons is because I believe the Bible is a book from God. Many people today see it as a book of myths. Others see the Bible as a book that can be picked apart. They keep what they like and cast aside what they don't agree with. The aim of the seminars is to get people back to reading the whole Bible. We want everyone to have confidence that the Bible is a book that can be understood. Each part of the Bible complements the other

---

[4] Religious views of Isaac Newton - Wikipedia
Socinianism - Wikipedia

parts. If you don't read and understand the Old Testament, you won't be able to understand the New properly. So, it's very important to…"

"But how do you know the Bible is true and not just a bunch of myths?" Thomas interrupted without thinking.

Verity was surprised, and glancing at Thomas she saw that he had surprised himself as well.

"Thomas, that's an excellent question!" Craig praised. He reflected carefully for a moment. "There are a few ways to prove this; I could easily talk for hours about the accurate and advanced medical knowledge in the Law of Moses,[5] the incredibly consistent message over 1500 years of authorship and 40 different scribes, the accuracy of the historical and archaeological record,[6] but… to answer you quickly, an easy one is prophecy. Over and over in the Bible, God said certain things would happen and they did—exactly as He predicted. The Old Testament is full of prophecies concerning Jesus, a thousand years before his birth. Everything happened as predicted, even though the Jews didn't understand or appreciate how the prophecies were all working out at the time, and often unwittingly fulfilled them.[7]

"God also made prophecies about particular nations hundreds of years before the events occurred. He predicted how certain ones would rise to glory and who would destroy them. There are several nations God clearly stated would never rise to power again—and

---

[5] The public health value of the Law of Moses (testimony-magazine.org)
Public Health And The Law Of Moses - 3500 years ahead of Its Time: Improved audio for 2020 -COVID-19 - ChristadelphianVideo.org
[6] (1) Why I Believe the Bible - Archaeology - YouTube
(1) Incredible - The Silent & Exciting Witness of Bible Archaeology - YouTube
[7] For example: Psalm 22; Isaiah 53

they haven't.[8] Babylon was condemned to be desolate forever.[9] Saddam Hussein tried hard to rebuild it before the Gulf War but the war stopped his efforts because it was against God's will."

"Wow! There are prophecies that are still coming true right now?" Verity asked in astonishment.

"Oh, yes!" Mr. Symons exclaimed. "And the best example is the modern nation of Israel! Before Jesus was crucified, he reminded the disciples of the prophecies which stated that the Jews would be scattered into all nations as punishment for their refusal to accept their long-awaited Messiah.[10] Yet other prophecies, in Ezekiel chapters thirty-eight to thirty-nine, promised that before Jesus comes back to earth again, the Jews will be re-gathered to the land of Israel and established as a nation once more. There are so many details in the re-gathering prophecies that have all come to pass exactly! I could easily spend an hour going through them with you. The Bible predicted, with complete accuracy, what nations would help the Jews return, what attitude the Jews would return with, how they would be 'hunted' back,[11] and so much more. Bible students in the 17 and 1800's were able to foresee that the Jews would return to their land, long before it took place."[12]

---

[8] YouTube - The Biblical Prophecy about Tyre
https://www.youtube.com/watch?v=K24uwdc-ato

[9] Jeremiah 51:60–64
A Prophecy about Babylon Confirms the Accuracy of the Bible by Beyond Today

[10] Luke 19:41–44 and Deuteronomy 28:15, 49–68
Online Article - Israel – A Powerful Witness to the Divine Inspiration of the Bible | Original Gospel
The MOST important video about Israel you'll ever see. by thelandofisrael YouTube

[11] e.g. Jeremiah 16:16

[12] See article John Thomas in Elpis Israel, page 349 Elpis Israel (wordpress.com).
isaac-newton-on-the-return-of-the-jews.pdf (wordpress.com)

Mr. Symons paused to pick up his fork but then laid it back down. "If you ever want to see the evidence that proves the Bible is inspired by God, please come and talk to me, Thomas!"

Looking over at Thomas again, Verity could see he was embarrassed to have shown interest. She was so glad he had asked the question.

Beth Symons, seeing that her husband was still sitting with a plateful of food, while everyone else had finished, carried on with the question of motivation. "There's also the hope we cherish," she began, "it's such a wonderful hope that we want to share it with everyone. We are fully convinced from God's Word that when Christ returns to this earth, the Kingdom he will set up will be more wonderful than anything we can imagine. Really, everything people are trying to find in this life—will be realised then. People don't want to die, they want good health, they long for peace, safety and a just government. The Bible promises all those things, saying also that the earth will be rejuvenated and produce food in abundance. There won't be wars or devastating plagues. It will be the perfect world so many are trying to obtain now but only God can bring."

Seeing that the children were growing fidgety, Beth asked them to clear the table. Then she suggested Taylor read Psalm seventy-two out loud before they served dessert. Jessica rushed to find everyone a Bible so they could follow along.

As Taylor read the Psalm, Verity noticed out of the corner of her eye that little Allan was pretending to be reading along intently – with his Bible upside down!

The Psalm was clear and simple, all about the wonderful promise of Christ's reign on the earth. It confirmed the words Mrs. Symons had spoken.

"That is our hope for the future," Craig stated, giving his empty plate to Lindsay. "As Beth said, it's such an exciting hope we can't keep it to ourselves. Everyone needs to have the opportunity to be involved."

"So why aren't there Christadelphians everywhere?" asked Aunt Judy, as Lindsay and Jessica began to bring around plates of raspberry pie and ice cream.

Craig looked thoughtful. "Why aren't there Christadelphians everywhere?" he repeated. "Well, Jesus said, *'Because strait is the gate, and narrow is the way which leadeth unto life, and few there be that find it.'*"[13]

He took a sip of his water, and continued, "Jesus was the best preacher there could ever be. He even performed miracles to demonstrate he was from God, and yet very few believed him during his ministry. In referring to the days just before his return, Jesus predicted that the world would be *'as it was in the days of Noah.'*[14] Verity would know from her reading," he continued with a nod in her direction, "that in the Flood, only Noah and his family were saved out of what was probably millions of people." He shrugged. "If you read through the whole Bible, you will see that the true way was never popular and often aggressively persecuted. There were only ever a minority of people that served God the way He wanted them to."

"And yet," added Beth, "there *are* Christadelphians found throughout the whole world in almost every country on earth." Her Bible was open to a relevant passage. "We were speaking about prophecies," she said, "I have another one for the last days before Christ's return." She read Second Timothy chapter three, verses one to five, *"'This know also, that in the last days perilous times shall come. For men shall be lovers of their own selves, covetous, boasters, proud, blasphemers, disobedient to parents, unthankful, unholy, without natural affection, trucebreakers, false accusers, incontinent, fierce, despisers of those that are good, traitors, heady, high- minded, lovers of pleasures more than lovers of God; having a form of godliness, but denying the power thereof: from such turn away.'* So you see," she said, "God predicted that most people would

---

[13] Matthew 7:13–14
[14] Luke 17:26–27

be following after other things than Him when Jesus returns. Serving God requires time and effort. Most people are too busy getting what they want for themselves out of this life. The life to come seems too abstract and requires faith and dedication."

"Read Second Timothy chapter four, verses three to four, as well, Dear, since it's just over the page," Craig asked.

She read, *"'For the time will come when they will not endure sound doctrine; but after their own lusts shall they heap to themselves teachers, having itching ears; and they shall turn away their ears from the truth, and shall be turned unto fables.'"*

"What does that tell you, Verity?" Craig asked.

Verity looked carefully over the verses again. "I guess it's saying that many people won't like what they read in the Bible and will choose to ignore God's truth in favour of what sounds better to them."

Craig nodded. "Does that make sense?" he asked Aunt Judy, as he also thanked Lindsay for the piece of pie she had handed him.

Aunt Judy and Kara nodded as they began their dessert.

Then Kara remembered one more question she had. "So, are you the minister of your church?" she asked.

Craig and Beth both shook their heads. "No," Craig smiled, "We don't have ministers or any other leaders, except Christ. The Bible, the Word inspired by God is the only authority we rely upon. All of us believe very strongly that the Bible can be understood with prayer and careful study. Brethren take turns leading the classes. As Jesus said, *'...be not ye called Rabbi, for one is your Master, even Christ; and all ye are brethren.'*[15] Every member also feels the responsibility of making sure that what they are taught is Scriptural truth—not mere opinions or man-made traditions."

---

[15] Matthew 23:8

Seeing that Kara looked sceptical, Craig continued kindly, "While the Bible refers to bishops, deacons, et cetera, Paul commended the Bereans because they diligently searched the Scriptures [16] to make sure that *he*, the apostle Paul, was teaching the truth! If everyone had this spirit and examined what they heard with what was written in the Bible, we wouldn't have so many false beliefs existing today."

Kara and Aunt Judy were nodding their heads, their fears dissipating. Allan had finished his meal and after sitting quietly for so long, he was anxious to go and play. Thomas thanked Beth for the meal and asked to be excused. The Symons children all followed suit.

"This is wonderful pie, my dear!" Craig complimented, finally getting to taste it.

Then he remarked to Kara, "I must say, I've been very impressed by your daughter. Verity wants answers and she's willing to put in a lot of effort to find them." He smiled at the dark-haired girl. "There aren't many young ladies your age who think so deeply about what life is all about!"

"Thanks, Mr. Symons," Verity said, turning a little pink.

"I suppose," remarked Aunt Judy, "not many girls her age have been through her experiences. Perhaps that is why she is thinking beyond her years."

After dinner, when the dishes had been cleared away, Mr. Symons talked quietly with Kara about how Thomas had improved in math since the new seating plan. Kara confided in him her concerns about the difficulties Thomas was having.

"He's very bright," he replied, as they observed the two younger boys wrestling with Thomas on the floor. "He just needs to work through those negative feelings. That may take time."

---

[16] Acts 17:10–11

Verity looked up from the beads she was stringing with Lindsay and Jessica and noticed the grin on Thomas' face as little Allan tried to tackle him. "How long has it been," she wondered, "since I last saw him look so happy?"

When Mr. Symons began to be concerned that his two boys were getting rather rough, he asked Thomas, "I have several heavy bags of grain to carry to the barn. Do you suppose you could lend me your strength?"

Flattered that Mr. Symons had asked him to help, Thomas readily agreed.

At least half an hour went by before the two came back in. Taylor and Allan, feeling greatly deprived, asked a few times when Dad was going to bring their friend back. Verity wished that she knew what they were talking about outside.

When they finally came in, Thomas was grinning, and Mr. Symons gave him a friendly pat on the back. Aunt Judy wanted to get home, so they all thanked the Symons and said good-bye. As they walked out the door, Verity looked back to see Mr. Symons shaking Thomas' hand and encouraging him to, "keep it up!"

"Keep what up?" she wondered, but when they got into the car Thomas sat sullenly looking out the window unwilling to give out any information.

Aunt Judy and Kara however, were mulling the evening over. "That was certainly a different approach than I'm used to," Kara replied. "Maybe I should write to Reverend Tobias and see what he thinks about all this." She paused for a moment and then spoke again, "I must say, I never thought the Bible could be so interesting. The discussion with Mr. Symons made me realise how many questions I have myself."

"So can I keep going to the seminars?" Verity inquired hopefully.

Kara nodded. "I think so. Just keep me informed of what you're learning."

With a deep sigh of relief, Verity sat back in contentment. The search would go on!

CHAPTER 20

A Lift Home

On Monday afternoon as Verity was stacking her homework into her backpack, hurrying to catch the bus home, Peter came around the corner with the 'soul' study- sheet and photocopies. "Sorry I've kept these so long," he apologized.

"Oh, that's okay," she replied. "Did you find them interesting?"

"They are very interesting but I'm not sure what to make of them. Actually, I called our pastor last night and had a long chat with her."

"And what did she say?" Verity asked, trying to zip up her bag. She wished she could just stop and chat about all of this, but there was hardly a person left in the school and she didn't want to miss the bus. Peter didn't need to worry about buses; he always walked home.

"Our Pastor hadn't looked into this before, but she felt it wasn't really important."

"Not important!" Verity echoed. "Peter, don't you want to know the truth of what happens when you die?" Hoisting her backpack over her shoulder she tried to head down the hall. Peter was walking so slowly! Didn't he realise that she needed to hurry to catch her bus? As Verity reached the front doors, she saw her bus pulling away from the sidewalk. "Oh no!" she wailed.

Peter looked out nonchalantly. "Oh, did you miss your bus?" he asked.

Verity set down her backpack with a thud. "Now what am I supposed to do?" she sighed, heading towards the pay phones.

"Who are you going to call?" asked Peter, smiling.

"The grocery store, I guess. I'll have to wait there till Aunt Judy finishes work."

"I could give you a lift home if you like."

"You have a car here?"

"No, but my parent's car is only a block away. My mom is quite happy for me to help poor stranded girls!" Peter said, failing to sound sympathetic and almost laughing instead.

"What's so funny?" she asked. Then, noticing how hard he was trying to keep a straight face, she grew suspicious. Was this why Peter had been walking so slowly? "Peter, did you plan this?" she asked.

Peter laughed out loud. "Well, I was sort of hoping we would get a chance to talk."

Verity shook her head in amazement. "Really, any time you want to drive me home, just ask. Riding the bus is no great pleasure!"

"Would riding with me be?"

It was a rather direct question and Verity was unsure whether he was teasing or not, so she just laughed. Honestly, he was too much today!

As they got into the car, the tall young man turned serious again. "Verity, after the talk I had with my minister last night, I really felt I had to talk to you in private."

"Oh?"

"Did you know," he asked rather nervously as they drove down the street, "that Mr. Symons' religion is a cult?"

"A cult?" Verity looked up in astonishment. "Peter, what do you mean by a 'cult'?"

"Well," he stammered, "I guess… well, a cult is a group that… that brain-washes people into thinking really radical, wrong beliefs! They always have a charismatic leader who makes everything sound good."

Verity paused for a moment to consider this. "But Peter, the only leader the Christadelphians have is Christ! Mr. Symons is constantly telling us to check everything he says with the Bible. He says that we shouldn't just accept his words without thinking but we should make sure they agree with the Bible."

"Yeah, that's what he says, Verity, but he's acting like a cult leader himself."

"A cult *leader?*" Verity was surprised Peter was speaking so strongly. "Mr. Henderson and he are the presenters for the seminars, but in their own church all the men take turns giving talks."

"Well," Peter argued, "they must have magazines, or books, or someone that tells them what to believe."

"Yes, they do have magazines and books," Verity replied, thinking back to a recent discussion at the seminars, "but Mr. Symons says they are only aids to help in studying the Bible. If they read something in them that they don't feel is based on the Scriptures, then they are quite free to disagree. The only book they accept as inspired by God is His own Word, the Bible."

For a few minutes both Peter and Verity were quiet, thinking things over. She realised that she was feeling defensive. The word 'cult' had sent off alarm bells in her head. Slowly she began to think more logically. "How do you think a person actually becomes 'brainwashed,' Peter?"

Shifting uncomfortably, Peter thought this through. "Well, I guess it can happen when someone keeps telling you something so often and so well that you eventually believe it," he replied.

Nodding, Verity asked, "If someone was trying to brainwash me into believing something that clearly contradicted the Bible—

would they feel free to send me home with a bunch of questions and tell me to find the answers in my Bible?"

Peter shrugged. "I don't know."

"Wouldn't it be more likely that they would tell me what they wanted me to believe and then warn me that I'm too uneducated to figure it out for myself? Wouldn't they want me to think that they were the only ones who were smart enough to understand the Bible and that my only hope was to listen to them?"

Then a sudden thought came into Verity's mind. "You know Peter," she said slowly, "I think back to my old church in Saskatchewan. We had one minister, one person giving all the talks. Everyone just believed whatever the minister said. Hardly anyone brought their Bibles along to look up the few references he gave. No one was encouraged to dig deep, or use Bible study aids to make sure they were right. Now that would have been the perfect environment for 'brainwashing'—if our minister had wanted to 'brainwash' people."

She turned in her seat to face him. "Peter," she said, trying to keep her voice gentle and calm, "look at you. All the references on that study-sheet showed clearly that the Bible does not teach an immortal soul. Shouldn't you be impressed by what you see for yourself in the Scriptures? Instead, when your Pastor says that what happens after death is not important and that the Christadelphians are a cult, you're just taking her word for it."

Peter clenched his jaw. Verity's words were spoken kindly but they made him flinch. He still had another challenging statement to make. "Did you know the Christadelphians don't believe in the Trinity?!" he asked. "The Trinity is the most important Christian teaching of all."

"The Trinity?" Verity felt rather uneasy about the Trinity. She remembered hearing lots about it in her old church but she wasn't sure she understood what it meant. "Okay, Peter," she sighed, leaning back against the seat. "I'm not completely sure what the

Trinity is—remind me. By the way," she said, noting they were coming to Sideroad Twenty, "turn right on this road. I live up this at the top of that hill."

Peter turned up the dirt road but before getting to her house, he pulled over to the shoulder and stopped. "Let's finish this discussion first," he begged, turning to face her. "The Trinity means that God, Jesus and the Holy Spirit are all One. They are Three in One—God the Father, God the Son, God the Holy Spirit."

Puzzled, Verity looked up at him. "God the Son? So, Jesus is God?"

Peter nodded.

"But Jesus was born, so how could he be God?"

"God came down from heaven and resided in a human form."

"But Jesus died."

"The human body that God lived in died. God didn't, of course," he said.

"So, who was in heaven, while God was on earth?"

"God the Father was in heaven."

"While God the Son was on earth?" she questioned.

"Yes."

"So wouldn't that mean there are two Gods?"

"No, God is One God," Peter stated emphatically, but then he smiled. "I know it sounds a bit confusing but that's because it's a mystery. We won't perfectly understand it until we get to heaven."

Sighing, Verity responded, "Peter, I really don't know much about this. Let me check it out and think about it and get back to you."

She turned to look out of the window for a moment. "I sure don't remember reading that Jesus is God in the Bible," she pondered, thinking hard, "but then again, I am only halfway through."

Peter headed back onto the road. "Verity," he said firmly, "I just don't think most people are capable of understanding the Bible for themselves. You need someone who's studied Theology, someone who has a degree in Divinity to explain it for you."

"Peter," she said softly, a moment later, "I may be wrong. I'm only just beginning to sort things out. But perhaps it's only when people have wrong beliefs that they feel they can't understand the Bible for themselves."

As they pulled into the driveway and Verity picked up her backpack to leave, Peter laid his hand on her arm. "Just one more thing…"

Verity glanced up wondering what he would say next.

He took a deep breath. "Your brother really concerns me. I've been trying awfully hard to get to know him but he has so much anger inside!"

"I know," she agreed sadly.

"Those friends he hangs out with are drinking most weekends, sometimes even at lunch hour during school."

Verity sighed deeply. "My mom has been making him work at the IGA on the weekends… but lunch hours are a problem! What can we do?" she asked earnestly.

Peter shrugged. "I don't know what we can do about lunch hours. I've been trying hard to get to know Thomas but I'm not having much success. My friends and I have invited him to play basketball with us at lunch, but he'd rather hang out with Hank."

"Thanks for trying so hard, Peter," Verity said gratefully, a little surprised that he was putting so much effort into this.

158

Peter hesitated for a moment and then added, "I know this is still a few weeks away, but I overheard Hank and Thomas discussing a big party during the Christmas holidays. I'm pretty sure it's going to be at Darcy Black's house just a block from where I live. Last year the police got called in and there were several arrests... drug possession, vandalism... you name it! Warn your mom. It will be easy for me to keep an eye out for him too, just in case he manages to slip over. He might be enjoying some social drinking now, but he likely has no idea what he's getting involved with."

Verity thanked Peter again and went to get out of the car—but she stumbled and fell. Her leg had given out on her once more.

"Are you okay?" Peter asked, jumping out of the car to help her.

Embarrassed, she let him pull her up. "I'm okay. My leg just lets me down now and again."

Peter looked concerned. "Have you seen a doctor?"

"Oh no," she replied, smiling. "I'm sure it's nothing to worry about."

She waved good-bye as he drove away, and then went into the house to warn her mother about the party.

CHAPTER 21

A History Lesson

When Verity rode with the Symons to the Bible study on Tuesday evening, she mentioned her discussion with Peter. She told them about Peter's claim that they might be part of a cult and that the Trinity was the most important Christian teaching of all.

"The Trinity is a concept that many Christians get very excited about," Mr. Symons replied, nodding. "I'm actually surprised we haven't had anyone ask about it yet during our Tuesday night classes. Now that we will be reading Genesis, it will probably come up. In the very first chapter there is a place where God says, *'Let us make man in our image.'* Most Trinitarians point to the word 'us' as proof that Jesus existed before creation and helped God make the world. If no one mentions it tonight, they probably will be when we get to chapter four."

"Will we get another study-sheet on the Trinity?" Verity asked, smiling.

"Certainly," he responded, with a twinkle in his eyes. "It's already made up!"

"Maybe Peter would do the study-sheet with you," suggested Mrs. Symons. Then she asked, "How did you answer him, when he said we were part of a cult?"

Verity explained what she had said and they nodded in agreement.

"Most people don't realise," Mr. Symons stated, "that according to the dictionary definition any group that follows a persuasive leader could be labelled a 'cult.' I think today when people hear the word 'cult' they associate it with being 'brainwashed.' But being 'brain-washed' can only happen if people give up their responsibility to think and let someone else do their thinking for them. Verity, if you always accept the Bible as your only authority, checking everything you hear with what's written there, you will have nothing to fear."

Almost a month went by before the topic of the Trinity came up. During that month they covered Genesis chapters one to three very slowly. Verity was amazed how much detail she had missed when she had first read it through. On several occasions, they also discussed Creation versus Evolution.

Quite a few people in the class had questions when they read through Genesis chapter three. Verity was most interested in Sarah's question about who the serpent was that tempted Eve and brought about the first sin. Mr. Henderson pointed out that the serpent only spoke words; therefore, it was Eve's thought processes that led to the sin. Eve examined the fruit and decided that it was good to eat. Eve saw that it was pleasing to the eyes—it looked beautiful. Eve believed the serpent when he told her that eating the fruit would make her wise.

Mr. Henderson showed them the passage in James chapter one, verses fourteen to fifteen: *"But every man is tempted, when he is drawn away of his own lust, and enticed. Then when lust hath conceived, it bringeth forth sin: and sin, when it is finished, bringeth forth death."*

"Whatever it is that begins the temptation," he stated, "it's our own thoughts and reactions to the temptation that lead to sin, or to *overcoming* sin."

It wasn't until a snowy evening in December, while they were finishing Genesis chapter three, that Mary, the mother of the little boy Jessica always sat with, asked the question Mr. Symons had been anticipating. "Who is God talking to in verse twenty-two, when He says, *'Behold, the man is become as one of us, to know good and evil...'* Is God talking to Jesus?"

161

"And what would bring you to that conclusion?" Mr. Symons asked kindly.

"Well, I'm wondering who the 'us' refers to," she responded. "Since Jesus was with God from the very beginning, I thought maybe God is talking to him?"

"In the first three chapters of Genesis that we've read together, has there been any mention of Jesus by name?" he asked, looking at everyone.

No one could think of an occurrence.

"Is there anyone else that God could be talking to here?"

The group was silent for a moment until Kelly finally answered, "The angels?"

"So, we have two possibilities," Mr. Symons replied. "I'd like to show you, Mary, from the Bible, why I would suggest that 'the LORD God' is speaking to angels. Remember, back in chapter one, verse twenty-six, we were told that God said, *'Let us make man in our image...'* We were made in the image of God, which is also the image or 'resemblance' of the angels. In fact, we look so much like angels that there are a few incidents in Scripture where angels were mistaken for men."[1] Mr. Symons had everyone turn up the incidents and look at them.

Then Mr. Symons continued, "We know that God's angels are His helpers. It says in Psalm one hundred and three, verses twenty to twenty-one, *'Bless the LORD, ye his angels, that excel in strength, that do his commandments, hearkening unto the voice of His word. Bless ye the LORD, all ye his hosts; ye ministers of his, that do his pleasure.'* [2] So, I believe that it was the angels who actively brought about God's creation of the world. God could have done it without

---

[1] Genesis 18, 19; Hebrews 13:2
[2] See also Hebrews 1:13–14

162

them, of course, but it would have been a great privilege for them to be involved."

"Where did the angels come from?" Henry asked.

"We aren't told the answer to that question in Scripture," Mr. Symons replied. "My suggestion would be that perhaps they came from a previous creation. God has been around forever with lots of time and creative power in His hands!"

Towards the end of the class, Mr. Symons said a few words about the history of the Trinity. First of all, he gave everyone copies of three creeds written in the early centuries after Christ.

Holding up the first one, he said, "The Apostles' Creed was originally written in about AD 120 and is completely free from Trinitarian concepts. Notice how simple it is; all the language that is used is straight from the Bible." He read it to the class.

The Apostles' Creed

I believe in God, the Father almighty, creator of heaven and earth.

I believe in Jesus Christ, his only Son, our Lord, who was conceived by the Holy Spirit and born of the virgin Mary.

He suffered under Pontius Pilate, was crucified, died, and was buried; he descended to hell. The third day he rose again from the dead.

He ascended to heaven and is seated at the right hand of God the Father almighty. From there he will come to judge the living and the dead.

I believe in the Holy Spirit, the holy catholic church,[3] the communion of saints, the forgiveness of sins, the resurrection of the body, and the life everlasting. Amen.

Mr. Symons turned to the next creed. "It wasn't until about the fourth century, three hundred years after Jesus had ascended to heaven, that The Nicene Creed was written. Now, as I read notice

---

[3] At this time 'catholic' was the universal Christian church.

the change in terminology used to describe the relationship between Jesus and God:

The Nicene Creed

We believe in one God, the father almighty, maker of heaven and earth and of all things visible and invisible. And in one lord, Jesus the anointed, the only begotten son of God, *begotten of the father before all worlds,* light from light, *true God from true God, begotten not made, being of one substance [homousion] with the father,* by whom all things were made. Who for us humans and for our salvation came down from heaven and *was incarnate* by the holy spirit and the virgin Mary, and was made man, and was crucified also for us under Pontius Pilate. He suffered and was buried, and the third day he rose again according to the scriptures, and ascended into heaven, and sits at the right hand of the father. And he shall come again to judge both the living and the dead. Whose kingdom shall have no end. [4]

And in the holy spirit, *the lord* and giver-of-life, who proceeds from the father, *who with the father and the son together is worshipped and glorified,* who spoke by the prophets. And in one, holy, catholic, and apostolic church. We acknowledge one baptism for the remission of sins. We look for the resurrection of the dead and the life of the world to come. [5]

"In here," Mr. Symons said, pointing to the creed, "we have the beginnings of the Trinity. You can look in any literal translation of the Bible, but you won't find the phrases *'true God of true God'* or *'incarnate,'* or *'Begotten not made,'* or *'being of one substance with the Father.'* That is not language from the Scriptures."

---

[4] This first paragraph was agreed upon at the Council of Nicea, 325 AD.
[5] This paragraph is supposed to have been adopted by the Council of Constantinople, 381 AD, although the records of that council are lost. The official recorded ratification of the creed as a whole took place at the Council of Chalcedon, 451 AD.
Microsoft Word - Creeds (washington.edu)

Pointing now to the third creed, Mr. Symons continued, "finally, in about the late fifth century, the Athanasian Creed was written. It was through *many* bitter debates, fighting and division within the church that this Creed was at last drawn up.[6] Since it is at least ten times longer than the Apostles' Creed, I am only going to read the relevant parts:"

The Athanasian Creed

Now the catholic faith is that we worship *One God in Trinity and Trinity in Unity, neither confounding the Persons nor dividing the substance.* For there is one Person of the Father, another of the Son, another of the Holy Spirit. *But the Godhead of the Father, of the Son, and of the Holy Spirit, is One, the Glory equal, the Majesty coeternal. Such as the Father is, such is the Son, and such is the Holy Spirit; the Father uncreated, the Son uncreated, and the Holy Spirit uncreated; the father infinite, the Son infinite, and the Holy Spirit infinite; the Father eternal, the Son eternal, and the Holy Spirit eternal. And yet not three eternals but one eternal, as also not three infinites, nor three uncreated, but one uncreated, and one infinite. So, likewise, the Father is almighty, the Son almighty, and the Holy Spirit almighty; and yet not three almighties but one almighty. So the Father is God, the Son God, and the Holy Spirit God; and yet not three Gods but one God. So the Father is Lord, the Son Lord, and the Holy Spirit Lord; and yet not three Lords but one Lord. For like as we are compelled by Christian truth to acknowledge every Person by Himself to be both God and Lord; so are we forbidden by the catholic religion to say, there be three Gods or three Lords.* The Father is made of none, neither created nor begotten. The Son is of the Father alone, *not made nor created but begotten. The Holy Spirit is of the Father and the Son, not made nor created nor begotten but proceeding*. So there is one Father not three Fathers, one Son not three Sons, and one Holy Spirit not three Holy Spirits. And in this Trinity there is nothing before or after, nothing greater or less, *but the whole three Persons are coeternal together and coequal. So that in all things, as is aforesaid, the Trinity in Unity and the Unity in Trinity is to be worshipped. He therefore who wills to be in a state of salvation, let him think thus of the Trinity.*

But it is necessary to eternal salvation that he also believe faithfully the *Incarnation of our Lord Jesus Christ.* The right faith therefore is that we

---

[6] When Jesus Became God - Ridhard E. Rubenstein.pdf (PDFy mirror) : Free Download, Borrow, and Streaming : Internet Archive

believe and confess that our Lord Jesus Christ, the Son of God, *is God and Man. He is God of the substance of the Father begotten before the worlds, and He is man of the substance of His mother born in the world; perfect God,* perfect man subsisting of a reasoning soul and human flesh; *equal to the Father as touching His Godhead,* inferior to the Father as touching His Manhood. *Who although He be God and Man yet He is not two but one Christ; one however not by conversion of the Godhead in the flesh, but by taking of the Manhood in God; one altogether not by confusion of substance but by unity of Person. For as the reasoning soul and flesh is one man, so God and Man is one Christ.* Who suffered for our salvation, descended into hell, rose again from the dead, ascended into heaven, sits at the right hand of the Father, from whence He shall come to judge the living and the dead. At whose coming all men shall rise again with their bodies and shall give account for their own works. And they that have done good shall go into life eternal, and they who indeed have done evil into eternal fire.

This is the catholic faith, which except a man shall have believed faithfully and firmly he cannot be in a state of salvation.[7]

"Did you notice that last sentence?" Mr. Symons asked, looking up. "Now if the Trinity was a doctrine necessary for salvation, why don't we find an explanation like this Creed, in the Bible itself? Why did the Apostle Paul never deal with this controversy in his epistles? He certainly devoted large sections of his writings to argue the reasons for why the Gospel of Christ superseded the Law of Moses. The Jewish people firmly believed that God is ONE. Surely, if this view needed to be overturned, this would be the subject of many Scriptural arguments. It's simply not there."

He added, "Did you also keep track of how many more words have now been added to describe the relationship between God and His Son? *'Substance, incomprehensible, uncreate, unity in trinity, co-eternal, co-equal.'* These words and ideas aren't found in the Bible. The reason that these philosophical terms were introduced was to exclude the Arians from fellowship in the church; they would

---

[7] The Athanasian Creed Circa 500 A.D. | Reformed Theology at A Puritan's Mind (apuritansmind.com)

not have been able to agree to these terms. However, in using this unscriptural language, the Trinity became a doctrine that could not be supported by the Bible.

"It's also important to understand," he continued, "that many of the 'church fathers' involved in this controversy were from Greek backgrounds – not Jewish. They didn't have the solid foundation from the Old Testament understanding that God was ONE God – the *only* immortal God.[8] Instead, their culture and thinking was replete with Greek mythology, full of 'demigods' with composite natures – part God and part man, and therefore these new, Trinitarian philosophical arguments were very plausible in their minds.[9] For the next fifty years this theological battle raged on, eventually splitting the church. Only three years after the Council of Nicea, many of its decisions were overturned and the Arians were reinstated into fellowship. But, year after year, church councils continued to overthrow previous decisions. Athanasius, who was instrumental in writing the Nicene Creed was condemned as a heretic at least five times, then reinstated later, and Arius had a similar experience."[10]

Putting down the Creed page and picking up another stack of papers, he continued, "What might surprise you even further is what some admit regarding the development of this teaching."

Handing out another page with two quotes on it, Mr. Symons said, "Here is a quotation taken from the Encyclopedia of Religion." He read:

"'Exegetes and theologians today are in agreement that the Hebrew Bible does not contain the doctrine of the Trinity.' And

---

[8] Isaiah 45:4-7, 11-12, 18-24; Deuteronomy 6:1-4
[9] List of Demigods in Greek Mythology • Greek Gods & Goddesses (greekgodsandgoddesses.net)
[10] For more info on the Greek influence: Jeff Deuble. 'Christ Before Creeds, Rediscovering the Jesus of History.' Published by Living Hope International Ministeries. 2021.

'Exegetes and theologians agree that the New Testament also does not contain an explicit doctrine of the Trinity.'[11]

He pointed out the quote from the New Catholic Encyclopedia, adding, "Keep in mind it was the Universal Catholic Church that eventually accepted the Creeds we just looked at." He read:

"'The formulation 'one God in three persons' was not solidly established, certainly not fully assimilated into Christian life and its profession of faith, prior to the end of the fourth century. But it is precisely this formulation that has first claim to the title the Trinitarian dogma. Among the Apostolic Fathers, there had been nothing even remotely approaching such a mentality or perspective.'"[12]

Craig Symons looked around at everyone in the group. "Those who promote the doctrine of the Trinity feel free to admit that it was not based on the Bible or the apostles' teachings. How important is it to you that your beliefs are founded on the Bible alone?"

With that, Mr. Henderson handed out the study-sheets, reminding everyone that it would be a couple of weeks before they would all meet again, as the December holidays were almost upon them.

After thanking the Symons for the ride home and giving the two girls a hug good-bye, Verity suddenly remembered the Creation book she had not yet returned. "I'm so sorry about that book, Mr. Symons! I don't know what could have happened to it. But I will keep looking!"

---

[11] Mircea, E, editor. The Encyclopedia of Religion. Trinity. New York. 1987; 15:54

[12] New Catholic Encyclopedia. New York: Guild Publishers; 1967–1974. Trinity; 14:299

"Don't worry," he said with a smile, even a little laughter in his eyes. "It'll turn up some day."

Verity wondered if Mr. Symons knew something that she didn't.

CHAPTER 22

Understanding Dad

Collecting the dishes from supper the next evening, Verity suddenly stumbled and fell. Plates and cutlery went flying everywhere. A tingling sensation had numbed her leg again and this time a sharp pain also shot up her back. "I'm so sorry!" she said in embarrassment, looking at the mess strewn across the floor.

Mom and Aunt Judy patiently helped her to clean it up. Trying to distract everyone from the accident, Aunt Judy said, "I was cleaning in the attic today, Verity, and I found some old stories that your father wrote in school."

"Really?" Verity started washing the pots and pans in the sink. "I'd love to read them!"

"They are quite funny, some of them," laughed Aunt Judy. "Kara, do you remember the 'Trial of the Big Bad Wolf'? I think you were going out with Dan when he wrote that play."

"Yes, I do! The teacher read it to the class, and everyone howled with laughter all the way through," Kara replied, smiling at the memory.

Verity glanced over at Thomas who was on the sofa looking intently at a magazine. She was sure he was listening. "What was Dad like when you were first going out, Mom?"

Kara gazed at Verity hesitantly. She wasn't used to discussing this topic. "He was very nice," she began slowly. "He could make me laugh and we really enjoyed being together." She picked up a dishtowel to dry the clean pots. "I always knew he had a temper, but I thought he had it under control. We went to church together and he tried to live a good life." She paused and then shook her head. "But he was always questioning everything, just like you, Verity."

Verity felt her mom's reproachful look.

"It wasn't until we had been married for five years," Kara continued, "that things began to go wrong. Dan started drinking a little too much!"

Kara stole a quick glance at Thomas, but his eyes were firmly fixed on the magazine. "When he lost his job after he went to work drunk, your dad became very depressed. All he looked forward to was the next drink. He stopped going to church with me and started mocking anyone who did. That's when he became abusive and out of control."

"Yet, you wouldn't leave him," put in Verity.

Kara Lovell put her hand over her face and sighed. "I couldn't! He was a sick man, Verity! I still loved him for what he had been." She shook her head sadly. "I guess I always hoped that one day he would get better."

Verity put her arm around her mother. "It's too bad he never found any answers while he was questioning everything," she said softly.

"But, Verity," her mom pleaded, teary-eyed, "that's why I'm so worried about you! You're questioning long-standing, traditional beliefs, those that all the churches have taught for years!"

"There's a huge difference between Dad and me!" Verity smiled. "I'm not just questioning. I'm finding out what the Bible teaches and that's the truth I'm going to hold fast to. I'm not *giving up* on God!"

A sudden thought occurred to her, and she ran to get the old King James Bible. "Mom," she said, coming back in and hastily flipping the pages, "I've been wondering who wrote all the little notes in this Bible. I wonder if you and Aunt Judy can tell?" She showed them a few. Most of them were question marks or comments like, "How does this fit?"

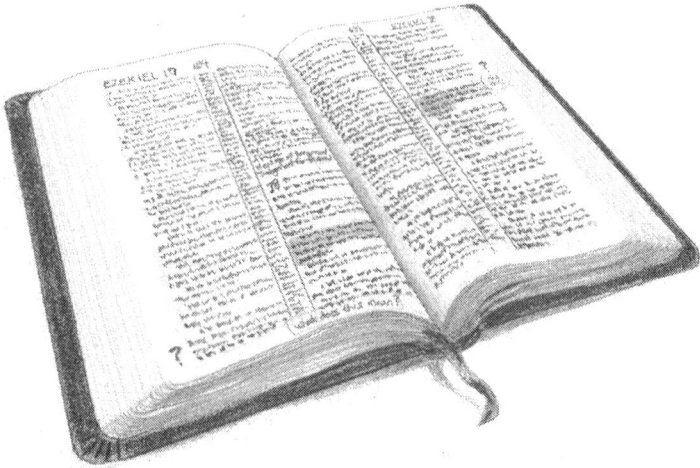

Aunt Judy and Kara studied a few of the comments and then looked at each other in amazement. "Your dad wrote these!" Aunt Judy stated.

"He always ran his printing together, just like this," said Kara, pointing it out. She looked up again astonished. "I never knew Dan read the Bible! He told me he did, but I didn't believe him."

Verity closed the old book up. She felt she had just given everybody one more reason to worry about her, but nonetheless, she was happy to know the notes were her dad's.

Hopping into bed that night, Verity turned on her reading light and settled down beneath her warm quilt to continue her quest. She loved evenings when she had the quiet of her own room and time to think. Night after night she was progressing through the Bible and now she was in the Psalms. It was with great delight that she came to Psalm seventy-two, the same psalm they had read together at the Symons' home. When Verity finished reading the visionary psalm, she lay back imagining what Jesus' reign on earth would be like. "I want to see this day," she reflected dreamily, "this day when Jesus will come back to the earth again. Imagine such a righteous man being the King over all the earth! Imagine a ruler that actually cares for the poor and oppressed! Imagine a ruler who knows what everyone is *thinking* and always makes the right decisions!"

Her curiosity about this time made her wonder if there were other chapters that could give her even more details. "Would I be able to find some using my cross- references?" she wondered. Sitting up again, she examined the centre column of her Bible. Sure enough, there were several cross-references in Psalm seventy-two. For a long while she flipped to one passage after another, making a list of all the relevant details she could find about the future promises.

It was way past midnight when she finally turned off her light and put her Bible away. She had discovered Isaiah was full of chapters about the Kingdom. The most vivid were Isaiah two and eleven. Now in her mind's eye she could picture all the nations of the earth going to Jerusalem to hear God's laws being taught. The hill of Jerusalem was going to be elevated way above all the hills around it, and a temple to God built there. Jesus was going to reign from this city, just like King David had so many years ago—yet Jesus would be the King of the World! It was a wonderful picture of peace and happiness for those who willingly chose to follow God. There were harsh judgments on the wicked though. Verity still found that side of God surprising.

In Isaiah chapter eleven, she had been amazed to read that even the animals were going to get along! The wolf would dwell with the lamb and lions would eat straw like the ox. What a lot of changes will have to take place in the world! "I want to be there!" she determined, "to see this day when everyone in the world will finally understand the promises God has offered. I want to see them fulfilled on the earth and appreciated as God's *gift.*"

It was difficult for her to fall asleep that night as she felt fully awake, but she knew she would be tired in the morning. As she lay there in the darkness, her eyes glanced over to the picture on her wall, lit up by the hallway light, with two smiling faces looking out at her. She thought back to the discussions she'd had with Aunt Judy and her mom that evening. So, all those little notes in the old King James Bible were her father's! Maybe she could relate to him after all. He'd had questions just like she did and he had tried to find the answers. Why didn't he find those answers? Didn't he dig deep enough? Did he pray to God for help? Or did he just give up when things didn't seem to make sense?

She remembered Mr. Symons' words: "It really comes down to our attitude on how we approach the Bible. Do we say, 'My beliefs are right, so the Bible has to fit around them?' or do we say, 'The Bible is God's Word; it's right, so I'll let it teach me?'" What attitude had her father had?

Whatever her dad's attitude had been, she had a new respect for him—at least he had tried! She wished he were still alive and that she could share all the answers she was finding with him.

Then with a shock she realised that for the first time she had just felt some sorrow over her father's departing!

Sitting up in bed, she looked at the picture again. With sadness, she focused on the eyes of the man smiling at her. "I think I understand you better, Dad," she said to herself. "I know you'll never hear me say this, but… I forgive you!" Tears began to fill her eyes as she continued softly, "I completely forgive you for all the pain you've caused our family. I know you didn't plan to become so scary to us. It just happened. I know I will never see you again, but from now on I will just remember the good things about you and let go of the rest."

The tears poured down her cheeks as she bowed her head and thanked God for all the help He had brought into her life and for the answers that she was beginning to find. Then she pleaded earnestly that He would help Thomas as well – and soon – before it was too late.

CHAPTER 23

Peter Thinks Hard

I can't believe that this is the last day of school for two whole weeks!" Emily exclaimed happily, as Verity sorted through the books in her locker.

"Oh, here comes Peter!" Kate announced.

Verity turned to look as Peter came up triumphantly waving a piece of paper. "This will answer all your questions, I'm sure!" he boasted.

Looking at the flyer, Verity read, "'The Mystery of the Trinity. Pastor Patterson will deliver a special address. All are welcome...'" she looked up. "Is this at your church, Peter?"

"Yes," he grinned. "My parents would be happy to have you come with us. It's to be held the first of February."

"Hmm," she said considering. "Well, I have a study-sheet to do on the Trinity. How about you do the study with me and then I'll go to this talk with you?"

Peter grinned. "Pretty hard bargain you drive, Miss!"

Verity waited for his response as she closed her locker door.

"Sure, I'll do it with you," he agreed. "When? Where?"

"I was hoping tomorrow evening at my place since you can drive and I can't!"

Peter laughed, giving his assent.

As he trailed off down the hall, Kate turned to Verity. "Emily and I have decided we'd like to go to the seminars too. You're always talking about such interesting things.

"That would be great!" Verity exclaimed. "They start up again in two weeks— after the holidays."

The girls walked out to wait for their buses. Thomas was already standing there alone, his winter toque pulled down to his dark eyebrows and the usual brooding look in his deep blue eyes.

"Have a great holiday, Verity," Purity called out cheerfully and then, mustering her courage, she added, "You too, Thomas!"

Thomas didn't even acknowledge he'd heard anything.

Verity turned and waved. "All the best to you, girls." Then, with a grin she called out a little louder, "Thomas hopes you have a wonderful holiday too!"

Thomas' eyes darted towards her furiously. "I'll speak for myself!" he whispered harshly.

"Then why didn't you?" she asked, shaking her head at his rudeness.

"I'm not going to speak to your snobby friend!"

"Well, she spoke kindly to you, so who's the real snob?"

"Why is she talking to me? Have you gone and made her feel sorry for me?"

Verity heaved a sigh. "I don't get you, Thomas. You're upset when people don't speak to you, and you're upset when they do!"

"I don't want anyone feeling sorry for me!" he retorted angrily as the bus pulled up in front of them.

"Then why don't you stop feeling sorry for yourself?" she taunted with frustration.

Thomas never answered. He found a spare seat at the back of the bus and continued brooding. Verity found a seat near the front next to a couple of younger girls and waved to her friends as the bus pulled away.

When Verity explained her plans for Saturday evening, Kara Lovell was quite concerned about the Trinity study-sheet. "I have no problem with Peter coming here," she began slowly, "but Verity, now you are questioning the Trinity! Is any church teaching safe?"

"As long as it's based on the Bible, it is!" she laughed. Then, remembering her own initial reaction, she queried, "Mom, what does the Trinity mean to you?"

Kara paused cautiously. "Well, I don't really know exactly, Darling. After all I'm not a Minister! But I think it means believing that Jesus, God and the Holy Spirit are three in one."

"So, they are all one and the same?"

"Oh no, Jesus is God's Son of course."

"Did you know, Mom," Verity inquired, "that the doctrine of the Trinity claims Jesus is God? When Jesus was on earth, he was supposedly God in a human body."

"I don't remember Reverend Tobias ever saying that! Are you sure?" Kara questioned.

Verity pulled the page on Church Creeds from her binder. "Look at this—it's the Athanasian Creed."

Kara read it over perplexed. "I don't recall seeing this before," she murmured. "It does sound very confusing." Glancing up at the Apostles' Creed, she pointed to it. "Now this one I memorized in Sunday School!"

"Yes," said Verity, "that is the earliest creed and in it there is no mention of the Trinity."

The snow was falling heavily as Peter arrived around seven that evening. After he had brushed the snow off himself, Verity introduced him to her mother and Aunt Judy. Peter was his usual friendly, good-natured self, and politely shook their hands.

"We can work at the kitchen table," Verity said, leading him towards it. She saw Aunt Judy and her mother retire into the living room to read.

Displaying the papers on the table, Verity first showed Peter the Creeds of Christendom, but he was not at all surprised. In fact, he knew them well. He objected though to the quotes from the two encyclopedias.

"There are lots of places in the Bible where the Trinity is spoken of!" he argued, shaking his head. "These quotes must be taken out of context. Anyway," he sighed, "let's do the study-sheet."

At the top of the page were the words, "Are Jesus and God Co-eternal and Co-equal?" In one column the characteristics of God were listed with Bible passages to support them. The other side, dealt with the characteristics of Jesus. Both sides had missing words in the titles, that required filling in.

"This first one is easy," Verity began, "James one, verse thirteen says God cannot be tempted. Obviously, Jesus was tempted."

"But he never sinned." Peter added warily.

"Is it sin to be tempted?"

Peter hesitated, unsure of the answer. He read Hebrews two, verses fourteen to eighteen, slowing down when he came to the words, *"in all things He had to be made like His brethren ... For in that He Himself has suffered, being tempted, He is able to aid those who are tempted."*

"He suffered being tempted," Peter read. Pondering the phrase carefully he then read Hebrews four, verses fourteen to fifteen, "*'For we do not have a high priest who is unable to sympathise with our weaknesses, but we have one who has been tempted in every way, just as we are, yet without sin.'*"

"So, temptation *isn't* sin," he deduced, "giving in to temptation is, I suppose. That's interesting…"

They filled in the next blanks without much discussion. There was no debate that God couldn't die, but Jesus had died and it was God who had raised him from the dead. However, Verity said, "If Jesus was just God inhabiting a human body, why did the human body have to come back to life?"

"I don't know," Peter grunted. "That does seem unnecessary…"

The next title made Peter frown. "Jesus is still referred to as a man, even after his resurrection. Really?" He read one of the passages, First Timothy two, verse five, slowly to himself, *"For there is one God, and there is one mediator between God and men, the man Christ Jesus."*

"He's become an immortal man," Verity clarified. "Just like we hope to be."

Perturbed, Peter looked ahead to the next set of passages. He read Matthew twenty-four, verse thirty-six, *"But concerning that day and hour no one knows, not even the angels of heaven, nor the Son, but the Father only."*

"Jesus doesn't know everything God knows," Peter agreed. "He was taught by God what he should say… his words weren't his own. I don't have a problem with that."

But Peter did find the next title disturbing. *'Jesus has a God. God has no god.'*

Verity read from John twenty, verse seventeen, *"Jesus said to her, "Do not cling to me, for I have not yet ascended to the Father… I am ascending to my Father and your Father, to my God and your God."'*

"This was *after* his resurrection," she considered. "He still referred to God as his God! Can you be God and have a God?" Looking over the other passages again, she added, "How did he pray to God, if he was God? And *why* would he pray to himself? That really doesn't make sense to me."

"It doesn't," Peter agreed reluctantly. Carefully, he read the passage listed from Hebrews five, *"Who in the days of his flesh, when he had offered up prayers and supplications with strong crying and tears unto him that was able to save him from death, and was heard in that he feared;"*

"I could understand this," Peter reasoned, "if Jesus was just praying as an example to his disciples, to teach them what they should do, but his prayers involved 'strong crying and tears', and 'fear' – or reverence. This is a prayer from someone who is sincerely begging to be heard from someone greater...and he has a need...he wanted to be saved from death!"

Hastily, Peter read the next two passages, both from Hebrews. *"'Although he was a son, he learned obedience through what he suffered... For it was fitting that he... should make the founder of their salvation perfect through suffering.'"*

"He had to learn things," Verity summarized. "He sounds very human to me. Jesus wasn't born perfect, God *made* him perfect by the experiences he brought him through – painful experiences!"

Peter nodded. "If he was God, surely he would have had God's infinite knowledge and wisdom, and not ever struggled to obey himself. But I guess that's just the 'human' part of Jesus, so he could sympathize with us," With a sigh, he asked, "What do think fills in the blank for the next one?"

Verity read it, "God has no...?" She skimmed through the passages. "No beginning!" She said. "He's always been there and always be." For a few moments she read through the passages that were listed, and then she summarized the facts, "Jesus' coming was promised all the way through the Old Testament – as someone who

181

would be from the genetic line of Abraham and David. That human decadency was such a big part of all the promises. His physical genetics are given vital importance. He is not just a body that was inhabited by God."

In agreement, Peter read through Revelation twenty-two, verse sixteen. *"I, Jesus, have sent my angel to testify ...I am the root and the descendant of David, the bright morning star."*

"He still refers to himself as the descendant of David, long after he's been in heaven with God," Peter observed. "I suppose that is why it was so important that his body was raised…that's why he's still called a 'man' – an immortal man."

"So, God gave him His Divine nature *after* resurrection," [1] Verity reasoned.

"And the Name above every name,"[2] Peter nodded, recalling a phrase he had heard numerous times at church. "He's been elevated now because of his victory, but, that First Corinthians fifteen passage, says he will give the Kingdom back to God in the future and be subject to his Father."

The last section made Peter think hard. He read the passage from Luke twenty-two about Jesus praying in the Garden of Gethsemane just before he was arrested to be crucified. Jesus had begged, *"'Father if You are willing, take this cup from me; yet not my will, but Yours be done.'"*

They both looked at the verse silently for a few minutes. "He had a different will than his Father's," Peter admitted. "He was struggling to do his part to fulfil God's plan. If he was God, he wouldn't have been asking *himself* if it was possible to change the plan."

---

[1] Philippians 3:20-21; Acts 13:32-37; Colossians 1:18; 1 Corinthians 15:53-54; 1 Timothy 6:16; 2 Timothy 1:10; Romans 6:23
[2] Philippians 2:8-11

"And sweating blood," Verity remarked, looking at the rest of the passage. "That's distress like I've never experienced!" She pointed out verse forty-four in her NIV Bible. "Look Peter, it says, he was *'in anguish.'* Going through with the crucifixion was against his will, yet he knew he had to submit to God's will. Surely if Jesus was God in a human body, he would be God in his thinking."

Peter took a deep breath as he looked at her gravely. With a groan, he slumped back in his chair. "I didn't realise that there was even a half decent case against the Trinity..." he began. [3]

At that moment, Thomas walked into the kitchen to grab a can of pop from the fridge. "Anyone else in need of a drink?" he mumbled.

Peter was happy to ask for one. "Say, Thomas," he began in a friendly tone, "do you have any plans for the holidays?"

Thomas looked up warily, his eyes narrowed.

Flushing slightly, Peter tried again. "I was only going to invite you over to my place after Christmas. We could play cards, or... actually, just a block down from my house is an awesome hill where we could do some snowboarding."

Thomas' guard was fully in place. "If you want to snowboard, you might as well come here. We have all the hills you could ever ask for! I'm sure Verity would be delighted to go with you."

Passing him a drink, Thomas slid out of the room and back downstairs. Peter looked baffled. "Did I say something wrong?" he asked Verity quietly.

She shook her head—but then Peter realised his mistake. "No, I did say something wrong," he half-whispered, covering his eyes with his hand. "He suspects I know about the party, and he thought I was going to confront him."

---

[3] See also Jesus – Son of God, Not God the Son. | Original Gospel

Looking at his watch, he picked up his papers. "I'd better go, I told my mom I'd be home around nine." He paused, "I guess we ran out of time to look at all the passages I had that *prove* the Trinity. I wish I could talk to Mr. Symons about them."

"I'm sure he would be happy to discuss them with you," Verity stated confidently. "I'll ask him," she offered. "Maybe we could get together after the holidays at lunch hour or something."

"That would be great!" Peter nodded, as they walked to the door. After he put on his coat and boots, he looked around carefully and then whispered, "That party is next Friday night. I overheard Thomas say he would be going for sure. Do your best to keep him from it and I'll do mine."

ARE JESUS AND GOD CO-EQUAL AND CO-ETERNAL?

son-of-god-worksheet-with-blanks.pdf (wordpress.com)

GOD	JESUS
GOD CANNOT BE _____	**JESUS WAS** _____
"Let no one say when he is tempted, "I am being tempted by God," for God cannot be tempted with evil, and he himself tempts no one." (ESV) James 1:13 "For You are not a God who takes pleasure in wickedness, nor shall evil dwell with You." (NKJV) Psalm 5:4	"... as the children have partaken of flesh and blood, He Himself likewise shared in the same, that through death He might destroy him who had the power of death, that is, the devil... Therefore, in all things He had to be made like His brethren ... For in that He Himself has suffered, being tempted, He is able to aid those who are tempted." Hebrews 2:14-18 "For we do not have a high priest who is unable to sympathize with our weaknesses, but one who in every respect has been tempted as we are, yet without sin." Hebrews 4:14-15
GOD _____	**JESUS** ____ **AND WAS** _____
See now that I, even I, am he, and there is no god with me: I kill, and I make alive; I wound, and I heal: neither is there any that can deliver out of my hand. For I lift up my hand to heaven, and say, I live for ever. Deuteronomy 32:39-40	For David speaketh concerning him ... moreover also my flesh shall rest in hope: Because thou wilt not leave my soul in hell, neither wilt thou suffer thine Holy One to see corruption.... Therefore being a prophet [David], and knowing that God had sworn with an oath to him, that of the fruit of his loins, according to the flesh, he would raise up Christ to sit on his throne;... He seeing this before spake of the resurrection of Christ, that his soul was not left in hell, neither his flesh did see corruption...This Jesus hath God raised up, whereof we all are witnesses. Acts 2:24-32

ARE JESUS AND GOD CO-EQUAL AND CO-ETERNAL?

son-of-god-worksheet-with-blanks.pdf (wordpress.com)

GOD	JESUS
GOD IS NOT A _____	**JESUS WAS A** _____ **AND IS NOW AN IMMORTAL** _____
"God is not man, that he should lie, or a son of man, that he should change his mind." Numbers 23:19 "And also the Strength of Israel will not lie nor relent. For He is not a man that He should relent." 1 Samuel 15:29	"For there is one God, and there is one mediator between God and men, the man Christ Jesus." 1 Timothy 2:5 "Men of Israel, hear these words: Jesus of Nazareth, a man attested by God to you by miracles, wonders, and signs which God did through Him in your midst, as you yourselves also know." Acts 2:22 "For if by the one man's offense many died... by the grace of the one man, Jesus Christ, abounded to many." Romans 5:15
GOD KNOWS _____	**JESUS HAS LIMITED** _____
I am God, and there is none else; I am God, and there is none like me, Declaring the end from the beginning, and from ancient times the things that are not yet done, saying, My counsel shall stand, and I will do all my pleasure: Isaiah 46:9-10 But concerning that day and hour no one knows, not even the angels of heaven, nor the Son, but the Father only." Matthew 24:36	"So Jesus answered them, "My teaching is not mine, but his who sent me." John 7:16 "Whoever does not love me does not keep my words. And the word that you hear is not mine but the Father's who sent me." John 14:24 "So Jesus said to them, "When you have lifted up the Son of Man, then you will know that I am he, and that I do nothing on my own authority, but speak just as the Father taught me." John 8:28

ARE JESUS AND GOD CO-EQUAL AND CO-ETERNAL?

son-of-god-worksheet-with-blanks.pdf (wordpress.com)

GOD	JESUS
GOD HAS NO _____	**JESUS HAS A** _____ **EVEN NOW.**
Thus saith the LORD the King of Israel, and his redeemer the LORD of hosts; I am the first, and I am the last; and beside me there is no God... I know not any...Thus saith the LORD, thy redeemer, and he that formed thee from the womb, I am the LORD that maketh all things; that stretcheth forth the heavens alone; that spreadeth abroad the earth by myself;" Isaiah 44:6-8, 24	"In the days of his flesh, Jesus offered up prayers and supplications, with loud cries and tears, to him who was able to save him from death, and he was heard because of his reverence." Hebrews 5:7 "Jesus said to her, "Do not cling to me, for I have not yet ascended to the Father... I am ascending to my Father and your Father, to my God and your God."" John 20:17 "the God of our Lord Jesus Christ, "Ephesians 1:17 (See also Rom. 15:6)
GOD IS _____	**JESUS WAS MADE** _____
"You therefore must be perfect, as your heavenly Father is perfect." Matthew 5:48	"Although he was a son, he learned obedience through what he suffered." Hebrews 5:8-9 "For it was fitting that he... should make the founder of their salvation perfect through suffering." Hebrews 2:10

ARE JESUS AND GOD CO-EQUAL AND CO-ETERNAL?

son-of-god-worksheet-with-blanks.pdf (wordpress.com)

GOD	JESUS
GOD HAS NO _____	**JESUS HAD A** _____
"You are My witnesses," says the LORD, "and My servant whom I have chosen, that you may know and believe Me, and understand that I am He. Before Me there was no God formed, nor shall there be after Me." Isaiah 43:10 "Thus says the LORD, the King of Israel, and his Redeemer, the LORD of hosts: 'I am the First and I am the Last; besides Me there is no God." Isaiah 44:6	"The Lord swore to David a sure oath ..."One of the sons of your body I will set on your throne." Psalm 132:11 "... you will conceive in your womb and bear a son, and you shall call his name Jesus. He will be great and will be called the Son of the Most High. And the Lord God will give to him the throne of his father David..." Luke 1:26-33 "I, Jesus, have sent my angel to testify ...I am the root and the descendant of David, the bright morning star." Revelation 22:16 "Now the promises were made to Abraham.... "And to your offspring," who is Christ." Galatians 3:16
GOD HAS A _____	**JESUS IN HIS MORTAL EXISTENCE STRUGGLED TO ACCEPT GOD'S _____, HE HAD A DIFFERENT ___ TO HIS FATHER.**
And I will put enmity between thee and the woman, and between thy seed and her seed; it shall bruise thy head, and thou shalt bruise his heel. Genesis 3:15 "But he was wounded for our transgressions, he was bruised for our iniquities: the chastisement of our peace was upon him; and with his stripes we are healed... Yet it pleased the LORD to bruise him; he hath put him to grief: when thou shalt make his soul an offering for sin, he shall see his seed, he shall prolong his days, and the pleasure of the LORD shall prosper in his hand." Isaiah 53:1-12	Saying, Father, if thou be willing, remove this cup from me: nevertheless not my will, but thine, be done. And there appeared an angel unto him from heaven, strengthening him. And being in an agony he prayed more earnestly: and his sweat was as it were great drops of blood falling down to the ground. Luke 22:41-44 Now is my soul troubled; and what shall I say? Father, save me from this hour: but for this cause came I unto this hour. John 12:27

CHAPTER 24

Reasoning Together

At Verity's request, Mr. Symons readily agreed to meet with her and Peter. In fact, he invited them over to his house the very next evening. Knowing that there would be many passages to get through, Mr. Symons phoned Peter that night and wrote down all the references that Peter wanted to talk about.

As her mother desired, Verity had been keeping her informed about everything she was learning. So now Aunt Judy and Kara were eager to go along and hear what Mr. Symons would say about Peter's verses. This meant of course, much to Thomas' annoyance, that he had to go as well.

The two younger Symons were getting ready for bed when they arrived, but Taylor was still up and very pleased to see his buddy again. With a pleasant 'hello' he plopped himself down right next to Thomas. Lindsay happily found a seat beside Verity and began telling her all about her day. Glancing over at Thomas, Verity had to suppress a smile when Taylor, seeing that his friend had come unprepared, generously went in search of a spare Bible and a notepad.

While they waited for Mr. Symons to finish getting his children to bed, little Jessica came down in her flannel nightgown to say 'good night' to Verity. She was running over to give Verity a hug when she saw Peter and stopped short.

Verity held out her arms. "Goodnight, Jessica."

Jessica came over shyly and whispered in Verity's ear, "Who is that boy beside you?"

"This boy," Verity laughed gently, "is Peter Bryant. Let me introduce him to you." Drawing the young girl in front of her, she formally introduced them to each other.

Peter shook Jessica's hand. "Nice to meet you, Jessica," he said very seriously, his kind brown eyes sparkling. "I hear you've adopted Verity as your big sister."

She nodded proudly.

"I don't have a sister either," Peter carried on, playfully sad. "I sure wish I did…" He would have said more but just then he noticed Mrs. Symons coming in with a large tray of hot drinks for everyone, so he jumped up to help her.

Jessica was reminded that she needed to be in bed, so she gave Verity a big hug and with a little wave to everyone, scurried off to bed.

When Mr. Symons came back downstairs, he began the evening as usual with a word of prayer for God's blessing on all of them and a plea that they would interpret the Scriptures accurately.

"Peter has given me many passages to go through tonight," he explained to everyone. "Since our time is limited, I would like to group these passages into four categories and deal with them together rather than one by one. Once we've done that, if Peter or any of you are still puzzled by individual verses, we can discuss those in more detail."

Nodding, Peter assented that this was a good idea and Mr. Symons began. "There are quite a few passages where Jesus is given titles that belong to God.

Isaiah chapter nine, verse six is one such place, and says in my version, 'his name shall be called Wonderful, Counsellor, The Mighty God, The Everlasting Father, The Prince of Peace.' Now, there are a few important things to understand here, but notice first that the verse says, 'his name shall be called.' What does that indicate?"

After a moment, Verity responded, "Jesus *will* be called this in the future?"

"Exactly. Isaiah isn't saying 'his name *is* Wonderful...' but 'his name *shall be* called Wonderful....' Verse seven indicates it will be in the future—during the time Christ sits as King 'upon the throne of David'—that is when all these titles will be addressed to him. Now, tell me, if you telephoned Bell Canada, and someone answered 'Hello, Bell Canada,' would you immediately think they were the president of the company?"

Peter wasn't sure where this was going but he answered anyway. "No, you would guess you were speaking to a receptionist."

"So, how can she answer as though she were the company itself?"

"Because she works for Bell Canada, so she represents them."

"Ah—that's it, Peter. Of course, she isn't Bell Canada herself, but because she is working for that company as their agent, she can answer in this way. This is also the way in which Jesus and others are called 'God' in the Bible. If you are familiar with the Old Testament, you may know that the judges of Israel were also called 'gods'. In Exodus chapter twenty-two, verses eight, nine and twenty-eight, the English word translated 'judges'—the name for the human rulers of Israel—is the Hebrew word 'elohim'. 'Elohim' is usually translated 'God' in the Old Testament, but not always. Jesus himself referred to this occurrence when the Jews accused him of saying he was God. Let's look at John chapter ten, verses thirty-four to thirty-six. Verity will you read that for me?"

Finding the passage where Jesus answered the Jews, Verity read from her translation. *"...Is it not written in your Law, 'I have said you are gods'? If he called them 'gods', to whom the word of God came—and the Scripture cannot be broken—what about the one whom the Father set apart as his very own and sent into the world? Why then do you accuse me of blasphemy because I said, 'I am God's Son'?"*

"Thanks," Mr. Symons nodded. "Now if Jesus really were God, this would be the exact place we would expect him to clearly confirm that. The Jews were accusing him of saying that he was God—so if he was—then he should have assented that 'yes, he was God.' Instead, he argues that if people in the Old Testament can be called 'gods' when they were only human judges with divine messages, then the Jews had no charge of blasphemy against Jesus; after all he was only claiming to be the 'Son of God.'"

"However," Mr. Symons went on to explain, "this title 'the Mighty God' will be given to Jesus when he is made King over all the earth."

Seeing that Thomas had a Bible now, Mr. Symons asked him to read Philippians chapter two, verses eight to eleven. With Taylor's help, Thomas found the passage and read, *"'And being found in fashion as a man, he humbled himself, and became obedient unto death, even the death of the cross. Wherefore God also hath highly exalted him, and given him a name which is above every name: That at the name of Jesus every knee should bow, of things in heaven, and things in earth, and things under the earth; and that every tongue should confess that Jesus Christ is Lord, to the glory of God the Father.'"*

"So how did Jesus get this exalted name?" Mr. Symons queried.

"He was given it," Verity replied.

"Right. God gave it to him after his obedient death and resurrection."

Turning up another Scripture, Mr. Symons asked, "Verity, do you mind reading First Corinthians fifteen, verses twenty-four to twenty-eight?"

When she had found it, Verity read, *"'But now is Christ risen from the dead, and become the firstfruits of them that slept. For since by man came death, by man came also the resurrection of the dead. For as in Adam all die, even so in Christ shall all be made alive. But every man in his own order: Christ the firstfruits; afterward they that are Christ's at his coming. Then the end will come, when he hands over the Kingdom to God the Father after he has destroyed all dominion, authority and power. For he must reign until he has put all his enemies under his feet. The last enemy to be destroyed is death. For he 'has put everything under his feet.' Now when it says that 'everything' has been put under him, it is clear that this does not include God himself, who put everything under Christ. When he has done this, then the Son himself will be made subject to him who put everything under him, so that God may be all in all.'"*

Mr. Symons looked up to see if they all had followed the sense of the passage. Everyone else's head was still down, trying to take it in. With understanding, he continued, "I know it's a bit hard to follow the pronouns here and understand which one refers to God and which one refers to Jesus. However, if you read the verses carefully a few times, you will see that they clearly point out that while everything in the future will be 'put under' Jesus, God is an exception to this. God does the putting under and God, Himself, is not put under Jesus. Now, do you see anything in this passage that indicates whether this exalted position is something Jesus has always enjoyed—or whether it is for a set time only?"

Verity had already considered this passage, so she spoke up. "It seems to be saying that after Jesus has reigned, he then becomes subject to God again."

"That's the right idea, Verity! And I think it is even a stronger point than that. The high position God gives Jesus in the Kingdom is not only for a limited length of time, but even during that time God is not subject to Jesus, he is excluded! Jesus is going to rule FOR God during this special limited time, as his representative or agent. This isn't an equal relationship—not at any time in the past, not now, *not even in the future.*"

Continuing to the next group of verses, Mr. Symons dealt with passages that describe Jesus as the Creator. He first inquired what everyone thought Jesus had created. Peter of course, believed that Jesus had been with God from the beginning way back in Genesis chapter one.

No one else could add anything to this, so Mr. Symons suggested that they look at Second Corinthians chapter five, verse seventeen.

Verity volunteered to read again. *"Therefore, if anyone is in Christ, he is a new creation; the old has gone, the new has come!'"*

They also read James one, verse eighteen and Ephesians two, verse ten. "What has Jesus created?" Mr. Symons repeated.

"It sounds like he created people like us," Peter offered.

"In the Genesis One creation?"

"Well...I believe he did, but this is maybe a secondary creation of believers."

Everyone looked puzzled, so Mr. Symons suggested, "Well, I'd suggest that these verses refer to the creation which involves redeeming men and women from sin and death and giving them the hope of being resurrected as he was, to immortality. Once individuals have become baptized," he explained, "they are *'in Christ'* and born again to a new life."

Mr. Symons could see that no one fully understood, so he tried to make things simpler. "How does this new creation happen? Well, it begins to germinate as a new life when a person first hears the true gospel message. When God's Word brings them to an understanding that they need to repent and accept God's way of salvation through baptism, they can become 'born again.' This is what Jesus tried to explain to Nicodemus."

Turning to the passage, Mr. Symons asked Aunt Judy to read John chapter three, verses one to eight.

"'Except a man be born again, he cannot see the kingdom of God. Nicodemus saith unto him, 'How can a man be born when he

is old? Can he enter the second time into his mother's womb, and be born?' Jesus answered, 'Verily, verily, I say unto thee, Except a man be born of water and of the Spirit, he cannot enter into the kingdom of God. That which is born of the flesh is flesh; and that which is born of the Spirit is spirit.'"[1]

"The spirit," he explained, "that Jesus is talking about here, is God's Word acting upon our minds.[2] The water is the water of baptism. This is the process we must go through to become new men and women. This process is called a Creation, with Jesus as the Creator, because it is through his death and resurrection that we can have this wonderful provision. Romans chapter six clearly shows us that baptism symbolises dying with Christ; we are crucifying our flesh, or our old way of life as he did. When we come up out of the water, we are symbolically rising from death, to be a new person, no longer following sin. Ultimately, if we follow Christ's ways in our life, we will be given immortality after the resurrection and judgment so that we will be truly like him, unable to sin or die any more."[3]

Noticing that Peter looked rather uncertain, Mr. Symons suggested, "Let's see if this model that I'm suggesting, works. Let's turn to the Colossians chapter one passage, that you gave me, Peter. This is the chapter most people would turn to if they believed Jesus created the literal creation in Genesis."

Mr. Symons first pointed out verse thirteen to demonstrate that this passage was indeed referring to God's Son. Then he had everyone read verses fifteen through to twenty in turn.

They read: *"Who is the image of the invisible God, the firstborn of every creature: For by him were all things created, that are in heaven, and that are in earth, visible and invisible, whether they be thrones, or dominions, or principalities, or powers: all*

---

[1] John 3:3–6

[2] John 6:63

[3] Luke 20:36; 1 John 3:1-3

195

things were created by him, and for him: And he is before all things, and by him all things consist. And he is the head of the body, the church: who is the beginning, the firstborn from the dead; that in all things he might have the pre-eminence."

"Thomas," Mr. Symons asked, "what does it say here that Jesus created?"

Thomas looked a little startled as though he had been daydreaming. Quickly he looked at the verses Taylor had turned up and was pointing out to him, "Well, things in heaven and earth, visible and invisible, thrones, powers, rulers and authorities," he read.

Mr. Symons nodded and looked around at all of them. "What was created in Genesis chapter one?"

Verity waved her hand.

"Yes?"

"It was more like plants, trees, sky, animals, birds, fish and people."

"So," Mr. Symons distinguished, "something's different here; this is not a Genesis creation. Peter, what do thrones, powers, rulers and authorities sound like to you?"

Peter thought for a moment. "It sounds like…well… a government, I guess, or…" he paused, "a kingdom."

"Yes," Mr. Symons nodded. "What is the whole purpose of Jesus creating new men and women?"

Verity saw the point. "Of course! We have to be new men and women to be a part of his Kingdom!"

"That's right, Verity," he said, looking pleased. "Now see if Revelation chapter five, verses nine to ten agrees with what you just said."

Verity read it. *"'And they sang a new song. You are worthy to take the scroll and open its seals, because you were slain, and with your blood you purchased men for God from every tribe and language and people and nation. You have made them to be a kingdom and priests to serve our God, and they will reign on the earth.'* Wow! It really fits!" she said.

Looking around again, Mr. Symons asked, "Is everyone okay with that?"

When they all nodded, he asked them to turn to Colossians one again. "The next group of passages deals with the idea that Jesus actually existed long before he was born to Mary. Many people get this from Colossians chapter one, verse fifteen and several other passages. I'll read it from my King James Version. *'Who is the image of the invisible God, the firstborn of every creature.'*"

Glancing up, he asked, "How do you understand this passage, Peter?"

"Well, just as it reads," Peter shrugged. "God created Jesus *first* before anything else in Creation."

"That is the popular understanding. Do you feel this happened way back before Genesis chapter one?"

"Yes."

"Now, we've already suggested there is an alternative creation in Colossians chapter one. Let's consider that this is not the Genesis One creation, but the process of redeeming men and women from death. How was Jesus the *firstborn* of all the spiritual creation?" Looking up he asked, "Peter, before you answer this, can you read from verse eighteen of this chapter?"

Peter read, *"'And he is the head of the body, the church: who is the beginning, the firstborn from the dead; that in all things he might have the pre-eminence.'"*

"So, what is Jesus the firstborn from?" Mr. Symons prodded.

Kara was catching on to this logic, so she piped up with, "The dead."

Nodding, Mr. Symons went further; "Now, was Jesus the first person to be raised from the dead?"

Aunt Judy and Kara nodded their heads, but Verity shook hers. "No, Elisha raised a little boy. Jesus raised Lazarus…"

"That's right, Verity," he agreed. "At least eight specific people were raised from the dead in the Bible record. So, in what sense was Jesus the *firstborn* from the dead?"

Everyone was quiet, mulling this over.

Finally, Peter spoke, "Well, if Jesus wasn't the first to rise *from the dead,* then I think this verse must be referring to him existing before the creation in Genesis one."

Mr. Symons smiled at Peter, but he tried to help everyone see the point by asking, "Are the people, such as Lazarus, who rose from the dead in Bible times, still living today?"

The group shook their heads uncertainly.

"What was different about Jesus' resurrection from all the others?" he prodded again.

A light suddenly dawned on Peter's face. "He was made *immortal* at his resurrection!"

"Exactly!" Mr. Symons beamed. "Had anyone else been raised and made immortal before Jesus?"

"No," they all exclaimed.

"Is this what the people who are 'new men and women in Christ,' hope to attain to?"

"Yes," they all agreed.

"So therefore, Jesus is working to make a new creation of men and women for the Kingdom. The process begins with God's Word acting on our minds.[4] This hopefully, leads us to repenting and being born again at baptism, willingly choosing to serve God, not sin. If we continue with the right attitudes, God's Word will continue to change us all through our lives to make us more like Him and His Son. If we die before Christ returns, we will be raised for the judgment, and in God's mercy, will be made immortal as Jesus was. Then we will truly be part of the perfect new creation."

A few times during the discussion, Verity had glanced over to see how Thomas was doing, but each time the expressionless look on his face made her think that he wasn't really following. "He doesn't even know what this is all about," she sighed to herself. "Unless you've asked yourself the questions, you don't appreciate the answers."

Peter, on the other hand—who was sitting beside her—had taken extensive notes and seemed quite amazed. As Mr. Symons had lumped together the numerous references Peter had given him, he now suggested that any specific questions could be asked.

Quick to take the opportunity, Peter brought up the passages he still had difficulties with. "How do you explain John chapter ten, verse thirty?" he asked. "Jesus says plainly, *'I and my Father are one.'*"

Nodding, Mr. Symons asked Peter to turn to John seventeen, verses twenty-one to twenty-three and read them aloud.

Peter read, *" 'That they all may be one; as thou, Father, art in me, and I in thee, that they also may be one in us: that the world may believe that thou hast sent me. And the glory which thou gavest me I have given them; that they may be one, even as we are one: I in them, and thou in me, that they may be made perfect in one...' "*

---

[4] 1 Peter 1:23–25; 2:2

Seeing the point, Peter quietly read the passage over to himself, again.

Mr. Symons asked, "What do you think is this 'oneness' that Jesus is referring to?"

After considering for a moment, Verity spoke up, "Could it be a 'oneness' in mind?"

"Yes," replied Mr. Symons, "belief and mind and purpose. As we discussed before, when God's Word is allowed to act upon our minds, we begin to think like He does. This is the oneness God wants to see in us. Jesus began his ministry with God's Word fully in his mind. Therefore, the words he spoke, the decisions he made, the compassion he showed—were all totally in accordance with what God would have said and felt and done. That's how Jesus could say, *'he that hath seen me hath seen the Father;'* and *'the word which ye hear is not mine, but the Father's which sent me.'*[5] The lesson for us in John ten and seventeen, is that God and Jesus expect us to try to develop the same mind that they have."

Peter had more questions. "I have to get an answer for John one, verses one to three," he said. "That passage is used more than any other to prove the Trinity."

"You're right," nodded Mr. Symons, "any discussion on the Trinity ultimately leads to this passage." He opened to the place and read, *"'In the beginning was the Word, and the Word was with God, and the Word was God. The same was in the beginning with God. All things were made by him; and without him was not any thing made that was made.'"*

Looking up at Peter, Mr. Symons asked, "Where do you see Jesus fitting into these verses, Peter?"

---

[5] John 14:9, 24

"He's the Word," Peter responded confidently. "In verse three it says, *'all things were made by him.'* The Word is a person—*him*—Jesus."

"All right," said Mr. Symons. "Firstly, this word 'word,' how can we find out what it means in the original Greek language?"

Seeing Peter frown, Mr. Symons smiled and passed him Strong's Concordance so that he could look up 'word.'

Finding it with speed, the young man looked over the definition carefully. "It's the Greek word 'logos' and it has the idea of *'something said (including the thought); by implication, a topic (subject of discourse) also reasoning (the mental faculty) or motive, by extension, a computation; specially, (with the article in John) the Divine Expression (i.e. Christ)' et cetera.'"*

"So, how would you put it in your own words, Peter?"

Reading the definition over a few more times, Peter summarised, "Well, I suppose 'logos' isn't only the spoken word, but the thought behind it."

"Right, and John chapter one tells us that at the very beginning of the world, this spoken word, including the thought, was with God. Now, how did God create the world, Peter?" Mr. Symons questioned.

"He spoke and it happened," the young man shrugged.

"Ah! God *'spoke'* and it happened." Mr. Symons repeated.

"Yes," replied Peter, not seeing the connection.

Mr. Symons had everyone turn up Genesis one. He briefly pointed out that over and over God said, *'Let there be...'* and it appeared. "So, the world was made by the 'word' of God – the spoken word," [6] he explained. "Now, Peter, when God created the

---

[6] Psalm 33:6

world, do you think He did it haphazardly or had He planned it all out ahead of time?"

"Well, I suppose He would have planned it out first."

"I agree," Mr. Symons stated, "because the Bible indicates that God had His creation so well planned that He knew sin would enter the world and that He would need to send His Son as a perfect sacrifice to redeem His creation from death. That's why Revelation thirteen, verse eighteen can say Jesus was *'the Lamb slain from the foundation of the world.'* We know that Jesus didn't die until about four thousand years after the earth was created, but because of God's foreknowledge He speaks as though this event happened when creation began."

"Are there other passages like that?" Peter questioned.

"Yes. First Peter chapter one, verses nineteen to twenty is another similar passage that mentions how believers are redeemed by the blood of Christ. Maybe you would read that for us, Judy?"

Aunt Judy was following attentively, and she read, *"'But with the precious blood of Christ, as of a lamb without blemish and without spot: Who verily was foreordained before the foundation of the world but was manifest in these last times for you.'"*

"What does 'foreordained' mean?" asked Kara.

"If you were to look it up in Strong's," Mr. Symons said, "you would see it has the idea of 'knowing beforehand.'"

"Knowing beforehand? So, wouldn't that refer to the relationship God had with His Son before creation?" Peter maintained.

"If that were the case, Peter, then believers must have pre-existed also," Mr. Symons answered with a smile. "Because, the same language is used of believers in Romans chapter eight, verses twenty-eight to thirty. Let me read it out to you. *"'And we know that all things work together for good to them that love God, to them who are the called according to his purpose. For whom he did foreknow, he also did predestinate to be conformed to the image of his Son, that he might be the firstborn among many brethren. Moreover, whom he did predestinate, them he also called: and whom he called, them he also justified: and whom he justified, them he also glorified.'"[7]*

Looking up at Peter, Mr. Symons asked, "Do you see how great God's foreknowledge is? Before He created the world, He knew the 'end from the beginning.'[8] He knew what His Son would come and do. He knew those who would choose to answer the call of the Gospel. He knew that the whole plan He had of filling the earth with His glory[9] would center on the forgiveness made possible through His Son. That is why from the very beginning of the Bible we find prophecies of the coming Messiah[10] and that is why so many rituals of the Law point forward to the greater sacrifice that Jesus would make.[11] Many faithful men and women throughout the Old Testament were brought through experiences in their lives to teach them about what Jesus would do when he came.[12] This is how 'logos' was with God at the very beginning of time as we know it. God's plan and purpose with His creation was already determined before Genesis one became history."[13]

---

[7] See also Ephesians 1:11; Jeremiah 1:4–6

[8] Isaiah 46:9–10

[9] Numbers 14:21

[10] Genesis 3:15; 13:14–17 – Galatians 3:14–16, 27–29

[11] Galatians 3:19–26; Hebrews 10:1–21. (i.e. A lamb without blemish sacrificed for a sin offering).

[12] 3 Melchizedek brought forth bread and wine to Abraham. (Genesis 14:18–20 – Hebrews 7:1–28). Abraham 'offered' his beloved son Isaac upon Mt. Moriah (Genesis 22:1–18). Joseph was sold and betrayed by his brothers and then became their saviour (Genesis 37; 45:1–11) etc.

[13] 2 Timothy 1:9–10. See also Proverbs 8 where WISDOM is personified as a woman with God at the time of creation.

Verity could see that Peter was thinking this through carefully, yet something was still bothering him.

"But this 'Word' in John chapter one is called a 'him,'" Peter responded.

"That's a liberty that the translators have taken," Mr. Symons stated, reaching for a small book that lay on the table beside him. "In the Greek language nouns have a feminine or masculine gender as they do in French or German. 'Chair' for instance, has a feminine gender in Greek, but because the *English* translators think of a chair as an *inanimate* object, they would simply refer to a chair as an 'it.'"

Having opened the small book in his hands, Mr. Symons explained, "This book I have here is called a Diaglott.[14] It is probably the most literal translation of the Greek New Testament that we can get today. Let me read how the Diaglott renders John chapter one: *'In the Beginning was the LOGOS, and the LOGOS was with GOD, and the LOGOS was God. This was in the Beginning with GOD. Through it every thing was done; and without it not even one thing was done, which has been done. In it was Life; and the LIFE was the LIGHT of MEN. And the LIGHT shone in the DARKNESS, and the DARKNESS apprehended It not.'"*

Passing the Diaglott over to Peter for him to examine, Mr. Symons continued on, "Now this translation has left 'logos' untranslated and uses a neutral gender. It might interest you to know that in the Greek language of today the word 'logos' is used casually to refer to the 'reason' behind a person's actions. The fact that 'logos' has a masculine gender would no more imply to *a Greek* that 'logos' is a man, than a feminine 'chair' is a woman."

Peter passed the small book on to Verity to examine. "So, how does Jesus fit into John chapter one?" he asked.

---

[14] The Emphatic Diaglott (Greek English New Testament) : Rev. Thomas Tilford : Free Download, Borrow, and Streaming : Internet Archive

"A fair question, Peter," Mr. Symons replied. "In the first few verses of John one, God's plan and purpose looks forward to the work that His Son would do. In verse fourteen that plan and purpose becomes reality, or flesh, when Jesus is born. It is then that everyone is able to see what God determined from the beginning. His plan was finally manifest to the world in a human being!"

After a moment's hesitation, Mr. Symons added, "Let me show you just one more passage on this. Kara perhaps you could read Second Timothy one, verses nine and ten?"

Kara read, *"'Who hath saved us, and called us with an holy calling, not according to our works, but according to his own purpose and grace, which was given us in Christ Jesus before the world began, But is now made manifest by the appearing of our Saviour Jesus Christ, who hath abolished death, and hath brought life and immortality to light through the gospel.'"*

"See the significance of that passage?" Mr. Symons asked the group. "Salvation was worked out for us *before* the world began, but it wasn't until Jesus came into the world that God's plan became manifest to all. Up until then, it was a mystery or secret that many had read about in the Scriptures, or written about under inspiration, or enacted in their lives, but didn't fully comprehend.[15] So, Jesus wasn't the 'word.' He was the *'word made flesh'* in verse fourteen!"

Verity was looking at the Timothy passage carefully. "There are those same words, 'life' and 'light,'" she pointed out.

"Yes," Mr. Symons agreed, "and do you see why, Verity?"

She looked long and hard at the passage, but it didn't immediately come to her.

"What was the 'logos' or purpose of God all about?"

---

[15] Luke 24:25–27,44–45; Ephesians 3:3–5, 9–10; Hebrews 1:1–3; 1 Peter 1:7–13

"Salvation."

"Right. The plan and purpose of God was all about the salvation of His creation. So, as it says here in Timothy, Jesus brought *'life and immortality to light through the gospel.'* The process by which God would provide a way for sinful human beings to attain to immortality was through the life, death and resurrection of His Son."

"The new creation," Verity recalled, "which we were speaking of earlier."

"Exactly," Mr. Symons affirmed. "Understanding how Jesus was in God's plan and purpose from the beginning to bring about the new creation of immortal saints in the Kingdom age, sheds a whole new light on all of these passages."[16]

When the discussion finished, after almost two hours, Verity could feel she was going to have trouble standing up. Her lower back had started to ache acutely. She waited until Peter left to get a drink of water, before she said quietly to Lindsay, "Do you mind if I lean on you when I stand up?"

Lindsay was only too pleased to help, and it saved Verity from what would certainly have been yet another embarrassing situation.

---

[16] For a study-sheet on the Pre-existence see did-jesus-pre-exist.pdf (wordpress.com)

CHAPTER 25

The Party

I t was great to have the holidays and spend time at home with her family and her Bible, but Verity felt a certain loneliness too. Thomas was so different than he used to be, and she felt their close friendship was a thing of the past. She also missed her school friends a lot!

Friday night, December twenty-seventh, arrived at last. Everyone in the family had been privately well-warned of the big party and so they kept a watchful eye on Thomas. As usual, Kara and Aunt Judy took him along to work that afternoon. To help even more, Verity went to work as well. Since most stores had been closed for Christmas and Boxing Day, Friday night was a very busy evening. Thomas was kept occupied stocking shelves, while Verity flew around helping to mop up slush-covered floors and tidy the vegetable stands. Aunt Judy was up in her office managing matters of importance while Kara stayed at the check-out counter, constantly ringing groceries through.

It was Verity's secret duty to check on Thomas every half an hour to make sure he was still there. For about three hours the plan worked quite successfully, until Verity suddenly realised that over an hour had passed since the last time she checked. Hurrying through the store, she looked down each row anxiously, hoping she would see Thomas, but to no avail. "Okay, I'll try the stock room," she thought. "Maybe he's getting a crate of goods."

Unfortunately, no one had seen him in the stock room for a while. In a state of rising panic, she searched each back room, asking all the employees if they had seen him. Finally, she came to the butcher, who remembered seeing Thomas head out the back door – for a break, he had assumed.

"How long ago was that?" she asked.

"I wasn't really watching the clock," he shrugged, "but I'd guess well over an hour ago."

Verity tried to hurry to the front of the store. Customers stopped her along the way to ask for help in locating certain items. Verity did her best to help politely but quickly. Up ahead, she saw that her mother had a line-up of at least six customers waiting to pay for their groceries. Her leg almost gave out on her again, but she managed to grab onto a bin of apples and steady herself till the jabbing pain subsided. With a forced smile, she finally reached the front and hung the "Next Cashier Please" sign on her mom's booth.

Kara, seeing the look on her daughter's face, tried to hurry serving the customer she was with. In her haste, of course, she messed up badly and had to do the woman's groceries all over again. Ignoring the grumbling customers who were angry about the long line-ups, Verity finally pulled her mother upstairs to the office.

"Mom, I can't find Thomas!" she said gravely. "The butcher says he saw him leave over an hour ago. In fact," she despaired, looking at her watch, "since I last checked on him, it's been almost two hours!"

Verity felt like she could be sick. Her mother was wringing her hands anxiously. "I'll phone Peter and see if he's seen Thomas," she suggested, grateful that Peter had the foresight to come up with this plan.

For fifteen minutes they tried over and over to phone the Bryants but Peter's line was busy. Kara was ready to give up and go in search of her son, when the call finally went through.

Mrs. Bryant answered the phone in tears. She explained that she had just finished talking to the police. Peter had been rushed by ambulance to the hospital in a serious condition. She didn't know exactly what had happened, but she was on her way to see him.

In shock, Verity put down the receiver and nervously relayed the message to her mother. Suddenly, the phone rang beside them.

Hesitating a little, Kara picked it up. "Kolmer's IGA," she said.

"May I speak with Kara Lovell," said a sober, authoritarian voice.

"This is Kara," she replied.

"Ma'am, your son is being held here at the Grandville police station. He's been charged with drinking under-age and will likely also be charged with aggravated assault."

The phone receiver dropped to the floor as Kara Lovell collapsed in a chair, sobbing, "Not Thomas! No, not Thomas!"

CHAPTER 26

It's Hard to Forgive!

Rushing to the police station, Aunt Judy had to keep consoling Kara. "Maybe this will be enough to wake that boy up and turn him around! Let's not despair!"

When they entered the police station, an officer kindly showed them to some chairs and went to get Thomas out of the cell. It was a very different Thomas who staggered out in handcuffs, sobbing. There was no sign of the wall he had been building so determinedly around himself. Weeping as though his heart had broken, he kept on babbling, "I'm sorry, Mom! I'm so sorry, Verity! I am so, so sorry!"

Verity's eyes quickly took in the scene. Why did Thomas have blood on his knuckles?! There was even blood splattered on his jeans! Wild-eyed she cried out, "What have you done, Thomas? There's blood all over you!"

Thomas sobbed even harder, if that was possible, and he tried to speak again, but couldn't form the words.

A policeman stepped forward and said gravely to Kara, "Your son and a few of his friends have been involved in a drunken brawl with another youth. Fortunately, we were called to the scene early by neighbours complaining of excessive noise. When we arrived, we were able to stop the assault and call an ambulance immediately. That probably saved the young man's life!"

It all came together too easily in Verity's mind—the party—an ambulance—a fight—Peter! "Was the young man... Peter Bryant?" she asked fearfully, trembling from head to toe.

Thomas sounded like he was going to choke.

"Yes," said another officer at the desk, glancing down at the report. "Do you know him?"

A sense of horror fell over Verity, and she burst into tears.

"Mrs. Lovell," the officer said sternly, "your son has been charged with 'minor consume,' that is, drinking under-age, which involves a fine of seventy dollars. I'm not sure what the final assault charges will be; that depends on the severity of Mr. Bryant's injuries. A court date will be set to sentence your son when we have finished our investigations."

Kara had become quite unresponsive. All emotion and colour had drained from her face. She sat stock-still, unable to believe she was going through all of this again, only now with her son! Thomas saw the look on his mother's face, a look that even in his intoxicated state, he remembered all too well. He tried to say something, but he was so choked with emotion that his words were incomprehensible.

"Shall we take him home?" Aunt Judy asked, not sure what was meant to happen in such a situation.

The officer next to Thomas shook his head. "No, he and his friends will spend the night here. We have police checks to do on all of them and we want to talk with them when they are sober. He'll probably be released tomorrow, on the condition that he promises to completely abstain from alcohol until his court date."

Verity was aware that the feelings inside of her needed to be restrained. Hatred and anger were bubbling up. What had Thomas done? Peter had only wanted to help! How could Thomas react so violently to someone so kind and good? And she was overcome with worry about Peter! What had happened to him? Would he be all right? What if he wasn't?!

As they turned to leave, the officer chose to assist Kara to the car, and Verity gave Thomas one last darting glance. Every bit of raw emotion came through in that look and instead of good-bye, she snapped, "You are just like Dad!"

Thomas turned away hastily.

All the way home, tears ran down Verity's face. Seeing the blood on Thomas's hands and clothes had been terribly frightening. Realising it was Peter's blood made her feel sick with fear. Her mind agonized over images of what might have occurred between them. How could Thomas have hurt Peter, when Peter had only gone to the party to try and help him? She reproached herself for agreeing to Peter's plan to help. It was crazy for one lone individual to try and intervene in a situation like that! Better to have let Thomas wallow in his drunken state than for an innocent person to risk his own life!

The image that kept replaying in her mind, of her drunken brother standing in the police station begging for forgiveness, struck only the faintest chord of pity. She was sure that in the morning when he was sober, he'd return to the same 'I don't care about anyone else' attitude that he'd maintained for so long.

When they arrived home, Verity tried to call Peter's house for what seemed like the hundredth time that evening, but the phone only rang and rang. No one was home.

All that night she tossed and turned. If only she knew what had happened to Peter! What did 'in a serious condition' mean? Would he make it? Did he hate her whole family now? She wished desperately for the light of day so she could phone to end the agony of her suspense.

There was still no one answering the phone at Peter's house the next morning and Verity doubted whether his mother would even think of calling her. Minutes seemed like an eternity, as she paced the floor wondering how she could find out what was happening. Finally, the phone rang, and she rushed to pick it up, but it was only the police stating that they could now take Thomas home.

Aunt Judy and Kara left immediately to get him, but Verity stayed home. She wasn't eager to see her brother and she certainly didn't want to miss any calls from the Bryants.

For an hour she walked back and forth in the kitchen, alone in silence, unable to collect her thoughts. She wished she had asked to be dropped off at the hospital and then perhaps she could have found out about Peter's condition herself.

When she heard Aunt Judy's Jeep pulling into the driveway, Verity decided to flee to her room. Seeing Thomas again without knowing about Peter would be too difficult to take.

As she was sitting there on her bed with her back against the headboard, a knock sounded on her closed door.

"Verity, it's me... Thomas. Please let me speak to you." The words were spoken so gently that she couldn't refuse.

Thomas came in hesitantly, his eyes red and puffy, tearstains still on his face. "I'm so sorry!" he said, his voice shaking. "I'm so sorry about last night!"

When she didn't answer, Thomas asked anxiously, "Have you heard anything... anything about... Peter?"

Shaking her head, she gazed at Thomas reproachfully, pondering how she felt towards him. His feelings were not a high priority.

Crushed by her look, Thomas collapsed into the chair across from her. "Verity, please forgive me!" he begged. "I know I've been horrible to you and to everyone!" He hid his face in his hands. "I saw myself last night in a way I never thought I would," he confessed earnestly. "I was so angry at Dad for how he treated us, and then," he sobbed, "last night I did the same thing to someone else!!"

Thomas looked up at her, his eyes desperate for understanding. "I don't know what came over me. I was just so mad that after all my efforts to get to the party—that Peter would come along and interfere."

"He was just trying to save you from yourself!" retorted Verity, angrily.

Thomas nodded. "Yeah, I can see that now, very clearly!" His chest heaved. "I guess he's been trying to help me for a long time."

"He has!" Verity burst out. "He's tried so hard, and you've been so mean, Thomas!"

Thomas shook his head in painful recollection. "I just lost my mind, Verity. All I could think of was my anger. And I didn't know that all the other guys would join in..." his voice cracked and he could say no more.

Horrified, Verity imagined a frightful scene with a violent crowd; she wanted to know more, and yet it was terrifying to think about it. With a quiet, trembling voice, she asked, "Was he badly hurt?"

Thomas looked at her, the fear in his eyes making her afraid to hear his answer. "I don't know, Verity," he said in anguish, turning away. "I only hit him a few times, then the others took over..." A huge sob escaped from his chest. "I just know he was unconscious and... and there was blood everywhere!"

With a sigh of agony, he reached across and laid his hand on her arm. "I have so much to apologise for. I've been so... so *rotten!* But if this turns out to be serious for Peter, I will never, ever forgive myself!!" The tears slid down his face again. "I'm so incredibly sorry!" he whispered.

They sat there looking at one another in silence for a few moments. Verity remembered how earnestly she had prayed for Thomas to come to a turning point in his life. Now here he was apologizing! He had finally understood that the path he was following had led him to this. Was she prepared to forgive him? Or would she grind him back into the despair and misery he had been under for so long?

Until this incident Verity had always thought of herself as a forgiving person. After all, she'd forgiven her father for all the pain he'd caused them! But this time it was so different—or was it? Had Thomas struggled with feelings as intense as what she felt now? If he had, then maybe she could understand why he had been so miserable. She took in his red, sorrowful, imploring eyes, his heaving chest. Maybe this had been God's way of helping Thomas. Maybe there had to be something this traumatic in his life to turn him around. In the back of her mind a little voice reminded her of Christ's command to forgive—even if your brother sins against you seventy times seven times.[1] Would she only forgive when she felt like it? Or would she forgive because Jesus wanted her to, even if it was incredibly difficult?

"Thomas," she said quietly at last, "I forgive you."

Relief flooded his eyes, as he got shakily to his feet. "Really?" he asked.

Going against every vengeful impulse she harboured against Thomas, she got up and gave him a hug.

It was then that the phone rang and Verity dashed downstairs to the kitchen to pick it up. "Hello, this is Verity," she said anxiously, rather out of breath.

"Verity, this is Peter's mother," said Mrs. Bryant slowly. "He asked me to call you to let you know he's going to be okay. He has a broken nose, several broken ribs and a punctured lung. There's swelling and bruises all over him; but he's going to make it, he'll be all right!"

"Oh!" Verity exclaimed, sobs of joy breaking her voice. "I'm so glad to hear he's okay! I was so worried!" She tipped the receiver partially away from her ear, so that Thomas, who was right beside her, could hear as well.

---

[1] Matthew 18:21–22

"Praise God!" Mrs. Bryant stated emphatically. "When I saw Peter last night, I thought things might be far worse! But thanks to God, he regained consciousness this morning and the doctor says he'll be okay."

An uncomfortable thought went through Verity's mind; should she say it or not? She decided she had to. "Mrs. Bryant... has Peter told you... who was involved in the fight?"

There was a long pause. "Yes, Verity, I know. We were informed by the police officers. Peter has managed to say a few things too." She paused again. "It's a little hard for us to understand right now, about your brother and everything..."

Verity's fears were realised. "He's very, very sorry..." she began, glancing nervously at Thomas, who had turned towards the cupboards, his face hidden behind his arms.

"Well, somehow Peter seems to be quite sympathetic towards your brother," Mrs. Bryant said cautiously. "Even though, supposedly Thomas started the fight. Anyway, Dear, let's worry about that later. When Peter is better, we'll let him speak for himself."

"Is it okay to visit Peter?" Verity asked, desperately.

"Well, I know he would love you to come," she hesitated, "but I think until his lung heals, it would be best for him to just keep very quiet."

The tears were flowing down Thomas' face again as Verity asked Mrs. Bryant to pass on her great concern and thanks to Peter.

"I don't deserve his sympathy," Thomas said shakily, after she hung up the receiver. "I haven't even told him that I'm sorry."

"Peter's been very forgiving with you all along," Verity reminded him. "Maybe now you can forgive someone else."

Thomas looked up at her soberly. "You mean Dad?" He paused, turning away again. "I have."

"You have?" she repeated in astonishment.

"I've finally realized how it all happened with Dad," he said sadly. "I never thought I would ever be a violent person and then last night, it just happened so easily. I am never going to drink again. Never!"

"I hope you mean that," Verity said, with uncertainty. Never was a very long time!

Thomas looked over at her with determination. "I do mean that! And furthermore, I'm going to start attending the seminars with you. I know I need to change my life."

"Wow!" Verity exclaimed, astonished. "You've made all these decisions in one night?"

Thomas shook his head, more in control now. "No, this has been building for a while, believe it or not. I've been so jealous of you—always happy about everything—so at peace. I'm not going to deny it any longer," he said earnestly. "I know I need to find what you have."

Verity hugged him again, spontaneously. How quickly life could go from the deepest darkness of night to the rising of the sun!

CHAPTER 27

A True Friend

Verity called Peter's home every other day hoping they could go to visit him but each time she was told to wait. Peter was now home from the hospital, but his mother was worried that if he laughed it would undo the healing. "He just needs total quiet for a little longer, Dear," she said.

So, Verity contented herself with sending a card and a book. Mr. Symons had lent her a book called, "When Jesus Became God".[1] It was an excellent historical account of the development of the doctrine of the Trinity, written in a dramatic story form. Having received Mr. Symons' permission, she passed it on to Peter.

They had been back at school for a whole week before Mrs. Bryant finally invited them over.

On the way, Mrs. Lovell picked up a fruit basket and a card. They were all feeling somewhat nervous. Thomas especially looked very pale, and Verity could see that his hands were shaking.

Mrs. Bryant greeted them all at the door with, what seemed to Verity, a determined look to be kind. Verity wished that she'd had an opportunity to meet Peter's mother before such a horrible incident had taken place. Nevertheless, the gentle lines on Mrs. Bryant's face gave evidence that she was more used to forgiving

---

[1] Richard E. Rubenstein. Published by Harcourt Inc. San Diego, CA USA
ISBN 0-15-601315-0
When Jesus Became God (Richard E. Rubenstein) : Richard E. Rubenstein
: Free Download, Borrow, and Streaming : Internet Archive

others, than holding grudges. Verity was surprised at how pretty and youthful she looked, even though her hair was perfectly snow-white.

Subconsciously, Verity had expected Peter to look like he did before the incident; after all, the fight had happened two whole weeks ago. However, he still had bandages over one eye and his nose. His face was discoloured with bruising and he was lying back on the couch very quietly. Seeing him like this brought reality to the whole ordeal. "Oh, Peter!" she exclaimed in dismay.

"Peter's just fine!" replied his mother in a cheerful voice as she closed the door behind them.

Smiling weakly, Peter quietly called out his own greeting and Thomas started nervously towards his couch. He broke down in tears halfway across the room. "I'm so sorry, Peter!" he blurted out, kneeling beside him. "I've been so selfish! I don't know what came over me that night! I know you were only trying to help. I hope you can forgive me!"

Peter looked surprised. This was certainly a very different Thomas to the one he knew! He laid his hand on Thomas' arm. "That's okay," he said awkwardly, "I understand... We'll be good buddies yet."

Verity sat down on the floor beside the couch. "Peter you were so brave to try and help Thomas that night!" she praised.

Peter managed something a little like a laugh. "Bravery?" he repeated, speaking weakly and short of breath. "Or foolish? One guy... wild party... trying to talk sense... to a drunken man!" He shook his head incredulously. "What was I thinking?!"

They all laughed sadly.

With his emotions now in check, Thomas said soberly, "Peter, thanks for being such a great friend. I know I can't possibly make up for what I've done but this has really turned my life around!"

Reaching out his arm to shake Thomas' hand, Peter replied, "If we're friends... this is worth it."

It was a generous response and Thomas was surprised. He shook Peter's hand gratefully.

Verity wished she could tell Peter all that had happened since that horrible night, but she knew she would have to wait until she visited him alone.

Meanwhile, she could hear her mother apologizing to Mrs. Bryant again. Kara had already had a few apologetic conversations on the phone with the Bryants. "Thanks again," Kara said, "for being so understanding towards Thomas. I appreciate that so much! This has really changed him already and he still has to face court sentencing in six months' time."

Verity would have liked to stay all afternoon with the Bryants. However, she soon got the feeling that Peter's mother was anxious for them to leave. Kara also seemed to feel this was the case, as she said, "Well, we should be going. Thanks so much for letting us apologise to Peter in person."

As his mother went to get their coats, Peter caught Verity's eye and held up the book that she had sent him. "This is great!" he said, straining to speak. "Entertaining... eye-opening! These bishops... so unchristian! Cheating... lying...hatred." He paused. "More concern... for status... and position... than truth." Taking a deep breath, he paused.

"We'll have to discuss it when you're feeling better," she said earnestly. "I *really* hope that will be soon!"

"It will!" he promised. "Another week or so."

Out of the corner of her eye, Verity saw Mrs. Bryant shake her head.

Thomas shook Peter's hand again to say goodbye. "Could I help you keep up with your schoolwork?" he asked.

Peter's eyes lit up. "Yes please! Exams are... two weeks away?"

Thomas nodded. "I could walk here after school and catch a ride home later with my mom from the store."

So, it was settled. Mrs. Bryant was very happy with the idea. Verity was too. She had long hoped that one day this friendship would grow.

CHAPTER 28

Who is to Blame?

School was busier now than ever before. Final exams were coming up fast, and major assignments were all coming due at the same time. Between all the schoolwork, going to the seminars, and keeping up with her goal of reading through the entire Bible, Verity had hardly a moment to spare.

However, a couple of months ago, in Matthew chapter six, she had come across the verses, *"So do not worry, saying, 'What shall we eat?' or 'What shall we drink?' or 'What shall we wear?' For the pagans run after all these things, and your heavenly Father knows that you need them. But seek ye first his kingdom and his righteousness, and all these things will be given to you as well."*

Since pondering the lesson of that passage, she had determined that no matter how busy her life became, she would always have time each day to pray and read the Bible. So, she continued reading at least four Old Testament chapters a night and one from the New. It was amazing how often when she sat down to read, that a verse or passage jumped out at her and was exactly what she needed to hear. No matter what she was wondering about, her answer was almost always found somewhere in the chapters she considered.

Not only was her notebook overflowing with questions, many now had answers written beside them. The seminars had fast-tracked her learning, but from her own diligent reading she had gleaned a much more personal understanding and a deeper relationship with God. Her reading was prompting her in prayer, as she came to a fuller appreciation of God's whole plan and purpose with the earth. Within her mind was developing a new perspective. A perspective that saw beyond the here and now, and focused instead on a hope that would be realized in the future. Sometimes with the pressure of so much to do, she read too quickly and then the words had no power to impact her life. But when she concentrated and gave God's Word the time it deserved, she was never disappointed; there was always some new insight to discover.

In all the hectic rush of those two weeks, Verity was so thankful that Thomas visited Peter every day. She herself had gone one day at lunch hour, but since then she had to content herself with sending him little notes. Peter was busy too, determined not to fail the courses he had already worked for so hard. Since Peter and Thomas shared three out of four classes that semester, Thomas brought home the day's work and studied hard with Peter until late every night. Mrs. Bryant, very thankful for Thomas' help, drove him home after their sessions. Once or twice, Thomas even stayed overnight.

Now that Thomas had changed his attitude, Hank and his group of friends had turned on him at school. However, since Thomas was no longer so fixated on himself, he was a lot happier, and the ridicule he endured didn't bother him much. One evening he had been quite open with Verity and explained that his friendship with Hank had only been one of convenience—nothing sincere. He'd been unwilling to develop any new meaningful relationships because he didn't want to have friends ripped away again when he moved back West. Now that didn't seem to be such an issue. A deep connection was being forged between himself and Peter. This was a friend he knew he could depend on and enjoy.

Verity was in the middle of finishing her last English essay, when Thomas came in at half past eleven on Thursday night. "Hey Sis, what are you doing up so late?" he asked sympathetically.

Weary-eyed she gazed up at him from the kitchen table. She was so happy to have the real Thomas back. Even Aunt Judy had remarked at dinner to Kara that it was as though Thomas was a totally different person.

She answered his question with a sigh. "I'm almost done this essay, I think… only I don't really like my conclusion. Maybe I should redo it."

Thomas took off his coat and gloves, and put them away in the closet. "Peter wonders what's happened to you. You haven't been to see him for *nine* whole days!"

She smiled. "He's counting?"

"He sure is!"

Reaching into his pocket Thomas produced a little note. "This is for you," he said, handing it to her.

Verity opened the piece of paper and saw the words:

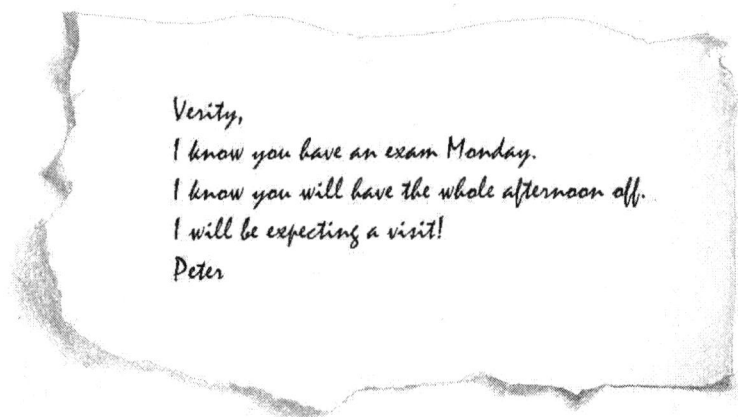

> Verity,
> I know you have an exam Monday.
> I know you will have the whole afternoon off.
> I will be expecting a visit!
> Peter

It was true. Verity's first exam was on Monday. So, after she had written it and done a little preparation for the math exam that she had to write the following day, she walked over to Peter's house.

Peter glanced up from the work he was doing as Mrs. Bryant opened the door and greeted her pleasantly.

"It's about time!" he called out.

"I'm sorry, Peter," she said, hanging her coat on the hook. She greeted Mrs. Bryant politely. "I'm so glad exams are finally here. Now I have time to breathe again!"

"It has been crazy," Peter agreed. "Without Thomas' help I would've have made it. He really is a great guy."

She nodded. "That fight with you was what turned him around, Peter. I'm awfully sorry though that you ended up so hurt!"

Peter looked serious. "It could've been worse. I'm glad no one had knives!"

Verity shuddered at the thought. Out of the corner of her eye, she saw Mrs. Bryant head quickly back into the kitchen.

"Everyone at school is asking about you," she remarked, sitting down in the chair opposite to him.

"I guess you wouldn't know what to tell them, since you're never here," he remarked flatly, with a twinkle in his eye.

She laughed. "Oh, I just tell them to ask Thomas!"

Peter was looking very much back to normal she decided. His nose had a slight new bump at the top and there was still some yellowish bruising on his face. Other than that, no one would know anything had ever happened to him. Around the couch lay exercise weights, textbooks, binders, tall glasses, some half full, and his Bible.

"You look so much better," she observed with relief. "In fact, I'd say you look great! How do you feel?"

"Like I need to get back to living!" he expressed with frustration. "I'm going to start jogging tomorrow."

From the kitchen, Mrs. Bryant piped up. "The doctor said Wednesday, Peter... just two more days."

Peter groaned.

With a shake of his head, he repositioned himself on the couch and motioned for her to sit down. "I have a new question for you, Verity," he prompted, unable to conceal a smile. "How come your brother is such a different person now than he was a month ago?"

Verity wondered why he was asking this. "I guess because he was angry and hurt," she shrugged. "His feelings showed through in his actions. I'm glad he's let all that go."

"What made him so angry?" Peter asked.

She could tell Peter was trying to get at something but what was it? "Well… I guess unfair circumstances provoked the anger… but it was also his decision to keep holding onto it."

Peter hesitated a moment. "Some people would say he was under the influence of the Devil!"

"The Devil? What do you mean?" She had never thought of it that way.

"Well," said Peter, "many people believe there is a fallen angel from heaven who has great powers. He goes about trying to take people away from God!"

"I don't understand," she replied, shaking her head. "How does that apply to Thomas?"

"The Devil was taking advantage of those unfair circumstances and stirring him up to act that way," Peter explained.

"So, you're saying that Thomas wasn't responsible for his own actions?" Verity asked, surprised. "How can that be right? I just read the other night in Romans where it says we aren't to serve sin but to serve God. It's a choice *we* have to make."

Picking up Peter's Bible from the coffee table, she took a seat beside him on the couch. "I have to show you this," she said, skimming through Romans. "Here it is, Romans chapter six, verses fifteen to eighteen. I'll read it to you: *'What then? Shall we sin because we are not under law but under grace? By no means! Don't*

226

you know that when you offer yourselves to someone to obey him as slaves, you are slaves to the one whom you obey—whether you are slaves to sin, which leads to death, or to obedience, which leads to righteousness? But thanks be to God that, though you used to be slaves to sin, you wholeheartedly obeyed the form of teaching to which you were entrusted. You have been set free from sin and have become slaves to righteousness.'"

She looked up to see if he had seen the point.

"Insert 'Devil' in place of 'sin' and you'll understand what I mean."

"But it doesn't say 'Devil,'" she laughed. "It says 'sin.' This is a choice *we* make," she argued, "whether we want to serve sin or serve God. Nothing is said here about a fallen angel."

Peter looked at her teasingly. "Ah—come on, haven't you ever heard of the Devil before? You know, all red with horns and hooves and a big pitchfork?"

"Yes, I've seen pictures," she laughed. "But I can't say it ever made much sense to me. I certainly haven't read any description like that in the Bible!"

"I've heard lots about him," said Peter, more seriously, as he pulled a small booklet out of the Bible she was holding.

"What's that?" she asked.

"This is a Christadelphian Statement of Faith," he replied. "I asked Mr. Symons for it. In this little booklet, all their beliefs are listed with a pile of references under each one as evidence for why they believe it. I was looking through here the other day and I discovered that they believe the Devil to be a personification of evil and our human nature."

"That's probably the next study-sheet," Verity mused. "Mr. Symons said the last one would be another important topic." An idea suddenly occurred to her. "Do you think you can come to the next seminar, tomorrow evening?" she asked, her eyes brightening.

"I was thinking I might," he nodded, putting down the booklet. "Say," he said, remembering, "that talk at my church on 'The Mystery of the Trinity' is this Sunday evening. I hope you're still coming with us."

"I'm looking forward to it," she smiled. "By then exams will be over and I'll be free!"

Glancing at the clock, she jumped up quickly. "I'd better go. The bus will be coming soon!"

Just before she headed out the door, she turned, paused and then quickly remarked, "School's just not the same without you, Peter. I'll be *so* glad when you're back!"

As Verity and Thomas stood outside waiting for the bus to come, large flakes of snow began falling from the sky. "Did you visit Peter?" Thomas asked curiously.

"Yes, we had a good chat. He sure looks a lot better now!"

Thomas glanced at her hesitantly. "He says he's quite proud of his new nose, it has more character."

Verity swallowed hard.

A voice from behind caused her to turn around quickly. "Oh Verity, I'm so glad you're still here! You left your math book in the library." Purity held it out to her, and then tried to catch her breath. "Hi, Thomas," she said timidly.

Thomas nodded back at her. "Hi!" he replied. Then remembering something, he reached into his pocket and pulled out his wallet just as the bus drove up. "I think I owe you this," he said, hastily finding a ten-dollar bill.

"Oh, you don't need to pay me back!" Purity protested, shaking her head.

Thomas stuck the money in her coat pocket and leapt onto the bus.

As the big, yellow vehicle pulled away from the curb, both he and Verity opened a window at the back to wave at her.

"Thanks for finding my book!" Verity called out, finally getting the opportunity. "I would have failed my exam tomorrow if you hadn't."

Purity waved back with a big smile.

Sitting down happily, Verity was elated. Thomas was really going out of his way to change. He was even talking to 'snobs'! Or rather, he had stopped being one himself!

CHAPTER 29

Who Was Blamed?

Throughout the month of January, Mr. Symons had led the seminar group slowly through Genesis chapters four and five, discussing every question that was raised. Verity had been thoroughly enjoying the company of Thomas, Emily and Kate, and this Tuesday evening, Peter had come as well!

Tonight, they were beginning Genesis chapter six. Mr. Symons had everyone read verses one to eight, and then they talked about the events that led up to the great flood.

Henry put up his hand and when Mr. Symons called on him, he asked, "These 'giants' in verse four," he began awkwardly, "Um, like do angels and humans often interbreed?"

"How does your version read in Genesis six, verse four?" Mr. Symons questioned.

Henry read from his Living Bible, *"'In those days, and even afterwards, when the evil beings from the spirit world were sexually involved with human women, their children became giants, of whom so many legends are told.'"*

Mr. Symons asked for anyone who had the KJV to read their translation. Peter read, *"'There were giants in the earth in those days; and also after that, when the sons of God came in unto the daughters of men, and they bare children to them, the same became mighty men which were of old, men of renown.'"*

"This is a really good example of how a loose translation – which is more like a paraphrase, can lead to major misunderstandings," Mr. Symons pointed out. "Henry, your Bible makes it sound like angels and humans produced giant offspring. However, Peter may not come away with that idea if he only reads the KJV. We do need to be careful with paraphrases like The Message and The Living Bible. They are easy to read, but full of translator bias. The more literal translations are the NKJV, the ESV, NASB and the NIV.

Working together with the class to research Henry's question, they discovered that the Hebrew word for 'giant' was 'nephilim.' When they did a search for the word, they found that the word nephilim was used again in Numbers thirteen, verse thirty- three, referring to the giants that intimidated the spies Moses sent out. Mr. Symons stated, "Gigantism existed long after the flood had destroyed the previous Nephilim, and still occurs today."

"So, who were the 'sons of God'?" Henry interrupted. "Doesn't that refer to angels?"

"Often it does," Mr. Symons agreed. "But believers are also called 'sons of God' in Romans chapter eight, verse fourteen." He reminded everyone that back in Genesis chapter four verse twenty-six, when Seth had a son called Enosh, men began *'to call upon the name of the LORD.'* "This was," he pointed out, "the beginning of a distinction between a group who worshipped God and those who followed Cain."

"So, these were men, not angels, who married the daughters of other men?" Henry asked, wanting further clarification.

"That's right, Henry. If you read Matthew chapter twenty-two, verse thirty you will see that this couldn't possibly refer to angels."

Henry read the passage. *"'At the resurrection people will neither marry nor be given in marriage, they will be like the angels of God in heaven.'*

"Oh, I see," he said, "angels don't marry. Wow, my version sure had me thinking something weird! I'll have to find a new one," he added, looking anxious.

As a group, they then carried on to examine the wickedness described in Genesis chapter six, verse five. That led to a long discussion on the cause of sin. Mr. Henderson, who always seemed to know what questions would be asked ahead of time, handed out a new study-sheet to everyone for homework, entitled "Who Are Satan and the Devil in the Old Testament."

Because Peter was well enough to drive now, he offered to come up to Aunt Judy's on Saturday evening so they could all do the study-sheet together. Huddled together around the kitchen table with steaming cups of hot chocolate, they chatted for a bit about their experiences writing exams that week. They were all greatly relieved that the last three weeks were now over.

"Do you think you did okay?" Verity asked Peter.

"Thanks to your brother I'm sure I passed at least three of my courses," Peter replied, clapping Thomas on the shoulder.

Then, picking up the study-sheet, he glanced through it briefly with a deep sigh. "Every time I do one of these, I have to re-examine all my basic beliefs!" He groaned, "I'd like to be *right* for once."

"Do you want to *be right*—or do you want to know what's right?" Verity teased.

"Hey!" Peter responded with mock indignation. "Is this what I get for hanging around a girl who asks too many questions?"

Even though Peter was only joking, Verity sensed he was stressed.

Thomas was listening to the interchange. "In some ways," he remarked, a little unsure of himself, "it's probably harder for you to do this study, Peter, because you're sure of your beliefs already. Verity and I never really knew what we believed.

Peter nodded with a slight laugh. "Yeah, let's just say I *was* sure of my beliefs! Anyhow, we should get started."

Thomas looked in the concordance and found out that in the Old Testament, 'satan' meant *'an opponent, an adversary...or to withstand.'*

Looking up the places where 'satan' was used in Englishman's Hebrew Concordance, Peter was very surprised to come across Numbers chapter twenty-two, verse twenty-two. After they had all puzzled silently over the context and verse, he finally said, "This is an interesting one. This is the story of the prophet Balaam who wanted to prophesy against Israel for money. God warned him that he could only go if the king's men called for him in the morning. Even then, he was only allowed to say what God would tell him to say. Instead of waiting for the men to call him, Balaam got up to go with them anyway. So, God was angry and sent an angel to stop him. Now, listen to this verse," he said, astonished. *'And God's anger was kindled because he went: and the angel of the LORD stood in the way for an adversary against him...!'"*

Peter looked up. "That word 'adversary' is the same Hebrew word 'satan,'" he remarked, "yet this angel was *stopping* Balaam from sinning! I thought 'Satan' only enticed people to sin!"

"That *is* interesting!" Verity remarked, taking note of Peter's reference. "So, a good angel was being a 'satan' in a good way!"

The next reference they looked up was Second Samuel nineteen, verse twenty- two. Verity read it. *"'David replied, 'What do you and I have in common, you sons of Zeruiah? This day you have become my adversaries! Should anyone be put to death in Israel today? Do I not know that today I am king over Israel?'"* Sharing her thoughts, she added, "That word 'adversaries' is the word 'satan.' David's nephews were trying to stop David from doing what he thought was right. So, maybe being a satan to someone means opposing what they are doing, whether for good or bad."

234

There were several other such passages.[1] None of them showed conclusively that satan refers to a fallen, supernatural angel.

Knowing which passage would give everyone difficulty, Mr. Henderson had made a special section dealing with the book of Job. The word 'satan' occurs at least fourteen times in the first two chapters of this book. When Peter saw they were looking at Job, he shook his head. "There's got to be a supernatural Devil in here! How can anyone explain this any other way?"

The first question on the sheet asked the participant to determine who 'the sons of God' were. They had already looked at this in the seminar class, but there were a couple of new references. In Job thirty-eight, the 'sons of God' definitely referred to angels celebrating the creation of the world.

Peter looked up Hosea one, verse ten, and read it out loud. *"'Yet the Israelites will be like the sand on the seashore, which cannot be measured or counted. In the place where it was said to them, 'You are not my people,' they will be called 'sons of the living God.'"* Looking up, he admitted, "And here the 'sons of God' definitely refers to Israel."

Looking up the third passage on the study-sheet, Thomas read First John three, verses one to three, from the old King James and then informed them, "This says we should be called 'sons of God' now."

Peter nodded. "All right. So 'sons of God' can refer to angels or believers."

They turned their attention to what it meant to 'present themselves before God'.

"I would have thought this only means coming before God in heaven," Peter stated uncertainly.

---

[1] 1 Kings 11:14; 1 Chronicles 21:1 compare with 2 Samuel 24:1

Thomas liked to do the concordance work. "'Present' means to *'station, offer or continue,'*" he read.

Verity looked up Deuteronomy chapter thirty-one, verse fourteen. *"'The LORD said to Moses, 'Now the day of your death is near. Call Joshua and present yourselves at the Tent of Meeting, where I will commission him.'* So, Moses and Joshua came and presented themselves at the Tent of Meeting.'"

She caught Peter's eye, and he shook his head wearily. "Wrong again," he grinned. "It looks like you *can* 'present' yourself to God *on earth*. I guess the next passage will prove the same thing," Peter sighed, but he turned it up anyway.

Looking quickly at the context of First Samuel chapter ten, verse nineteen, he summarised, "Okay, Samuel is speaking here, telling the people of Israel off because they asked for a king, when God was their king. So, he says, *'And ye have this day rejected your God, who himself saved you out of all your adversities and your tribulations; and ye have said unto him, Nay, but set a king over us. Now therefore present yourselves before the LORD by your tribes, and by your thousands.'"*

Peter shrugged. "God is telling the tribes of Israel to 'present' themselves to Him. I guess you don't have to be in heaven to 'present' yourself to God."

When they looked up the three passages in Job[2] they discovered that Job always attributed his sufferings to God, never Satan. To further emphasise the point in question number three, Mr. Henderson had specifically asked them to state who was carrying out the suggestions that Satan was making.[3] When they looked these up, they saw that each one referenced Job's troubles as coming from God's hand.

---

[2] Job 1:21; 2:10; 19:21
[3] Job 1:11; 2:3 and 42:11

Thomas read the last passage on the sheet, which was Job chapter forty-two, verse eleven. *"'Then came there unto him all his brethren, and all his sisters, and all they that had been of his acquaintance before, and did eat bread with him in his house: and they bemoaned him, and comforted him over all the evil that the LORD had brought upon him: every man also gave him a piece of money...'"*

Verity noted from the concordance that there weren't any further references to Satan in the book of Job after the first two chapters.

Peter sat back trying to sort all this out. "If Satan wasn't the red guy with a pitchfork, then who was he?"

Verity reasoned, "Well, he was among the 'sons of God,' so he could have been just a man that believed in God."

"And if he was 'presenting himself before God,' maybe he was a man that believed in God, coming to worship God," Thomas added.

Tilting his head to one side, Peter frowned. "So, if he was a believer, then why did he want to do such awful things to Job?"

"Maybe he wasn't a very good believer," Thomas offered.

"That could be, Thomas!" Verity nodded. "Lots of believers in the Bible had times where they did things that were wrong. Think of David," she suggested. "He ended up taking another man's wife and then trying to figure out how to kill the man!"

It was slowly becoming more plausible to Peter. "Okay," he began, "so you mean that this Satan was a believer who had an issue with Job? Like maybe he was jealous of him?"

Verity nodded excitedly, feeling they were on to something. "Yes, jealousy might be the reason, Peter! Remember in chapter one God was telling Satan how wonderful Job was?"

Peter looked sceptical again. "That bothers me," he said, "God actually *talked* to this Satan!" He paused and considered, "But I guess back in the Old Testament, God talked to lots of people – good and bad. He talked to Balaam, he talked to Cain…"

Verity could see that Peter was carefully thinking this all through, so she waited to hear what he was going to come up with. Finally, he gave it a try. "All right, if Satan can be anyone who tries to oppose someone else, then Satan could have been an enemy of Job's that was jealous of him." He pondered this further. "God did talk directly to people in those days, so maybe after their conversations, God carried out this enemy's ideas to show him how faithful Job was."

"Maybe it was one of the *friends* who gets rebuked at the end of the book?" Verity suggested.

"Or Elihu," Thomas interjected. "He just appears – says his bit, and then is gone, just like Satan." [4]

They were all surprised that the word 'devil' does not occur at all in the entire Old Testament, although the plural 'devils' does— meaning a 'goat' or 'demon' and referring to idols.

"A goat," Peter reflected. "Maybe that is why the horns and shaggy goatee became part of the devil's appearance!"

As they worked through the rest of the study-sheet, they discussed the fact that there were no warnings about the devil or satan throughout the entire Old Testament. If this supernatural being was a danger to believers in the first four thousand years of history, surely God would have felt it was important to explain this enemy's presence and how to combat his influence. Instead, the Old Testament characters attributed the source of temptation to their own fleshly hearts.

---

[4] An excellent book on this topic: Job's Quest: Student Edition: Archard, Ethel: 9798367264463: Christianity: Amazon Canada

"God destroyed the whole world at the time of the flood," Verity mused, "because He *'saw that the wickedness of man was great in the earth, and that every imagination of the thoughts of his heart was only evil continually.'"*[5]

Peter was looking in Genesis chapter three. "You know," he pondered, "even after the temptation of Adam and Eve, God only blames the serpent, not a supernatural force inhabiting that serpent, as I've always been taught. It's the serpent who cops the punishment, and he doesn't make any attempt to blame another source."[6] It's not until Revelation – *the end* of the Bible, where we are told the serpent is the Devil."[7]

"In a book that is full of symbols and visions," Verity added. "Why did God wait so long to reveal this to everyone? Or is that vision symbolic of something else?"

No one knew the answer, but they wrote everything down on their study-sheets. Perhaps they could ask the question at the seminar.

Bent over her papers, Verity suddenly remembered something she had read in the New Testament. "Remember when Jesus said, *'Get behind me Satan'*[8] to Peter?" she asked. "I guess he was calling Peter 'Satan' because Peter was trying to stop Jesus from doing what was right."

A glance at the guys' puzzled faces indicated they didn't understand why she was saying this.

"Well, I always wondered why Jesus would call his own disciple such an awful name," she explained, "but Peter was being

---

[5] Genesis 6:5
[6] Genesis 3:1-15; 2 Corinthians 11:2
[7] Revelation 12
[8] Matthew 16:23

an adversary to Jesus. So that's why he deserved to be called 'Satan.'"

Stretching his arms out, Peter confessed, "I still have a lot of questions about this. But I must say, with so much time to think lately, it has started to bother me that there could be such a thing as a supernatural Devil or Satan. It certainly wasn't taught in the Old Testament. So, why is it so prominent in the New?"

No one had an answer, but it was certainly a good question to ask at the next seminar.

WHO ARE SATAN AND THE DEVIL IN THE O.T.?

satan-and-the-devil-in-the-old-testament.pdf (wordpress.com)

1. Consider the meaning of the word "satan" in the Old Testament using a Concordance or a Bible program: MySword - Free Android Bible

Satan – Hebrew # _____ Word _____

Strong's Definition _____

2. Examine these passages in the Old Testament where the Hebrew word "satan" is used. (You could find these yourself searching for the Heb. #)

Passage	English Word	Who or what is being satan?	How or why is this satan an adversary?
Numbers 22:22,32			
1 Samuel 29:4			
2 Samuel 24:1			
1 Chronicles 21:1			
1 Kings 5:4			
1 Kings 11:14,23,25			
Job 1:6,7,8,9,12; 2:1,2,3,4,6,7			
Psalm 109:6			
Zechariah 3:1, 2			

3. Do any passages in the chart show **conclusively** that 'satan' refers to a fallen angel/supernatural being? Y / N

4. Give your own brief definition of the word 'satan':

_____

_____

WHO IS 'SATAN' IN THE BOOK OF JOB?

"Now there was a day when the sons of God came to present themselves before the LORD, and Satan came also among them." Job 1:6
(It would be helpful to read Job 1 and 2 to get the context.)

1. Who are the 'sons of God' in Job? (These references use this phrase)
Genesis 6:2-4 _____
Deuteronomy 14:1 _____
Job 38:7 _____
Hosea 1:10 _____
1 John 3:1-3 _____

2. How did 'the sons of God' present themselves before God?
'PRESENT' – Hebrew # _____ Hebrew word _____
Strong's definition _____

3. How else is this word 'PRESENT used?

Deuteronomy 31:14 _____

1 Samuel 10:19 _____

4. To whom did Job attribute his sufferings? (Job 1:21; 2:10; 19:21)

_____

5. Who was actually implementing Satan's suggestions? (Job 1:11; 2:3; Job 42:11) _____

6. Who did God rebuke at the end of the book of Job? (Job 42:7-9)

_____

7. CONCLUSION: Who do you think was the 'satan' (adversary) in the book of Job? _____

WHAT ARE 'DEVILS' IN THE OLD TESTAMENT?

1. Do a search for "devil" in the Old Testament. Does it appear? Y / N

2. However, 2 different Hebrew words are translated as 'devils' in the KJV.

'DEVILS' – Hebrew # _____ Word _____
Strong's Definition _____

'DEVILS' – Hebrew # _____ Word _____
Strong's Definition _____

3. If you do a search for these numbers in the O.T., you will find the following occurrences and others. Comment on the use of 'DEVILS':

SAIYR (TRANSLATED MANY X AS 'GOAT' AND 2X AS 'DEVILS')	Comments
Leviticus 9:3 ... Take ye a **kid** <sa`iyr> of the goats for a sin offering; and a calf and a lamb, both of the first year, without blemish, for a burnt offering;	
Leviticus 17:7 And they shall no more offer their sacrifices unto **devils** <sa`iyr>, after whom they have gone a whoring. This shall be a statute for ever unto them throughout their generations.	
2 Chronicles. 11:15 And he ordained him priests for the high places, and for the **devils** <sa`iyr>, and for the calves which he had made.	
Daniel 8:21 And the rough <sa`iyr> goat is the king of Grecia: and the great horn that is between his eyes is the first king.	

4. What is significant about the Hebrew word 'saiyr' being translated 'goat'? (Think of the popular image of the 'devil') _____

SHED (ONLY APPEARS 2X IN O.T as 'DEVILS')	Comments
Deuteronomy 32:17 They sacrificed unto **devils** <shed>, not to God; to gods whom they knew not, to new gods that came newly up, whom your fathers feared not.	
Psalm 106:36-38 And they served their idols: which were a snare unto them. Yea, they sacrificed their sons and their daughters unto **devils** <shed>, And shed innocent blood, even the blood of their sons and of their daughters, whom they sacrificed unto the idols of Canaan: and the land was polluted with blood. 39 Thus were they defiled with their own works, and went a whoring with their own inventions.	

5. What are both 'saiyr' and 'shed' associated with in the Old Testament?
_____

6. Can you find the cross-reference from Psalm 106:36-39 to a New Testament passage, and what does it say? _____
_____

CONCLUSION: 'Devils' in the Old Testament refer to:
_____

243

ISAIAH 14 – WHO IS LUCIFER?
Isaiah 14 speaks of "Lucifer" (meaning 'daystar') in the KJV. Read through the entire chapter to get the context and determine who Lucifer is. (Comment on anything helpful, especially in verses 4, 11,16-17)

EZEKIEL 28 – THE KING OF TYRE
Ezekiel 28 speaks of the King of Tyre. Chapters 27 & 28 give the context.
1. Comment on any helpful verses: _____

2. What special connection did the King of Tyre have with Israel and the Temple in Jerusalem?
2 Samuel 5:11_____
1 Kings 5:1 _____
DOES GOD HAVE A SUPERNATURAL RIVAL?
1. Does God indicate He has a supernatural rival?
Isaiah 45: 5-7, 20-21 _____
Isaiah 46: 9-10 _____
2. Can you find any Old Testament passage that cautions us to fear someone other than God? _____
3. Compare your answer with 2 Kings 17:33-41_____

4. The O.T. was the only Scripture record for 4000 years before Jesus Christ. If God has a Supernatural rival, would it be important to warn believers of this dangerous being? **Yes / No**

WHAT IS THE SOURCE OF EVIL?
1. In the O.T. , what source of evil did God tell/warn His creation about? And what did believers perceive was the source of temptation?
CAIN: Genesis 4:6-7 _____

NOAH: Genesis 6:5-13 _____

Genesis 8:21 _____

SOLOMON: 1 Kings 8:38 _____

JEREMIAH: Jeremiah 17:9-10 _____

MESSIANIC PROPHECY: Isaiah 53 - is there anything in this prophecy about Jesus conquering a supernatural being who is opposed to God?

These definitions at left are taken from *Strong's Concordance*.
Below this is a selection of relevant verses extracted from
Englishman's Hebrew Concordance.

[H7853] (satan/saw-tan') a primitive root; to attack,
(figuratively) accuse:--(be an) adversary, resist. [H7854]
(satan/saw-tawn') from 7853; an opponent; especially (with
the article prefixed) Satan, the arch-enemy of good:--
adversary, Satan, withstand. see H7853

Nu. 22:22 the angel of the LORD stood in the
way for *an adversary* <07854>
　　32 I went out *to withstand* <07854> thee,
　　(marg. *to be an adversary*)
1Sa 29:4 lest in the battle he be *an adversary*
　　<07854>
2Sa 19:22 ye sons of Zeruiah, that ye should this
　　day be *adversaries* <07854>
1Ki 5:4 there is neither *adversary* <07854> nor
　　evil occurrent.
　　11:14 the LORD stirred up *a n adversary*
　　<07854> unto Solomon, Hadad
　　23 God stirred him up another *adversary*
　　<07854>, Rezon the son of
　　25 he was an *adversary* <07854> to Israel
1Ch 21:1 *Satan* stood up against Israel.

Job 1:6 *Satan* (marg. *the adversary*) came also
　　among them.
　　7, 8, 12 the LORD said unto *Satan*
　　—9 Then *Satan* answered the LORD
　　12 *Satan* went forth from the presence of
　　2:1 *Satan* came also among them
　　2, 3, 6 the LORD said unto *Satan*,
　　—,4 *Satan* answered the LORD,
　　7 So went *Satan* forth from the presence of
　　the LORD, and smote Job with sore boils
Ps 109:6 and let *Satan* (marg. or, *an adversary*)
　　stand at his right hand.
Zec 3:1 and *Satan* (marg. or, *an adversary*)
　　standing at his right hand to resist him.
　　2 the LORD said unto *Satan*, The LORD
　　rebuke thee, *O Satan*;

CHAPTER 30

Does It Matter?

On Sunday evening, February the first, Verity went with the Bryants to the special talk at their church in Amberhill. Walking up to the building with Peter, she marvelled at the building itself, which was huge, modern and beautiful. Rays of light shone through a lovely stained-glass window over the door. There was a large meeting hall in the centre with many benches, a proper stage and a massive pipe organ.

"So many people must go here!" she thought. "Can they really all be wrong?" Uncertainty flooded her thoughts. How could she, one little person with a Bible, be finding fault with the teachings of a huge church like this? She was no one special, still just a teenager—and here in this church were pastors who had trained for years in Theology! Quietly she followed Peter past all the wooden pews to find a seat at the front.

As they sat there waiting for the program to begin, Verity started thinking back on what she'd read in the Bible. Was there ever a time when the majority of people were right? She remembered how over and over in the Old Testament the majority of people had disobeyed God. In Noah's day, only eight people were saved in the ark. With the destruction of Sodom and Gomorrah, only Lot and his two daughters escaped. Of all the Israelites whom God brought out of Egypt and tested for forty years in the wilderness, Joshua and Caleb were the only adults which left Egypt and also entered the Promised Land. It went on and on throughout the whole Bible. So many of the prophets that God sent to his own people Israel were rejected by them—sometimes even killed because the majority of people hated hearing what God had to say.

Even in Jesus' day, huge crowds of people had called for Christ's crucifixion. The Jews were people who claimed to follow God! They read and studied the Scriptures. They trusted that they were God's chosen people—yet they killed the Messiah that they were all waiting for! There were only a few faithful followers at the foot of the cross and even they didn't understand why Jesus had to die.

Disconcerted, she recalled that it was the Jewish religious leaders, those who professed to know the Old Testament the best, who were instrumental in putting Jesus to death!

Verity remembered Mr. Symons' words about checking everything he said with the Bible. She remembered how he had told them in one of the sessions that the Jewish people had volumes upon volumes of their own writings and traditions, which blinded them to understanding the simple truth in the Scriptures.

"How easy it is," she thought, "to give up our own responsibility to think and just trust those we esteem as 'the experts.' A person would have to have a strong desire to find 'the truth' in the Bible, in order to put in the effort to search for it."

Peter nudged her arm, and she became aware that he had probably nudged her a few times. "What were you thinking about?" he laughed quietly, his brown eyes teasing. "You were a million miles away!"

She gave her head a little shake and said, "Let me show you a verse."

"Already?!" Peter questioned, exaggerating his astonishment. "The talk hasn't even begun yet!"

"I know," she smiled, as she flipped through Matthew. "But you asked me what I was thinking about!" Finding the highlighted passage in chapter seven, she pointed out the words of Jesus to him. *"Enter through the narrow gate. For wide is the way and broad is the road that leads to destruction, and many enter through it. But small is the gate and narrow is the road that leads to life and only a few find it."*

Looking very puzzled, Peter asked, "And what does that have to do with anything?"

Before she could explain, she noticed that the program was about to begin so she just whispered in his ear, "I'll tell you later."

Lively, up-beat singing began the evening. The performers were impressive. In the church Verity had attended in Saskatchewan, there had only been a piano. Tonight's program was true entertainment and she realized how attractive that would be for many people.

Once the presentation began, the Pastor did turn up several Scriptures and make a good case for the Trinity. John one, Colossians one, Philippians two were powerfully presented, but having already discussed these with Mr. Symons, Verity knew there was more than one way to view them. There were also many quotations from Church Fathers who had written elaborate and extensive treatises on the subject, which were hard to understand. Over and over the Pastor referred to the Trinity as a Mystery that would only be perfectly understood in heaven. However, she also stated that anyone who didn't believe the Trinity was degrading the person of Jesus by not exalting him as God; therefore, they could not be considered 'Christian.'

Finding a small scrap of paper in her Bible, Verity wrote a note to Peter. "But, Mr. Symons says if you believe in the Trinity, you don't see the victory Jesus had over sin. If Jesus was God, then he couldn't be tempted. If he was a God-man, like the legendary Greek heroes, then overcoming sin and submitting to death would be like an Olympic athlete winning a race against a two-year old. It would be simply a 'given,' not an incredible feat."

Peter nodded thoughtfully and wrote back on the other side. "I never noticed before just how many times the Trinity is referred to as a Mystery!"

Verity returned, "If it's wrong, then it certainly doesn't have any chance of being understood."

When the presentation was over, the congregation rose to sing a hymn. Scanning the words in Peter's hymnbook, Verity decided she couldn't participate. The phrases in the hymn were exalting Jesus as God, and the Holy Spirit as God. That was not what she believed was true, so how could she sing them as praise to the one true God?

Peter however had sung the hymns of praise since he was a small boy and joined right in with a strong, tenor voice.

Verity pointed to some of the phrases, but Peter just looked at her and shrugged. The prayer made her uneasy too. There were several references to God, Jesus, and the Holy Spirit being one and the same. How could she join in worship with someone who was praying to a different God than she believed in? Would God be pleased with a prayer that praised Him for things that weren't Biblical?

On the way home in the car, Mr. and Mrs. Bryant had a lengthy discussion about how good the evening's talk had been. This left Verity and Peter a chance to chat privately in the back. She didn't need to say a word to Peter about how she felt; she could tell he had sensed her discomfort.

"Verity," he appealed in a hushed tone, "I know that hymn was saying things about God that I'm not sure I believe anymore, but…" He stopped, trying to think of how he could explain. "I've done a lot of thinking, and praying and reading these last few weeks," he carried on quietly. "I've come to realize that at least a few of my beliefs have been wrong. But, my parents, my pastor, my brother… they'd all be so upset with me if I were to leave their church!"

"*'Anyone who loves his father and mother more than me, is not worthy of me…* '"[1] Verity began, quoting Jesus' words.

---

[1] Matthew 10:37

Peter sighed. "I know that quote and I know you've done that in your own life, but I don't think God cares so much about what we believe or who we fellowship with, as how we *act,* how we *live* our lives."

This didn't sit completely well with Verity. "Peter," she exclaimed in a half-whisper, "why wouldn't you want to know what's true? I know how important honesty is to you! Why wouldn't you want to tell others exactly what God has said?" Frowning anxiously, she added, "The Bible has been given to us by God—a God who says He hates lying.[2] Don't you think He would want us to be extremely careful not to misrepresent Him?"

Pondering this for a moment or two, Peter at last shook his head and replied firmly, "No, I think that God is more concerned that we live a good life, that we honour our parents and are kind to our neighbours. God doesn't want us to argue and fight about what He's said or hasn't said."

Verity was perplexed. She wondered what had caused Peter feel this way? "Is that what you'd like to believe?" she asked quietly. "Or have you come to that conclusion from reading the Bible?"

Peter stared at her blankly for a few moments. "Okay," he said, a grin spreading on his face, "and where would you turn in the Bible to prove to me that beliefs matter?!"

She smiled, admitting, "I might need to do some research."

A few minutes later, she spoke up quietly. " I'm not saying that our actions and behaviour are not important," she clarified, "Of course they are. We are to honour our parents and be kind to people. God doesn't want us to fight and argue and be mean to people. But," she was searching for the right words, "...our actions have to be based on the truth about God, who he really is, otherwise it's just based on our own human thought."

---

[2] 2 Proverbs 6:16–17 and 12:22; Revelation 21:8, 27

Peter's frown indicated that he didn't see the distinction. It was all so clear in Verity's mind, but she was struggling to put her thoughts into words.

For a few minutes they sat in silence, gazing out the window at the traffic speeding by. With her mind in a whirl, Verity tried hard to think of a verse to answer Peter's question. Where had she got the idea that beliefs mattered to God? Was there a passage somewhere that would prove it? Opening her Bible, she began flipping through the Gospels, scanning the pages quickly. Peter leaned over to see what she'd find. At last, she came to John chapter four, verses twenty-two to twenty-four, where Jesus was talking to a Samaritan woman who was very confused about what she should believe. Here was a verse! She pointed out Jesus' words to Peter. *"You Samaritans worship what you do not know; we worship what we do know, for salvation is from the Jews. Yet a time is coming and has now come when the true worshippers will worship the Father in spirit and truth, for they are the kind of worshippers the Father seeks. God is spirit, and his worshippers must worship in spirit and in truth."*

"Not bad," Peter smiled. But Verity could see in his eyes that this was a very serious issue to him, and it would take a lot more than one verse to convince him otherwise.

After another period of silence, he spoke quietly so that his parents wouldn't hear. "Verity, this is a huge step for me. It's one thing to realize that some of my beliefs have been wrong, but to leave the church that my whole family attends… is… is *major!* I'd need to be convinced beyond any shadow of a doubt, to do that."

When they drove up to her house, Verity graciously thanked the Bryants for the ride and the presentation, and then reached over to open the door. Peter jumped out and ran to her side to help her out. She was quite thankful, for the weak feeling had come again and it was so embarrassing to fall.

Noticing that she was limping slightly, Peter begged, "You know, this is becoming a regular occurrence. If you don't go to see a doctor soon, I'll have to drag you there myself!"

"I just have a weak leg, Peter," she said colouring slightly. "It doesn't really seem to be getting any worse."

"It is worse," he said, with real concern in his voice. Gravely, he observed, "You're limping. I don't remember that happening before."

She opened her front door and promised, "I'll go to the doctor when things slow down." Then she added with a little smile, "But that may not be until school is over!"

CHAPTER 31

In the Heart

The wind was howling up the driveway and around the house when Verity and Thomas stepped off the school bus Tuesday afternoon. All the way home visibility had been poor, as snow squalls passed over the area, causing near-whiteout conditions. Normally, Verity didn't mind a good snowstorm if she could stay safe and warm at home. Tonight, however, was the seminar night; the night they were to discuss the 'satan' study-sheet. She really didn't want to miss it.

"How was the ride home?" Kara asked anxiously, as the two of them entered the house.

"Not great," Thomas replied. "I'm surprised that the Highway isn't closed. Some places were pretty bad."

"I doubt the seminars will be on tonight," Kara remarked, as she carried on cooking supper.

Verity took a deep breath. "Oh, maybe it will calm down by six-thirty."

Aunt Judy came into the kitchen with a plate of cookies. "They're calling for the storm to last all night, Dear," she said. "Missing one session won't hurt. Besides, Mr. Symons might not even make it."

Verity waited patiently until six o'clock. She knew it was nasty out, but she'd seen weather worse than this. After all, it was only a ten-minute trip. Finally, she decided to call Mr. Symons and see what his plans were.

"Yes, I'm hoping to go tonight," he replied. "I drove home from school, and it was bad but I could still see fairly well." He added, "Most of the people who come to the seminars live right in town, so they won't have any trouble making it. Do you still want a ride?"

Kara was hesitant to let them go but at last she gave in. It wasn't so terrible that she felt it was impossible to drive safely.

Shortly thereafter, Mr. Symons arrived alone at their house. He explained that his wife had stayed home because their two daughters were coming down with colds. Verity and Thomas piled into his car before their mom could change her mind. The snow was gusting wildly across the road, but as they came up to the highway, a big snowplow with its flashing blue lights passed in front of them.

"Now there's an answer to prayer," Mr. Symons chuckled.

"You prayed for a snowplow?" Thomas asked.

"Well," he smiled, turning onto the highway, "I prayed before I left that God would go with us and keep us safe. Perhaps a snowplow is His way of helping us."

"So, if I wanted to jump over Niagara Falls, would I only need to pray to God for safety?" Thomas questioned.

Mr. Symons looked across at Thomas, who was sitting in the front with him, in a serious manner. "That actually raises quite a deep issue..." he began.

Thomas nodded. "Well, when is a person just acting crazy and when is he or she doing what's right?"

"The line between acting foolishly or acting in faith *is* sometimes hard to see," Mr. Symons agreed, following very slowly behind the huge, lumbering snowplow. "We have to carefully examine our motives before choosing to do something dangerous. Remember, that *was* one of Jesus' temptations. He knew that if he threw himself down from the temple in front of all the people, the angels would have to rescue him. Then all the people would see how important he was. If what we are doing is for our own self-glory or to get praise from others, we would be sinning to test God in that way."

A huge transport truck passed them at that moment, throwing slush all over their windshield. For a moment, Mr. Symons concentrated on driving carefully; then he continued, "Tonight, for instance, requires some discretion. If it were so bad that the highway was closed, then no, I wouldn't risk it. However, I'm not heading out to the seminars for my own glory but to try and share God's Word with others. If I shrink from this because of a little bad weather, where is my faith? If I know in my heart that I would take the risk to go to a fun family outing, how can I not try just as hard for the things of God?"

"Sometimes," Verity put in, "we think if we are doing God's Will, then everything should be made easy for us."

"That's true, Verity," Mr. Symons said. "Yet, when we carefully consider people's lives in the Bible, we come to appreciate that God tests good people with bad times to strengthen their faith. Poor Abraham came to the land God had told him to go to and found himself in a famine!"

"And Joseph," added Verity. "He refused to commit adultery with Potiphar's wife and then spent years in prison because she lied about him."

"Right," nodded Mr. Symons, "or Daniel who prayed to God, even though it was forbidden by the King's laws, and was then thrown into the lion's den."

"And his three friends who wouldn't bow down to the idol were thrown into the fiery furnace."

"All right," said Thomas, eager to feel a part of the conversation. "I have one. How about Jesus, who did everything God asked him to and then was beaten and crucified?"

"That is the ultimate example, Thomas," Mr. Symons nodded, as they pulled up to the library. "All those people were able to have faith even in difficult times because their eyes were on the future age to come. What happened to them in this life was trivial, compared to the joy they believed the Kingdom age would bring."

Since they had driven so slowly, they arrived a few minutes late. Most people were already seated and waiting for the class to begin. As they trooped in, Verity saw Peter, Emily and Kate sitting in the middle row. They waved and she smiled back.

"I wasn't sure you'd make it tonight," Peter whispered, as they sat down in the seats he'd saved.

"If it hadn't been for Mr. Symons and his faith in God—we wouldn't have," she said smiling. Before she could explain further, Mr. Symons stood up to start the class.

The evening began as usual with a reading from Genesis. Verity loved reading the Bible at the seminars. Sometimes just a few verses provided enough questions and answers to last a whole hour. She was amazed how much they could discover by using cross-references. The whole Bible was truly tied together from start to finish.[1] Tonight's reading of Genesis six led to a further discussion on what causes people to sin. Mr. Symons pointed out that before the great flood, the world was becoming a terrible place, 'filled with violence.' He explained that because the flood is recorded in the sixth chapter of Genesis, it seems to come quite quickly after creation; but in reality, approximately one thousand, six hundred and fifty years had elapsed! Demonstrating with a few mathematical calculations, he showed the group that the population of the earth at this time could easily have been in the millions, if not billions of people. "During this time period," he said, "the world environment was likely vastly superior to what we presently experience, and

---

[1]

people were living up to nine hundred years! Knowledge would surely have increased at an alarming rate."

"Today," Mr. Symons contrasted, "people spend twenty years of their life just learning what is already known. Then they have perhaps thirty to forty years to discover new inventions and search out greater understanding. Imagine if you had five hundred years to be productive in this way?" Because of this, Mr. Symons felt the world in Noah's day was very much like our modern world. People were becoming more and more concerned with acquiring fame, wealth and reputation. They were highly successful and independent, no longer seeing a need for God in their lives. In the midst of all this, Noah alone was singled out to be righteous.

"Where did God say the source of all this wickedness was?" Mr. Symons asked.

From doing the study-sheet, Verity knew the answer. She raised her hand. "In verse five of Genesis chapter six, God blames it on the thoughts and imaginations of the people."

"Exactly," nodded Mr. Symons, "so whether there is a supernatural devil or not, it *is* possible for man's *own* thoughts and imaginations to lead to wickedness so great that God has to destroy them!"

Mr. Henderson reminded everyone of the first sin they had read about in Genesis chapter three, when Eve had taken the forbidden fruit. The serpent in the Garden of Eden had tempted Eve to disobey God. Reading aloud Genesis chapter three, verses one to four, Mr. Henderson pointed out that the serpent contradicted God by saying that Adam and Eve would not *'surely die.'* In other words, the serpent lied.

As a group they recalled the process Eve went through in her temptation, noting: her desire to taste the fruit, that it was pleasant to her eyes, and it appealed to her pride—she would *'be like God'*!

Turning to First John chapter two, verses sixteen to seventeen, the same three types of temptation were referred to again, with no mention of a supernatural 'devil' being involved. *"For all that is in the world, the lust of the flesh, and the lust of the eyes, and the pride of life, is not of the Father, but is of the world."*

Finally, Mr. Henderson concluded the class, by going over their answers to the study-sheet on 'Who Are Satan and the Devil in the Old Testament?' Most people had come to similar conclusions as Verity, Peter, and Thomas. Mr. Henderson suggested a few other possibilities for who the 'satan' could be, but he agreed that the idea of 'satan' being a believer who was jealous of Job's success was quite plausible. "It's very interesting to note," he said, "that Job remained faithful through all of the painful losses he endured in the first two chapters. However, beginning in chapter four with the false accusations of these three friends, Job ends up saying things that he greatly regrets later when God rebukes him. His 'friends' nasty insinuations provoked him to sin with his lips, which the hardships did not. So, whether or not they were the 'satan' of chapters one and two, they certainly were a 'satan' to him for the rest of the book! At the end of the story Job is instructed by God to pray and sacrifice for his friends, so that God will forgive them!"

Mr. Henderson then proceeded to give some guidelines for examining the subject of the devil in the New Testament. "Firstly, we need to remember that the Old and the New Testaments do not contradict one another," he began. "The New is the fulfilment of the Old, not a contradictory revelation. The people living during the four thousand years of the Old Testament weren't given false information.

"If you read the Old Testament," he continued, "you will notice that none of the Old Testament characters ever plead with God that they have been tempted by the devil. All of them freely acknowledge that they sinned because they gave into their own wicked thoughts. As we read tonight, the serpent that lied to Eve was punished for his lie and he didn't blame anyone else. If a 'supernatural Devil' was really the voice behind the serpent, then God should have had something to say against this Devil, as well.

"Before the flood," he continued on, "God *'saw that the wickedness of man was great, every imagination of the thoughts of his heart was only evil continually.'* Here, God didn't say that people were being led away by a rebellious angel; no, it was their own hearts leading them away from God. Even after the flood, God's assessment of their thoughts was the same. In Genesis chapter eight, verse twenty-one, God says, *'I will not again curse the ground any more for man's sake; for the imagination of man's heart is evil from his youth.'*

Giving examples, he referred to Job. "As we've just considered—through all his trials and suffering Job always identified his troubles as coming from God's chastening hand.

"The prophet Jeremiah states, *'The heart is deceitful above all things, and desperately wicked: who can know it?'*[2]

"So, all the way through the Old Testament, it is clearly acknowledged that 'satan' refers to that which is adversarial to another—for good or evil. Unfortunately, bound up within each one of us is our own human nature, which is often adversarial to God and His ways!

"Clearly the concept of the Devil doesn't occur in the Old Testament. So why is it so much more prevalent in the New?" Mr. Henderson looked around at the group, but no one offered an explanation. Instead, Verity and Peter waited eagerly for the answer.

After a pause, Mr. Henderson continued, "Again, the influence of the Persian culture and folklore was prevalent on the Jewish people at this time, especially up in the north where foreign ideas were rife.[3] If you research Persian dualism, you will find it is similar to the concept of the Devil, as a supernatural evil being,

---

[2] Jeremiah 17:9
[3] 2 Kings 17

dueling with the God of good.[4] But, ask yourself one critical question," he encouraged. "The question is—What did Jesus accomplish for mankind in his life and death?"

Peter, who had been following the discussion intently, spoke up. "He died to conquer sin and provide a way of salvation for us."

"Good answer," Mr. Henderson replied. "As Peter said, the whole focus of Christ's mission was to *'destroy him that had the power of death, that is, the devil.'*[5] His sacrificial death provided a way of escape from the *'wages of sin [which] is death.'*[6] He also needed to show us the example of how to overcome sin ourselves. Jesus came to fight and overcome the battle with sin – personal sin."

Turning again to the audience, Mr. Henderson asked, "Is it sin when a wrong thought comes to our mind?"

Nobody was quite sure.

"Well, no," he answered, "the thought itself is not counted to us as sin—it's what we do with that thought. If we allow the temptation to stay in our minds, and we enjoy its presence, fan the flames or commit the actual sin it suggests, then we have sinned.[7] However, if we overcome it by banishing it from our thoughts, as Jesus did by the power of God's Word in his mind, [8]then it is not sin. In order for us to appreciate the daily struggle we all undergo with our human nature, that little 'bad' voice is described as 'the devil.' It is to be seen in parable form, an analogy or metaphor, if you will, as an enemy who is always trying to draw us away from loving our Father. We need to see our own nature in that light and go to 'war' with it, as the Bible says. Now if we were instead to view this enemy as a powerful, evil angel, suddenly we would no longer be taking

---

[4] Persian Dualism - The Atlantic
[5] Hebrews 2:14
[6] Romans 6:23
[7] James 1:14–15
[8] Luke 4:1–13

full responsibility for our own actions but blaming them on something else."

Peter glanced over at Verity with a little smile, remembering their conversation not so very long ago.

After the seminar was over that evening, Verity was eagerly discussing the study-sheet with Emily when she noticed Thomas walking up to Mr. Symons with a book. It was the book she had been looking for! The one she had borrowed from Mr. Symons for the creation presentation! So, Thomas had been reading it all this time? She laughed to herself. Had her brother actually been interested enough to start reading that book way back when she had practised her creation presentation at home?

Mr. Symons graciously received the book back and the two of them stood chatting for quite awhile.

CHAPTER 32

Snowed In

Walking out of the library that evening to go home, they were all surprised to see how much worse the storm had become. At least twenty centimetres of snow had fallen and Mr. Symons' car was completely covered with drifts. Thankfully, in the winter he always carried a shovel, so Peter and Thomas set to work right away to help him move away the snow. Verity found the ice-scraper in the car and did her best to brush all the snow off the windows. After twenty minutes of hard work, Mr. Symons tried to back up out of the parking lot but he was still quite stuck. All three of them had to help push the car out. It took several tries before they finally pushed it back on to the road.

"You know," said Peter anxiously as they were about to leave, "it looks a lot worse now than it did before. I think you should all stay over at my place. My mom won't mind."

"Thanks, Peter," Mr. Symons nodded appreciatively, "We'll give it an honest try, but we'll definitely keep that in mind."

Peter left, and the rest of them climbed into Mr. Symons car. They prayed for God's guidance and protection on their trip home and then they drove slowly through town. The roads were deeply covered in snow and the wind made it hard to see, even with the shelter of houses on each side. When they finally came to the intersection with the Highway, barriers were up, declaring the road closed.

Mr. Symons hesitated. "I do know a back way home... but I think it might be better to take Peter up on his offer!"

Back they drove across town. Following Thomas and Verity's directions, they made it at last to Peter's house. A welcome light glowed from the living room window. They were all relieved not to have to drive any further.

Peter came quickly to the door at the sound of their knock and happily ushered them in. Mr. and Mrs. Bryant greeted everyone pleasantly and shook Mr. Symons' hand. "You must be cold," Mrs. Bryant said compassionately. "I'll make you all a hot drink."

Mr. Symons asked if he could make a couple of phone calls to explain to his wife and Kara Lovell why they wouldn't be coming home. While he was doing this, Peter led Thomas and Verity into the living room to warm up in front of the fire.

Sitting down on a big sheepskin rug, Verity soaked in the heat. Thomas stretched out on the carpet and Peter sat down between them.

"This is a bonus!" Peter said with a grin. "I was just thinking on the way home, that I had another question to ask Mr. Symons."

While they were waiting for the adults to join them, Verity noticed several photograph albums on a big bookshelf against the wall. One in particular attracted her attention. It was a mid-sized album with gold letters on the spine that spelled 'PETER.'

"Ooh, do you mind if I have a look at these photo albums?" she asked excitedly.

Peter shrugged. "Not at all."

Verity walked over and picked up the 'PETER' album.

"There are better ones," Peter groaned. "My mom put that one together."

She smiled. "This one looks interesting to me!"

As she opened it up, Thomas jumped to his feet and came to sit on the other side of her. "Ah, baby Peter," he commented as they turned to the first picture. Two small boys—with 'big-brother' smiles—were holding a little baby wrapped in blue.

"Your brothers!" Verity remarked with interest.

"Yes, they're older than I am. Andrew is five years older," he said, pointing to a scrawny-looking boy with blond hair and freckles, "and James is three. They both live in the Maritimes now and work for my mom's brother."

The album seemed to be a sampling of Mrs. Bryant's favourite pictures, for the next photo was of Peter learning to walk. Then there was Peter pulling the cat's tail and Peter making a mess with chocolate cake.

"What a *cute* little boy you were," Verity murmured.

Thomas and Verity flipped slowly through the pictures of a small lad being read stories, attempting to hold a baseball bat, and playing with his brothers.

Suddenly, on the next page, Peter slapped his hand down over the photo before they could see it.

"You can look at all the rest but not this one!" he said, with laughter in his eyes.

Very curious, Verity exclaimed, "Now I have to see it!" She tried hard to pry his hand off. "Help me, Thomas," she called out, but Thomas shook his head.

Realizing she didn't have the strength on her own, she gave up, saying, "Okay, I'll turn the page."

Peter turned it for her carefully, so he could keep the picture from view. School photos were next. Verity and Thomas had fun picking out which boy was Peter among all the other students. Since this was their first year in Grandville, it was also interesting to see many of their classmates as youngsters. Some they recognised right away, but others Peter had to point out. A few of them had changed so much that Thomas roared with laughter.

When Verity felt Peter's guard was down, she quickly flipped back to the page with the secret photo. Both she and Thomas burst out laughing as Peter tried to cover it in vain. A darling three-year old boy with straight, blond hair in a pageboy cut and big, brown eyes, smiled out at them. He was all dressed up to go somewhere special. Between the haircut and fancy little outfit, he looked much more like a girl than a boy.

Thomas doubled over in laughter. "I can't believe you haven't burned that one, Peter!"

"I can't," moaned Peter. "It's my mom's favourite. She always wished she'd had a girl."

Verity was studying it carefully. "I think it's gorgeous," she said, "you would have made a pretty little girl."

Peter looked at her sideways. "Thanks for the compliment!" he said sarcastically.

As they flipped through the last part of the album, Verity realized how much she didn't know about Peter's life. There were a lot of camping, canoeing and fishing pictures. His brothers were in many of the photos and they all looked so happy together as a family. Now she appreciated a little more how close he was to his parents and the siblings she had never met.

"Is this James or Andrew?" she asked him, pointing to one of the brothers whose dark colouring was in great contrast to Peter's. "He seems to be with you the most."

"That's James," Peter replied. "He's only three years older than me so we were pretty close growing up. Andrew's kind of a typical firstborn—thinks he knows everything. But James is just a really good friend, kind of goofy, kind of serious but always right there for anyone who needs him." Peter paused and then added, "I wish he didn't live so far away!"

This was all a surprise to Verity. Until tonight she hadn't thought much about his family. She continued turning the pages with growing interest.

"How come you're not saying, I'm 'so cute' anymore?" Peter teased.

Verity laughed.

"She's probably trying to think of a better word," Thomas laughed. "You could use handsome, good-looking, drop-dead gorgeous... or just 'photogenic' if you wanted to be subtle..."

Feeling that she was being set up, Verity kept her head down studying the pictures and thinking of how best to respond. There was no doubt that Peter was handsome, but he was so much more than that!

"That's not *all* that I like about him," she murmured quietly, a smile spreading across her face.

"Pardon me? I didn't quite hear what you said," Peter said, leaning over, and trying to sound like he was still just teasing.

Laughing, Verity repeated herself a little more loudly.

"Like, or *love?*" Peter prodded with a grin.

She giggled. "The 'v' word might be more accurate."

Peter squeezed her hand meaningfully. Thomas raised his eyebrows, but just at that moment, Mr. Symons and the Bryants came back into the room. Handing each of the teens a hot drink, the adults settled down on the couch.

Becoming serious again, Peter remembered the question he had been pondering. "Mr. Symons, a few classes ago you mentioned something about the nation of Israel, that they were fulfilling Bible prophecy right now. I don't understand why God would give the land of Israel back to the Jews, when most of them don't even believe in Him, and the ones that believe in God, don't accept Christ."

With an understanding smile, Mr. Symons nodded. "That's one of my favourite questions to answer, Peter! What we have seen happen with the nation of Israel in the last century is a miracle! Right before our very eyes, we've been able to see Bible prophecies fulfilled to the letter. Do any of you know why there *wasn't* a nation of Israel for almost two thousand years?"

Mr. Bryant commented, "I suppose because the Jews rejected Jesus as their Messiah, so God allowed the Romans to totally overthrow them."

"Right," Mr. Symons agreed. "Many places in the Gospels Jesus warned them that this would happen because they refused to accept him for who he was.[1] So, God punished His people. Now the question is, did God ever intend to show favour upon the Jewish nation again, or was He completely finished with them?"

"I thought that God is working with all nations now," Peter replied, stretching out his legs comfortably and leaning back on his arms. "Aren't we in the 'times of Gentiles'? Or something like that?"

Mr. Symons nodded. "Yes, Peter, that's true. Maybe Romans chapter eleven is a good place to start." He opened up the Bible that he had brought in with him and Peter jumped up to grab his own.

To give them a sense of the context, Mr. Symons tried to show them from the beginning of the chapter that Paul was discussing this very issue. *"Hath God cast away his people?"* was the opening question of the chapter. The following verses explained that God had stopped working nationally with Israel for a period of time, nearly two thousand years, giving the Gentiles—the other nations— the opportunity to be guardians of the Gospel message and take it to the world. "But look at verses twenty-five to twenty-eight," he continued. "Thomas, maybe you could read verse twenty-five?"

Thomas read, *"'For I would not, brethren, that ye should be ignorant of this mystery, lest ye should be wise in your own conceits;*

---

[1] e.g., Matthew 8:8–12

that blindness in part is happened to Israel, until the fullness of the Gentiles be come in.'"

"So, is there an end to Israel's blindness, Thomas?" Mr. Symons asked.

"Yes," he replied, "it says they'll be blind *'until the fullness of the Gentiles be come in.'"*

"Right; and 'fullness' just means 'full number.' Peter, can you read verse twenty-six?"

He read, *"'And so all Israel shall be saved: as it is written, There shall come out of Zion the Deliverer, and shall turn away ungodliness from Jacob.'"*

Mr. Symons looked around. "Does anyone know who this Deliverer refers to?" When he saw everyone shaking their heads, he explained, "This refers to Christ, returning to the earth. He is the Deliverer! Notice that this deliverance connects with Israel being saved and ungodliness being turned away from the Jews. The word 'Jacob' is commonly used in the Bible to refer to all of Israel. Verity, could you please read verses twenty-seven to twenty-eight?"

She did. *"'For this is my covenant unto them, when I shall take away their sins. As concerning the gospel, they are enemies for your sakes: but as touching the election, they are beloved for the fathers' sakes.'"*

"Why would Paul say the Jews were enemies for the believers' sakes?" Mr. Symons questioned.

Mr. Bryant spoke out again, "Well, the Jews were persecuting the believers at that time."

"That's right!" said Mr. Symons, impressed. "And why are the Jews beloved for *the fathers'* sake?"

Verity had the answer to this. "Because of the promises God made to their forefathers, Abraham, Isaac, Jacob and David."

"Yes," he agreed. "The Jews called these Old Testament individuals their fathers. So, God is saying here that He loves the Jews because of what He had promised long ago to their early fathers. Now, I could take you to passage after passage in the Old Testament prophecies where God talks about restoring the Jews to the land that He promised to Abraham.[2] Verity has been quite interested in these promises," he stated, with a smile in her direction, "and she knows Abraham was promised the land of Israel for his descendants and also for himself!"

Turning back in his Bible, Mr. Symons continued, "I'll just take you to one of these prophecies—Ezekiel chapter thirty-six. If you read this chapter and the next three, you will find it very exciting reading. These four chapters only began to be fulfilled in the twentieth century, and they won't be completely fulfilled until Jesus has returned to earth to deliver Israel from a massive, northern invasion."

Reading through Ezekiel chapter thirty-six, verses seventeen to twenty, Mr. Symons showed them that this prophecy explained how God would scatter Israel into all countries of the earth because they had displeased Him so much in their own land. Everywhere the Jews were driven it would have been a slur against God. They were supposed to be the people of God and now it would look to other nations as though God couldn't protect His own people. Not many people understood that the Jews' scattering was a fulfilment of God's prophetic Word.

Mr. Symons asked Peter to read verses twenty-two to twenty-four.

Peter turned his page and read, "*'Therefore say unto the house of Israel, Thus saith the Lord GOD; I do not this for your sakes, O house of Israel, but for mine holy name's sake, which ye have profaned among the heathen, whither ye went. And I will sanctify my*

---

[2] Isaiah 14:1–3; 51:2–3; 54;1–17; 60:1–22; 62:1–12; 66:19–24; Jeremiah 23:3–8; 32:37–42; 33:6–26; Ezekiel 20:40–44.

great name, which was profaned among the heathen, which ye have profaned in the midst of them; and the heathen shall know that I am the LORD, saith the Lord GOD, when I shall be sanctified in you before their eyes. For I will take you from among the heathen, and gather you out of all countries, and I will bring you into your own land.'"

Noticing a few confused looks, Mr. Symons asked, "Why is God choosing to gather Israel out of the nations again?"

Peter had seen the reason. "Because of *His Name's* sake. He clearly says it wasn't for their sake."

"That's good, Peter," Mr. Symons encouraged. "And notice that God doesn't say He will do this 'IF' they are faithful – but He will do this regardless of their behavior! By 'God's Name,' Yahweh – *'I will be who I will be'* - God is also referring to His reputation – His reputation to keep His word. God made promises way back in the Old Testament— the promises that Verity referred to. He promised to give the land of Israel to the forefathers and their descendants. What else did He promise, Verity?"

Remembering back, she added, "God promised that Jesus would sit in Jerusalem on David's throne. He promised that Abraham would inherit the land of Israel and those who are baptized into Jesus would also have a part."

"That's great!" he nodded. "And those promises to Abraham and David were made with no conditions attached. So, God has a lot planned for the land of Israel when Jesus returns. What we see happening in Israel today is in preparation for the exciting events of the future. God didn't establish Israel again as a nation because the Jews were faithful to Him; but rather because the time period of the Gentiles is almost at an end! God is bringing everything into place for His promises to finally be fulfilled in the earth! The prophecy carries on into chapter thirty-seven explaining how the nation of Israel will once again have a King! They will once again be righteous and willing to follow God's laws.[3] They will have peace, and a new temple will be built among them for the whole world to come and worship.[4] When this happens then all the nations around will eventually come to know that God has accomplished what He promised so long ago. He keeps His promises."

"So, when will Israel become righteous, or godly?" Peter asked, trying to put it all together.

"Peter, if you look up Zechariah chapter twelve and read it through, you will see that there is a time of trouble coming for the nation of Israel. Ezekiel thirty- eight also speaks of this trouble and indicates it will come when Israel is dwelling in *'peace and safety.'*[5] At this time of great destruction in Israel, when many nations gather against Jerusalem for war, Jesus himself will save the Jews. He will be the *'Deliverer from Zion'* we read about in Romans chapter eleven. The Jews who survive this war will look on Jesus and realize in shock that the man who their forefathers crucified many years ago has delivered them from total obliteration! These extremely humbling experiences will turn the Jews around nationally and they will want to change their lives. From this point on, they will choose to serve God in truth and accept Jesus as their Messiah."

Peter nodded thoughtfully. It was coming together in his mind. "So, you're saying," he reiterated, "that God didn't bring the Jews back to the land of Israel because they were doing anything good. Instead, they were regathered because of God's plan to set up a Kingdom for His Son on the earth."

"Yes, exactly!" Mr. Symons nodded, pleased that Peter had understood.

---

[3] Ezekiel 36:25–31; 37:21–28; 39:21–29; Zechariah 12:2–10
[4] Zechariah 14:16–21; Ezekiel 37:21–28; Isaiah 2:2–4
[5] Ezekiel 38:8, 11, 14

Mrs. Bryant was looking rather disturbed. "Where do faithful Christians fit into this whole picture? I always thought that those prophecies referred to 'spiritual Jews' – Christians."

Mr. Symons could see that he needed to explain how all this would fit together in the Kingdom. "You have to understand, firstly, that the thousand-year reign of Christ on the earth has various components. There will be a King—Christ, there will be rulers—the immortal believers, and there will be subjects—those people who survive Armageddon. The faithful Christians' hope is to be one of the immortal rulers with Christ in this Kingdom. The Jews will be just like any other mortals on the earth at this time - privileged to live during the time of this Kingdom but still subject to sin and death. At the end of this thousand-year period there will be a second resurrection, spoken of in Revelation chapter twenty. That is when all the mortal people who have lived during Christ's millennial reign, will be brought before a final judgment and given eternal life if they lived a faithful life, or eternal death if they were unfaithful."

Thomas had been trying to understand all of this and he thought he might have a point to add. "I guess the Jews will be privileged to live in Jesus' capital city?'"

Nodding, Mr. Symons agreed. "Yes, so much could be said on this subject! You are right, Thomas. The capital city of the whole earth will be a glorified Jerusalem as it says in Isaiah chapter two, verses one to three. Jesus will be there ruling on his throne and all nations will have to make yearly pilgrimages.[6] The Jews will be in the land promised to their forefathers, and be very privileged to be in the midst of so many spiritual leaders and spiritual activity."

Glancing at the clock on the wall, Mr. Bryant got up. "Thanks for the discussion," he said politely. "I'm not sure I agree with all that's been said but it's been interesting to consider. Perhaps, though, it's time we all went to bed."

---

[6] Zechariah 14:16–20

"Yes, I see it's past eleven," Mr. Symons agreed. "Where would you like us to sleep?"

Mr. Symons was given Peter's room and Mrs. Bryant kindly showed Verity the guestroom. "I hope you'll be comfortable dear," she said. "Just call me if you need anything."

Thomas and Peter found sleeping bags and stretched out on the carpet right in front of the fireplace.

CHAPTER 33

More Questions, More Answers

The following Saturday night, Peter brought Emily and Kate with him to work on the study-sheets. Mr. Henderson had suggested that before Tuesday, it would be helpful if everyone could get through questions one to four.

"Good evening," Verity said with a smile as she held open the big front door.

They all came tramping in, bringing the wind and snow.

She took her friend's coats to hang them up as they left their boots by the door and followed Thomas into the kitchen.

"How are you?" Peter asked with a playful tug of her hair.

"Great! I love these get-togethers. This is what I call fun!"

"You would," Peter responded with a grin.

"Don't you?"

Hesitating, Peter looked at her thoughtfully. "It's great spending time with *you*—but these study-sheets are hard work!"

Thomas had the idea that they break up into two groups and come together at the end to share their results.

Agreeing that this would be good, Thomas, Emily and Kate stayed in the kitchen and Peter and Verity chose to work at the coffee table in the living room.

"I've got to admit," Peter began as they sat down on the carpet, "the little speech Mr. Henderson gave the other night about Satan has really made me think. Why *did* God wait four thousand years before He finally explained about the Devil falling from heaven in Revelation – the last book of the Bible? If the Devil was the serpent way back in Genesis, why wouldn't God warn people about him right at the beginning of the Book?"

Verity picked up her photocopied sheet from the Greek concordance and looked up at him. "Those are great questions, Peter!" she encouraged. "And most people who believe in a supernatural Devil, believe that he was thrown out of heaven before Genesis, don't they?"

Peter agreed. "And yet," he sighed, with a shake of his head, "I'm still not completely convinced one way or the other."

They began the study-sheet by finding the Greek numbers and looking them up. "'Devil' means 'false accuser' or 'slanderer,'" Verity repeated. "There are actually a few different numbers used in Strong's Concordance, but the one used the most is 1228— 'diabolos.'"

Peter wrote the information down in the space provided. He picked up the photocopy with all the places the Greek word 'diabolos' was translated into English. "Hmm, it's mostly translated 'devil' but there are three places where it isn't… First Timothy three, verse eleven says wives shouldn't be slanderers." With a laugh, he teased, "Is that a problem for women?"

Verity laughed and gave him a push.

"Second Timothy three, verse three, and Titus two, verse three," he continued more seriously, "are telling people not to be false accusers." He examined the verses for a few moments, and then he said, "I guess this is saying that anyone can be a devil if they falsely accuse or slander someone else."

Verity leaned over to see the passages in Peter's Bible and then made notes on her study-sheet. "So, people can be the devil," she repeated thoughtfully, "just as in the Old Testament, people can be 'satan'.

Looking at the next question, she said, "Now, Mr. Henderson has asked us to see if the Old and New Testaments agree about where temptation comes from. I'll look these up, Peter."

The first one Verity looked at was James one, verses thirteen to fifteen. *"When tempted, no one should say, 'God is tempting me.' For God cannot be tempted by evil, nor does He tempt anyone; but each one is tempted when, by his own evil desire, he is dragged away and enticed. Then, after desire has conceived, it gives birth to sin; and sin, when it is full-grown, gives birth to death."*

"The Devil isn't even mentioned here," Peter observed, "and yet that verse is clearly explaining how we come to commit sin!" He leaned over to look at Verity's NIV version of the verse more carefully. "Hey, this is an example of personification," he pointed out. "Look, it says 'he is dragged away,' as if this 'desire' was an evil monster taking the person captive! That's a figure of speech—personification! Did you learn about that in English class?"

"Yes," Verity replied. "Personification is when something inanimate is spoken of as though it were human. And not only is this 'desire' dragging someone away, but a child 'sin' is born!"

Peter nodded. "Right! And the blame is entirely on the 'evil desire' as being the initiator of the sin." He pondered the matter. "This verse would be the perfect place to insert the 'Devil' instead of 'evil desire,' if he were a real being."

"Instead," Verity added, realising this paralleled the Old Testament view of sin, "this verse describes our 'own thoughts' as being the cause of sin, just like in Genesis chapter six, at the time of the flood."

Galatians chapter five, verses seventeen to twenty-one was the next passage. Verity read, *" 'For the sinful nature desires what is contrary to the Spirit, and the Spirit what is contrary to the sinful nature. They are in conflict with each other, so that you do not do what you want. But if you are led by the Spirit, you are not under law. The acts of the sinful nature are obvious: sexual immorality, impurity and debauchery, idolatry and witchcraft; hatred, discord, jealousy, fits of rage, selfish ambition, dissensions, factions and envy; drunkenness, orgies and the like.'"*

"So, all these sins come from our own sinful nature," Peter marvelled. "We are quite capable of all of this evil without any supernatural Devil's help!"

Mark seven, verses twenty to twenty-three were the words of Jesus himself. *"What comes out of a man is what makes him 'unclean.' For from within, out of men's hearts, come evil thoughts, sexual immorality, theft, murder, adultery, greed, malice, deceit, lewdness, envy, slander, arrogance and folly. All these evils come from inside and make a man 'unclean.'"*

"That's another good summary of all the bad things people could possibly think of and do," Verity stated. "Again, Jesus says it all comes from our own hearts."

The next section was on angels. Looking up the passages, Psalm one hundred and three, verses twenty to twenty-one and Hebrews one, verse fourteen, they saw that God spoke of his angels as beings that *do* His commands and *listen* to the voice of His word. *"All are ministering spirits."*

"God doesn't speak about any exceptions here," Verity noticed. "He could have said, 'except for the devil and his angels, all the rest of my angels have followed my commands,' but He doesn't."

Peter nodded, looking up from the Hebrew concordance. "Yes," he replied, "if there was an exception, you'd think it would be mentioned there."

He pointed to the concordance. "I thought I would look up the word 'angels' and it's interesting that the word doesn't always mean a 'divine angel.' It can also be translated as 'messenger.' Sometimes this same Hebrew word 'malak' is used for *human* messengers – like

John the Baptist!"[1] He shook his head. "Wow! I'm not sure how that fits."

Question six of the study-sheet dealt with people who were delivered over to Satan in the New Testament in order to turn their hearts back to God. After looking up the passages, Peter was thinking them through aloud, when he became aware that Thomas had walked over. He turned around to see Thomas standing behind him.

"Did you get question six?" Thomas asked excitedly. "We've figured it out, I think." Emily and Kate stood by eagerly as well.

"All right, tell us what you think," Peter nodded, pleased to see Thomas enjoying Bible study so much.

"Well, it doesn't make any sense if those passages refer to a Satan who wants to take people away from God," began Thomas. "But if Satan represents our own sinful desires—then 'delivering someone to Satan,' could mean giving people over to the consequences of their own sinful desires."

Seeing that Peter looked uncertain, Thomas tried to explain. "It's like this, Peter; let's say that I had a problem with wanting lots of money. All of you would try your hardest to explain to me that this was wrong from the Bible's perspective. But if I wouldn't listen and I was spending all my time making money instead of serving God, then you would need to give me over to my obsession. Let me pursue it all I wanted. You would have done all you could. Now, it would be up to God to use the bad experiences in my life to show me that making lots of money isn't going to bring me true happiness!"

Peter was nodding now, thinking that this had happened to Thomas in a different pursuit not so long ago. "Yeah, that fits better than a rebellious Devil turning people back to God. Maybe that's it."

---

[1] Matthew 11:10; Mark 1:2; Luke 7:24; James 2:25

Seeing how fast time had flown by, they decided to finish the evening by looking at Romans five to seven together. Throughout Paul's extensive doctrinal discussion about the battle with sin, nowhere does he mention the devil or satan. Referring to the temptation of Adam and Eve, Paul says, *"Wherefore, as by one man sin entered into the world, and death by sin; and so death passed upon all men, for that all have sinned"*

"So, Paul doesn't blame the serpent or the devil," Peter observed. "Instead, he blames Adam. He blames the humans who made the choice to disobey God."

It was the same in Romans seven, verse eleven, where Paul says, *"For sin, taking occasion by the commandment, deceived me, and by it slew me."*

"It sounds like he is talking about a person slyly figuring out a way to deceive Paul and then killing him," Thomas considered.

"That's personification!" Verity piped up. "Just like we read in James chapter one."

"I wonder why the Bible doesn't just speak in really simple terms?" Emily questioned. "Then there wouldn't be so many misunderstandings."

"No," Kate argued. "Then it wouldn't be a classic book, like we ones we admire written by intelligent human authors. The Bible uses exciting and advanced literary devices because the author is God."

"Whew, that's deep," Thomas replied.

"Well, think about it," Kate continued. "We don't have courses on 'Little Red Riding Hood,' in Grade eleven. We study Shakespeare or Ben Hur, because they are full of so many interesting and challenging thoughts and analogies – that's what elevates them to advanced study. Why would be expect God's Word to be anything less?"

"I like that," Peter nodded. "We'd despise God's Word if it was just written in simple terms. We'd think He was less intellectual than ourselves."

Peter read the last passage in Romans seven, verse seventeen to the end, *"For I know that in me (that is, in my flesh,) dwelleth no good thing: for to will is present with me; but how to perform that which is good I find not. For the good that I would I do not: but the evil which I would not, that I do. Now if I do that I would not, it is no more I that do it, but sin that dwelleth in me. I find then a law, that, when I would do good, evil is present with me. For I delight in the law of God after the inward man: But I see another law in my members, warring against the law of my mind, and bringing me into captivity to the law of sin which is in my members. O wretched man that I am! who shall deliver me from the body of this death? I thank God through Jesus Christ our Lord. So then with the mind I myself serve the law of God; but with the flesh the law of sin."*

After a moment, he paused and then said, "I'm going to insert devil in here and see if it makes sense." He read, *"For the good that I would I do not: but the evil which I would not, that I do. Now if I do that I would not, it is no more I that do it, but the devil that dwelleth in me. I find then a law, that, when I would do good, the devil is present with me."*

"That's how I've always seen it," he said, "But instead Paul refers to sin as a beast that has us under control. So, the devil and sin seem to be interchangeable. They both can control us, dwell in us, deceive us, kill us…"

Everyone was looking up at him with expectation.

"That's all I've got," he shrugged. "I don't know why…"

They weren't finished the study-sheet, but it was time to head home. Everyone had to get up for school in the morning.

As Emily and Kate were going out the front door, Peter hung back for a second. "This is all very interesting," he confessed to

Verity, "but I'm still having a hard time with it. There are so many passages in the New Testament that I don't understand now. I don't see how they could be explained other than by a belief in a supernatural Devil."

Verity patted his arm. "Don't worry, I'm sure Mr. Symons will let you ask questions next Tuesday."

Nodding, Peter continued, "I'm sure he will, but there are so many passages, I think I'll need at least three nights!"

Laughing, Verity encouraged him to bring his best ones.

"Don't you have any?" he inquired.

"No, this makes sense to me," she replied. "I'm really enjoying all your questions though! You make me think."

"What's happened to me?" Peter laughed. "I didn't used to have any questions about the Bible."

"But think how many answers you now have," she encouraged. "Both of us! That's the value of asking questions."

Nodding thoughtfully, he said goodbye.

WHO ARE THE DEVIL & SATAN IN THE N.T.?

satan-in-the-nt-worksheet-chris-mods-1.pdf (wordpress.com)

1. Using Strong's Concordance look up the word for 'satan.'

Greek # _____ Word _____

Strong's Definition: _____

2. Using Strong's Concordance look up the word for 'devil.'

Greek # _____ Word _____

Strong's Definition: _____

Scanning through the listings of 'diabolos' (list attached) in the N.T.,
record any instances where the Greek word is used for humans.

_____

3. Scanning through the listings of 'satanas' (list attached) in the N.T.,
record any instances where the Greek word is used for humans.

_____

4. What do the following passages say about the 'source of temptation'?

James 1:13-15 _____

Galatians 5:17-21 _____

Mark 7:21-23 _____

1 John 2:15-17 _____

5. What does the Bible say about God's angels? Is rebellion possible?

Psalm 103:20-21 _____

Hebrews 1:14 _____

Luke 20:35-36 _____

Romans 6:23 _____

6. Explain how delivering someone 'over to Satan' could bring them back
to God?

1 Timothy 1:20 _____

1 Corinthians 5:3-5 _____

7. Read through Romans 5 to 7. This is the Apostle Paul's discussion on sin, temptation and salvation. List any verses where the Devil or Satan are blamed for our sins. Record anything else of interest:

_____
_____
_____
_____

8. Romans 5:12 Through whom did 'sin' enter the world? _____

9. Romans 7:11 What seized Paul, deceived him, and in a sense 'put him to death'? _____

9. b) What figure of speech is being used here? _____

10. Romans 7:17-25 Who does Paul blame for his wrong actions?

_____

WHO TEMPTED JESUS IN THE WILDERNESS?

"And Jesus being full of the Holy Ghost returned from Jordan, and was led by the Spirit into the wilderness, Being forty days tempted of the devil. And in those days he did eat nothing: and when they were ended, he afterward hungered." Luke 4:1-13 3.

1. What important event had just occurred in Jesus' life before he was 'driven into the wilderness' and what had he received?
Luke 3:22 & 4:1 _____
(This incident is also recorded in Matthew 4:1-11& Mark 1:9-13)

2. If this gift was suddenly given to you, what temptations would you face? _____

3. What does the N.T. tell us about the way in which Jesus was tempted? Hebrews 4:14-15 _____

4. How are we tempted?

James 1:14-15 _____

Mark 7:21-23 _____

Romans 7:14-24 _____

5. What were the three temptations that Jesus faced?

_____

6. Did Jesus face these same 3 temptations again later in his life?

Matthew 14:15-23 _____

Luke 4:28-31 _____

Matthew 26:52-54 _____

John 6:14-16 _____

7. Was it necessary for these temptations to be given by a supernatural being? Why or why not? _____

8. If 'satan' or 'adversary' in Luke 4 is not a supernatural being, who or what could it be? _____

9. Romans 5:12 Through whom did 'sin' enter the world? _____

10. Romans 7:11 What seized Paul, deceived him, and in a sense 'put him to death'? _____

10. b) What figure of speech is being used here? _____

11. Romans 7:17-25 Who does Paul blame for his wrong actions?

_____

The definitions below are taken from *Strong's Concordance*.
Below this is a selection of relevant verses extracted from
Englishman's Greek Concordance.

[G1228] (diabolos/dee-ab'-ol-os) from 1225; a traducer;
specially, Satan (compare 7854):--false accuser, devil,
slanderer. see G1225 see H7854

Mat. 4:1 Then was Jesus led up of the Spirit into
the wilderness to be tempted of the devil.
  5 Then the devil taketh him up into
  11 Then the devil leaveth him,
  13:39 The enemy that sowed them is the
    devil;
  25:41 prepared for the devil and his angels:

Joh 6:70 you twelve, and one of you is a devil?
  8:44 Ye are of your father the devil,
  13:2 the devil having now put into
Acts 10:38 all that were oppressed of the devil;
Acts 13:10 thou child of the devil, thou enemy
Eph 4:27 Neither give place to the devil.
Eph 6:11 to stand against the wiles of the devil.
1Ti 3:6 the condemnation of the devil.
  11 wives be grave, not slanderers <1228>,
    sober,
2Ti 2:26 out of the snare of the devil,
  3:3 trucebreakers, false accusers <1228>,
    incontinent,
Tit 2:3 not false accusers <1228>, not given to
    much wine,
Heb 2:14 power of death, that is, the devil;
Jas 4:7 Resist the devil, and he will flee

1Pe 5:8 because your adversary the devil,
1Jo 3:8 He that committeth sin is of the devil; for
the devil sinneth from the beginning.
  —might destroy the works of the devil.
  10 manifest, and the children of the devil:
Jude 1:9 when contending with the devil
Re 2:10 the devil shall cast *some* of you
  12:9 that old serpent, called the Devil,
  12 the devil is come down unto you,
  20:2 that old serpent, which is the Devil,
  10 the devil that deceived them was

The definitions below are taken from *Strong's Concordance*.
Below this is a selection of relevant verses extracted from
Englishman's Greek Concordance.

[G4567] (Satanas/sat-an-as') of Chaldee origin corresponding
to 4566 (with the definite affix); the accuser, i.e. the devil:--
Satan. see H4566

Mat 4:10 Get thee hence, Satan:
    12:26 And if Satan cast out Satan,
    16:23 he ...said unto Peter, Get thee behind
       me, Satan:.
Mar 1:13 forty days, tempted of Satan;
    3:23 How can Satan cast out Satan?
      26 And if Satan rise up against himself,
    4:15 Satan cometh immediately,
    8:33 Get thee behind me, Satan:.
Lu. 4:8 Get thee behind me, Satan:
    10:18 I beheld Satan as lightning
    11:18 If Satan also be divided a
    13:16 whom Satan hath bound,
    22:3 Then entered Satan into Judas
      31 behold, Satan hath desired to have you,
Joh. 13:27 Satan entered into him.
Acts 5:3 Ananias, why hath Satan

Ro. 16:20 shall bruise Satan under your feet
1Co 5:5 unto Satan for the destruction
    7:5 that Satan tempt you not
2Co 2:11 Lest Satan should get an advantage.
    11:14 for Satan himself is transformed
1Th 2:18 but Satan hindered us.
2Th 2:9 after the working of Satan
1Ti 1:20 whom I have delivered unto Satan,
    5:15 already turned aside after Satan.
Rev. 2:9 but are the synagogue of Satan.
      13 where Satan's seat is: a
      —where Satan dwelleth.
      24 known the depths of Satan,
    3:9 them of the synagogue of Satan,
    12:9 called the Devil, and Satan,
    20:2 which is the Devil, and Satan,
      7 Satan shall be loosed

CHAPTER 34

Look in the Mirror

After missing a couple of the Seminar sessions due to illness, Lindsay and Jessica were happy to be well enough to go out again. They had missed their little friends and the big ones too. As a group, everyone was getting to know each other and many good conversations occurred both before and after each class. Verity found a seat at the front with her school friends. She looked back to see the two young Symons setting up their crayons and papers, making sure the little girl and boy next to them would have lots to do. Who were they planning to draw pictures for tonight? Lately, Peter had become very popular with the children. Last week, Peter had received more pictures after the class than Verity had! Jessica seemed to feel Peter needed extra attention, probably because he kept sadly reminding her that he 'didn't have a sister.'

They began the class with reading about the onset of the Flood in Genesis chapter seven. As usual, there was a lively discussion. Once again, Mr. Symons went through the details of the inspired record, showing where the water came from that flooded the earth. They analysed the geological effects the flood would have had on the earth during the actual flood and especially afterwards, as the water drained away into the seas creating massive erosion. Mr. Symons also explained that the geological record of fossils could be better explained by an instant flood, than by millions of years of slow burial and evolution.

After everyone had opportunity to ask questions on Genesis chapter seven, Mr. Symons went over the important lessons from the study-sheets. He was pleased to have so many people participate.

Thomas was happy to share his analogy of being 'delivered over to Satan.'

"It's very encouraging to see all of you thinking these things through and coming to such good conclusions!" Mr. Symons praised. "You're finding out by experience that the answers to your questions about the Bible are found within the Bible. I hope all of you are developing confidence that with enough searching and prayer, you can find the answers you are looking for."

Turning to the New Testament, he continued, "I'm going to go over Romans chapters five to eight tonight, as it very helpful in understanding the source of temptation. Here in Romans, Paul is dealing with the specific issue of our struggle with sin and the forgiveness God has provided. This is the main place in the whole Bible where the subject of sin is dealt with; and yet, there is no mention of the 'Devil' or 'Satan.'"

As a class they discussed many of the points that the young people had studied the night before. "This is the struggle we all face day by day," Mr. Symons stated. "When we want to do good, evil is right there with us. For instance, if we wanted to do something kind, say, bring a meal to a family in need; no sooner do we think to do this good deed when the little, 'bad' voice in our minds suggests a whole host of reasons why we shouldn't do it. 'Oh, it's probably going to snow and anyway I haven't got the right ingredients, and on and on. Or, after delivering the meal, the voice pats us on the back, puffing up our pride and telling us what wonderful people we are to be so kind! That voice never leaves. It's always there trying to take any good thoughts we have and turn them against loving God. It is a war, but we can't blame it on a 'rebellious angel-devil'; it's our own human nature we're fighting against."

Peter couldn't hold back any longer. "What is Revelation chapter twelve about then, if it's not about a supernatural, fallen-angel Devil?"

Turning it up in his Bible, Mr. Henderson said, "I would love to spend an hour or more on this chapter, Peter!" He glanced up at the clock. "For tonight, I'll try to give you a brief overview."

Mr. Henderson explained that Revelation is a book of symbols and signs, a vision 'signified'[1] – given by Jesus after his ascension to heaven, about things that would *'shortly come to pass,'* as is clearly stated in Chapter one, verse one. "Therefore, whatever chapter twelve is about," he explained, "it was not about history *prior* to Christ but that which would occur *after* Jesus had given this revelation to John.

Peter wrote the comment down. Verity could tell this was new to him.

"I think we should read Revelation twelve around," Mr. Henderson suggested. "Just so we all know what the chapter is about." When they had finished reading, he pointed out that verse one demonstrated that this was a symbolic vision, as a woman couldn't be literally clothed with the sun and have the moon under her feet. "Now I realise Peter that you want to know who the 'great red dragon' is," he smiled, looking over at him, "but let's start at the beginning of the chapter and first figure out who this woman is. Do you have any ideas?"

"Well," Peter replied, "I think the man-child she gives birth to is supposed to be Christ... so I suppose the woman is Mary?"

"Do you think this is a good description of Mary?" Mr. Henderson questioned. "A woman clothed with the sun and the moon under her feet? And did Mary have to flee into the wilderness for one thousand, two hundred and sixty days after bearing Christ?"

"Maybe symbolically?" Peter offered.

Thomas chipped in, "But if Revelation is about things that happen *after* Christ's ascension to heaven, this couldn't be about his birth!"

"That's right," Mr. Henderson agreed. "Now, Peter, if you read through the whole book of Revelation, you will notice that two

---

[1] Revelation 1:1

contrasting women are part of the symbology. One is a faithful, chaste virgin—the bride of Christ,[2] the other woman becomes a harlot and represents those that have gone astray from Christ.[3] In fact, these two contrasting women are used throughout the whole Bible.[4] So, the symbol of a woman in this book represents the church of Christ, either the faithful or unfaithful believers at this time. Here in chapter twelve, the church gives birth to a man-child. This man sounds like he is Christ, as he is caught up to God and everyone shouts when he rules, saying that the Kingdom of God has come. But remember that this is a symbolic book. If Jesus is truly taking the throne of his Kingdom in verse ten, then why does the woman— in verses thirteen to seventeen—continue to be persecuted after this Kingdom of God has come?"

Peter shook his head. "I honestly don't know."

"Well, Revelation chapter twelve," Mr. Henderson continued, "describes the church as a woman giving birth to a man who was going to bring the church to political prominence. I'll just point out that she's not a faithful woman, as she is giving birth to a child, when she is supposed to be a 'chaste virgin' to Jesus Christ until his return.[5] 'Heaven' is used symbolically in the Bible to represent rulership, power or government.[6] This huge battle between the church's man-child and the dragon took place in the political heavens."

"So, who was the dragon, then?" Peter asked, looking bewildered.

---

2 Revelation 14:1–4 and 19:7–9
3 Revelation 17:1–8 and 18:1–9
4 i.e. Ephesians 5:23–33; Proverbs 7 and 8
5 2 Corinthians 11:2-3
6 Isaiah 1:2, 10—God speaking to the 'heaven' and 'earth.' In verse 10 He clarifies this as the 'rulers of Sodom' and 'people of Gomorrah.' See also Deuteronomy 32:1.

Mr. Henderson noticed the look on his face. "This is very involved, Peter, I know." He glanced around at all the faces in the class. "Revelation is a highly symbolic book. You aren't going to find clear, simple stories here. To truly understand Revelation, you need know and understand the rest of the Bible to see how each symbol should be interpreted correctly. The book of Daniel, for instance, is a small, easier prophecy that gives us many clues we can use to understand Revelation."

"So," he went on, somewhat apologetically, "let's turn to Daniel chapter seven, where in a similar vision to Revelation, God also used beasts symbolically. Here the beasts represent various nations." Mr. Henderson read Daniel seven, verse seventeen, *"'these great beasts, which are four, are four kings, which shall arise out of the earth,' and verse twenty-three, 'the fourth beast shall be the fourth kingdom upon earth, which shall be diverse from all kingdoms...'"*

"We need to appreciate," he continued, "that in a vision, a creature like this dragon in Revelation is meant to be understood as symbolic of something. Beasts in prophecy refer to nations or empires. Nothing in Revelation, nor the rest of the Bible, explicitly defines the dragon as a rebellious angel. He is spoken of in verse nine of chapter twelve as being the Devil and Satan, and an old serpent, and having angels—but he isn't called an angel himself. Rather, if you follow the pattern in Daniel—where a beast symbolises a nation—then the dragon fits very well with pagan Rome. This was the power in control of the world around the third century AD, which was when the Christian Church gave 'birth' to a man who led the Church in a war against pagan Rome, and the Church won! The Church then became ruler over the Roman Empire, with its 'man-child' as emperor."

A look of astonishment passed over Peter's face. "I think I read about this in that book Verity gave me, 'When Jesus Became God.' Was this man-child the Emperor Constantine?"

Mr. Henderson looked impressed. "Yes, Peter! Can you tell us how it all happened?"

"Well," Peter began, "I remember reading that before Constantine came along, the Christian Church was fiercely persecuted by the pagan Roman government. Constantine decided to take the side of the Church because he thought the Christian religion would help to unite his empire. At the battle near some famous bridge, the Christians defeated the Pagans, and from that time on the Christians were in power over the mighty Roman Empire."

Mr. Henderson and Mr. Symons nodded enthusiastically. Mr. Symons added a comment, "Do you know that at that famous bridge—the Milvian Bridge—where they won the war, there is *actually* a statue of a woman with a crescent moon under her feet with a slain serpent dragon draped over it?"

Peter and the others in the class were astonished. "A woman, a moon and a serpent-dragon?" Henry echoed. "Why that's just like here, in Revelation twelve!"

"Not only that," Mr. Symons continued, "but Constantine himself wrote to Eusebius, and in reference to his victory over the pagans, spoke of *'that dragon having been deposed from the governance of affairs, by God's providence.'*[7]

Mr. Henderson nodded. "Constantine was not a true Christian but he applied this chapter of Revelation to himself, and rightly so. He saw the dragon as symbolic of the pagan Roman world and he even displayed this on the coins minted at that time! A Vatican painting of this very war also shows the Pagan Romans holding a serpent-dragon standard. So, you see, the Christians believed that this great victory, which put the Church in the position of ruling the ancient world, *was* the Kingdom of God on the earth."

"Right," said Mr. Symons. "The Christians forgot the promises we've discussed so much in previous classes, that Jesus had to return, that there had to be a resurrection of the faithful, that the Jews had to return to Israel, et cetera. Instead, they proclaimed that the Kingdom of God on earth had come through their Church. Unfortunately, it was a counterfeit kingdom that led to many biblical beliefs being altered and new traditions being brought in to help win over the pagans. Sadly, after the Church came into power, she began to persecute any who disagreed with her teachings – which is why the 'woman' – the faithful remnant of the church, had to go into hiding."

---

[7] The Bible Magazine, volume 13, Issue #1, page 16.
See also <u>Bible Magazine Volumes 10-19 – Bible Magazine</u>

"One more thing," begged Peter, knowing his question had already taken up much of the time. "How was the man-child caught up to God?"

"Remember, this is a symbolic vision, Peter," said Mr. Henderson. "Do you know what the Caesars were called at the time of the Roman Empire?"

"Well, I know they were worshipped as gods," Peter offered.

"That's right," said Mr. Henderson. "The name Michael, in this chapter twelve, means 'Who is like God?' People in pagan Rome actually worshipped and sacrificed to the rulers of the Roman 'heaven.' Constantine took over the position of Caesar. Those who came to power in the Church after him began to ascribe titles to themselves that essentially meant they were 'God on earth.'"

Verity watched as Peter added to his extensive notes. She was in awe of how the symbols of the chapter were matched by real-life occurrences in the fulfilment of the prophecy. There was no doubt that Peter was also impressed.

"I'd just like to ask a question about all this," Henry spoke up. "Why is this dragon called the 'old serpent,' and the 'devil,' and 'satan' in verse nine?"

"It's an allusion back to Genesis chapters three and four that I would love to take up with you in more depth later," Mr. Henderson explained. "For now, do you remember who told the first lie in the Bible, Henry?"

"The serpent in the Garden of Eden."

"Right, so this dragon is associated with lies. What have we shown that the Devil and Satan represent?"

"Human nature."

"So, suffice it to say at this point," Mr. Henderson continued, "that a nation or kingdom governed by lies and the thinking of flesh—human nature—is opposed to God and can be described by the words used in verse nine."

"Who were the dragon's angels?" questioned Sally.

"Well, what does the word 'angels' mean?" Mr. Symons asked.

Verity raised her hand, remembering Peter had looked this up. "Messengers."

"Is the word always used for Divine angels?" he inquired again.

"No," said Peter, well-informed, "sometimes it can mean human messengers."[8]

"Therefore," replied Mr. Symons, "in the symbolic language here, I would say that the 'angels' refers to the *agents* of this pagan Roman power. Its messengers, if you like."

Leaning over, Peter whispered, "I can't believe how well this fits."

Verity nodded, amazed.

Henry had his hand in the air. There was a question he wanted to discuss. "Back to the study-sheet," he implored. "When Jesus was led into the wilderness to be tempted, who was the Devil he spoke to?"

Mr. Symons nodded, agreeing that this part of their research was important to go over. He asked everyone to look up Luke chapter four, verses one to thirteen. "I want all of you to notice verse one," he said. "Here it says that the 'spirit' led Jesus into the wilderness. Matthew four also says *'Then was Jesus led up of the*

---

[8] The word 'aggelos' is translated 'messengers' in Luke 7:24; James 2:25; and Matthew 11:10, referring to human messengers.

spirit into the wilderness to be tempted of the devil.' Does this seem a little odd to anyone?"

"Well, if the Devil was God's arch-enemy, why would God's Spirit direct Jesus to him?" suggested Peter.

"Hmm, good point," said Henry.

"Yes," said Mr. Henderson. "Why would God's Holy Spirit lead Jesus to the Devil? Wouldn't God be trying to keep His son from this being? —if it is a Supernatural being? What else could be happening here?"

"Was this 'devil' the voice of human nature in Jesus' mind?" inquired Verity.

"That's how I've always understood it," replied Mr. Henderson. "Remember that Jesus had just received God's Spirit without measure. Think of what a temptation that would be; Jesus could now do anything he wanted! Imagine the voice of his human nature suggesting to his mind all the possibilities that there were to use this power wrongfully. Jesus needed time to think carefully about the appropriate uses of this limitless power."

He paused. "I see the three temptations given here as examples of the struggle in Christ's mind during the forty days he stayed in the wilderness. How Jesus conquered the voice of his nature is an example for us—Jesus quoted Scripture! He had put God's Word so deeply into his mind that the temptations didn't deceive him. He had developed a spiritual mind that could overcome the flesh. When the voice spoke, he knew right away from God's Word why it was wrong. And as you discovered with the study-sheet, all three of these temptations occur in similar ways later in his life."[9]

---

[9] BREAD TO SATISFY HUNGER—Made bread to satisfy others, but not for himself – Luke 9:12–17
KINGDOMS OF THE WORLD—Short cut to Kingdom power—the people want to make him King –John 6:14–15.

Turning to and reading Hebrews four, verse fifteen, Mr. Symons carried on, "We are told that Jesus *'was in all points tempted like as we are, yet without sin.'* He provided a way of forgiveness for us and showed us how to defeat sin in our lives. While we will never be perfect, God wants us to try our best to overcome sin and follow His son's example."

In closing, Mr. Symons took everyone to Hebrews two, verse fourteen and asked Verity to read it.

"*'Since the children have flesh and blood, he too shared in their humanity so that by his death he might destroy him who holds the power of death—that is the devil.'*"

"If this is referring to a supernatural 'Devil,'" Mr. Symons said, "then he should be gone, for he was destroyed at Jesus' death, as stated here. He should have no more power over anyone! We can only understand this verse if we see the 'devil' as Jesus' *own human nature*. In his life he never gave in to this nature and at his death it was finally destroyed—silenced. It could no longer tempt him; he was dead and he had overcome. Now that he has been resurrected and made immortal, Jesus no longer has this struggle. He shares God's Divine, incorruptible nature.[10] It is our hope that we will be made immortal also, after the resurrection and finally get rid of this 'sinful nature.'"

"So," he said with a little smile. "If you want to know who the 'devil' is, go home and look in the mirror!"

Not long after the class had ended, Peter and Verity were sitting discussing what had been said when little Jessica came running up with three pieces of paper.

"Hey, are those all for me?" Peter teased, picking her up to sit on his lap.

JUMPING OFF THE TEMPLE TO PROVE HE WAS GOD'S SON—"If thou be the Son of God, come down from the cross" – Matthew 27:40–43.
[10] 1 Corinthians 15:42-50

She looked at him hesitantly for a moment, her pretty blue eyes full of concern. "Well, these two are," she said at last, "but this one is for Verity." With great seriousness she divided the pictures between them.

Peter looked at his and gave a low whistle, and then he compared them to Verity's. "I definitely got the best ones," he joked. "These are just beautiful—lots of colour! I think you must want to be *my* little sister now."

Jessica didn't fully comprehend that Peter was teasing her. She looked like she was in a great dilemma.

"She can't be your sister," Verity responded, continuing the game. "She's already promised to be mine!"

"Is that true?" Peter asked, pretending to be very sad.

Little Jess thought carefully. "Well, I did tell Verity I would be hers first," she explained hesitantly.

"Then I guess I'll just be all sad and lonely," Peter sniffed.

Anxiously Jessica looked over at Verity. Verity mouthed the words, 'You can still be his friend.'

Patting his arm, she said earnestly, "I'll still be your friend!" Then she hopped down to play with the other children.

It was a beautiful March evening when Peter walked with Verity out to the parking lot following the Symons. She had asked him what he thought of the class and he was trying to describe that it made sense, "and yet," he explained, "I've had this fear of the Devil since I was a child. It's hard for me to let it go!"

Without warning, Verity's leg suddenly gave way and she fell down hard onto the snowy sidewalk. She hoped Peter would think she had just slipped but he didn't. Gently pulling her back up, he put his arms around her and said firmly, "Either I'm taking you to the hospital right now, or you're making a doctor's appointment tomorrow!"

"All right," she said, feeling rather silly. "I'll make an appointment tomorrow."

"Do you promise?"

"Yes."

Only then did he open the car door for her and help her inside. Before he shut it though, he leaned in with a grin saying, "I'm going to call tomorrow night and check on that appointment!"

CHAPTER 35

Tobogganing!

It was difficult to get an appointment with the doctor when Verity's mom called the next day. Amberhill was renowned for its doctor shortage. Every family doctor had far more patients than they desired and anyone making an appointment usually had to wait at least a week, if not two. On top of this, with the March break coming up, the doctor had a vacation planned with her family. However, an appointment was finally fixed for a date two weeks later.

While Kara felt concern over Verity's leg, her anxiety had been eased with Aunt Judy's words. "Oh, I know exactly what's wrong with her!" Aunt Judy had stated confidently. "When I was in my twenties, my right leg… actually, perhaps it was my left leg… started giving out on me—just like Verity's. I went to doctor after doctor and no one could find out what was wrong. I must have put up with that leg for almost a year and then I decided to try a chiropractor. After seeing him four times a week for a good six months, the problem completely went away. It was just a pinched nerve in my lower back."

Kara wanted Verity to see their family doctor first, but she didn't feel it was an urgent situation. After all, Aunt Judy had put up with her bad leg for a whole year!

"Hey, Verity," Thomas spoke up at supper that evening, "when Peter calls to check on your appointment, why don't you invite him over for some tobogganing during the holidays? It's a shame we haven't had a chance to ask him before."

So, Peter was invited and all involved hoped eagerly that there would still be enough snow.

When the March break finally arrived, three other school friends had been invited to come as well. Purity, Emily and Kate were also excited to see what the big hills were like.

Late one afternoon, bundled up in layers of warm clothing, they grabbed their sleds and trudged up the pathway to the tobogganing hill. The snow was fluffy and quite deep. It lay on the tall, dark pines like sparkling-white icing on a cake. Above them the sky was a beautiful blue.

"I'm glad there isn't a wind!" Thomas exclaimed. "When the wind starts blowing out here it can be too miserable to do anything."

The four newcomers were very impressed by the graceful, rolling scenery all around them. "Oh, Verity," Emily breathed, having reached the ridge where she could see down into the valley, "I would love to live here! You are so lucky!"

Verity glanced over at Thomas, and saw he was nodding his head in agreement.

"We are lucky! We know it!" he stated with pleasure. "Our old place in Saskatchewan was in the middle of the city. We didn't know what a view was back then!"

When they reached the hill crest, the girls looked down the steep slope with alarm. "You actually sled down here?" questioned Emily, looking like she was about to do something extremely dangerous.

Verity laughed. "This is Thomas' run. He loves the challenge. It's a bit gentler over on the other side of the hill."

Peter suggested that he and Thomas help get a track started for the girls on the easy slope and save the steep one for later.

It was a lot of fun piling onto the sleds and tobogganing down with the boys. At first, they went down quite slowly, as they kept sinking into the snow. But after a few runs, the surface became hard and well-packed, so the slide down was good and fast.

Verity was secretly having quite a struggle walking back up the hills. She hadn't tobogganed for a couple of months and she felt very out of shape. There was a lot of pain in her lower back especially, but she kept a smile on her face and no one seemed to notice. "I really should do this more often," she told herself, "I need the exercise."

After an hour, the guys decided to try out the more daunting side. For a while the girls watched Peter and Thomas whoop and holler as they flew over the jumps on the steep hill, but then they began to feel chilled. Emily suggested another slide down the hill. The long walk back up soon made them feel toasty-warm again. It was great a great workout. Aside from the pain, Verity was enjoying the visit.

Laughing and chatting, they were all quite happily keeping company with one another—until they became aware of a strange quietness! The girls had almost reached the top of the hill when they noticed the absence of noise. Hurrying to the top, they looked over the edge to see Peter and Thomas sprawled out down below, lying very, very still! Their toboggan lay upside down some yards away. It looked as though they had collided with a tree and gone flying off in different directions!

"Oh no," Verity cried. "Peter, Thomas," she hollered down, "are you okay?"

There was no answer.

The girls turned wild-eyed to one another, panic setting in. "Do you want me to run back and call an ambulance?" Kate asked, her voice wavering.

"Not yet," said Verity shakily. "Let's go down first and see just what is wrong."

"What? Go down this hill?" questioned Emily in fear. "Look at what happened to them! Now we know how dangerous it really is!"

"Well, I'm going down, right now!" Verity said firmly, feeling there was no time to waste. "If you don't want to come, you can stay up here and be ready to run for help if we need it."

"Wait, I'll come with you," said Purity, trembling. "Oh, I hope they're okay!!"

"I'll come too!" said Kate anxiously. "But go slowly!"

Emily stayed back, as the rest jumped on the toboggan and slid down the hill. With Kate's feet dragging in the snow on both sides, it wasn't a very fast ride.

Verity was feeling tremendously anxious. All this time the boys hadn't moved at all! What ever could be wrong? And if something were seriously wrong, how would they ever get Peter and Thomas back to the house? It would take hours for the four of them to pull the boys all that way up the hill!

As soon as they reached the bottom they dashed over, their hearts pounding.

"We'd better not move them in case their spines are injured!" Kate exclaimed.

Verity hadn't considered this. What a scary thought that was! But on the other hand, the boys would freeze just lying in the snow waiting for medical help!

Purity and Kate were already at Thomas' side, so Verity ran to where Peter lay sprawled. With tears in her eyes, she took off her mitts and put her hand above his mouth. He was still breathing at least! She touched his head; she couldn't feel any lumps. There was no sign of blood anywhere. How would she ever know where he was hurt? Or whether his spine was injured?

"Please Peter, tell me what's wrong!" she sobbed, not knowing what else to do. All of a sudden, Peter's face broke into a grin and he burst out laughing.

303

Thomas too, quickly lost his 'dead' look and sat up with a smile.

Sitting back on the heels of her boots, Verity realised they had been cleverly duped! Slowly a smile crossed her face as she wiped the tears from her eyes and pondered how well the boy's scheme had worked.

"Peter, that was mean!" she said reproachfully.

Peter was laughing so hard he could only look up at her; he couldn't answer.

"It was so mean," exclaimed Purity, "that I think we ought to snow them!"

So began an intense battle of who could rub the most snow into the others' face. Three against two, the girls had an advantage. Finally, worn out from a good day's worth of exercise, they all collapsed in the drifts. Emily eventually found the nerve to join them, sliding slowly down without a sled.

Above the hills the sky was turning a deep, indigo blue and the sun was low in the horizon. The hours had gone swiftly by.

"So, whose wicked, little voice thought up that deceptive scheme?" Verity taunted, although she was pretty sure that she knew the answer.

Thomas and Peter just looked at each other, laughing again at the memory. They weren't going to tell.

"Don't you know we almost called the ambulance?" remarked Emily.

Peter grinned. "Oh, we wouldn't have let it go that far. We just wanted to see if you'd worry about us or not."

"Worry about you!" Verity retorted. "We were scared to death!"

The first, little stars were twinkling in the ultramarine sky and a full moon lit up the evening, reflecting off the white of the snow. All around, the lights of the cities far away, sparkled and glittered. There was a peaceful sense that everything was all right.

Gratefully, Verity looked around at the friends that she loved. She felt that they had something very special in common. The times they had spent together trying to understand God's Word had deepened their friendship. Looking over at Thomas, she noticed the warmth and laughter in his face as he talked and joked with the girls.

"What are you thinking?" Peter asked, gently tugging on the frozen locks of her hair that had escaped from under her hat.

She hugged her knees, ignoring the pain in her back. "I'm just thinking how happy I am that God has given us life and this beautiful world to enjoy." After a pause, she added, "And I'm thankful that Thomas and I have so many good friends here. Look at my brother—he's really enjoying himself. I know he's glad we came here now."

Peter nodded. "Yeah, Thomas and I are good buds. We see eye to eye on a lot of things." He paused and looked at her. "Then again, he's a different person now than when I first met him."

"When he was choosing to be a slave to sin?" Verity smiled, quoting Romans.

Peter sighed. "I guess that's an ongoing struggle we all have," he remarked thoughtfully.

Emily and Kate stood up to head back. Now that they were all just sitting in the snow, the cold dampness was seeping in quickly. Reluctantly, Verity tried to pull herself up.

Holding out his hand, Peter helped her to her feet. "How's your leg?" he asked quietly.

She turned hesitantly, wishing Peter didn't notice when she had difficulty with it and yet appreciating that he cared. "It's okay," she said cheerfully. "At least it's still working!"

They trudged back up the steep hill, hand in hand. The guys were kindly pulling the heavy sleds and Verity was thankful that Peter was also pulling *her* up the hill. With the full moon it wasn't too hard to see where they were going. Verity's heart felt full of joy and peace. God had been so good. So many of her prayers had been answered. She had found the answers she had been looking for and so many more as well. Now, in her thankfulness, she wanted to respond in obedience to Him. She hoped Peter would want to join her.

CHAPTER 36

A Decision Made

The month of March went by quickly and they were well into April when Verity stepped off the bus one afternoon. Here and there little blades of tender, green grass poked through the dead, yellow thatch. Up near the house, daffodils nodded their sunny heads to her as she went in through the front door.

There was a slight limp to her walk that was frequently evident now. A couple of weeks ago she had been to see the doctor, but after a rather quick examination, Dr. Filbert had agreed that it was probably a pinched nerve. She had suggested that the chiropractor in town may be able to help and that he would first take an x-ray to see if that was truly the problem. Just to be sure, Dr. Filbert had filled in a lab form so that Verity could get some blood tests done. "Probably a little more exercise would do her good, as well!" she suggested brightly.

Kara had wanted Verity to go and see the chiropractor right away but Verity had disagreed. There wasn't a chiropractor in Grandville, so she would have to go to Amberhill, which was over half an hour away. She'd heard that for the first two months she'd have to have four treatments a week. In her mind she didn't know how she would fit in that many visits. Her life was already full enough. If she could just get school finished first, then she felt the intensive visits could begin during the summer holidays. That was only a couple of months away. Surely, she could put up with the pain until then. After all, Aunt Judy had put up with it for a year. The pain in her back didn't seem as urgent to Verity as something else. There was another matter that was pre-occupying her thoughts from day to day.

"Mom," she said without hesitation that afternoon as she limped into the kitchen, "I've decided I want to be baptized."

Kara looked up from preparing dinner. This was unexpected. "You've already been baptized, Dear," she said.

"You mean, when I was christened?" Verity asked.

"Yes, we made sure that you and Thomas were both baptized when you were babies," Kara replied.

"Where in the Bible does it say that *babies* should get baptized?" Verity asked not too gently, wishing earnestly that her mother would read the Bible some day.

Kara glanced at Verity reproachfully. She always felt at a disadvantage in these conversations.

"I'm sorry, Mom," Verity apologized, "but there aren't any examples of babies being baptized that I've come across. Every baptism in the New Testament is always of adults. Jesus himself didn't get baptized until he was thirty! He's supposed to be our example."

"Verity," Kara returned, trying a different tact, "I'm sure that Reverend Tobias always said a person should only be baptized once! You've been christened, so you've been baptized."

"Mom," Verity replied softly, not wanting this to become a heated argument. "When you christened me, I had no choice—I wasn't even aware of what was happening. I had no idea why I was being sprinkled with water. Baptism in the New Testament always follows belief and repentance."[1] She paused for a moment, thinking back to the discussion she'd had with Mr. Symons about this. "God's Word has to first work on a person's heart before they can understand the need for baptism. That's how we are born again by water *and the spirit*.[2] "A baby can't understand the Bible; a baby can't believe or repent."

---

[1] Mark 1:4; Mark 16:16; Acts 2:38
[2] John 3:1–6 & John 6:63

"Repent," echoed Kara. "What do you need to repent of? You're not a murderer or a thief!"

Leaning against the table, Verity replied, "Sin isn't only horrible crimes like those. Sin is also anger, impatience, pride, desiring what others have, selfishness...[3] and so many other things. I know all those things are in my mind and I struggle with them. Lots of times I give in to them. I need to have God's forgiveness and His help to overcome sin."

"Well," said Kara, remembering another option, "You can be confirmed when you are old enough to understand and repent, and then your baptism will be complete."

With a sigh, Verity pondered whether to continue the discussion or not. Her mother didn't seem very open to this whole idea, but then again, she needed to know about these things. "Mom," Verity persisted, "baptism is a full immersion in water, not a sprinkling."

"Oh?" Kara questioned.

"The Bible speaks of people being baptized where there was 'much water.'[4] People went down into the water and came up again. Jesus himself was baptized in the river Jordan."[5]

"I don't see that it matters how much water there is," Kara returned. "It's only a symbolic thing."

"Yes," Verity continued, "but it's symbolic of Jesus' death and resurrection. When Jesus died on the cross his human nature was put to death. When we go beneath the water, we are symbolically putting our old way of life 'the flesh' to death. When Jesus was resurrected from the dead he rose to a new life—in his case immortality. When

---

[3] Mark 7:20–23; Galatians 5:19–21
[4] John 3:23 "Baptizo" means 'to immerse, submerge, to make whelmed (fully wet)'
[5] Mark 1:10–11; Acts 8:36–39

we come up out of the water, we are rising to a new life—a life in which we will try to follow God's ways and not our own desires."[6]

It was obvious that Verity had thought this through completely. "Well, if you feel this is so important, Dear," Kara said wearily, "then I'm certainly not going to stand in your way."

"Important?" Verity echoed, "That's an understatement." How could she ever help her mother to see just how important this was? "Mom, I have to show you Galatians chapter three!" Leaving the room, Verity collected her Bible and brought it back to the kitchen.

"Look at verses twenty-seven to twenty-nine," she said excitedly. *"'For all of you who were baptized into Christ have clothed yourself with Christ. There is neither Jew nor Greek, slave nor free, male nor female, for you are all one in Christ Jesus. If you belong to Christ, then you are Abraham's seed, and heirs according to the promise.'"*

She looked up, puzzled that her mother couldn't see how clear and simple it all was. "It's baptism that makes us belong to Christ, and it's being Christ's that allows us to share in Abraham's promises. Without this, we have no hope for eternal life. Don't you want to have a part in the life to come?"

Kara was anxious to terminate the conversation. "Have you told Mr. Symons that you want to be baptized?" she asked flatly.

"No, but I plan to!" And with that, Verity dialled the number and happily conveyed the message.

Mr. Symons was very pleased. He arranged for he and Mr. Henderson to meet with Verity the next evening to see that she properly understood the truth of the Bible. Their discussion went well, and the next Sunday was set for her baptism.

---

[6] Romans 6:1–14; Galatians 5:24

At school the following day, on the way to class, Verity met Peter at his locker. "I'm getting baptized this Sunday, God willing!" she said with a smile, and then she pleaded, "I hope you can make it!"

With a look of concern, Peter asked. "Really? I don't get why you're rushing this."

There wasn't time to discuss it as they both had to get to class. "Let's talk later," she said quickly. Verity knew he needed time to think it over. She understood he felt she was making the decision too soon, and perhaps she was. However, it was hard to explain the urgency she felt deep inside. As she hobbled to class, she knew it would be hard for him to be there for her baptism. Peter always went to his own church on Sunday. If he asked to go somewhere else, she knew it would not go over well with his family.

Confident that this was to be the most important day of her life, she invited all her friends at school to come to witness her decision. A new beginning was going to take place for her, all her sins would be forgiven and she would now have an ongoing hope for forgiveness and salvation! She would be included with those whose names were written in the 'book of life.![7] How simple a ceremony it would be—but how much would take place that only those who read God's Word could appreciate. "I will be a new creation in Christ[8] and have a part in the promises to Abraham!" she thought joyfully.

When Peter finally caught up with her at the end of the day, he asked sceptically, "Are you really sure you're ready to do this?"

"Why are you so amazed?" she replied. "I'm very sure that I have discovered the true hope, so now I need to respond to God's invitation."

---

[7] Malachi 3:16 and Revelation 21:27
[8] 2 Corinthians 5:17

"It's just so soon," he argued. "Why don't you just give a few more months? I'd like you to come talk to my Pastor and hear another side…"

"Peter," she said gently, "We've gone over everything ourselves to make sure we understand what the Bible teaches. Why wouldn't I choose to take part in such a wonderful hope? And choose now? There are no guarantees on this life."

He shook his head. "It's a huge commitment!"

Verity laughed, looking up with compassion into his troubled, brown eyes. "How is it going to be any different than the way I'm living now? I'm already committed!" Slinging her backpack over her shoulder, she reached over and took his hand. Strolling down the hall together, so she could catch the bus, she added, "I've come to a point in my life where I know that I need to 'repent and be baptized.' Right now, I'm not part of God's promises and then, I will be!"

With a sigh, Peter didn't answer.

Before she got on the bus, she gave one last appeal. "I know it's really difficult for you to come on a Sunday but please be there if you can! We've worked through so much of this together." She paused, searching for the right words. "You're my best friend…"

He understood. "I'll see what I can do," he nodded gravely, as she boarded the bus.

Sitting down beside a little five-year old, Verity looked out through the window. Peter was still standing there, looking so… so serious! Why wasn't he more excited for her? Did he disapprove? Did he still doubt they had found the true Gospel message? Was he worried what his parents would think?

Finally, as she lay in bed that night, a new idea came to her. Was Peter struggling with his own response to the call?

CHAPTER 37

Belief and Action

On the morning of her baptism, Verity sat with Thomas and her mother at the front of the Christadelphian Hall. Aunt Judy couldn't make it as she was short-staffed that morning at the IGA. Peter and her friends hadn't yet come and she didn't know for sure that any of them would, but she had saved a few seats just in case.

Contemplating the 'huge commitment' she was about to make, Verity thought back to the day when she had stood outside this very building, looking at the sign and wondering what God's promises were all about. Now she knew how important they were and how much she wanted to be a part of them.

A man called Brother William was to give the exhortation that morning to prepare everyone's minds for taking the bread and wine in remembrance of Christ, as well as to prepare her for her baptism. Verity had never met Brother William before. Curiously, she watched him walk up to the front podium. He was an older man with silver-grey hair, yet he looked very young at heart. With a few energetic strides he took his place at the front.

"Good morning, Brothers and Sisters in our Lord Jesus Christ," he began. "Good morning, young people, and especially Verity and her family. It is my great delight that we meet here today to remember our Lord in the memorials as he has asked us to,[1] and to witness Verity Lovell's confession of faith. I don't know Verity personally yet, but I have heard of her great love for truth and her efforts to search for it, and the life it brings." He went on to discuss

---

[1] Luke 22:17–20; John 6:53–57; 1 Corinthians 11:23–29

how impressed he was that such a young girl could see the importance of serving God so early in her life.

Brother William discussed at length the joy of making the decision to follow Christ and the help and sustaining power God would give to those who chose this path. "Baptism is only the beginning of a faithful walk in Christ," he continued. "Up ahead, Verity will face trials and difficulties as every believer must." He explained that this is how God tests our progress and helps us to develop godly attitudes. Reading from James chapter one verses two to five and verse twelve, Brother William gave evidence that God has promised a crown of life to those who overcome their trials faithfully.

"How can we overcome trials in our lives?" he asked. "What are the things we should remember when troubles beset us?"

Answering his own question, the older man explained there were two things to never forget—prayer and reading. "The one asks for God's help and the other gives us His answers," he exhorted. "One of the places this is best demonstrated is in the Garden of Gethsemane—where Jesus prayed to his Father in his anxiety over the cross ahead of him. Here our Lord faced his greatest trial and overcame; his disciples also faced trials and failed. What was the difference? What helped our Lord to be successful? Why did the disciples fail?"

"To answer these questions," Brother William continued, "this morning I would like to contrast the disciple Peter to our Lord Jesus Christ."

Brother William then proceeded to outline the background of Peter's life. Looking up a few incidents in the gospels, he showed that Peter was usually the first disciple to speak, act, and show faith. "It was Peter who tried to walk on water. It was Peter who said Jesus was God's Son when most Jews felt it was blasphemy to say so. It was even Peter who, just before they left for the Garden of Gethsemane, bravely stated that he was willing to die for Christ! So, what went wrong? Why did this faithful, bold disciple lose his conviction and end up denying his Lord three times that very night?"

Suddenly, a tall young man took the seat beside Verity. Kate and Emily slid in beside him.

"Sorry, I'm late," he whispered.

Squeezing his hand, Verity's face lit up. "I'm so glad you're here!" she whispered. She smiled at her other two friends as well.

"Peter didn't pray," Brother William was saying. "In Luke chapter twenty-two, we have recorded that Jesus clearly told all of his disciples to *'pray that ye enter not into temptation.'* Instead of heeding his advice, the disciples kept falling asleep. They didn't see the need for God's help at that time. Jesus, on the other hand, prayed so intensely to his Father, that his sweat was like great drops of blood. Jesus poured all of his inner wrestling out to his Father. He pleaded that there might be another way to save the world, another way that didn't involve the pain and torture of the cross; yet he was also fully prepared to submit to his Father's will. There in the garden, he struggled greatly against his own flesh and he brought God into that struggle. Prayer is an essential part of overcoming any trial. God helps those who ask—Peter didn't ask. Because of this, he wasn't fortified to meet the challenges of the night."

"However," Brother William continued, "there was even more to Peter's problem than his failure to pray."

By turning up a few other incidents in Peter's life, Brother William showed that Peter, like the other disciples, didn't understand what the Lord came to do. "They expected that Jesus would immediately establish the Kingdom of God on earth, by overcoming the Roman authorities. Like all the other Jews at that time, they didn't understand that their Messiah had to suffer and die first, to save the world from sin. Yet Jesus had told them very clearly what he had to endure, explaining carefully that he would be delivered to the Gentiles, mocked, spitefully entreated, spat on, scourged and put to death. He even promised that the third day he would rise again!² So why didn't they understand that this had to happen?"

Turning up Luke nine, verses forty-four to forty-five, the grey-haired man at the front, demonstrated that this wasn't what the Jews had been taught to believe about their Messiah and the disciples were afraid to ask him about it. "Why were they afraid? Because what Jesus was saying sounded horrible and they didn't want to believe it! They chose to cling to the exciting hope of the Kingdom being established right away, rather than hear more about this awful experience Jesus was speaking about."

Turning to Mark chapter eight, verses thirty-one to thirty-three, Brother William read an example of this. *"'And he (Jesus) began to teach them, that the Son of man must suffer many things, and be rejected of the elders, and of the chief priests, and scribes, and be killed, and after three days rise again. And he spake that saying openly. And Peter took him, and began to rebuke him. But when he had turned about and looked on his disciples, he rebuked Peter, saying, Get thee behind me, Satan: for thou savourest not the things that be of God, but the things that be of men.'"*

Looking at everyone in the audience, Brother William went on, "Imagine being called Satan by our Lord! Why did Jesus speak so strongly to Peter? Well, here, Peter with his mistaken beliefs was trying to stop the Lord from accepting the cross. Peter's words would have been harmful to the Lord's resolve. It was difficult enough for Jesus to fortify his own mind to be able to endure the horror of crucifixion, it would be even harder to hear these words from his close friend; that was why he rebuked Peter so strongly. This rebuke should have been a warning to Peter that his beliefs were mistaken and that he needed to change them."

Verity felt a tingle go down her spine. She and the young man beside her exchanged knowing looks. They had discussed this incident, and they both appreciated how awful it would be for Peter

<hr>

² Luke 18:31–34

to look back on his words to Jesus and see himself as a satan to the Lord he loved. Yet being a satan to someone else seemed incredibly easy to do. In her mind, Verity considered how often she herself might say words to others that would reinforce their natural way of thinking, rather than strengthen their spiritual resolve.

Continuing on, Brother William reiterated, "Any Jew that read the Old Testament should have been familiar with prophecies indicating that their Messiah would be tortured and killed, but yet rise again. Prophecies such as this were clearly laid out in Psalm twenty-two and Isaiah fifty-three. But these words weren't what the Jews wanted to believe. They looked forward to their traditions of the Messiah coming as a hero, to fight the Romans and establish his kingdom right there and then. This, after all, was what the religious leaders of the day—the Scribes and Pharisees—taught. These leaders were heavily schooled in religion but they failed to appreciate that the cross had to come before the crown. Their mistaken beliefs led them to crucify Christ, *their Messiah* – the one they were waiting for, losing out on their opportunity for eternal life and ultimately bringing destruction upon the whole Jewish nation."

He paused a moment and then continued, "How did Peter's mistaken beliefs affect him? Well, because Peter didn't understand what was happening, he ended up losing faith at the most crucial time in Jesus' life. Instead of standing by Jesus as a friend through his terrible sufferings, Peter forsook him with the others and denied three times that he even knew the man! Jesus on the other hand was well prepared for the trials he had to face. The prophecies concerning his death and resurrection were firmly fixed in his mind. Undeniably, his relationship with God as his Father gave him the strength to overcome this time of trial. God even sent an angel to strengthen his son in Gethsemane, while the disciples slept.[3] Isaiah indicates that God woke Jesus every morning of his life to speak to him.[4] Fortified as he was by the Word of God, he endured the blows,

---

[3] Luke 22:43
[4] Isaiah 50:4–9

and submitted faithfully to God's will, even the torture of the cross. As it says of Jesus in Hebrews twelve, verse two, '...*who for the joy that was set before him endured the cross, despising the shame, and is set down at the right hand of the throne of God.*'"

In closing, Brother William said, "We act based upon our beliefs. If our beliefs are wrong, then we will eventually act in wrong ways. If we act wrong – yet think we're right, then we won't be pleasing to our Heavenly Father. So how do we develop the kind of faith that will lead us to serve God in the right way?"

Brother William quoted Romans chapter ten, verse seventeen, "*'So then faith cometh by hearing, and hearing by the word of God.'*"

"When our faith is weak," he continued, "and all of us have times in our lives when our faith is weak—we need to turn back to God's Word. We need to see the examples of how God has worked with people in the past and take courage that whatever our trials, God will bring us through them for our good, if we hold fast to Him. We need to make sure that our beliefs are solidly based on God's Word, that we understand His character properly and the character of Christ. We need to appreciate the plan and purpose God has for this whole earth. We need to develop our minds to think as God does, so we can understand how He works in our lives. All that *will* happen if we spend time reading and contemplating God's Word. In conjunction with reading the Bible, we need to pray; to pray earnestly, deeply, sharing our struggles with Him and asking Him for wisdom to understand His hand in our lives."

Directing his last words to Verity, Brother William encouraged her to grow in her faith, using the peaceful times in her life to prepare for the trials that would surely come. "Let me leave you with the words of Hebrews twelve, verses five to thirteen," he said. "*'...My son,'* or today, my daughter, Verity," he added in, "*despise not thou the chastening of the Lord, nor faint when thou art rebuked of him: for whom the Lord loveth he chasteneth, and scourgeth every son whom he receiveth... Now no chastening for the present seemeth to be joyous, but grievous: nevertheless afterward it yieldeth the peaceable fruit of righteousness unto them which are exercised thereby.'"*

After the exhortation, the presiding brother asked Verity to go downstairs and prepare for her baptism. While she did this, the others sang a hymn and read a portion of Scripture.

Sitting in the warm tank of water in a long white gown, Verity kept her gaze fixed in front of her. Everyone was now gathered around to witness her confession of faith. She wanted to focus on the death and resurrection she was about to undergo. To do this she needed to concentrate.

Brother Symons gave a prayer and then asked Verity if she believed the *"things concerning the Kingdom of God and the name of Jesus Christ."*[5]

Understanding this to mean the whole gospel message bound up in these two aspects, Verity said happily, "I do believe! With all my heart." Then, after saying that she was baptised into the saving name of the Lord Jesus Christ for the remission of her sins, Mr. Symons gently lowered her backwards under the water and she came up a 'new creation.'[6] Her sins were now forgiven and covered in Christ!

Everyone went quietly back up the stairs to read another chapter from the Bible, giving Verity a few minutes to get into dry clothes again. Then in the company of her new brothers and sisters, she partook of the bread and wine for the first time, in remembrance of Jesus Christ's sacrifice for sin.[7]

After the service had ended, lots of people came over to welcome her as part of a worldwide family. There was a special joy in greeting Mr. and Mrs. Symons now as Brother Craig and Sister

---

[5] Acts 8:12
[6] 2 Corinthians 5:17; Ephesians 2:10-15
[7] Luke 22:15-20; 1 Corinthians 11:20-28

Beth. Purity and the Hendersons were very happy to welcome her also.

Peter, Kate and Emily stood talking to the others while Verity was occupied. Finally, there was a call for everyone to come downstairs for lunch. "That was really special this morning," Peter said to her, as they walked down the stairs. "Your baptism was so simple, yet... it seemed totally complete."

"Peter, I'm so happy!" she said, as they entered the line to help themselves to a variety of casseroles and salads. "It's like a huge weight has gone from my shoulders and now I can just be thrilled to think of Jesus coming back soon."

He nodded rather solemnly. "It was a little disconcerting to hear my name so often in that sermon, or exhortation – or whatever you call it here," he laughed. "I knew it wasn't about me, but all the same..."

With her eyes twinkling, Verity looked up and laughed. Once they had a plate of food they headed towards some empty chairs. Happily, Verity noticed that her mother and Thomas were chatting with the Hendersons, Kate and Emily.

"It must have been so awful," she replied to Peter soberly, sitting down at the table, "for the disciple Peter to look back on his life and see how he had been a satan to Jesus, just when Jesus needed him the most!"

"Yeah," Peter agreed. He looked like he was about to say more, but just then the Symons came over to join them.

"Good to see you, Peter," Mr. Symons said, as he pulled out a chair. "Did you have any trouble coming out this morning?"

"With my parents?" Peter asked, buttering his bun. "Yes. They weren't too happy about it, but since Verity was getting baptized, they understood it was a special occasion and important for me to come."

The Symons nodded.

"I'm really having trouble with... well, knowing if it really matters," Peter blurted out. "I agree with you on most matters of belief but I don't really think it's important what church I go to, or what I call myself, as long as I'm leading a good Christian life."

Mr. Symons leaned forward. "I understand how you're feeling," he empathized. "And like anything that we've discussed so far, it's not my opinion that matters; it's only what the Bible says. Really, it would be good for us to get together and examine this in depth." He paused, rising from his chair. "For now, let me just show you a passage or two. I'll just get my Bible."

As they waited for his return, Verity remarked to Mrs. Symons, "Mr., I mean... *Brother* Craig is so good about dropping everything to answer our questions."

She nodded pleasantly. "It's his life; he loves to talk about the Bible." Taking a sip of water, Beth added, "That's what happens when you spend lots of time reading the Bible. The more you read and understand, the more you come to love it. The Psalms are filled with verses that say, *'Oh how I love thy law! it is my meditation all the day.'*[8]

"All right," said Mr. Symons, taking his seat again at the table. "I actually brought your Bible down, Verity, as maybe your version is a little easier to understand. Now, I'd like to show you a passage in Galatians. These Galatians that Paul was writing to were Gentile believers who were being influenced by Jewish believers that still wanted to keep the Law of Moses. There was a specific problem here with beliefs. Let's see if Paul feels it's important whether the Galatians believers had the exact truth, or not." He read chapter one, verses six to nine. *"'I am astonished that you are so quickly deserting the one who called you by the grace of Christ and are turning to a different gospel—which is really no gospel at all.*

---

[8] Psalm 119:97, 127, 129, 140, 162, 174

Evidently some people are throwing you into confusion and are trying to pervert the gospel of Christ. But even if we or an angel from heaven should preach a gospel other than the one we preached to you, let him be eternally condemned!'"

Looking up at Peter, he asked, "What do you think? Is preaching a different gospel a serious matter, or not?"

Peter reread the passage a few times and then said, "Well, if eternal condemnation is the opposite to eternal life—this *is* pretty serious." Looking puzzled, he asked, "But why would Paul say *an angel* would preach another gospel?"

"Paul is just trying to make the point using hyperbole," Mr. Symons explained, "What he is saying is that it doesn't matter what credentials the person has, he will be condemned if he preaches a different gospel. You see," Mr. Symons said earnestly, "we could give up all we own, travel to a far away country and spend our whole lives preaching; but if we are teaching a different gospel than Christ taught, then we are promoting false ideas, not the truth."

Craig Symons continued kindly, "There are many New Testament passages that warn the believers about a great falling away from the truth. It was even starting to happen right then while the New Testament was still being written." He turned to Second Thessalonians two, verses ten to twelve. "This passage shows how important it is to have actual truth." Seeing that they were all busy eating their meal, he read it out loud, *'...they perish because they refused to love the truth and so be saved. For this reason God sends them a powerful delusion so that they will believe the lie and so that all will be condemned who have not believed the truth but have delighted in wickedness.'"*[9]

Verity had been following the conversation with great interest. She could sense, however, that Peter was edgy.

---

[9] 2 Timothy 4:3–4; 2 Peter 2:1–3; 2 John 7–11

"Do you see the point?" Mr. Symons asked.

Hesitating, Peter responded, "Well, I see that it says you will perish unless you love the truth. But what is this 'truth'? Isn't it enough to believe that the Bible is God's Word and that Jesus died for us? Isn't that what is *most* important. Paul says that if you believe in Jesus, you will be saved.[10] Why does it have to be anything more than that?"

"I appreciate what you are saying," Craig nodded. "There are passages that seem to indicate that a simple belief is all that matters. However, this morning William talked about the importance of what we believe and how it affects our actions. The Jews in Christ's day thought that because they were Abraham's descendants, read the Scriptures, and worshipped in God's temple, they would be pleasing to God. Jesus told them very plainly that they would all perish unless they responded to *his* teachings."[11]

Reaching out to hold Peter's arm, Verity added, "The exhortation also brought out the point that because the Jews didn't understand the Messianic prophecies, they put God's son to death."

Mr. Symons continued, "And that's another discussion we could have later, Peter. You see, many Christians today only see the gospel message as being one of love and peace. They don't appreciate the full character of God, or of Christ. There are a few prophecies that indicate when Christ Jesus returns to earth again, many people will mistakenly think he is the 'antichrist,' and refuse to submit to him as King. There will be a war after Christ becomes King. Jesus' rule will be a righteous *monarchy,* not a democracy.[12] Many people will refuse to accept him as their Messiah because they don't understand prophecy correctly nor the judgmental side of his character. Jesus came the first time as a lamb when the Jews were

---

[10] Romans 10:9

[11] Luke 13:1–5; John 5:24, 45–47; 6:63; 12:47–50; Mark 7:6–13

[12] Psalm 2; 2 Thessalonians 2:8; Revelation 19:11–21; Daniel 7:9–14

looking for a Lion. He will return to earth as the Lion, when many Christians are looking for a Lamb!"[13]

Still not fully convinced, Peter said, "I always thought those passages in Galatians and Thessalonians referred to religions that weren't Christian. The church my parents go to is always talking about Jesus and the Gospel."

Mr. Symons nodded understandingly. He didn't want to press the point, so he picked up his fork to eat.

"Do you think my church has it all wrong?" Peter challenged.

Laying his fork back down, Mr. Symons hesitated. "That's not really for me to say."

"But that is what you are saying," Peter protested. "Isn't it?"

With a sigh, Mr. Symons looked at Peter kindly. "The next time you read the New Testament," he encouraged, "take note of just what was preached as the 'Gospel message.'" He turned up another passage. "I'll just show you one quick example from Acts eight, verse twelve." He read, *'But when they believed Philip as he preached the good news of the kingdom of God and the name of Jesus Christ, they were baptized, both men and women.'*[14]

"Now, what was the 'good news' that Philip was preaching?" Craig asked.

"He was preaching about the kingdom of God and Jesus," Peter responded with a shrug.

"All right," Craig nodded, "so one aspect of the gospel that is important for us to believe concerns the Kingdom of God on earth, in Jerusalem."

---

[13] Revelation 5:5-10; 2 Thessalonians 1:7-10; Revelation 17:12-14. For more about this, see "Who Are You Looking For?" – Book 2 in this series.
[14] See also Matthew 24:14; Acts 4:10–12; 28:30–31; Luke 24:44–47

"But when people talk about heaven, it's sort of the same idea..."

With his head cocked to one side, Mr. Symons looked up earnestly. "The Kingdom of God was an essential half of the Gospel message. The Bible is full of references as to *where* it will be and the capital city of worship, who will be there, how and when it will come, who the King is, the changes that will occur on this earth—the list goes on and on. Jesus himself went everywhere preaching the *'gospel of the kingdom of God.'*"[15]

Peter shifted uneasily in his chair.

"Now what about the name of Jesus Christ?" asked Mr. Symons. "That is the other half of the gospel message. What do you think that involves? Does it matter what you believe concerning him?"

"But that passage in Acts only states that Philip preached *'the name of Jesus Christ.'* How does that involve more than the fact the Messiah's name was Jesus?"

"When you get home, read through some of the speeches in Acts, Peter. I think you will see that the apostles did more than just tell people what Jesus' name was. They talked about how he fulfilled the Old Testament scripture, how he died for us, how he overcame sin, his elevated status both now and in the future.[16] At the very end of Acts, it records that Paul was *'teaching those things which concern the Lord Jesus Christ.'*"

Looking rather uncomfortable, Peter sighed heavily.

"Peter," Verity said gently, "if your church is teaching that Jesus is part of a Trinity then don't *you* think they are preaching a different gospel than the one the disciples taught?"

---

[15] Matthew 4:23; Mark 1:14; Luke 4:43; 13:24–29
[16] Acts 2:22–40; 3:12–26; 4:8–12; 5:29–32, 42 etc.

For a moment or two Peter didn't respond. He sat quietly drumming his fingers and thinking through their words thoughtfully. At last, he said, "So you're saying that to preach the *true* gospel we need to teach the right things about the Kingdom, and God's relationship with his Son."

With another nod, Mr. Symons clarified. "That's what I believe *the Bible* is saying. I realise that to speak this way today— is to come across as rather bigoted and exclusive. But don't just take my word for it, do some searching on your own. Read the New Testament, especially the Epistles that the apostles wrote, and see how many times they warn the believers to be careful what they are being taught—to make sure it agrees with the true gospel.[17] That way *you* will determine if the Bible presents 'doctrine' as something of vital importance, or whether I'm just giving you a misguided opinion."

Peter thanked Mr. Symons for his help, adding that he would examine the whole New Testament more carefully. "I do need to go," he said apologetically, "my mom is expecting me home at two o'clock."

"Did that help?" Verity asked, as she followed Peter to his car.

Regarding her thoughtfully, Peter replied, "It certainly has given me a lot to think about!"

Opening the door of his car to get in, Peter stopped abruptly and turned back. "I know this day has been very exciting for you," he began, "and I feel like I should be showing a lot more happiness, but I'm still just trying to sort this all out." Looking at her uncertainly, he asked, "Do you understand?"

---

[17] 2 Timothy 2:15–18; 3:14–17; 4:1–4; 2 Peter 2:1–3; 3:14–17; 1 John 4:1–3; 2 John verses 7–11; Jude verses 3–4

Verity smiled. "I do understand," she assured him. "And I'm really thankful you made the effort to come today. That means *a lot* to me! Thank you!"

As she waved good-bye, Lindsay and Jessica came running up to her with a bunch of freshly picked dandelions. "We've been wanting to say 'hi' to you all morning," Jessica said, taking her hand, "but you've been talking with the adults the whole time!"

Verity looked at them with a smile. "I have been talking a lot," she admitted, putting her arms around their shoulders, "but now I can talk to you!" Then she went back in with the girls to enjoy her new family.

CHAPTER 38

The Lowest Low

The weeks that followed Verity's baptism were filled with highs and lows. She was very happy she had been baptized but at times she felt discouraged that her 'old self' was still alive and well. Mr. Symons – who had asked that she now just call him 'Craig,' reminded her that baptism is only the beginning of a life of crucifying our old nature and praying for forgiveness. Yes, there will still be the same anger rising within, or selfishness demanding its rights, but overcoming sin means mastering these impulses daily by developing a spiritual mind from God's Word. This is the example Christ left for us to follow.[1]

In between school and homework, Verity was having a wonderful time making the acquaintance of her new brothers and sisters in Christ. Last week she had stayed over at Purity's house again and they'd had a deep, heart-to-heart talk until way past midnight. Purity had told her about a Young People's week to be held on Manitoulin Island in August. She had explained that everyone would study a certain topic from the Bible before they went, and then at the camp there would be discussion groups every morning based on their study. Young people came from all over the world and it was a great place to make long-lasting friendships with other believers. The whole idea seemed wonderful to Verity and she hoped Peter and Thomas would be willing to come along.

Peter, however, was another of Verity's lows. He had become very quiet and distant. At the seminars he listened and occasionally asked questions, but his early enthusiasm just didn't seem to be there. Even so, she had high hopes that once Peter sorted everything out in his mind, he would return to his happy, good-natured self.

---

[1] Luke 4:1-13

Life seemed to be full of promise and hope. There were so many things she was looking forward to in this life and the one to come! If only she didn't feel so... *sick!* No longer was it just a rare occurrence for her to fall. Now her leg frequently felt weak and unable to support her weight. Her lower back was constantly in pain. She had lost her appetite and often felt sick to her stomach. Yet, the Doctor's tests had been fine; at least, Verity assumed they were fine, because there had never been a phone call to state otherwise. Her mother had even called to check on the results—just to be certain. But Dr. Filbert's secretary had assured her that if she hadn't received a phone call there was no reason to worry. Yet Kara did worry—she didn't like to see Verity limping. Verity was convinced in her own mind that she was suffering from a pinched nerve, just as Aunt Judy had so many years ago. She had visited a chiropractor, but it had only seemed to make things worse. Aunt Judy encouraged her to persist; apparently it had taken three adjustments before Aunt Judy began to feel relief. However, to her alarm, Verity was now having other symptoms she knew were more serious. After a short phone call, another appointment with the doctor was made for the first week of May.

April twenty-sixth was a Saturday and the forecasters were predicting a beautiful, sunny day with a high of eighteen degrees Celsius. Peter was to leave that afternoon for a week in Nova Scotia. His brother's wife had just given birth to twin boys and they already had two small girls at home. The Bryants had decided to go for a visit and bring their two granddaughters back to stay for a month.

As Verity was sitting in the living room contemplating what she should do that day, the phone rang.

Thomas was the first to pick it up and she could hear him talking. "Oh, Hi Peter... Well, actually I just agreed to help the neighbours fix their fences today... Yeah, Verity's just sitting in the living room. I'm sure she'd love to go for a walk! ... Sure ... Hey, have a great time on your trip out East! I'll see you when you get back! ... Bye."

Elated that Peter was coming to say goodbye, Verity was also apprehensive about how far she could walk. Uncertain as to what was wrong, she didn't want Peter to know how awful she felt.

By the time her friend had arrived, Thomas was already working hard on the fences down the road. Together, Peter and Verity walked out to the ridge. She did her best to hide the pain and enjoy the opportunity for a good chat. Since her baptism Peter had been rather distant. She was eager to know what his thoughts were and what was bothering him.

Having forced herself to walk as normally as she could, by the time they reached the ridge Verity was exhausted and nauseated. "I've got to stop, Peter," she said abruptly, "I'm not feeling well."

A strained look came over Peter's face.

"Verity," he appealed, "I know you don't want to listen to me, but something is wrong with you!" He paused, looking at her with a puzzled expression. "You're only sixteen. You're in the prime of your life! Yet, you're looking really pale... and thin." Then with deep concern, he stated, "I think you are really, seriously ill!"

Verity sat down with her head resting on her arms. She concentrated hard to avoid being sick... that would be too embarrassing with Peter so close by! Several times she had argued before that she had a pinched nerve, something a chiropractor could fix... but she wasn't so sure anymore. She could tell him again that the doctor had said she was fine; that her blood tests must have been okay or the doctor would have called. Instead, she gazed at the grass waving in front of her and didn't reply.

Peter sat down beside her, looking out over the valley. Almost two months ago they had been tobogganing out here in the cold. Now all the snow was gone and the hills were covered again with little blades of new grass. The trees in the forest down below were fully attired with pale green buds ready to burst into leaves in a couple of weeks' time. Robins and sparrows were all around, chirping happily away as they brought dead grass and twigs to make their spring nests.

"I think," Peter began slowly, "that you should go and see a different doctor." He turned to face her. "Sometimes doctors are wrong. A second opinion can't hurt."

Verity looked up into his eyes. The kindness was still there but the laughter had gone. Instead, she thought she saw fear. "You're right," she said sadly, "I have an appointment with the chiropractor and my doctor next week… but maybe I should see someone else as well."

Peter smiled a short, forced smile. "You just agreed to see three doctors in *one* week without any argument!" he laughed. "I'm proud of you!" But his laughter sounded hollow and filled with dread. They were silent a long time, as the breeze blew softly against their faces.

Finally, Verity said, "What's bothering you, Peter?"

He put his arm around her shoulders and drew her close. "It really bothers me," he confided anxiously, "that you're so sick and we don't know why!"

Verity laughed a little and gratefully rested her head on his shoulder. "Hopefully, we'll find that out soon," she assured him. "Is there anything else? You haven't seemed yourself lately."

There was another deep sigh. "I guess I'm still trying to sort out whether it matters what you believe or not. There are lots of passages that warn about the gospel message being corrupted, but I just don't know…if everything we've discovered is truth – the *original* truth – that impacts so many people, so many churches… my whole family!" He paused. With his free hand he picked up a small rock that lay beside him.

Nodding compassionately, Verity agreed.

Peter threw the rock trying to hit an old stump with it. "My parents don't want to talk about it," he continued. "But I'm hoping that this week I can have a good chat with my brothers. Andrew is studying to become a pastor so he should be up on what the Bible has to say."

Verity smiled. "I'll look forward to hearing all about it when you get home."

He nodded. "Maybe it will help me figure it all out. I would like to hear both sides."

They watched as a little rabbit suddenly jumped out in front of them on the pathway. It sat still for a few minutes, gazing intently in their direction, before it took off at high speed into the wild raspberry canes.

Glancing up with a smile, Verity encouraged, "Maybe when you get back—we'll have the answers to everything!"

With a light laugh, Peter glanced at his watch. "I guess we should head back," he said regretfully. "My parents want to leave in an hour." He helped her up and then tucked his arm around hers.

As they walked through the budding orchards, he expressed with dismay. "I feel really badly leaving you right now. I hope you're going to be okay. A whole week away from you is a very long time!"

The walk back to the house wasn't all that far but it took tremendous effort on Verity's part. She was thankful for Peter's strong arm, but she still didn't want to show him how weak she was. An encouraging thought was now in her mind, though. Perhaps by the time Peter returned, she would have figured out her illness and he would have sorted through his questions. Then this strange sadness could end.

Suddenly, her leg gave out and she stumbled. Without a word, Peter picked her up and carried her the rest of the way. It was a tearful, very difficult goodbye.

Tuesday morning as they were eating breakfast, the phone rang. "Oh, Hi, Dr. Filbert," Kara responded cheerfully.

Verity looked up expectantly. Then she watched as her mother's face changed from a pleasant expression to one of concern, then to alarm and finally, to absolute shock.

"You can't be serious!" Kara exclaimed. "How sure are you about this? ... Oh, I can't believe it! ... This is *dreadful!* ... So, you'll meet us at the hospital then? ... No, no, of course I won't."

Many things rushed through Verity's mind. Had something happened to one of her mother's friends? Or was someone hurt in a car accident? Maybe someone from school was injured?

As she hung up the receiver, Kara was visibly trembling.

"What happened?" both Verity and Thomas called out at the same time.

Kara came over and put her arms around her daughter. That's when the thought crept into Verity's mind that this phone call might have something to do with her. For what seemed like an eternity, Kara couldn't speak. Then finally, tearfully she managed to get the words out. "Verity, somehow your lab results, they... they got mislaid! Last night," she sobbed, "Dr. Filbert was tidying up her office and she... she found them in a place where they never should have been put." Kara had to stop and compose herself. "She realised that they had never been brought to her attention!"

Verity sat in trepidation as her mother choked up again. She wondered where this was heading!

"It turns out," Kara said weakly, "that you have a very high white blood cell count..."

"Well, great!" Verity replied, confused. "If they've found a problem, then she'll be able to help me!"

Her mother looked tense. "I hope so, Dearest," she replied gently, "but Dr. Filbert suspects you have... have something very serious!"

The words were said quietly but Verity felt as though they had been shouted. She knew she wasn't perfectly healthy but was it really something serious?

Thomas stood up in alarm.

Kara hugged Verity tightly. "Dr. Filbert made an emergency booking for a CAT-scan. She's most apologetic that these results went unnoticed for over six weeks. We're to meet her at the hospital at ten o'clock."

"Can they tell much from a CAT-scan?" Verity asked fearfully. If something was seriously wrong with her, then she wanted to know exactly what it was and she wanted to know soon!

Still deep in shock but now back in control, Kara was hoping for the best. "Dr. Filbert says this scan will give us a lot of information."

Verity looked across at Thomas, realising he had taken her hand. His eyes were full of fear but he spoke gently. "Don't worry," he assured her. "Maybe we'll find out it's nothing to worry about. Let's wait until we know for sure."

Time went by so slowly while they waited to leave. Verity couldn't concentrate on anything. The pain and nausea were overwhelming. She sat in a daze by the living room window as Kara called Aunt Judy to ask for the day off work.

Suddenly, Verity realised Thomas had sat down beside her. He put his arm around her shoulders. "Verity," he asked hesitantly, "Do you want me to say a prayer for you?"

Nothing could have touched her heart more. She didn't feel focused enough to pray for herself. Her Bible lay on the coffee table, but she knew right now she wouldn't be able to take a word in. "Please, Thomas!" she begged.

He prayed a simple prayer that God would be with them and help Verity to recover from this illness, regardless of what it was.

Verity was surprised at his earnestness. "Thank-you, Thomas," she said, gratefully. "My head's in such a muddle, I can't even think straight!"

It took a couple of days to get the results from the CAT scan. Dr. Filbert was extremely upset that such an oversight had been made and knew she was to blame. She didn't try to excuse herself on the basis of patient overload. It was true that she was trying to handle too many patients at once, but she realised that she should have taken Verity's symptoms more seriously in the first place. It was a human error—and unfortunately a devastating one. With grief, she slowly explained that Verity had cancer.

"Cancer?!" Verity exclaimed. Suddenly, she needed to be sick and thankfully the doctor had a bag on hand. She had been preparing herself for something serious, but this was far worse than she could have imagined! She gazed in utter terror at her mother. Her mom pulled her close, with tears in her eyes.

"Oh, Verity!" Kara mourned, "Dr. Filbert warned me that it could be cancer, but I didn't want to alarm you."

Dr. Filbert continued on, her voice shaking, to explain that Verity had a tumour deeply embedded in her spine. That was what was causing her to limp and giving her lower back pain. The report stated that the tumour was so entwined around Verity's nervous system that it would be impossible to remove it. The cancer had also invaded other organs. "This looks to be a particularly aggressive form," Dr. Filbert stated sadly. "The CAT-scan showed that Verity's liver is much bigger than it should be."

"What does that mean?" Verity begged.

"I'm sorry, Verity," Dr. Filbert apologized sincerely. "Advanced liver cancer means we can't use chemotherapy. The liver is the organ that filters the blood. Once cancer has spread to other organs, especially the liver, we have to look at alternative treatments. There are a number of experimental trial drugs that have been used with quite good success."

Her eyes suddenly filling with tears, Dr. Filbert wiped them away. She explained that she didn't usually get emotional about her patients, but she felt personally responsible for the advanced state of Verity's disease. "I don't know if six weeks would have made a favourable difference in the outcome," she expressed sadly. "I don't have any miracle drug," she cautioned, "but I will prescribe a trial immunotherapy, that has been showing promising results in some cases."

"How long does she have if it isn't effective," Kara inquired, trembling.

"Possibly only a couple months," the Doctor replied, "but let's try to think positively. I'll get right to work to find the best trial drug available and…well… miracles do happen!"

Verity sat in absolute disbelief as Kara and the Doctor discussed whether Verity should see another doctor for a second opinion, or if she should be hospitalised, or kept at home with a full-time nurse.

Many decisions were made, and later Verity didn't know if she had been consulted about them, or not. She felt completely in a daze. Since Tuesday, her optimistic outlook had steadily eroded away. From feeling positive that she would get better—she now was fearful she was going to die!

CHAPTER 39

Wrestling with God's Will

When Verity arrived home that afternoon it was with a very different perspective than when she had left. She looked around at everything and everyone in the house, wondering how much time she had left. "Will it only be a couple of months?" she asked herself. "Or will the immunotherapy drugs kick in and help me fight this? Could it really be God's will that I die so young? Why would he take my life so soon? Surely, He will do a miracle and save me!"

Aunt Judy was beside herself when they told her the news. "I can't believe it!" she said over and over. "There can't be a God!" she stated at last emphatically. "How could a loving God ever let this happen to you? You've tried so hard!"

Her aunts' words were difficult for Verity to hear; it only reinforced the voice she was trying to suppress.

Verity had lost her appetite completely. They all tried to coax her to eat and drink, but the thought of food made her gag. After dinner they all stayed with her until late, trying to divert her thinking and help her to forget. Once she glanced up to see Thomas trying to call someone on the phone. "Who are you calling?" she asked, certain that she knew.

"Peter," he answered with a serious look on his face.

"He won't be there," she reminded him. "I think they were supposed to be leaving Nova Scotia today. In fact," she added sadly, "he probably won't be home until late tomorrow." The thought of telling Peter this terrible news filled her with anxiety. How would he take it?

Finally, night came, when everyone else was asleep and Verity had to face her own thoughts. They had all given her big hugs and told her to call them if she needed to talk at any time. She dreaded being alone, but knew it was necessary. Sleep was the last thing on her mind; she felt she might be awake all night.

Aunt Judy had openly stated Verity's worst, insidious thoughts. Why had God let this happen to her? Hadn't she tried to do His will? Was she wrong in thinking she had found the truth? Did God not like her? Was God even in control? Did He actually exist?

She had been in such a state of shock all day that she had been unable to face these questions. Now, in the blackness and loneliness of the night, she could only think the worst. This was it; her short life was about to end. She would leave all the people she loved and they would carry on without her. Tears poured down her cheeks in self-pity, her shoulders heaved with sobs. "Why did You let this happen to me?" she cried out to God. "What have I done wrong? Do You even care about me? Are you even out there?!"

After a long, long while, her anger and hurt subsided; there were no tears left to cry. She sat on the couch, staring out her open window. The soft, warm breeze blew through her long, brown hair and dried her tear-stained face. In the darkness of the night sky, little stars twinkled peacefully, stable, and steadfast. A full round moon shone brightly in the deep blue heavens. The quiet stillness was comforting.

Gradually, an encouraging thought dawned on her tormented mind. She remembered the exhortation Brother William had given on trials and their purpose in a believer's life. The verses he had quoted were coming back to her. She took her Bible from the night table and found the passage she had highlighted from his talk, James chapter one, verses two to five. *"Consider it pure joy, my brothers, whenever you face trials of many kinds, because you know that the testing of your faith develops perseverance. Perseverance must finish its work so that you may be mature and complete, not lacking anything. If any of you lacks wisdom, he should ask God, who gives generously to all without finding fault, and it will be given to him."*

A little way down, she had highlighted verse twelve, as well. *"Blessed is the man who perseveres under trial, because when he has stood the test, he will receive the crown of life that God has promised to those who love him."*

She stared at the words on the page. Slowly, they began to make sense to her. "If I don't understand why God is doing this to me," she thought, "then I guess I should pray and ask for wisdom." With her head bowed low, she opened her heart to God and laid bare the thoughts she was struggling with. Never had she prayed more earnestly, begging God to help her see His plan. It was an incredible relief to lay all of this before a much Higher Being. A little confidence returned, that God controlled all, knew all, and had truly answered her prayers so many times in the last year.

"Now," she thought, "I must go in search of His answer to me." She smiled, remembering that she was very close to reaching her goal of reading the whole Bible through. There was only the book of Malachi and the last three chapters in Revelation left. "Tonight, I must finish!" she determined.

Having left her troubles in God's hands for the moment, she was better able to focus on what she was reading. As always in her reading, a few verses leapt off the page—exactly fitting her situation: *"You have said, 'It is futile to serve God. What did we gain by carrying out his requirements and going about like mourners before the LORD Almighty? But now we call the arrogant blessed. Certainly the evildoers prosper, and even those who challenge God escape. Then those who feared the LORD talked with each other, and the LORD listened and heard. A scroll of remembrance was written in his presence concerning those who feared the LORD and honoured his name. They will be mine, says the LORD Almighty, in the day when I make up my treasured possession. I will spare them, just as in compassion a man spares his son who serves him. And you will again see the distinction between the righteous and the wicked, between those who serve God and those who do not."[1]*

A smile passed over her tear-stained face. "How could I have forgotten?" she asked herself. "It's not about this life—it's all about the life to come. That's when the reward will be given! Now is only my probation, my time to serve faithfully in whatever way I am asked, for however long I'm asked to do so."

Drifting into her mind came the stories of faithful, godly servants that she had been reading about for almost a year. How many of them had lived lives full of good things and pleasant days? Some yes, but many were persecuted, hated, and cast out of society. Then, of course, there was Jesus. His existence had been devoid of most common human pleasantries. He'd given up his life on a daily basis for everyone else around him. She remembered reading how he had pleaded with God for another way to save the world. He had prayed, sweating great drops of blood, feeling the terror of crucifixion and fearing the mocking and pain he was to endure.

Slowly her mind searched for a passage that she remembered reading not so long ago. "I'm sure it explained how Jesus was able to overcome the trial he had to go through," she thought. Flipping through the New Testament, she looked at all her highlighted passages, until at last found the one that she wanted. Hebrews twelve, verse two: *"Let us fix our eyes on Jesus, the author and perfecter of our faith, who for the joy set before him endured the cross, scorning its shame, and sat down at the right hand of the throne of God."*

"It was the joy," she whispered, "the vision he had of the wonderful Kingdom God would give him! That was what gave him the strength to go through his crucifixion."

Finally, she read the last chapters of Revelation. To her great delight they were all about this exciting time to come when Jesus

---

[1] Malachi 3:14–18

Christ will reign on earth. *"And I saw the souls of those who had been beheaded because of their testimony for Jesus and because of the word of God. They had not worshipped the beast or his image or received his mark on their foreheads or their hands. They came to life and reigned with Christ a thousand years."*[2]

"Imagine how I would feel as a believer if I had to face *beheading* for my beliefs!" she thought astonished. "Would I have been baptized if it was at the risk of my life? Yet these people kept their faith in God's promises. They didn't question whether God existed just because He wasn't protecting their lives right then. Their vision of the future Kingdom must have been very strong—their faith a confident, sure belief in what was to come."

She read about the Book of Life and smiled. "I know that my name has been written there."

Chapter twenty-two lifted her mind to the vision she struggled to keep. The great city of the Lamb... the water of life... no longer any curse... no more a need of light... for God will give them light and they will reign for ever and ever.

"'Behold I am coming soon!'" she read over and over. "And yes," she thought, "he is! If I die from this, my next waking moment will be with Jesus in His Kingdom! In one sense, I am privileged not to have to wait any longer for that day to come."

Her heart peaceful and her faith restored, she slept the last few hours of the night.

---

[2] Revelation 20:4

CHAPTER 40

Another Dark Day

The next day was spent making a comfortable spot for Verity in the living room. A hospital bed had been ordered, which arrived just before Dr. Filbert came over to hook up the immunotherapy in an IV drip. The kind doctor explained how to help ease Verity's suffering and nausea, and gave Kara liquid painkiller that was easy to swallow. With the medication, Verity felt a considerable measure of relief.

Since both her legs were becoming unreliable, Verity gathered what she needed around her so that she didn't have to walk far. Dr. Filbert recommended a nurse, and with her assistance and expertise Verity felt confident that she would be well taken care of.

During that day, there were still occasional bouts of tears and self-pity, but on the whole, the long night of wrestling with God's will had prepared her to accept whatever would come. She was hoping for a miracle, but trying to fortify herself for the worst. "Your will, not mine," was her constant prayer. Her family was having more trouble coming to terms with their shock and sorrow than she was. It was hard for them to see it from the 'eye of faith.'

As she lay in the comfortable hospital bed, she reflected on how privileged she was to have found a hope for life beyond death, before this tragedy came upon her. If she hadn't spent the last ten months searching earnestly for life and truth in the Bible, she wouldn't be able to face death so graciously now. In fact, when she visualised how she would have felt had this cancer occurred a year ago, she couldn't imagine anything other than absolute terror and self-pity. That brought her to a measure of thankfulness —realizing God had brought her to a full understanding before all this had overtaken her! Even now, facing almost certain death, she had found true life.

Aunt Judy continued to be rather outspoken about the tragedy. "I just can't believe this has happened to you, my dear!" she said tearfully again and again. "If anything like this happens to me before I get my chance to retire—I couldn't cope! I just know I couldn't cope!"

Verity understood that Aunt Judy was trying to sympathise with her. But the words did anything but help! In fact, it reminded Verity of how easy it was to be a 'satan' to someone else.

"How can you be so calm about this," she had asked later in amazement at Verity's peaceful composure. "This is so unfair for you!"

Verity tried explaining but she could see that Aunt Judy wasn't taking it in. As she lay on the bed, hour after hour, fading in and out of sleep, Verity reflected that Aunt Judy was like the builder in one of Jesus' parables, who *'built his house upon the sand.'* [1] When the rains came, the sand was washed away and down fell the house. Aunt Judy had focused all her hopes and dreams solely on this life. A crisis like the one Verity was undergoing would wash away everything she had. She would crumble to pieces, like she said she would. There would be no way to see a brighter side. While Verity still held onto hopes and dreams for her teenage years, she had one vivid, solid, wonderful Hope of the Kingdom to come! With this vision in mind, she could be dashed by the storms and still have a house that stood strong on the rock.

She tried to explain this to Thomas that evening but like Aunt Judy, he was having trouble getting past the same feeling that God had let her down.

---

[1] Matthew 7:24–27

"It would have been worse if I was killed instantly in a car crash. It happens so often in the news. This way I get to say goodbye to all the people I love... and maybe I'll get better." But she wasn't feeling any improvement... not yet!

Thomas turned away as tears welled up in his eyes. Minutes went by before he looked at her again and then he asked hesitantly, "Are you going to tell Peter, or would you rather I did?"

Verity sighed deeply. "I think it would be better if you phoned him, Thomas, and told him everything" she said slowly. "Tell him that I hope he will think it over and pray before he says anything to me. I know it's going to be really hard on him."

Saturday morning, Thomas decided to drive into town and tell Peter personally. Forty minutes later, Verity's mom called out to her that Peter was driving into their driveway.

Feeling very uneasy, Verity wondered how Peter was going to handle the news. There was no way he could have taken time to think this through. Just how was he going to react?

When Kara opened the door, Peter stood there ashen, his brown eyes desperately hoping the news wasn't true. But the look on their faces confirmed Thomas' words. "I can't believe this!" he exclaimed stormily, striding over to where Verity rested against the cushions, looking so thin and wasted. "You have less than two months to live? Why didn't you tell me sooner?!" He tried to say more but emotion overcame him and he burst into tears.

Verity started out calmly. "Peter, we only found out Thursday. By then we knew you were on the road driving home. And I might get better if the new drugs work... I might have longer."

Sitting down on the floor beside her, Peter buried his head in his arms and sobbed.

She tried to explain how she was trying to view it from a different perspective, but Peter didn't seem to hear. So instead, she just passed him tissues and stroked his head. At last, he gained control, but his anger burned on. "How could God do this *to you?* I've never seen anyone give up their life so completely and now He strikes you with this! Why? *Why?!"*

Verity didn't say anything. The night she had wrestled in her mind with God's will was clearly before her, but she didn't know how to bring Peter to feel the same peace? Perhaps he could only come to it himself.

"Verity," he implored tearfully, "how many times did I *beg* you to go to the doctor? If you had only gone three months ago, maybe they could have done something!"

Peter's words hurt but what could she say? He was right.

"I know!" she agonized. "Peter, I wish so much that I'd listened to you! I wish I'd realised how serious this was! But I can't change that now. I am trying to accept it…"

Angry at her peaceful resignation, Peter vented, "What? Why? How can you just lie there and *blissfully* accept death? Don't you *care* that you're leaving us all behind?"

It was all too much for Verity. She had fought her own battles with this but dealing with Peter's grief was causing her to slip from her resolve. The look on his face crushed her to the core. Where was the kind, patient, forgiving Peter? She had never seen him this upset before and she felt confused and a little betrayed. Waves of self-pity began to sweep over her.

"I do care!" she protested, as tears slid down her cheeks. "I love you! I don't *want* to leave you, ever! I didn't *ask* for this, Peter!" Overcome with deep emotion, she picked up the bowl beside her and was violently sick.

Anxiously, Kara came running over to help.

Flustered and bewildered, Peter stood up. "I'm sorry," he apologized earnestly. "I didn't mean to make things worse…"

Pulling herself together, Verity begged tearfully, "Peter, I need you to go home and pray and read. I need you to think about this before you come back."

Incredulous, Peter shook his head. In his turbulent state of mind, he was unable to think clearly. "You're asking me to pray and read when God has allowed *this* to happen to you? I don't get it! I just don't get it! And *now* you want me to leave?"

She nodded with a sob. Their conversation had gone so poorly. She wished she knew how to smooth things over, but she didn't. "Please, Peter," she begged, "please go—but come back *as soon* as you can! You know I love you!"

CHAPTER 41

The Visitors

Monday night, Thomas brought home a huge card for Verity from everyone at school. All her friends and many other students had written little messages expressing their love and sympathy. Even the teachers had signed their names and written messages. Many asked if they could come and see her. Kara offered to phone them and plan times.

Later that evening, as Thomas sat close beside her reading the various messages, Verity reflected, "It's *very* kind of everyone to send me this card. But I'm not *just* a sick girl!" she protested. "I have a new hope of *eternal* life." With a laugh, she added, "I wish everyone was congratulating me... not just feeling sorry for me."

Thomas looked up from the card, deep in thought. No one in the room said a word. Soon the nurse came over to help her get ready for the night. Verity was glad she was a kind lady, as it was quite different having a stranger in their home. "At least," she reminded herself, "I'm not in a hospital full of strangers!"

Being at home with her mother all day was also a new experience for Verity. Kara had requested time off from work to spend the days with her and Aunt Judy had agreed, of course. With lots of time to talk and not much else to do, her mother seemed much more open to discussing the Bible than she ever had before. Urgency lay in Verity's heart to share her hope with everyone she loved. Yet, even with the great discussions they had, Kara didn't seem to view the Bible as anything more than an interesting historical account, with good morals and lessons – but not a life-changing force.

Aunt Judy was still unable to deal with what was happening. Like Peter, she couldn't understand Verity's faithful perseverance. Every day though, she brought home a healthy drink for her niece from the store. That was about all Verity could keep down, and only if she drank it very slowly.

After Mom and Aunt Judy had retired to bed that night, Verity lay on the hospital bed with a soft light shining onto her Bible. Thomas approached hesitantly to sit in the chair next to her. "Peter is really taking this hard," he relayed. "We've had some talks about it and he's so angry that God would let this happen."

Looking up with a pained expression, Verity wasn't sure what to say.

"He's afraid to come here and upset you again," Thomas added. "Actually," he confessed softly, "I don't understand why *you* aren't angry about it."

"I was at first," she admitted, "and those feelings do keep coming back; but, Thomas, I have a hope for a *wonderful* future in God's Kingdom. I know I will be raised to life again and I pray that Jesus will accept me to live *forever!*"

Pointing to the big card that sat on the table beside her, she asked, "Do you feel sorry for any of the people who signed this?"

Thomas looked confused.

She tried to help him understand. "They are the ones to be truly sorry for. I have the hope of eternal life, Thomas. Some of these people here," she said, waving her hand in front of the card, "at this point in their lives, they don't even see their need for God. At any moment, their lives could end and then they will perish... forever."[1]

"Like me?" Thomas asked seriously.

Verity contemplated that for a moment. "Well yes, Thomas, unless you do something about what you've come to know... Yes, you, and Peter, and Mom, and Aunt Judy are all in a much sorrier state than I am."

---

[1] Ephesians 2:12-13; Psalm 49:12-20

"Where does it say that again?" Thomas asked, touching her Bible.

It didn't take Verity long to find a passage in her NIV Bible. It was highlighted in yellow. "Paul is talking to the Gentile Ephesians," she told him. "He's recalling the state they were in before they learned the Gospel. He says, *"remember that at that time you were separate from Christ, excluded from citizenship in Israel and foreigners to the covenants of the promise, without hope and without God in the world. But now in Christ Jesus you who once were far away have been brought near by the blood of Christ."*

"But didn't Jesus solve that problem when he died for the world?"

She looked at the passage again more carefully. "It says, *'you were foreigners to the covenants of promise,'*" she reasoned. "I'm pretty sure we only inherit those promises if we repent and are baptised into Christ."[2]

"How sure are you?" he smiled.

With a smile, she shrugged. "You and me, we're both new to this, Thomas," she admitted. "I wish I had longer to learn more. But from what I have read and heard, it seems that all that we are born with is mortality. We live, we die – that's it. If you want something more than that, God expects you to follow His directions. Even then, eternal life isn't something we can earn but a gift that God gives us."[3]

Looking at Thomas slouched in the old armchair, his face so sensitive and sad, she again felt the sorrow of leaving. "Oh Thomas," she sighed with great agony, "there are so many people I

---

[2] Galatians 3:27 (put on Christ); Colossians 3:2–10 (put on the new man cp. Romans 6:3–13); Matthew 22:1–14 (the man without a wedding garment); Revelation 19:7–9.

[3] Romans 6:23; Acts 2:37-38; 16:30-33

want to see again after I die! I do hope that what's happening to me makes them all come to God, not turn away!"

Getting up, her brother sat down beside her on the floor. Tears filled his eyes. He took her hand. "Verity, this last year," he began, emotionally, "you have made all of us think—think really hard about life! What's happening to you right now has already made me realise that I can't take life for granted! Thanks for looking out for me when I was in trouble. I'm not sure yet about everything but I am seeing the importance of a life with hope, *real hope!*" Wiping his face, he added with a sad smile, "You can know for sure that you've made a huge difference in my life!"

"Thank you for letting me know that," she said gratefully. "I really want to see you again, Thomas! I want to share *forever* with *you* and mom, and Aunt Judy and... and *Peter!*" She swallowed hard. "Please help Peter get through this! I don't want him to wait too long. I hope he and I can have at least one more good talk..."

Thomas nodded seriously. "I'll do my best," was all he could promise. "Goodnight, Sis," he said affectionately, squeezing her hand, and then he headed to his room.

There were many visitors to Verity's bedside in the next little while. Many friends from school came. She told each one, "I may be leaving this life but I've found the hope for the life to come—when Jesus returns and resurrects me."

Even a few of her friends from Saskatchewan sent cards. Ken actually phoned to talk to her, but as thoughtful as he was, it was very difficult for either of them to know what to say.

Verity was so relieved one day when her mother told her that the Symons had arrived. She had been rather down that morning and was in need of their company. At home and amongst her friends, Verity had done much of the giving during the last week, helping others to feel better about her situation. Today she felt her focus dissipating and she needed to talk. As soon as Craig Symons asked her how she was, tears welled up in her eyes. It was wonderful to have the freedom to express her fears to those who didn't need her to stay strong.

Beth Symons took Verity's hand and cried some tears of her own. "You've been so brave and faithful through this dear," she said.

"Well," Verity said between sobs, "as long as I keep the right perspective, I can see things the right way. I know God has been so good to let me find this hope before I die, but..." she dissolved in tears again for a few minutes.

"The struggle in our minds stays with us to the very end," Craig encouraged gently, as he pulled up a chair to sit close by. "Verity, you've found the source of faith, don't let go of your reading and prayer."

"Sometimes though," she said, eager to pour out all her inner anxieties, "sometimes I wonder if I'm good enough to be in the Kingdom. Sometimes I feel this sickness means God isn't..." she broke down again, "isn't pleased with me!"

"Verity," said Beth soothingly, "we all go through periods of self-doubt, but at times like this, you need to keep remembering how God has *blessed* you and been there for you. Look at how He has lovingly guided you! He knew your urgent situation before you did, and He sped up your search for the truth in the Bible. Look at how He answered your prayers about Thomas. God has shown you all along that He loves you. What you are going through is very sad but perhaps some greater purpose is being worked out, one that we know nothing of now."

Craig nodded. "God's ultimate purpose is to fill this earth with His glory, forever.[4] Sometimes the trials that come upon us are not only for our benefit, but also for the benefit of others. When we stand immortal in the Kingdom, I'm sure we will at last understand why God chose to work in our lives the way that He did. You've done the

---

[4] Numbers 14:21; Psalm 72:17–19

right things, Verity—you've followed His commands. Just trust Him to the end. God knows what is best. Some of the most faithful people in the Bible had to endure the most terrible trials."

Picking up a piece of coloured cardstock that she had brought with her, Beth held it out. "There are some verses on this that I think will comfort you," she told her. "They will encourage you to have confidence that God is working in your life, that this is part of His plan, and that he wants you in His Kingdom. The girls did the decorating!"

Verity accepted the gift. Three verses were neatly printed in the middle, and lots of colourful stickers surrounded them. The verses were from the NIV:

"And I am sure that God who began the good work within you will keep right on helping you grow in his grace until his task within you is finally finished on that day when Jesus Christ returns." Philippians 1:6

"And we know that all that happens to us is working for our good if we love God and are fitting into his plans." Romans 8:28

"So don't be afraid, little flock. For it gives your Father great happiness to give you the Kingdom." Luke 12:32

Just hearing the Symons' complete confidence in God's plan, re- affirmed the faith Verity had been trying to keep. They talked with her a long while, and read a few well-chosen passages from the Bible. After a very sincere prayer, they left.

More than a few times in the next two weeks, the Symons returned to help bolster her faith and share in remembering Christ with her, since she couldn't go out on a Sunday. A few times they brought Jessica along, and sometimes one of the other children. Verity wasn't sure just how much Jessica understood about what was happening. She had developed a special relationship with the little girl and she worried how Jessica would react when she was gone. There was a cute little picture hanging on her wall that Jessica had drawn. A tall girl and a short girl stood hand in hand with rainbows in the background, wolves and lambs playing beside them.

"This is the Kingdom!" Jessica had explained, "and that's you and me together."

Verity had given Jessica one of her school photos and written a big, "I love you!" on the back.

On one of the visits, Verity gave the Symons a little note and asked them to read it when they got home. "It's just a few requests I have for... for the end," she said.

Craig Symons swallowed hard. He nodded, solemnly tucking the note into his pocket.

"Please help Peter through this!" Verity begged.

Beth Symons asked gently, "Has he come to see you yet?"

Sadly, Verity shook her head. "I want to see him so much... but... but..." She searched for the right words to explain, only she couldn't find them. How could she explain how his anger had made her feel incredible self-pity? She longed to help him, but she didn't know how!

"I didn't think it would take so long..." she replied, her voice breaking. "What if Peter isn't in the Kingdom?" she questioned as tears slid down her cheeks. "Sometimes I wonder if I will always feel sad and miss him if he's not there. And my family, I love all of them. Will I be lonely if none of them are there?"

Beth clasped her hand. "All of us have certain people that we'd like to keep with us," she empathized, "who for whatever reason don't choose to follow God's ways and therefore won't be accepted. But human nature will be done away with when we are immortal—there won't be destructive emotions. Yes, you will remember the people you loved who aren't there, but God has promised to take away all sorrow and tears.[5] It's hard for us to believe now but we need to trust His promise."

She paused, looking at Verity earnestly. "I think Peter is a very wise young man. With enough time, and God's help, I'm quite certain he'll come to choose the right way."

Verity smiled. "I do hope so! But please keep praying for him and don't...don't let him go. I know he has a lot of respect for both of you."

"We'll do our best to be there for him and everyone else in your family," Craig Symons promised.

Before they left, Craig gave her one more thing to think about. "You know, Verity," he said thoughtfully, "your worries aren't unique. A lot of people wonder how they could possibly be happy in the Kingdom without certain ones they love. But think for a moment of Jesus. After all, he is our example to follow. Jesus knew his Father's plan for the future age much more completely than any of us ever will. Think about what Jesus was prepared to give up so that he could have a part in the life to come. He gave up every pleasure in his mortal existence. He had no home, no wife, no children, no fulfilling occupation or hobbies; he even gave up his own life in torture! Jesus felt the future age was worth the loss of all these things. Yes, he gets to be the King—but our promise is to rule with him!" He rose, giving Verity a gentle pat on her shoulder. "You will be happy, Verity! Of that there is no doubt."

Purity and her parents also came to visit. Verity wasn't sure how she had earned Purity's respect, but it was always there, deep and real in her soft, green eyes. Verity loved her friend deeply, but this crisis made it difficult for either of them to know what to say. A slight feeling of envy struck through Verity's heart. She hated to feel this way, or even to admit it to herself, but it was there. Purity had grown up with this wonderful hope. It had been taught to her from

---

[5] Revelation 7:14–17

the time she could first understand. Did she even fully appreciate the jewel she held? Purity got to live on, healthy and strong, enjoying the happy teen years ahead of her... "Stop it!" Verity told herself, "I've got to be thankful for what God has given me!"

Today, there was something Purity wanted to say. She had been looking at Verity with big, sad eyes, and suddenly she clasped her friend's arm and started to cry. "It's not fair!" she wailed much to Verity's surprise. "God should have taken *me,* not you! You're the one who talks to everyone about the Bible. You're so good at explaining things. You've made so many people think! I wish so much that I could be like you!"

"Oh, Purity!" Verity exclaimed, as they held each other and cried. She was so surprised at her friends' outburst. "One day you will see just how precious the treasure is that God has given you. Then you won't be afraid to tell anyone. It will just flow out of you."

Purity wiped her eyes. "Verity, I hope so much I can be like you," she sobbed. "If only you could stay with me!"

Verity had to focus hard. *"Forever,* Purity!" she reminded her friend and herself. "It will be forever in God's Kingdom!

CHAPTER 42

Good-bye in a Letter

As the days passed, the sickness grew worse. Verity lost the use of her legs. Inside, she could feel the grip of the horrid disease taking its toll there as well. Her skin was turning an awfully dark yellow colour. The immunotherapy was not having any effect. Nurses came and went. No one talked about months left to live anymore; instead, she overheard a nurse tell her mother it might be a matter of days.

The pain medication doubled, then tripled. Verity slept more than she was awake. Knowing she must look terrible, she was afraid to look in a mirror. Whenever visitors came, she covered herself in blankets as much as possible.

In between all the visits and the hours of sleep, she began reading the Bible from the beginning again. She smiled, remembering many of the old questions she had begun with. "No wonder I had such difficulty understanding," she thought to herself. "I came to the Bible with so many wrong ideas!" Prayer and reading continued to give her the strength to keep her faith.

Time was running out and Peter had not come. Thomas talked to him everyday, so Verity knew he was still struggling with the same feelings and didn't want to upset her again.

At last, Mrs. Bryant came over, with a big pot of purple and pink pansies. The card simply said, "Love Peter". Verity felt comfort every time she looked over at those flowers. That little gesture meant a great deal.

Mrs. Bryant apologized for her son's state of mind. "I'm so sorry!" she said, taking Verity's hand. "I don't know how to help him. He's beside himself! He's only just barely passing his courses. He's lost interest in all the things he once enjoyed."

"Please tell him I love him," Verity begged. "And so does God."

Then one night Thomas brought home a note, it said:

Dearest Verity,
You mean everything to me!!
I can't bear this.
Love, Peter

That night she told Thomas she would write Peter a letter, even though she would rather have spoken in person. Somehow, she had to say her last good-bye. She had thought a lot about what she wanted to tell him if he came, but she knew it might come out better on paper anyway. Then she could express her real feelings without hesitation. Thomas left her a stack of paper and a pen. She chose not to take the pain medication that evening so she could focus better. Having slept most of the day, she was wide awake when everyone else headed for bed. Picking up the pen she wrote:

Dearest Peter,

You've been my best friend, even if we haven't always listened well to each other. I'm sorry, Peter! I wish I had listened to you earlier and realised how serious this illness was.

I'm so thankful for all the support you've given me, your cheerful presence in the last year, your friendship and the care you have shown to Thomas and I. If there's anyone I hate to leave, it has to be you!

I hope that my influence on your life won't be to turn you away from God—or my friendship will have had no value and you would've been better off without it. How I hope that my friendship has been God's opportunity for you to find the hope of life forever!

I don't see this as the end, Peter. My next waking moment will be the day I've longed for, when Jesus will stand again upon this earth and grant us immortality. Never again will there be sorrow, or pain, or tears. I pray that if God sees fit to grant me eternal life, I will also see you there, Peter!

There is a day coming soon, when many who lie in the grave will awaken from their sleep. Some of them have been waiting thousands of years to enjoy the promises they looked forward to. When they rise, it will seem to them as though they just awoke from a good night's sleep!

Imagine, Peter, how wonderful it will be to hear the words, 'Come you who are blessed by my Father; take your inheritance, the kingdom prepared for you since the creation of the world!'

Imagine running on legs that never grow weary, with bodies sustained by God's Spirit, knowing that never again will we face death or pain or temptation.

Imagine talking to all the people we've read about in the Bible, asking them why they chose to do what they did and finding out more about their lives. There are so many people I've come to love in the Bible! Maybe we'll be sent by Jesus to work side by side with them on some exciting project. Perhaps they will end up being our good friends!

You and I, Peter, we might be asked by Jesus to go and help in countries and villages that we've never seen before. Or maybe we'll even come back to Grandville, to help those who have survived God's judgments on this earth.

I can't wait to see the temple built in Jerusalem and God's righteous Son set up as King. Peter, think how amazing it will be to have a man like Jesus as King over all the earth! There will be perfect justice, kindness, and peace. Happiness will have a new meaning!

Please always remember, I've found my life! Maybe it seems to all around me that God has taken life from me, but the reality is He's blessed me with the discovery of eternal life!

It's not about this life, Peter. This is only the preparation for something so much grander. What are a few years of mortal existence in comparison to eternity in God's Kingdom?

Peter, please be there! I love you!

Verity

As tears streamed down her face, she folded the letter, put it in an envelope and set it aside to give to Thomas the next day.

The next morning when Verity awoke, she knew her time was very near. Her abdomen was swollen like a balloon. She felt extremely weak and ill. For the first time, she hoped that there wouldn't be much longer to wait.

With all the great talks she'd had with her family lately, Verity would have felt completely at peace—if it weren't for Peter. Where was he? Surely, he must have come to terms with this by now? She regretted ever telling him to leave. In her mind, she had thought perhaps he would stay away for a day or two—but it had been over two weeks!

Thomas gazed at her anxiously as he took the letter she handed him. Feeling a sense of urgency, Verity tried to speak. To her surprise, her words came out thick and slurred. With much difficulty, she struggled to say, "Tell Peter to come, no matter how he feels!" After a few attempts, Thomas finally understood. Reaching out, he squeezed her arm affectionately before he left for school.

An hour later, Peter came, with a bouquet of red roses. Kara had popped out for a minute to get some more medication, leaving Verity alone with the nurse.

Verity thought she must look terrible and the look on Peter's face confirmed it. Shocked and dismayed, he stood stock-still for a moment, taking in the change in her condition.

She thought to herself with a pang of sorrow how haggard he looked. Had he eaten in the last two weeks? His face was so thin and grave. For someone who had always been so cheerful and such a tease, there wasn't much sign of it now.

Peter set the roses down on the table nearby and Verity smiled gratefully. "Beautiful!" she said.

Sitting down sadly in the chair beside her bed, he apologized. "I'm sorry I didn't come sooner. I didn't want to make things worse for you and I'm *still*... still struggling. But I read your beautiful letter..." Tears began sliding down his face. "And Thomas said if I didn't come now, I... I might not get... to say good-bye!" He tried to say more but only choked.

Verity nodded and reached out for his hand.

Gripping hers firmly with both of his, he carried on telling her how he had tried to read the Bible but it wasn't helping.

"You need... faith," Verity tried to say. She had to say it a few times before Peter heard her.

"How do I get faith?" he asked wearily. He didn't want to argue.

She glanced over at her Bible.

"It's not working for me," he protested sadly. "I'm not even sure I believe anymore."

"Keep trying," she smiled.

Looking at her through his tears, he protested gently. "I don't know how you can smile, when you're lying there in pain, knowing that life is almost over."

Again, she struggled to speak. "My vision…"

Peter was realising the effort it took for her to speak. He tried to put it together for her. "You believe that if I read the Bible and pray, I'll have a vision like yours of the Kingdom?"

She nodded, attempting another smile but she was quickly tiring.

"I've got to admit," he added, "you have a wonderful vision. You see all this… and I appreciate how helpful you find it… but I don't. I don't see it… I just see a God who doesn't… answer…" He choked up and could say no more.

For a long while they sat in silence while Verity rested, her eyes closed. At last, she opened them and rallied one more time. "Hebrews twelve," she begged.

Peter finally understood that she wanted him to read it to her. As he read, he understood better what she wanted to say. *"'Let us fix our eyes on Jesus, the author and perfecter of our faith, who for the joy set before him endured the cross, scorning its shame, and sat down at the right hand of the throne of God… And you have forgotten that word of encouragement that addresses you as sons; My son, do not make light of the Lord's discipline, and do not lose heart when he rebukes you… No discipline seems pleasant at the time, but painful. Later on, however it produces a harvest of*

362

righteousness and peace for those who have been trained by it... Therefore since we are receiving a kingdom that cannot be shaken, let us be thankful, and so worship God acceptably with reverence and awe...'"

Verity was smiling at him as he finished but her eyelids were heavy, and she was fighting to keep them open.

With concern for her patient, the nurse quietly suggested that it would be best for Peter to go.

"Good-bye, Verity," he said tearfully and gently kissed her forehead.

He was just heading towards his car when Kara arrived back home. Seeing he was leaving, she said to him hesitantly, sorrow in every line of her face, "Peter, the nurse says Verity won't make it through tonight. Please stay... *if you can.* I know Verity would want you to..." She tried to say more but faltered.

The realisation that it was so near to the end hit Peter hard. Numbed and speechless, he followed Kara back into the house. Sitting down heavily in the chair beside Verity, he took her hand once again.

Verity's consciousness was fading fast, yet she heard Peter come back and she squeezed his hand as tightly as she could. Full peace settled over her. She was ready to leave Peter and all her loved ones in God's care. Mrs. Symons' words from so long ago had come back to her. "When things are beyond our control, sometimes all we can do is pray." In her last conscious moments, she prayed in her mind one last prayer that God would take care of Peter and all the ones she loved.

Verity's eyes barely even fluttered again. Soon Thomas, Kara, and Aunt Judy joined Peter around the bed. Kara held her daughter's other limp hand as they watched her breathing become more and more erratic.

Sitting there in agony, watching her life slip away, Peter thought about the letter that he had stuck in his shirt pocket. He didn't understand, or even know if he wanted to understand. He was just so angry, and weary, and sad. Tears slid down his face profusely. How he wished that he could have been more of a support, and not abandoned his best friend when she needed him the most. But he still had nothing positive or uplifting to say. Pulling out the note with his free hand, he reread it. "Maybe," he thought to himself, "If I'd just listened, Verity would have encouraged my heart!"

Not long after the clock struck one, the dark-haired girl breathed her last. Her little mortal existence was ended, and she lay completely still in the bed. They all cried and hugged each other, knowing nothing more could be done. Nothing more would be said or felt by her. It was over. She would now lie silent and unconscious until the day came that she had looked forward to so much.

CHAPTER 43

"I Know that My Redeemer Liveth"

P eter sat alone in his room. His straight, brown hair was still wet from a shower and carefully combed into place. It was a Monday evening, but he wore his crisp, white shirt and tie. A black suit coat dangled from the hook on his closed door. In a couple of hours, the funeral would begin. Right now, he just wanted to be alone with his thoughts. Downstairs, he could hear his nieces running around happily without a care in the world.

Loneliness seemed to fill his heart so full he thought it would break. Verity, his best friend, was gone. It had all happened so fast! He hated the way he had reacted. Yet even now he wasn't sure he could've said or done anything differently. If only he could turn to someone who would understand, someone with the wisdom to help him through this. Yet at this crucial time, his family—whom he had always relied on before—was only making things worse.

He'd never had a chance to tell Verity of his week out East. He was no longer sure of anything. Andrew had undermined everything he thought he'd figured out. Deep into his theology studies, his older brother didn't take lightly to Peter questioning the Trinity. He had answers for every verse that Peter showed him, which seemed quite convincing. Outnumbered by Andrew, James and his parents, and not fully familiar with the new way of understanding God's relationship with Jesus, Peter felt he lost every debate. Writings from church fathers in the past held a lot of weight in his family and were difficult for to Peter to refute. Most evenings they had been up until past midnight discussing the issues that Peter raised, but Andrew had always done most of the talking. Now Peter felt like his whole family were against him. Who was Peter, to question the teachings of the church? Had he attended Theological College? Was he preparing to be a Pastor like Andrew was? The study-sheets he tried to show them were quickly dismissed. Andrew had warned him, again and again, not to get involved with such a radical group! But was it a radical group? How could it be radical to read the Bible for oneself and believe what you read?! Wasn't Christianity based on the Bible?

In many ways Peter just wanted to give up on religion all together. The pain in his heart made him angry with God. He wanted to lash out. A part of him chafed against the whole concept of any so-called 'loving' Heavenly Father who answered prayer. His desperate pleas had not been heard! How could someone as faithful as Verity die so *tragically?*

Wiping away the tears, he shook his head in dismay. Grabbing his Bible from the bedside table, he placed it up on a high shelf. There were so many different 'Christian' groups all insistent that their own teachings were the 'truth' and that others were false. Was religion supposed to lead to such conflict? Was it all about arguments and division? If God was really in control, why would He allow His church to be so full of confusion? Nothing made sense anymore! Yet a line from Verity's letter kept repeating itself in his head; *"I hope that my influence in your life won't be to turn you away from God—or my friendship will have had no value and you would have been better off without it."* Those words echoed around inside and he wished that he could shut them out. Picking up the letter, he carefully folded it up and tucked it away inside the drawer of his desk.

Rising from his chair, Peter picked up his jacket and decided to walk out to the cemetery. The funeral was to be held at the graveside on the outskirts of Grandville. It was only a few kilometres away.

With his jacket slung over one shoulder, he shuffled despondently down the stairs. His mom looked up from reading a story to her little granddaughters. He could see the love and concern in her eyes, and he knew she wished she could help. So many times in the last few days, she had tried to tell him that Verity was in heaven, looking down in peace and happiness on all that was going on. Sadly though, those words no longer provided any comfort.

"I don't know why you keep saying that, Mom," he had remarked just yesterday in frustration. "Firstly, it isn't even what our church would say. Verity doesn't believe in the Trinity so our Pastor... *even Andrew*... would say she's not a Christian. Secondly, as I've tried to show you, Verity won't be thinking or feeling anything until the resurrection."

"Oh, Peter," his mother had implored, "No wonder you're struggling so much with all of this. Of course, Verity is in heaven."

"Is that what you'd like to believe?" he'd asked, "or have you come to that conclusion from reading the Bible?" Then he had stopped in shock—realising he had just echoed Verity's words to him not so very long ago.

All these things went through his mind as he stood there on the stairs. "Mom," he said flatly, "I'm going to walk to the service, I'll see you there."

His mother seemed very concerned. "Peter, we'll be leaving in half an hour or so. Why don't you just wait and get a ride?"

"It's okay," he stated firmly. "I need some time to think."

It was a balmy June evening as he set out on foot. All around the town children were outside playing games; people were barbecuing their dinners; life carried on as though nothing had happened. Peter was relieved to finally walk past all the houses and down a long, quiet dirt road. Coming around the corner he saw the cemetery. Monuments and gravestones stretched from one end to the other under tall, stately maples and oaks. Lots of cars were lining the road and hundreds of people stood around. Peter was surprised how many students, neighbours and church members had come to pay their last regards. Putting his suit jacket on, he swallowed hard. This was it—this was the final, official good-bye.

Strains of music reached his ears, but he didn't recognise the tune until he was quite close. "That's Handel's Messiah playing," he thought, "I wonder if Verity requested that?" Listening to the words, he realised it was the piece, 'I Know That My Redeemer Liveth.' It seemed rather fitting; it had been her hope to the very end.

Peter saw Kara and Thomas standing together and they motioned for him to join them. A long, dark coffin lay close by, covered in flowers. It was painful to look at. Tears streamed down Thomas' face and Peter's eyes filled up. Putting their arms around each other they stood silently waiting for the service to begin.

As Peter glanced around, he recognised several friends from school. Even Mr. Connor stood far back in the crowd. Several faces were friends he recognised from the seminars. There were also people that Peter didn't know at all. It was plain to see that Verity's death had touched many lives.

Mr. Symons prayed to God and then opened his Bible to begin his words of comfort. "It's very fitting to remember that Verity began her search *at* a funeral, less than a year ago," he said. "A time such as this reminds all of us, that sooner or later, we will all come here. The writer of Ecclesiastes tells us, *'It is better to go to a house of mourning than to go to a house of feasting, for death is the destiny of every man; the living should take this to heart.'* "[1]

"As sad as such an occasion as this is," he went on to say, "good may come from pondering these things. We need to realise that unless we do as Verity did and search diligently for the hope and the promises God has offered—when death overtakes us—we will simply die and be no more.

"Many of us wish that Verity had realised earlier the seriousness of her health condition," he stated, pausing momentarily as grief contorted his face. "Perhaps then, she would still be with us today," he added, choking up.

---

[1] Ecclesiastes 7:2–4

Peter couldn't stop the tears that flooded down his face.

Keeping himself together, Mr. Symons continued, "However, while we might be saddened that Verity didn't seek medical treatment sooner, we rejoice that she urgently sought a cure from a much greater Physician, for a much more serious problem. We thank God that He allowed her to come to Him before it was too late. She found the 'water of life'[2] our Lord has prescribed, which will in the end bring forth life forever!

"Verity left this life with a smile on her lips, knowing that this is not the end. She wanted everyone to hear today the words of Job; *'I know that my Redeemer lives, and that in the end he will stand upon the earth. And after my skin has been destroyed, yet in my flesh I will see God; I myself will see him with my own eyes—I, and not another. How my heart yearns within me!'*[3]

"Without the resurrection of the dead, we would truly have only sorrow for Verity's untimely death. But she hopes to be a partaker of life again in the near future when Christ returns to earth to set up his Kingdom. In the words of Thessalonians, *'Brothers, we do not want you to be ignorant about those who fall asleep, or to grieve like the rest of men, who have no hope. We believe that Jesus died and rose again and so we believe that God will bring with Jesus those who have fallen asleep in him.'*[4]

"Till that day then, dear Verity, we say good-bye." Mr. Symons voice faltered again and Peter looked up through his tears wondering if the older man would make it through to the end. The last few words were hard to hear, "May God graciously give all of us the *hope* of seeing each other again and partaking in the promises that will surely come upon this earth."

Then Mr. Henderson stepped forward to explain that the closing hymn they were about to sing had also been a special request

---

[2] John 4:10–15
[3] Job 19:25–27
[4] 1 Thessalonians 4:13–14

from Verity. It was a rousing hymn, and Peter felt uncomfortable. This was a song of rejoicing, not one of mourning! He couldn't bear to sing, but he listened to the words,

"Lift now your voice and sing, Hallelujah, amen.
Sing loud of Israel's King, Hallelujah, amen.
Sing of the better day,
When earth shall own his sway, All nations him obey,
Hallelujah, amen.
Hail! Jesus comes again, Hallelujah, amen.
He comes o'er earth to reign, Hallelujah, amen.
True Heir to David's throne, He'll claim it as his own;
His power shall then be known, Hallelujah, amen..."

Mr. Henderson then closed in prayer.

The clouds in the sky were beginning to turn pink as the casket, covered in flowers, was lowered into the ground. Peter, Thomas, and Kara embraced and cried. Aunt Judy talked sadly with the Hendersons. Purity came over and hugged them all, and then for a while, everyone just stayed around and talked.

Feeling he needed to be alone once more, Peter was thinking about leaving when he felt a small hand reach into his. He looked down to see little Jessica Symons looking up at him. Her big, blue eyes were clouded over and there were tearstains on her face. "I'll be *your* sister now," she said generously.

Peter realised that Verity's death was as difficult for the little girl as it was for him. Gratefully, he knelt down and gave her a big hug. "Thanks," he managed to say. "I'll need you to be!"

"We'll see her again in the Kingdom," Jessica sobbed.

"You will," Peter consoled her.

Mr. Symons had been following his daughter and he put his arm on Peter's shoulders. "If you need a listening ear," he said, "just let us know. We really feel for you!"

Peter stood up and embraced the older man. "Thanks," he said, "I'll probably take you up on that... at some point."

The sky was becoming darker, with just the last few streaks of brilliant colour disappearing on the horizon. Most people were heading out to go back to the hall. Peter accepted the invitation to go as well but he didn't want a ride. "I'd just like to walk, if that's okay," he said, trudging off with his head down low.

Thomas looked over just in time to see Peter leaving. "Hey, Peter Bryant," he called out, "wait up! I'm coming with you!"

Peter turned around, with just a hint of a smile. Together, arms around each, he and Thomas made their way up the dusty, dirt road.

With one glance back at the graveyard, words flooded through Peter's mind. He might have hidden the note away in the drawer of his desk, but he couldn't remove it from his heart. "It's not about this life," she had pleaded. "This life is only preparation for something much grander. What are a few years of mortal existence in comparison to eternity in God's Kingdom?"

"Peter, please be there! I love you!"

That was how the letter ended. Verity had written it—and lifting up his tearstained face, Peter knew deep, *deep* down, that there was truth to her words.

Acknowledgments

I have had a tremendous amount of help in putting this book together. There have been so many people who have been wonderfully generous with their time and encouragement!

I'm very grateful first of all to God, who has given all of us life, opportunities and His sustaining spirit. I'm thankful that He has given us His Word, the Bible, the best book ever written.

I'd like to thank the people who have been influential in the ideas for In Search of Life, namely: Gerhard and Carolyn Runge, Perry and Nancylee Braux, Jim and Nancy Milner, and Allan and Jessica Crandlemire. We came together as a group of people from various religious backgrounds, with a common interest in reading the Bible. Thanks so much for all your great questions and comments in the last five years. Much of what is written in this book is based upon the discussions that we shared as we read through Genesis, Luke, and Acts.

Thanks to my husband (a real Mr. Symons) who patiently welcomed any questions and always directed everyone back to the Bible for their answers.

I'm very appreciative of all the encouraging words, opinions and great advice from many "proof-readers". Carol Link (a real Mrs. Symons) was most influential in gently guiding me along with her many thoughtful comments. I'd also like to thank Dorothy Link and Anna Moore for reading through the first, "bare-bones", grammatically incorrect, rough draft and giving me encouragement to carry on. Thanks also to my in-laws, my family, Perry and Nancy-Lee Braux, Hannah Abel, Laura Spry, Carolyn Runge, Jim and Nancy Milner, the Luke family, Sue Catchlove, Rhonda Saxon, and Dave Ormond for their unique insights and great suggestions! Thanks to three special ladies—Cathy Allen, Mona Findlay and Grace Lloyd. With different religious persuasions, they kindly gave me many useful comments and their honest feedback. A big thank-you to Rebecca Lines who gave this book a final grammatical inspection and to my amazement, spotted errors on almost every page! Let's hope she found them all! Lastly, but certainly not least, thanks to Aleck Crawford for his months of patient typesetting. His sharp eyes and wise counsel sorted through several potential problems and added the finishing touch.

The revision and fourth printing involved many more people: Thank you to Abiyah Snobelen for modelling so many of the illustrations, and also Chris, Faith and Verity, along with Johnnie Abel and Priscilla Adair who modelled for the original pictures. A special thank you to Cilla Tuckson and Jessica Fish for their help with the newly redesigned cover.

Please feel free to email me at the address below. I welcome any questions or comments you may have after reading this book. To the best of my ability, all meaningful correspondence will receive a reply.

annatikvah@yahoo.ca

"Know also that wisdom is sweet to your soul; if you find it there is a future hope for you, and your hope will not be cut off."
Proverbs 24:14

If you have enjoyed this story, you will want to read the sequel, **Who Are You Looking For?**

Find out what happens when Peter returns home for Thomas' wedding after almost ten years overseas. How have life's experiences changed him? And what will be the outcome of the tumultuous year ahead?

At first, Peter wants nothing to do with the religious understanding he rejected after Verity's death. However, he soon discovers his family is enthralled by the popular Christian concept that a future Antichrist will take over the world. A series of unusual circumstances, and his best friend's warnings, force Peter to revisit his grudge against God. As he investigates what the Bible says about Antichrist, he encounters opposing views between his brother Andrew – now a highly esteemed Pastor – and Craig Symons, his former mentor. Forced to search deeper into the Scriptures for truth, Peter discovers real answers and a wonderful new friendship.

FREE ONLINE RESOURCES

BIBLE COURSE

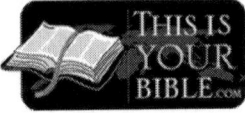

https://www.thisisyourbible.com/courses

AUDIO BOOKS and RESOURCES,
including the Anna Tikvah series

 https://www.magnifyhimtogether.com/

PODCASTS & YOUTUBE

 https://goodchristadelphiantalks.com/

 http://essentialbiblestudies.org/

 http://www.bibleinthenews.com/Podcasts

 https://www.youtube.com/@biblestudieswithchris

Printed in Great Britain
by Amazon